As a child, **Jennifer Haymore** travelled the South Pacific
with her family on their homebuilt sailboat. The months

Praise for Jennifer Haymore

'Jennifer Haymore's books are sophisticated,
deeply sensual and emotionally complex'
Elizabeth Hoyt, *New York Times* bestselling author

'Sweep-you-off-your-feet historical romance!
Jennifer Haymore sparkles!'
Liz Carlyle, *New York Times* bestselling author

'[Haymore] perfectly blends a strong plot that twists
like a serpent and has unforgettable characters to
create a book readers will remember and reread'
RT Book Reviews

The Duchess Hunt

Jennifer HAYMORE

piatkus

PIATKUS

First published in the US in 2013 by Forever, an imprint of Grand Central Publishing,
A division of Hachette Book Group, Inc.
First published in Great Britain as a paperback original in 2013 by Piatkus

A CIP catalogue record for this book
is available from the British Library.

ISBN 978-0-349-40125-6

Printed and bound in Great Britain by
Clays Ltd, St Ives plc

Papers used by Piatkus are from well-managed forests
and other responsible sources.

MIX
Paper from
responsible sources
FSC® C104740

Piatkus
An imprint of
Little, Brown Book Group
100 Victoria Embankment
London EC4Y 0DY

An Hachette UK Company
www.hachette.co.uk

www.piatkus.co.uk

For Lawrence, who tells the kids, "Shhh, be quiet. Mommy's not home," even though they all know very well that I'm in my office a few feet away, typing furiously on my next book.

Acknowledgments

To Selina McLemore, my editor, and Barbara Poelle, my agent: thank you for believing in me and in my work. To all the people who helped me with this story, especially Kate McKinley, Tessa Dare, and Cindy Benser: thanks for your support and for taking the time out of your busy schedules to help me create a better book. And to all my readers: thank you so much for your support. Without all of you, I wouldn't be able to do what I love. You have my heartfelt thanks.

Prologue

❧

Sarah Osborne had only lived at Ironwood Park for a few days, but she already loved it. Birds serenaded her every morning, their trilling songs greeting her through the little window in the cottage she shared with her father. Each afternoon, the sun shone brightly over the Park, spreading gentle warmth to her shoulders through the muslin of her dress as she ran across the grounds. And in the evenings, lanterns spilled golden light over the façade of the great house, which sat on a low, gentle-sloped hill and reigned like a king over the vast lands of the Duke of Trent.

If Sarah looked out the diamond-paned window of the cottage she shared with her father, she could see the house in the distance, framed by the graceful, curving white branches of two birch trees outside the cottage. She gazed at the house often throughout the day, always giving it an extra glance at night before Papa tucked her in. It stared back at her, a somber, massive sentry, and she felt safe with it watching over her. Someday, she dreamed, she might be able to draw close to it. To weave through those tall, elegant columns that lined its front. Someday, she might even be able to go inside.

But Sarah wasn't thinking of Ironwood Park right now—she was thinking about a butterfly. She dashed down the path in pursuit of the beautiful black-and-white speckled creature flitting from leaf to leaf of the box hedge that marked the outer boundary of the garden. She hiked up her skirt and chased it through the wrought-iron gate that divided the garden from the outer grounds.

Finally, the butterfly landed, seemingly spent, on a spindly branch. Sarah slowed and approached it cautiously, reaching her hand out. She let out a long breath as her finger brushed over one of the wings. The butterfly stared at her. So delicate and gentle. It seemed to nod at her, then in a soft flutter of wings, it flew away again, leaving Sarah gazing at the bush.

"Oooh," she murmured in delight. It wasn't just any bush—it was a blackberry bush. Last summer, when Mama had been so ill, Sarah had picked blackberries nearly every day. Blackberry root tea had soothed Mama's cough-weary stomach, but Sarah loved the berries' bumpy texture and burst of sweetness when she bit into one.

It was early in the season for blackberries, but among the ripening berries that loaded the bush, Sarah found a small handful that were ripe enough to eat. She gazed at her surroundings as she ate them one at a time, savoring the sweet taste edged with the slightest tinge of sour.

Not only one blackberry bush grew here—there were many. They sprawled from the ground in no orderly fashion along the bank of a trickling stream.

Sarah turned to glance in the direction she'd come from to make sure she wasn't lost. The domes of the roof of the great house peeked through the elms, a reassuring beacon.

Her handful finished, she went back to searching for ripe berries, picking through the thorn-covered branches. She searched and picked and ate until her belly was full, light scratches from the thorns crisscrossed her arms, and the dark juice stained her hands. Looking dolefully down at her skirt, she realized blackberry juice had stained her dress as well. Papa would be displeased if he saw, but she'd scrub out the stains before he came home.

Her braid was being unruly again—strands had fallen out of it, and her dark hair wisped across her cheeks. She blew upward, trying to get them out of the way, but that didn't work, so she pushed them away and tucked them behind her ears with her dirty hands.

And then she saw the butterfly again.

At least, it looked like the same butterfly. Beautiful and enormous, its wings speckled like a sparrow's egg, it had settled on a twig deep and high inside one of the black-berry bushes.

Sarah stepped onto a fallen branch. On her tiptoes, she leaned forward, peering at it. "Don't fly away," she murmured. "Don't be afraid."

She reached out—this time not to touch it, but to catch it. She wanted to hold it, feel its delicate, spindly legs on her palm.

Just a little farther... *Crack*! The branch snapped under her feet, and she lurched forward, her hands wheeling against the air as she tried to regain her balance. But it was no use. With a crash, she tumbled headfirst into the blackberry bush, gasping as thorns grabbed at her dress and tore at her skin.

She came to a stop on her knees inside the bush, her hands clutching the thorny undergrowth.

Panting against the smart of pain, she squeezed her eyes shut as she freed one hand and used her fingers to pick the thorns from the other. Blood welled on her arms, a hot stream of it sliding down around her forearm. Each breath she released came out in a little moan of pain. Her knees hurt horribly, but she couldn't regain her balance without something to hold onto, and there was nothing to grab except painfully thorny branches.

"Can I help you, miss?"

She tried to look over her shoulder toward the voice, but a thorn scraped over her cheek, and she sucked in a breath.

It was a man's voice, she thought. A kind voice. "Yes, please, sir."

"All right. Stay still."

It seemed to take forever, but slowly, using a small dagger, he cut away the thorny branches that twisted around her. Holding her by the waist, he gently extracted her, pausing to cut away any branch that might scrape her on the way out.

Finally, he settled her onto her feet on solid, thorn-free earth. Taking a deep breath, she turned around and looked up at him.

He was a boy. A big boy—far older than she was. Freckles splashed across his nose, and dark blond hair touched his shoulders. He gazed at her, concern denting his forehead between his crystal-green eyes.

"Are you all right?"

Sarah wasn't accustomed to talking to boys. Especially handsome boys wearing breeches and fine dark wool coats. And boys whose voices were deepening with the imminent arrival of manhood.

Speechless and wide-eyed, she nodded up at him. His expression softened.

"Here." He crouched down and withdrew a handkerchief from his coat pocket. Ever so gently, he swiped the cloth over her cheek, dabbing up the blood that had welled when she'd tried to turn to him. Then he folded it and tried to clean her hands. Then he looked at her knees. Following his frowning gaze, she looked down, too.

"Oh no," she whispered.

Her skirt was rent from her knees to her feet, and her stockings, also ruined, showed through. Worse, caked blood stuck her dress to her torn stockings.

Papa would be furious.

She must have made a sound, because the boy's brow furrowed. "Does it hurt terribly?" he asked, his voice grave.

Sarah swallowed hard. "N-n-no."

The edges of his lips tilted up in a smile. "You're very brave, aren't you?"

At those words, her fear melted away. She squared her shoulders, and, standing tall, she looked directly into his green eyes. "Yes, I am."

"Where do you live?" he asked.

She pointed toward the grand domes of the roof of Ironwood Park. "There."

"Well, isn't that something? I live there, too. Can you walk?"

"Of course I can."

Side by side, they walked down the path that led toward the house. Sarah's knees hurt, and she couldn't help it—she hobbled just a little. Without a word, the boy put a firm arm around her waist, steadying her.

They passed the gardener's cottage where Sarah lived with her father and headed toward the back side of the great house itself. Sarah didn't speak, and neither did the boy. She bit her lower lip and glanced at him from the corner of her eye, watching him walk. He was tall and strong, and she liked the way the sun glinted on his hair.

But as they drew closer to the house, and it looked more and more like he actually intended to enter it, her body grew stiff. She didn't know where Papa was, but he'd be very angry if he discovered she'd ventured too close to the house. Above all, he'd stressed the importance of her staying out of the family's way. If she bothered anyone, he might lose his position.

The boy slowed as they walked beneath the shadow of the enormous house, and then he looked down at her. "Are you all right?"

"Mm hm." Her voice wasn't much more than a squeak.

He stopped altogether and pulled away from her, watching her carefully to make sure she was steady.

"What's your name?" he asked.

"Sarah."

"I'm Simon." He glanced at the back of the house, which now loomed over them, so massive and heavy she could hardly breathe, and then back to her. "Come inside and I'll make sure you're taken care of."

She licked her lips, unsure. Then she whispered, "My papa said I mustn't disturb the family."

"You won't be disturbing the family." He said it like a promise.

She gazed up at him. She didn't know why, but she trusted him completely. He could have told her he took daily walks on the surface of the moon, and she would have believed him.

He continued, "I've been a rather poor doctor, so I'd like Mrs. Hope to take a look at those cuts. She has a salve that cures scratches like those in a trice."

Sarah had no idea who Mrs. Hope was, but the scratches still hurt—they stung and ached and itched. A salve that could cure them fast worked as sure as a lure into the forbidden.

She gave a little nod.

He took her least-affected hand, gentle with her scratches. "Come, then."

He led her up the stairs and into a vast room that made her hesitant steps grind to a halt. It was the largest room she'd ever seen. Open and cold and vast, lacking furniture except for a few benches and tables lining the walls. But those were too ornate to even be called benches. Metal legs shaped into vines held enormous slabs of marble. The tables held beautiful vases and busts of important-looking men. The room was almost overwhelmingly pale—the giant stones that made the walls were of an off-white color, and the plasterwork that adorned the walls and ceiling pure white. The only color was provided by the black checks on the tiled floor, the metalwork of the benches, and the enormous gilded chandelier that hung down in the center of the room.

Sarah tilted her head up, looking past the chandelier

and gallery rails at the elaborately carved ceiling—it seemed as high as heaven itself.

Simon stood beside her, and he looked up as well. She stole a glance at him, watched the considering look passing over his face—as if he were seeing the room for the first time, too.

She gripped his hand tighter. "Are you sure it's all right?" Her whisper seemed to echo in the cavernous space.

Simon shook off whatever he'd been thinking and smiled down at her. "Of course. This is the Stone Room. We don't spend much time in here. Come."

Holding her hand, he tugged her along. It seemed to take forever just to cross the vast area and reach one of the two doors that flanked a magnificent metal sculpture of a bearded, naked man and two naked boys. An enormous snake twined around their bodies. From the expressions of agony on their faces, she was sure the snake was crushing them.

He paused just in front of the door, no doubt seeing that her jaw had dropped as she stared at the statues. "Do you know the story of the Laocoön?"

She shook her head, unable to speak. She'd never heard of "Laocoön." She'd never seen a naked man or naked boys before. She'd never seen anything quite so *vicious*, either.

"Have you heard of the Trojan War?" He hesitated while she shook her head again. "Well, there was a war between Troy and the Greeks. Laocoön was the son of the Trojan King. When the Greeks tried to trick the Trojans by bringing them a gift of a giant wooden horse, Laocoön didn't trust them at all. He warned them to 'beware of

Greeks bearing gifts.' But the gods were on the side of the Greeks, and Laocoön's warning made them angry. Poseidon, the god of the sea—"

"I've heard of him!" Sarah exclaimed, seizing on the one element of the story that was familiar to her. Mama had told her nighttime stories of Poseidon and the other gods.

"Well, Poseidon sent a giant serpent from the sea to kill Laocoön and his two sons. And that's what this statue represents."

Sarah stared at the statue. She had seen real death. Recently. Real death was bad enough, so why on earth would people choose to remind themselves of it on a daily basis?

Simon turned from her to gaze at the statue again. "I don't like it either," he said in a low voice.

After another minute during which they both frowned at the gruesome thing, Simon opened the door and led her into another room, this one smaller but equally magnificent. In contrast to the echoing cavernous feel of the previous room, this one was warm and colorful and full of laughter. Children's toys covered a carpet containing a design of reds and golds and browns, and a large fire crackled heartily in the enormous hearth.

The room seemed to be brimming with people, and Sarah came to a dead stop at the threshold, her heart surging to her chest. For as soon as she and Simon entered, all eyes turned to them.

Oh no, she thought with a sinking heart. Except for the woman standing in the middle of the room and the toddler she held in her arms, the room was filled with children ranging from about her age to one who looked older than Simon—all of them boys.

This was the family. It must be. Servants didn't wear satin frocks or the fine wools and linens that these boys wore. Servants never played in spaces with silk hangings and Persian carpets. Servants' toys weren't carved of ivory and adorned with gilt.

Papa was going to be so angry.

Sickness welled in Sarah's gut. Simon had led her right where her father had told her never to go. And nothing weighed on her more heavily than the idea of disappointing her father. Now that Mama was gone, he was all she had.

She tried to tug her hand from Simon's grip, but he held firm, keeping her standing beside him.

The woman who stood in the center of the room had mahogany hair speckled with gray coiled elaborately on her head, but a few curls bounced down at the sides of her face. All that lovely blue satin she wore accentuated her voluminous bosom and narrow waist. The toddler was darker-haired than his—or her, Sarah couldn't be sure— mother, with soft ringlets brushing his—or her—nape and a round, pink-cheeked face.

Sarah blinked hard. The lady of the house was a duchess. One day, she'd dreamed about meeting a duchess.

There was no doubt in Sarah's mind. Though children surrounded this woman, and she even carried one on her hip, she was no nursemaid. She was far too elegant, far too regal. She had to be the Duchess of Trent.

And here Sarah was, finally face to face with a real duchess. But Sarah was bleeding and dirty, with torn stockings and a ripped dress, and her traitorous fingers itched to stroke that blue satin that clung to this beautiful lady's body.

If it were possible to die of mortification, Sarah would have dropped dead right then and there.

The duchess looked at her hand holding Simon's—her grip had tightened as she'd realized exactly who she was facing—then smiled. "What sort of creature have you brought us this time, darling? A forest nymph?"

Sarah's brows crept toward her hairline. *Darling?*

Simon shrugged, a little chagrin seeping into his expression. "Not sure. I found her under attack from a blackberry bush by the stream."

"Come closer, child." Hitching the toddler higher on her hip, the duchess approached them. What a contradiction—such a fine lady doing something so common as adjusting a babe on her hip. Weren't such actions reserved for more lowly people, like Sarah herself?

Simon stepped forward to meet the duchess, pulling Sarah along with him.

"What's your name? Where do you come from?"

Sarah opened her mouth but no words would emerge.

"She said her name is Sarah, and she's from here," Simon supplied.

The duchess cocked a dark brow. "Is that so?"

"Down, Mama!" the toddler complained, squirming. "Down, down, down."

With a sigh, the duchess lowered the child, never taking her gaze from Sarah. The toddler stared at Sarah curiously for a moment, then ran toward the cluster of boys, but Sarah couldn't drag her eyes away from the duchess long enough to see what was happening on the other side of the room.

"I don't recall having any little girls in residence at Ironwood House," the duchess mused. "Do you, Trent?"

"No, ma'am. But I've not been home. There have been no new arrivals this summer?"

"No, only the..." The duchess's brown eyes brightened. "The new gardener. Fredericks hired him. I had naught to do with it. I'd wager she belongs to him."

Simon looked down at Sarah. "Are you the gardener's daughter?"

Biting her lip and looking down at the beautiful carpet her dirty feet had trod upon, Sarah knew she'd made a horrible mistake. She should have stopped Simon when they'd passed the gardener's cottage. She should never have come into the house. What on earth had she been thinking?

She hadn't been thinking.

"Yes," she whispered.

Firm fingers grasped her chin, forcing her to look up into the stern face of the duchess. Tears sprang to Sarah's eyes. Now was her only chance.

"Please," she whispered. Her throat opened just enough for her to speak in a croaking voice. "Please don't dismiss my papa."

The woman's eyes narrowed, and Sarah's heart sank so low, she could feel it beating in her toes.

"What has your Papa done?"

Sarah stiffened. "Nothing!"

"Then why should I dismiss him?"

Sarah's eyes darted toward Simon, pleading for help.

"Mother," he said quietly, "you're scaring her."

The duchess dropped her chin, leaving Sarah with blazing cheeks. *Mother?* Simon was one of the family, too, then. Oh, she was a royal idiot.

"I brought her here because she needs medical attention." A touch of irritability had seeped into Simon's smooth voice. "Where is Mrs. Hope?"

"I've no idea." The duchess turned away toward the group of boys. "Mark, my love, will you go find Mrs. Hope? Tell her to bring some of the salve she uses on you ragamuffins when you get a cut. Sam—run and fetch the new gardener, will you? Explain that his daughter has been injured, but do let him know it's not serious. Bring him back to the house if he wishes it."

Sarah flinched. Her father had never beaten her before, but she had committed a severe enough infraction that she was entirely deserving of a whipping. Hopefully he would wait until they had some privacy. Nothing would be more disgraceful than being beaten in front of Simon.

"Can I go with Sam, Mama?"

"Yes, Luke, but stay with him and come straight back here. Understand?"

"Yes, ma'am."

"Me too?" said the smallest of the boys. "I want to go with Sam, too, Mama."

"All right, Theo, but do stay with your brothers."

As the door swung silently shut behind the four boys, the toddler wandered back to the duchess—a girl, Sarah thought, deducing from the child's features rather than her dress. Taking her plump little hand, the duchess turned back to Sarah. "Really, child, there's no reason to be afraid. You've done nothing wrong." A hint of a smile touched her lips. "The duke said the bush attacked *you,* after all. You probably didn't even encourage it."

Slowly, as if through a bucket of thick syrup, Sarah turned to Simon. "The *duke*?" she whispered.

Not quite meeting her eyes, Simon gave a one-shouldered shrug, and Sarah's heart began to kick its way back up her body.

"I see he didn't introduce himself properly." The duchess turned on her son. "Really, darling, must you always ignore the fact that you're the duke now? It has been almost three years."

"We didn't exactly have a proper introduction. Trust me, Mother," he added dryly, "whenever I am involved in a proper introduction, the title is *never* forgotten."

The duchess stared at her son for a moment, then smiled. "Of course it is not." She held her free hand out to Sarah. "Now, come, child, and sit down. Your leg is still bleeding. It must pain you to stand upon it."

Sarah glanced at the pristine silk sofa that the duchess was gesturing to and shook her head. It was so beautiful, the deepest color of purple she had ever seen, and shining in the sunlight streaming in from the window. "Oh, no, ma'am. I can't. I'm too dirty."

"If I was afraid of a bit of dirt and blood, I'd have never been able to countenance raising one child. But I am raising six, and I assure you, you are *not* too dirty to sit upon my sofa."

Simon gave her an encouraging look. "I think you should sit."

So she took the duchess's hand and allowed the great lady to guide her to the sofa. Simon helped Sarah to settle on the sleek silk upholstery before he sat beside her, and the duchess took an elegant armchair across from them while the toddler wandered toward a pile of shiny toys in the corner of the room. Sarah studied the duchess. She looked like a beautiful fairy tale ice queen regally sitting upon her throne. That was, until she gave Sarah a smile that rivaled her son's in its kindness. "Do you like tea, Sarah? I'll ring for some."

"Um...?" She glanced at Simon for guidance.

He nodded, then winked, making her feel like she'd just exchanged some communication with him that she hadn't yet deciphered, before turning to his mother. "Some warm milk?"

Sarah looked into her lap, smiling. That did sound nice.

"Of course." The duchess rang a bell, and a dainty maid came in to take the order for a bit of warm milk from the kitchen. The maid didn't even slide a disparaging look toward Sarah, just hurried to do the duchess's bidding without comment.

When the door closed behind her, the duke and his mother looked at Sarah expectantly, and the absurdity of the situation washed over her.

She was lounging in the parlor of a duke. She'd just been offered tea, and now a duke and a duchess were gazing at her as if expecting her to begin some sort of important conversation. And here she sat, torn and bleeding, her legs dangling from the adult-sized sofa, smearing dirt and blood onto the fine silk.

Feeling a little desperate for a completely different kind of saving, Sarah glanced at the door.

"She's charming, isn't she, Simon? And lovely, too, I imagine, underneath all that grime. The best thing that's happened to us all day." The duchess made a face as if reconsidering. "Well, aside from those wretched abrasions."

Just then, the door opened, and an older woman with fluffy white hair bustled in. Simon rose to his feet. "Mrs. Hope. Thank you for coming so quickly."

The woman curtsied. "Your Grace."

Sarah should have curtsied and said, "Your Grace," too, to both the duke and duchess, but it was too late now. She would have at least risen from the sofa, but the older lady came bustling toward her brandishing a bottle, and she shrank back against the cushions.

"Here now, little one, let's have a look at all those cuts." Mrs. Hope crouched in front of the sofa, first taking each of Sarah's arms in her gentle hands, then carefully peeling her stocking away from the worst of the scratches on her knees. "We'll have to wash them first. Binnie, hand me a towel."

Sarah hadn't noticed the young, dark-haired maid who had entered with Mrs. Hope before now. She stood at attention near the sofa holding a basin and several small white towels, one of which she handed to Mrs. Hope. Mrs. Hope finished removing Sarah's stockings and cleaned her knee, muttering about how the injuries looked horrible, but they were really quite minor, and once she'd cleaned them and applied a bit of salve, Sarah would feel as good as new. At one point, when Mrs. Hope had pulled Sarah's dress up over both her knees, she glanced up at Simon. "If she were any older, Your Grace, I'd have you leave the room."

Simon's expression didn't falter. "I found her, so I am responsible for her. I'll stay until I'm certain she'll be all right."

She gave him a shy smile. She was already all right, thanks to him. She wouldn't have ever imagined that a duke could be so kind. Or a duchess, for that matter.

Ever since she'd come to Ironwood Park with Papa and lived under the shadow of the enormous house and his dire warnings should she go anywhere near the family, she'd formed an image of the House of Trent as a group of cold, unkind aristocrats who would brush her aside like an annoying fly—if they'd even bother to look down their noses at her. But they were nothing like that. Beneath the great gabled roofs and beyond the marble and silk and gilt, they were a shockingly regular family.

One of the boys—Mark, Sarah remembered—stepped forward, cradling a steaming cup in his hands, which the duchess took and handed to Sarah after blowing a bit upon its surface. It was sweet and warm and soothing, and Sarah sipped at it and held her body as rigid as the statue of the Laocoön while Mrs. Hope applied the woodsy-smelling salve. If the Laocoön could be so still while being strangled by a gigantic serpent, then she could be still while her cuts stung and burned.

And if Simon had thought her brave, then she would be.

Just then, the door opened, and yet another servant stepped in, followed by her father. He rushed inside, then halted suddenly, drawing himself up and fumbling to remove his wide-brimmed gardener's hat as the boys tumbled in behind him.

"Your Graces." He bowed low toward Simon and his mother. "Please forgive me. My daughter—"

"Ah, you must be Mr. Osborne." The duchess rose from her chair to greet him. "Welcome to Ironwood Park. I do hope you have found its landscape to your liking."

Papa's gaze flitted to Sarah, who gave him a fearful look, but she was still trapped behind Mrs. Hope's ministrations, her leg being held down, and she couldn't move to his side despite the fact that his expression summoned her.

"Ironwood Park is an idyllic setting, Your Grace. I am

honored to be employed here. The landscape is nothing less than an artistic masterpiece, and I will do my best to maintain its glory."

Sarah swallowed hard. She knew what Papa was doing. Trying to convince the duchess that despite his daughter's wayward behavior, he was determined to perform his duties well.

He was trying to keep his position. And it was Sarah's fault he had to do this.

"It *is* quite lovely, isn't it? Boys"—the duchess waved her hand toward the door as she addressed her sons— "you are excused. You may remain outdoors until dinner. Keep an eye on each other, and please try not to ruin your clothes today."

"Yes, Mama!" The four boys tumbled back out of the room, but Simon didn't move from his mother's side. He stood quietly, his shoulders straight and hands clasped behind his back. He gazed at her father with solemn green eyes, his face a mask of politeness.

The duchess smiled at Sarah's father. "The duke rescued your daughter from the throes of a blackberry bush attack." Her dark brows rose into perfect arches. "No one informed me when we took you on that you were in possession of a family, Mr. Osborne. Fredericks has been remiss. I have told him time and again that he must tell me everything about everyone who makes their home at Ironwood Park."

Papa bowed his head. "It is only Sarah and I, Your Grace. My wife, she—died last year." Papa still couldn't talk about Mama without a catch in his voice. "I gave my assurances to Mr. Fredericks that I would keep the child out of the family's way."

The duchess waved her hand. "The more children frolicking happily about this cold and desolate place, the warmer and friendlier it becomes. And your daughter, despite her ruffian appearance, is quite the epitome of sweetness. Not to mention that this house lacks in female blood."

Simon turned to his mother. "We do have Esme," he pointed out.

The duchess laughed. "I tend to forget that my youngest is female sometimes. But that poor child—with five older brothers, she's more likely to turn into a ruffian like the rest of them than into a proper young lady."

Papa gazed at the little girl, then looked back to the duchess, clearly unsure how to respond.

"Now," the duchess said, "back to the problem of Sarah. As I told you, she suffered a brutal attack from a thorned assailant. However, the housekeeper has assured me that the damage is minor. I am relieved to report to you that the scratches are not deep and, thanks to Mrs. Hope's miraculous salve, will not scar, save the one on the knee, perhaps."

Papa gave a short nod, then cleared his throat. "My daughter has a tendency to wander. However, I can assure you that it will not happen again. She will remain in our cottage from now on." There was a note in his voice that promised future discipline, and Sarah cringed inwardly at the sound of it.

"Oh, but Mr. Osborne, it is natural for children to wander, to explore their surroundings and to discover. Especially in an unfamiliar place. I have always encouraged my children to explore to the extent of their curiosity."

Papa gaped a little at that, but then he gathered his wits

and bowed his head, clutching his hat to his chest. "Nevertheless, ma'am, my daughter should not be gallivanting about the grounds as if she owned them. She will refrain from doing so henceforth."

The duchess's expression softened. "Can you truly expect a child of her age and disposition to sit in that tiny cottage of yours every day while you go about your duties? No child should be constrained so, Mr. Osborne."

Papa glanced toward Sarah again but didn't answer. Clearly he wanted to be out of this great house and back to tending his beloved bushes.

The duchess's gaze moved from Sarah to her father, an odd glint in her brown eyes. "Tell me, does Sarah know her letters?"

Papa's body jolted at the change of topic, then he straightened a little. "Why, yes, ma'am. Her mother was quite learned—she was the schoolmistress at the parish's charity school before we were married. She taught the girl to read and to write."

The duchess clasped her long-nailed hands together in front of her. "Ah! I thought there was something about the way both of you speak..." Musingly, she turned toward Sarah, who was holding out her arm to Mrs. Hope while the older woman dabbed salve over a cut on her forearm. "Would you like to continue your studies, dear?"

Unsure how to respond, Sarah glanced at Papa. The answer was yes, of course she'd love to learn more. About everything. Especially the Trojan War Simon had mentioned earlier. If Mama were still alive, Sarah would run home and beg her to tell her the story right away.

But how would Papa want her to answer?

The duchess followed her gaze. "I see she turns to

you, Mr. Osborne. Well, then, did your daughter enjoy her mother's teachings?"

"She did," Papa admitted reluctantly. "Very much."

"Good!" the duchess exclaimed, clapping her hands. "It's settled, then."

Everyone stared at her, including Simon. "What's settled, Mother?" he asked.

"Starting tomorrow, Miss Sarah Osborne will join your brothers in their studies with Miss Farnshaw."

No one said a word. Sarah watched as her father's jaw slowly fell open.

And that was how a gardener's daughter ended up being educated with the offspring of a duke.

Chapter One

❦

Sixteen Years Later

"Welcome home, Your Grace."

Simon looked down at the stable hand who'd taken the reins from him. "Thank you, Tanner. Have my brothers arrived?"

"Yes, sir. All but Lord Lukas."

Simon ground his teeth as he dismounted. He shouldn't be surprised that Luke had ignored him—hell, Simon had sent the note to his brother's residence in London not even knowing whether Luke was there. He could be off carousing in some bawdy house or on one of his drunken revels. It was possible the directive Simon had sent had never entered his brother's hands.

Tanner led the lathered animal toward the stables as Simon approached the enormous columns that flanked the front door of the house. It had been almost three years since he'd last visited his ancestral home, but Ironwood Park hadn't changed. He hadn't expected it to. Ironwood Park never changed.

Mrs. Hope didn't change, either. She stood at the top of the steps to welcome him, her face awash with pleasure, looking the same as she always looked, with her pale skin, rosy cheeks, and white hair piled high on her head.

A feeling of rightness swept through him. It was always this way—not Ironwood Park itself but the people who resided here who made him feel like he'd come home.

"Your Grace," Mrs. Hope said warmly. "Welcome home." And then concern furrowed her brow, and he understood. He was sorry to be home under these circumstances. Sorry that he was so busy these days that the only thing that could drive him home was an emergency of this magnitude.

He took Mrs. Hope's clasped hands in his own and squeezed. "Thank you, Mrs. Hope."

And then Esme appeared behind the housekeeper, her dress as somber and dark as her hair, and he turned to greet her.

"Esme. You look well."

And she did. With a jolt, Simon realized it had nearly been a year since he'd last seen her. Since then, she'd grown even taller and filled out with womanhood.

"Thank you," she murmured, eyes downcast. "You, too."

"Come inside, Your Grace," Mrs. Hope commanded. "You'll wish to change before you see your brothers. They have planned to meet in the parlor before dinner, and dinner will be served in..." She glanced down at her fob. "Just over an hour."

Dusk had settled like a soft blanket over the house—

dinner at Ironwood Park was always earlier than in London. "Excellent," he said. And to his sister, "I'll see you in the parlor in a few minutes."

She gazed up at him, and it was only then that he saw the shine in Esme's eyes. On impulse, he laid his hand on her shoulder, only to feel her stiffen beneath him. His intention had been to comfort, but his touch was so unknown to Esme, perhaps it had become unwelcome. He removed his hand and said in a low voice, "Don't worry. We'll find her."

Esme nodded, her gaze shining, then looked away, blinking rapidly. At that moment Fredericks appeared in the archway leading to the grand staircase. After Simon exchanged a greeting with the steward, Mrs. Hope bustled him upstairs and into his dressing room, where a basin steamed on the bureau and clothes for him to change into were laid out on the clothes press.

He washed and shaved himself. The silence of the room seemed loud after the bustle of London and Burton's incessant chatter. Due to the urgency of this visit, he'd left his valet in London, probably happily fussing over some new outfit he was having tailored for Simon during his absence.

Simon dressed in buff pantaloons and buttoned on a wine-striped waistcoat and a dark tailcoat before combing his hair and gazing into the looking glass at the somber visage staring back at him. The crow's feet at the edges of his eyes spoke of his exhaustion—he'd ridden straight from London at the close of Parliament yesterday, changing horses but not stopping to sleep. His eyes appeared dull, the green of them not as light as usual, but dark and mossy.

It was time to face his brothers and sister and reveal his plan of action. Unfortunate that he didn't have one.

He left the dressing room and returned downstairs, taking slow, deliberate steps to the parlor. When he reached the door, he didn't hesitate but stepped inside and closed it behind him before turning to survey the room.

Everyone was present. Except Luke.

Samson, Simon's older half-brother, leaned against the casing of the enormous rectangular-paned window on the far side of the room. Mother had given birth to Sam out of wedlock the year before she married the Duke of Trent. One of her conditions upon marrying the duke was that she would be allowed to keep Sam and raise him alongside any other children she might have. For reasons unknown to Simon, his father had agreed—he had even given Sam the Hawkins name—and it was one promise he'd never reneged upon, though he had never gone so far as to treat Sam like a son.

Sam had been gazing outside but turned toward Simon as he entered. This was the first visit home for Sam in nearly five years. His work in the service of the Crown kept him busy, though Simon did see him from time to time in London. Sam had always possessed a serious demeanor, but the army had hardened him, given him a seemingly permanent cold and detached expression that Simon expected would never go away now. His brother had simply seen too much.

Simon's younger brothers, Theodore and Markos, sat side by side on the plum-colored silk sofa, their sandy brown heads and eyes so similar, people had always thought them twins. But they were very different in disposition. Theo was quiet and studious like Esme, and Mark was the one person in the family who could bring levity to any conversation. Today, however, Mark's face was grim and set, his normal exuberance dampened by the gravity of the situation.

Simon turned to the table in the center of the room, where Esme was pouring tea, his gaze finally coming to rest on Sarah Osborne, who stood at his sister's side, assisting her.

His body came instantly alive at the sight of her, even after all this time. Even under the circumstances. *Lust. Desire. Need.* All of it barreled through him in a hot rush.

Damn. She was more beautiful than ever.

When he'd last come home to Ironwood Park, he hadn't been able to keep his hands off her. God knew he'd tried.

Her mouth caressing his, the feel of her body under his hands…It had been three years. He should have forgotten all of it by now.

But how could he forget the sweetest lips he'd ever tasted? How could he forget the curve of her bottom, the feel of her soft, plump breasts under his hands?

How could he forget that he'd taken advantage of an innocent? Someone who worked in his house, under his employ? How could he forgive himself for crossing a line he never, ever should have crossed?

She turned the full force of her wide smile on him and then dipped her head as she dropped into a curtsy. "Your Grace."

"Good evening, Sarah." He gazed at her, taking in her dark, dark hair, her black-fringed blue eyes, her porcelain complexion, her willowy stature, for perhaps a second too long before forcefully returning his attention to his brothers. "I'm glad you all came so quickly," he told them.

"Where's Luke?" Theo asked. "You wrote to him as well, didn't you?"

Taking the china teacup and saucer that Sarah held out toward him, Simon thanked her then stepped forward. "I did. Evidently he chose not to respond."

Everyone was struck silent by that, until Sam spoke up from his position near the window. "Or he didn't receive the missive. We all know how Luke feels about Mother."

"It's possible he didn't receive it," Simon acknowledged. It was true—despite all of his shortcomings, Luke adored their mother. "I wasn't sure where to find him. You know Luke. He could be anywhere."

Theo gave a low whistle as Sarah handed him and Mark their tea. "Thank you, Sarah. Right. Well, then, it's just us. But Luke won't be happy we met without him."

Simon arched a brow at his youngest brother. "He should either visit his lodgings once in a while or let us know where he is located in the world if he wishes to be privy to important family news."

Theo raised his cup. "True." He took a sip before setting the cup and saucer down on the oblong carved teak table that squatted low in front of the sofa.

Simon lowered himself into the Egyptian-styled bronze and silk-damask empire chair across from Theo and Mark. He looked at his sister and gestured to the identical chair beside him. "Please sit, Esme."

As Esme approached, Sarah set down the teapot and turned to leave the room.

"Sarah, you will stay." His tone was clipped and

brooked no argument. He glanced at his brothers. No one reacted to the out-of-place command, which meant they understood exactly why he wanted Sarah in the room with them.

This was a family affair, and while most might dismiss a maid after she'd finished with the tea, this particular maid had embedded herself so deeply into life at Ironwood Park that she sometimes knew things that occurred here that none of the rest of them did. His brothers understood as well as he did that her presence might prove valuable.

Plus... well, damn it, he just liked having her close. His brothers didn't need to know that.

"Yes, Your Grace." Her answer was automatic, as was her bobbed curtsy. She stayed where she was, standing behind the silver tea service, attentive but silent.

When he had everyone's full attention, Simon turned to his sister.

"Tell us what happened, Esme. We must hear every detail. From the beginning."

She nodded. Fixing her gaze on the teak table and clutching the carved arms of her chair in her hands, she began. "I don't see Mama every day anymore—not since she moved into the dower house. So I don't know when it happened, but... but... I should have been paying closer attention. She is my mother. I should have been visiting every day, making sure she was all right..."

"When was the last time you saw her?" Sam's voice, as always, was cool and detached.

Esme's eyes filled with tears. "A week ago."

Simon nodded. "Go on."

"Well, the day before yesterday I realized I hadn't seen

her in a few days, so I went to the dower house for a visit. And..."

"And?" Theo prompted, leaning forward, his elbows on his knees, his eyes narrowing on their sister.

She turned her focus to Theo. "There was no one at home. Binnie and James weren't there, and Mama wasn't there. All three of them had simply vanished."

Simon frowned. Binnie and James were the two servants his mother had taken with her when she'd moved to the dower house. He hadn't known they'd also disappeared.

"I knocked and knocked. I tried the door, but it was locked, and you know Mama rarely ever locks her door. I ran back to the house and asked Mrs. Hope for the key. Sarah came with me, and we went inside, but no one was there."

"Why didn't you go straight to the constable?" Mark asked, his brow creased in a rare frown.

"I...I..." Esme broke off, and sent a helpless glance in Sarah's direction.

"We thought it best to send His Grace a message before we involved anyone outside the family," Sarah explained. "Because once we contact the authorities, everyone will begin to speculate. We thought it would be more prudent to allow His Grace to decide whether to involve them."

"You made the right decision," Simon told her. And he wouldn't involve the authorities at all in this matter, if he could help it. Sarah knew him well enough to understand that he preferred to keep private family matters private, because when it came to the Hawkinses, the gossipmongers tended to take facts and embellish them to the point of outlandishness. In any case, he possessed more resources to use to find his mother than any constable would.

Sam pushed off from the window casing and took a step forward, his cool gaze focused on Esme. "What was the state of the interior of the dower house? Was it clean? Ransacked? Were any of Mama's things missing?"

"It was clean," Esme whispered.

"As far as we could tell, most of her possessions were untouched," Sarah added. "But her safe was open and empty. All her money was gone, as well as her jewels."

Hell. His mother had enough jewels to keep a small village living in luxury for years.

Mark's frown deepened. "A robbery?"

If someone wished to rob Ironwood Park, the dower house would be the best place to start, considering that not only was it secluded—hidden in a copse of trees on the northern edge of the property—but it wasn't well guarded, and everyone acquainted with his mother knew she wasn't one to pay much heed to such frivolous things as locks.

But if someone had entered the dower house with the intention of stealing jewels, what had the thief done with his mother and her servants? The thought brought bile into Simon's mouth.

"Possibly," he told Mark, but his voice held doubt.

"Who originally searched the dower house?" Sam asked Sarah.

"Mrs. Hope, Lady Esme, and me, sir. We were out there this morning again while we awaited your arrival."

Sam met Simon's gaze. "We'll do a thorough search. Leave no stone unturned."

"And not only of the house," Simon added, "but also the woods and the surrounding areas. And"—he took a fortifying breath—"we'll need to drag the lake."

Esme sniffed. The stream running through the property fed the small lake near the dower house... dragging the lake was akin to admitting their mother might have been drowned. Turning toward his sister, Simon saw her shoulders slump as a tear carved a trail down her cheek.

Hell, he'd been raised with brothers. Esme hadn't been born until he was ten years old and already at Eton. His mother had always been the epitome of strength—she'd never shed a tear in his presence. He'd never learned how to comfort a weeping female.

He glanced up and realized he wasn't the only one at a loss as to what to do about this. His brothers appeared frozen in place. Even their expressions didn't change as they stared at their whimpering sister.

Sarah broke the stillness. She hurried over to Esme, knelt beside her, offered her a handkerchief and put an arm around Esme while the girl sobbed into Sarah's shoulder. Sarah looked up at Simon over Esme's head, stroking Esme's dark hair. Her blue eyes, usually sparkling with vivacious warmth, had darkened with sympathy... and with her own worry. Sarah loved their mother as much as any of her children did.

"Hush." She looked back down at Esme and rubbed her back in gentle circles. "If anyone can find her, His Grace can."

Esme's shoulders shuddered. When Sarah looked up at him again, the knowledge of what he must say flooded into him. "We'll find her, Esme. That is a promise."

He glanced at his brothers, all of whom nodded their agreement.

Esme took a great gulping breath, her voice muffled in Sarah's shoulder. "But what if she...if she isn't...what if she is..."

"There's no evidence whatsoever that points to the conclusion that Her Grace has come to any harm," Sarah soothed.

"That is correct," Sam said, his voice a notch lower than his usual cold detachment. "And that is how we must approach finding her."

"Mama wouldn't—" Theo broke off, frowning.

"She wouldn't what?" Simon asked him.

Theo gazed at him with bleak eyes. "She wouldn't run off, would she?"

Everyone stared at Theo. Even Sarah looked at him with parted lips. Finally, Mark asked, "Why would she run off?"

Theo shook his head. "Couldn't say." He shrugged. "It was just a thought."

"If Mama simply decided to leave Ironwood Park, one would assume she'd let *someone* know where she was going," Mark said.

Simon looked to Esme, whose tears had abated. Sarah still crouched beside her, though, keeping that comforting arm around his sister, and he was glad he'd told her to stay. "Has our mother been behaving erratically in any way?"

Mark snorted. "What kind of a question is that, Trent? Our mother is always erratic."

"I mean more so than usual."

Esme shook her head somberly. "No. No more than

usual. She was excited about the ladies' luncheon she was going to hold next week. She'd embroidered kerchiefs for each of the ladies and was planning to give them as gifts."

"So she wasn't planning to run off, then," Theo said thoughtfully.

"But you know her. She'll change plans on a whim," Mark pointed out.

"True," Sam agreed. "We should check her house near Lake Windermere as well as her townhouse in London."

"And her sisters' houses as well, in case she decided to make a last-minute visit," Simon said.

Theo shook his head. "If our mother went somewhere on a whim, she could be anywhere in England."

"But someone would have seen her, somewhere," Mark said. "Collectively, we know her favorite haunts and the routes she'd take to travel to them."

"We will check them all," Simon said.

A knock on the door heralded a footman, who told them dinner was served. Simon dismissed the man, then turned to his siblings, his stomach growling in anticipation of a hot meal. He hadn't eaten since yesterday.

"We'll formulate a solid plan after dinner." He turned to Sarah. "Thank you for staying. Will you meet us back here at nine o'clock?"

"If you wish it, Your Grace."

"I do."

She inclined her head and looked at him with her big, blue eyes. "Then I will be here."

Chapter Two

❧

The midnight hour had descended over Ironwood Park when Sarah finally left the great house for the night and walked toward the cottage she shared with her father.

Yesterday it had rained, but tonight the waxing moon shone bright, sparkling over the trees, shrubs, and flowers her father was responsible for keeping beautiful. He'd done an excellent job of it, and the duchess loved to tell him so. She always laughed and said that when he'd been hired, she hadn't actually expected him to *improve* Capability Brown's famous landscape.

But improve it he had. The gardens around the house were beautiful to look upon year-round, constantly emitting the fresh, sweet scents of flowers and herbs. The outer garden was a study in geometric forms, its boundary keeping a strict separation between it and the landscape beyond, which Papa constantly assessed and modified to provide a haven of nature that flowed naturally with the contours of the land.

Despite the beauty and perfection of the grounds through which she walked, Sarah was brimming with a feeling of dread.

The duchess's strange disappearance had knocked the small universe of Ironwood Park out of kilter. The Duchess of Trent was a constant here. Sure, she traveled often, visiting London and her family scattered throughout England. But Ironwood Park was her home, her anchor, and when she was gone, everyone felt her absence keenly. And this absence was different from a mere holiday—everyone knew it in their bones. The servants were all on edge. Even Mrs. Hope—a woman in possession of an inherently positive nature—was scared.

Worst of all was the family. Sam, Mark, and Theo had all rushed home, their concern obvious in the speed of their arrival. Luke hadn't come, though no one was worried—he made an appearance either in London or at Ironwood Park once every few months, but Sarah knew how upset he'd be when he ultimately heard the news. Of all of them, Luke was closest to their mother.

Poor Esme had discovered her mother missing, and for some reason she blamed herself for the odd disappearance. Esme was terrified something dire had happened. So was everyone else, but Esme wasn't able to push that fear aside like the rest of them had.

And Simon.

Sarah's step faltered. She gazed up at the spray of stars that made silver pinpricks in the dark velvet of the sky.

Simon.

She couldn't speak his name out loud anymore. That wouldn't be proper. But she'd never stopped speaking it in her mind. Not since the day he'd encountered her in the blackberry bush long ago and had gifted her with it.

It had been almost three years since she'd last seen him. He was more handsome than she remembered. It was like that every time—she convinced herself that he wasn't as appealing as he truly was, only to be overwhelmed by his allure when next she saw him.

When he'd walked into the parlor earlier this evening, her heart seemed to have stopped cold for a few seconds, and when it had started up again, it had beaten like a hundred horses galloping through her chest. Images of his lips and hands on her, hot and breathless, slammed through her head. She'd managed--only barely—to finish pouring the tea and hand him the cup and saucer without her hand shaking violently enough to splatter tea all over the carpet.

His straight hair had grown an inch or two—but it was the same color it had been since he'd reached adulthood—light brown with golden streaks. His penetrating green eyes had always been serious, but now they looked a little darker than she recalled, the full irises as dark as the moss green ring that usually circled around the edges. Shallow lines were etched into the corners of his eyes—she didn't remember those at all, but she liked them. They lent additional character to his face.

The freckles scattered across his nose as a youth had vanished, leaving his face with a uniform golden hue. His patrician nose and high cheekbones topped a square jaw, the lines of his facial structure coming together in a way that no one would deny was handsome, punctuated by the slightest cleft that dented the center of his chin, difficult to see unless he smiled. Sarah hadn't seen it since he'd arrived. She hoped he'd smile at least once before he left Ironwood Park.

The way his strong thighs strained against the wool of his pantaloons tonight had drawn Sarah's eye so often she kept having to remind herself to look away. The way the muscles in his shoulders and broad back flexed beneath the wool of his coats had stolen her breath.

She remembered how those muscles had felt under her hands. How she wanted to touch them again, to explore every facet of his strong body.

But the way he walked into the parlor and took control in that calm, self-possessed way of his—that was most appealing of all. He wasn't overbearing or obnoxious or self-indulgent. He allowed everyone to speak, took everyone's opinions and suggestions under review. Even hers.

And as she'd struggled to focus on the problem at hand, Simon's presence had constantly distracted her, constantly brought her back to that night. The memory of that kiss—the heat of it. Goodness, she still dreamed about it. Still woke craving his arms around her, his lips on hers.

She'd resolved that she was no longer besotted with him. Now, tilting her head to the sky, she gave a self-deprecating puff of laughter up to the heavens. How silly she'd been. Three years had passed since she'd last seen him, but she was as besotted with the Duke of Trent as she'd ever been. More so, probably.

She closed her eyes and let out a long, slow breath. Sarah was well aware of her place. Simon was aware of her place, too, and of the vast distance that separated him from her. Everything Simon did was well thought out and cautious—he was very cognizant of his family's image and in a constant struggle to wipe it clean of the tarnish his parents had caused to mar it.

Whenever he and Sarah were in the presence of others, Simon was careful never to cross those deep, thick lines that society had drawn between them.

It wasn't right for her to so desperately want someone so far out of her reach. It had never been right, but it was especially wrong now, when the duchess was missing. The duchess was Simon's priority right now, and she should be Sarah's, too.

She began walking again, hesitating at the fork in the graveled walkway. The right fork would take her home to Papa and the cottage. The left fork led to a path that wandered along the bank of the stream. On impulse, she went left. She couldn't sleep. Not yet. Her head was too busy, too muddled by the events of the past few days. She needed to clear her mind before sleeping, and it would be easier to do so outside in the crispness of the spring air.

The moon splashed silver over the path, lighting her way. As Sarah walked, she considered the fact that robbers might have been at Ironwood Park—that perhaps very bad men were responsible for the duchess's disappearance.

Sarah couldn't conjure any fear of a similar horror happening to her. This was Ironwood Park, her home, and if there were intruders near, she'd hear them. She'd *feel* them. And they wouldn't be after the gardener's daughter, anyhow.

She walked along the stream for about half a mile, soothed by the gurgling and bubbling noises the water made as it rushed over stones.

When she reached the familiar marble bench that had been placed at a bend in the bank wedged between two blackberry bushes, she hesitated again. Set on the bank a bit of a distance from the path, it glimmered pearly white in the moonlight, beckoning to her.

She didn't come out here as much as she used to. Sitting on that bench made Sarah dream things a practical girl like her had no business dreaming. But sometimes she came anyhow, just to remember.

Tonight, she wanted to remember. So she sat, breathing slowly in and out, curling her toes in her shoes as she gazed out over the stream. Moonlight glistened over the ripples and eddies the water made as it slipped past her.

She gripped the front edge of the bench and straightened her back, stretching this way then that, then rolling her neck in each direction, trying to rid herself of some of the stiffness that had built up since Esme had come rushing into the Stone Room, where Sarah had been supervising the annual deep cleaning of the marble, to tell her the news about the duchess.

"Sarah?"

She stilled, then stiffened. Then she looked over her shoulder.

He was standing in the path, his body partially obscured by the dark fingers of branches. Moonlight dappled his coat and threw a gold accent over the masculine slope of his nose.

Simon, her body whispered. Her chest tightened, all that pent-up love for him that she'd locked tight within her pressing to be set free.

"Your Grace," she said, keeping her voice mild.

"I couldn't sleep."

"Nor I." She turned back toward the stream, scooting over to make room for him on the bench.

They'd met at this very spot more than once over the years. Each of them had made it their personal place of peace and solitude, and that hadn't changed when they'd begun to discover each other here from time to time.

But the last time they'd met here, Simon had kissed her. It had been a long kiss, hot and drowning. His lips had ventured far from hers—over her jaw and neck and down to her breasts, which he'd kissed over her dress and pelisse. And he'd touched her, too. His hands had stroked her breasts, moved over her nipples, cupped her behind and pressed her body against his.

He had returned to London the very next day, and she hadn't seen him again until tonight.

Now, his tall form cast a shadow over her as he settled beside her.

She hadn't expected him. He must be tired from his hard ride from London, and she'd assumed he'd go straight to bed. Even if he hadn't been exhausted, she knew his association to this place must have changed three years ago. Hers certainly had. It was no longer a place of quiet tranquility, because their last encounter had charged it with something hot and needy and frantic. Something *carnal*.

But here he was. He'd had the opportunity to turn away without her noticing his presence, but he'd chosen to stay. To sit beside her.

They gazed out over the swirling silver-washed flow of water. Slowly, Sarah's tension eased. There was no further need for her to roll her shoulders or twist her neck. The warmth emanating from Simon and the cedar-and-spice essence that she inhaled with every breath when she was beside him was enough.

Eventually, she slid a glance in his direction. "I'm sorry you had to come home like this, Your Grace."

"I'm not sorry to be home. It is ... good to be here. It's been too long. The circumstances, though ..." He sighed. "I don't believe I'll ever understand my mother. Why she didn't warn one of us that something was amiss is beyond my comprehension."

"You can't be certain she had aught to do with it," Sarah reminded him gently.

He blew out a breath from between tight lips. "True. Still, I have a feeling she did."

It was always like this out on the grounds when they were alone. They could talk freely without the constraints their respective positions placed upon them. And they always did. There was an ease out here in plain privacy that there would never be in the presence of others. Out here, those thick, deep lines that separated them seemed insubstantial and unimportant. Out here, ever since that very first day when he'd rescued her, they'd been friends.

Until the last time, when they'd suddenly become something more.

"After you and Esme left the parlor tonight, I had an idea," Simon said.

She turned to him and met his eyes, trying to ignore the heat that licked through her at his proximity. She remembered how they'd been sitting just like this, and then suddenly he'd groaned. "I can't stop it anymore, Sarah," he'd said. Then his arms went around her and his lips clashed with hers. She'd immediately fallen into the kiss, a slave to the sensations he aroused in her. Kissing Simon was *right*. As natural as breathing, but far, *far* more exciting. She'd known instinctively what to do. Her arms had slipped around him, and she'd kissed him back, touching him through his coat, exploring him as his lips and hands explored her, kissing her all over, licking her earlobe, suckling her breast through layers of material.

Now, his serious gaze didn't waver from her as he said, "If we don't find my mother right away, I think it'd be best if Esme accompanied me when I return to London."

Snapped out of the memory of their kiss, Sarah sucked in a breath. If Esme left Ironwood Park with Simon, all of the siblings would be gone, all of them heading in different directions to broaden the search for the duchess.

"Esme is nineteen years old," Simon continued, a musing tone in his voice. "She's a young woman, and she ought to be in the company of her peers and friends during the Season. She ought to be in London, not isolated out here in the country. I know my mother believed it would be best for her to remain at home this year, but I disagree. Keeping her locked away isn't going to help her in the end."

Esme had been quite content to stay at Ironwood Park rather than go to London for the Season. She'd had her come-out last year, and though Sarah hadn't been given details, by all accounts it had been disastrous. Esme had told Sarah that everything about the marriage mart made her insides curdle. "I find it barbaric," she'd told Sarah, "that we are forced to lay ourselves out like slabs of meat at the market to be inspected and discarded if found lacking."

"But what if you aren't found lacking?" Sarah had asked.

"Even worse!" Esme had exclaimed. "Then it's a competition between the hungriest gentlemen, and if the poor lady is unlucky, a feeding frenzy."

At social events held at Ironwood Park, Esme was quiet and desperately shy. When Sarah thought of Esme in London, something inside her tightened with sympathy, because she just couldn't imagine Esme thriving amongst a bevy of beautiful and elegant ladies whinging about which jeweled necklace to wear for that night's ball.

"There is also the concern that Ironwood Park might not be entirely safe right now," Simon added.

"I'd be here with her. I'd keep her safe," Sarah said. So would the other servants.

The corner of his lips tilted upward as he studied her. "I believe you could protect her, Sarah, if I gave you that responsibility. Which is why I'd like you to come, too."

"To...London?"

"Yes."

"I...I..." *London*. Sarah had never been to London. Even when she was a little girl, she'd wanted desperately to see the city someday.

"I would like to employ you to be Esme's companion."

"Her companion? But I can't!" She said the last word over a heavy lump in her throat.

He frowned. "Why not?"

Heat tightened over her cheeks. "I am not of genteel birth."

He shrugged. "But you comport yourself as if you were. No one needs to know that you're a gardener's daughter. The moment you open your mouth, no one will question your upbringing."

"But *I* know I am not a lady," she said. "And so do you. And Esme, too."

He met her eyes again, utterly serious. "I really don't care."

She sat back, stunned. Simon *always* cared about matters of propriety.

He continued, "You are the best choice to be a companion to Esme. You're very good with her—I watched how you calmed her tonight. She adores you, and she'll listen to you." He rested his hands loosely over his knees. "London is a very busy place. For me, especially. I am rarely home. I couldn't countenance leaving her without proper companionship."

Sarah swallowed hard and forced herself to say it, because as much as she wanted to go to London and be with Simon and Esme, it was the right thing to say. "You could easily find someone else, Your Grace."

Someone more qualified. He would only need to tell a few people that he was searching for a companion for Esme, and potential candidates would come running in droves hoping to fill the position of companion to the Duke of Trent's sister.

"I thought about it, but no."

"Why not?"

He broke her gaze to look down at his hands. "You're sensible. I trust you with Esme. More than I would trust any stranger."

The way he said the last word made the breath whoosh from her lungs. When she'd caught it again, she asked, "What if someone should find out I'm just a housemaid?"

With a sigh, he said, "If the *ton* is that hungry for gossip, let them. In the end, it won't make any difference to our lives. And the rumors will eventually fade. People in lesser positions than head housemaid have been raised to higher positions than lady's companion."

"But you...you despise scandal," she whispered.

"True. But there are things more important than risking a small scandal, Sarah. My sister's happiness and safety, for one."

"But Lady Esme? It might not be such a minor risk to her." It was Esme's reputation ultimately at stake, and unlike Sarah's, Esme's reputation mattered.

Simon's gaze searched her, probing. "Do you find my sister so weak?"

"Esme is tenderhearted, yes, but this has little to do with a person's weakness or strength, Your Grace. It is more about how the *ton* can sink its poison-tipped claws into a person and never let her go."

"Ah. I see you have listened to our stories of Town." He leaned toward her slightly, his expression somber and serious. "I am willing to risk it in this case, again, because the threat is slim and vastly outweighed by the benefit of you being in London with Esme. I can lay it all out for my sister if you'd prefer, but if she has any sense at all, she'll come to the same conclusion."

Sarah sighed. She knew Esme well enough to believe that she would indeed agree with this plan—to Esme, Sarah was as comfortable as a well-worn old blanket and preferable to a stranger any day—but whether her agreement would be based on sense, Sarah had her doubts.

Still, she understood Simon's logic. He was willing to risk a relatively minor scandal, in this case, for the ultimate good of his family.

It warmed her that he thought her presence would be for the good of his family.

"Very well," she told him. "I'll go."

He raised a brow. "But you don't wish to?"

She hesitated, then smiled. "I haven't ventured beyond the village since I first stepped foot into Ironwood Park sixteen years ago. During those years, I have watched you and your siblings come and go again and again, and..." Her voice dwindled.

"And...?"

She squeezed the front edge of the bench, the marble cold and hard under her palms. "Well," she admitted, "I've always wished I could go with you."

He smiled at that, showing that slight cleft in his chin. She'd pressed her lips there three years ago. She averted her gaze.

"You should have told one of us sooner," he said.

She laughed softly. "Lord knows what people might have thought if I accompanied Lord Luke to the Continent or Lord Theo to Cambridge."

A shadow passed over his face. As he looked away, Sarah saw a muscle twitch in his jaw, and it struck her then exactly what people would have thought.

"Oh," she whispered. "I didn't mean in that way."

He was silent for a moment before his gaze swung back to her. "I know you didn't."

But the way he looked at her, his eyes narrowing, turning dark green and hungry and possessive, stole her breath.

In three years, Simon's skin hadn't come in contact with hers. But it did now, warm and firm, his fingers heavy and blunt and so masculine as he cupped her face in his palm. His cedar scent wrapped around them both like a cocoon, and his heat radiated through her.

She tried so hard not to close her eyes, to sink into his palm. But the pleasure of touching him was so overwhelming, she couldn't help herself.

"The last time we were here...on this bench..." His voice was a husky whisper. "It was so long ago, but I've craved your mouth ever since."

Heat emanated from him. His breath whispered across her cheek. She released a shaky sigh of pleasure at his words.

"I've wanted to touch you everywhere. Kiss you all over."

She opened her eyes, because she wanted to see him as she leaned closer in—

He dropped his hand from her face, jerking back as if she'd burned him.

"God." A low groan emitted from his throat as he thrust his hand into his hair and turned away. "I'm sorry. I shouldn't have said that."

"It's...all right..." she managed to say through her dry throat. Her skin was still buzzing from the contact, her cheek tingling and warm where he'd touched her.

"Sarah—it was a mistake. I shouldn't ever have touched you. It was disrespectful of me...and wrong."

"Oh...Your Grace. No." She had felt anything but disrespected that night. She'd felt...*desired*. And for the last three years, she'd savored that feeling.

"It was late at night, and I took advantage of you."

"No," she repeated.

"I shouldn't have."

He rose to his feet. She, stubbornly, remained seated.

He clenched his hands at his sides. "I've spent three years reminding myself of how wrong it was to touch you, and yet I sit here and all I can think about is putting my hands all over you. Tasting you all over again."

His words sent a delicious shudder through her body. She wanted that, too. She gazed up at him, waiting, wishing he'd give in and sit beside her again, take her into his arms, and drown her in his kisses.

Raising his hand, he bent his head and rubbed his temple, then blew out a breath and met her gaze again. "I shouldn't—mustn't—touch you. I want to do right by you, Sarah. It is morally reprehensible for me to have these feelings for someone who is under my care."

If she were a London debutante, it might be different. But she was Sarah Osborne, his head housemaid, and she understood exactly why Simon felt like it would be morally reprehensible to touch her again. It had everything to do with those vast chasms that separated her social class from his.

Damn them, she thought brutally. Why must it matter? He was hungry for her—she could see it in his eyes, hear it in his words. And, Lord knew, she was hungry for him, too.

Her gaze dropped to his fist, clenched so desperately at his side. He really did believe it would be wrong to touch her. She knew Simon's deepest fear was that he'd become like his parents, whose lives had been replete with scandal, betrayal, and flagrant promiscuity.

Above all, she didn't want him to lose sight of who he was, who he wanted to be, who he never intended to be.

If he ever did touch her again, she didn't want him to regret it afterward.

So she took a deep breath and rose, brushing the wrinkles from her skirt to keep her shaky hands occupied. Giving him a slight smile, she asked, "Walk me home?"

"Of course."

They walked down the path side by side. Awareness of him still resonated through her, stronger than ever. She watched him from the corner of her eye as they walked.

She knew there was wisdom in his reluctance. His brother Luke had boldly ventured into an affair with one of the maids at Ironwood Park once, and it had turned into an unpleasant situation all around. What could come of a relationship between a housemaid and a duke? Very little but heartbreak for the housemaid. Sarah knew this. She wasn't stupid.

Her traitorous body clearly had no intention of listening to her mind, though, because it desperately longed for more of his touch. For another of those hot, passion-filled kisses of three years ago. For *more*.

Simon stared ahead, silent and brooding, his gaze never wavering from the path. When it narrowed in spots, he stepped aside to give her a wide enough berth to pass before falling in behind her.

The distance to Papa's cottage felt interminable when it usually seemed so short. When they finally reached the cottage door, Simon finally spoke. "I don't want you walking the grounds alone anymore. Not until we discover exactly what happened to the duchess. I should have had someone walk you home tonight."

"But—"

He raised his hand. His gaze drilled into her. "From now until we leave for London, a footman will accompany you where you need to go."

She sighed. "All right."

Stepping forward, he bent low over her, his eyes narrow. "I know you, Sarah. You haven't stopped wandering about since you were eight years old. Promise me you won't until we're sure it's safe."

He was close enough that she could wrap her arms around him and pull him to her. Her gaze flickered to his parted lips, so close, so deliciously edible. Her heartbeat spiked in anticipation. And for the first time, she realized she could do it, if she chose to. She could bring her lips to his and take them. He wasn't the only one who could initiate a kiss. She could kiss him, too.

But before she had a chance to adequately process this new information or to consider her options further, he repeated in a low growl, "Promise, Sarah."

"I promise," she breathed. She didn't take her eyes from his lips. Her voice could have fluttered away on the wings of a butterfly.

He straightened and took a step back. "Good." He gave a short nod, but his eyes had lightened, and his hungry gaze burned hot under her skin. "Good night, then. I'll see you in the morning."

With that, he swiveled and retreated down the path, leaving her to watch his broad, wool-covered shoulders recede into the darkness, her heart galloping again.

Chapter Three

✦

$\mathcal{S}$imon and Sam woke at dawn the next morning to search the dower house. As Esme had said, everything was in its place, with no sign of a struggle or anything untoward—besides the empty safe and the items missing from it.

After breakfast, Esme and Sarah joined them to continue the search, while Theo and Mark rode to question the villagers.

From the moment Sarah walked through the door of the dower house, Simon's awareness of her sharpened, honing in on the small things about her he found so fascinating. The fresh scent of her, like a meadow after a spring rain. The curve of her waist, the rise and fall of her bosom, the pale turn of her ankle when her skirt lifted slightly as she leaned over something. Her pink lips pursed in concentration as she filed through a sheaf of papers. The way black curls kept falling over her eyes...how his fingers itched to smooth the hair back, tuck it behind her ear.

When he'd touched her last night, felt the soft flesh of her chin pressing against his fingertips, his body had hardened and his cock had stirred, straining against the material of his pantaloons. He'd looked into those wide blue eyes, had studied the contrast of her dark lashes and brows against her porcelain skin, and he had grown uncomfortably hard. He'd wanted to brush his fingers over the slant of her cheekbones, press his lips to that soft, pink mouth, lay her down on the bench...

Hell.

He wished that part of him that had become so wildly attracted to Sarah Osborne would retreat. This was neither the time nor the place, and as much as his body told him otherwise, Sarah was most certainly not the woman.

And, for God's sake, his mother was missing.

They were all in the duchess's bedchamber, Sarah and Esme going through the bedside tables while Simon and Sam searched their mother's desk drawers, when Sarah said, "Ooh. They didn't take all the jewelry, then."

Simon turned to see her holding up something small between her thumb and forefinger. He frowned. "What is it?"

"It's a ring," she said. They all gathered around to see the object she transferred to her palm so they could view it more clearly.

"Mother's ring." He gazed at the diamond-encrusted gold. She never took it off—hadn't since the day his father had given it to her as a wedding gift. Simon's grandfather had purchased the ring for his grandmother on a long-ago trip to the Continent.

After a long silence in which no one moved, Esme asked warily, "Why is it not on her finger?"

"Perhaps she removed it before retiring at night?" Sarah suggested. "It was in her bedside table."

"Although her bed is made," Sam said, "so we know she wasn't forcefully taken from it."

"She could have been...taken...just before she went to bed." Esme nearly garbled the word *taken*. "Everything is laid out on her dressing table as if she was preparing for bed."

That was true. There was a basin full of water and soap scum, long since grown cold. A cosmetics jar was open on the dressing table, and the duchess's brush had strands of hair in its bristles as if she'd just finished combing her hair.

"Yes," Sam agreed. "Though if she was removed from this house against her will, she didn't put up much of a struggle. If she had, things wouldn't be so orderly."

"And yet if she knew she would be leaving," Sarah mused, "she wouldn't have been preparing for bed."

"Perhaps the person she left the dower house with was someone she knew," Simon said.

"Oh, that doesn't help at all," Esme whispered. "She is acquainted with *everyone*."

"It does narrow the field a bit, though." Simon took the ring from Sarah's open hand and slipped it into his pocket. "I'll keep it safe until she returns to us."

Simon met Sarah's gaze. He stared into her lovely blue eyes for a long moment, heat creeping beneath his skin, before he returned to himself and looked away.

"Let's finish here," he said in a brisk voice.

After he'd gone to bed last night, he hadn't been able

to push the images from his mind. He'd lain there, wide awake, his skin crawling with need, craving Sarah Osborne under him. Now, as he sifted through the duchess's papers, none of them providing a clue as to what had happened to her, worries about his mother's fate battled with fantasies of Sarah's warm, naked, slender form arching against his.

Every nerve in his body heated, reaching out for her. Craving her. Every time she glanced at him, heat scorched through him. Need, rising and burning, aching and demanding.

His body paid no heed to his strict attempts at discipline, to his notions of honor and responsibility.

He wanted her.

God help him.

After a quick luncheon, Simon began to question the staff. Over and over again, he asked the same questions and received the same answers.

"When was the last time you saw the duchess?"

"'Bout a week ago, Your Grace."

"Where?"

"Out and about on the property."

"Did anything seem odd about her? Was she behaving differently in any way?"

"No, sir."

"Have you seen anyone besides the staff and family on the grounds of Ironwood Park recently?"

"No, sir."

And on and on. Until one of the coachmen entered the saloon through the double doors of dark, heavy oak.

He was a new employee, tall, dark-haired, and dark-eyed, and clearly he had never been inside the saloon before, for he gazed in unabashed wonder at the octagon-shaped ceiling painted with an image of Apollo driving into the sun.

Simon had not been introduced to this man, and evidently none of his brothers had either, for none of them greeted him. Sarah was the one to rise from a gilded red velvet armchair, one of several arranged about the vast room. She came forward to stand beside the man and make the introductions.

"Your Grace, this is Robert Johnston, the new coachman. He has been at Ironwood Park since September of last year."

"Mr. Johnston," Simon acknowledged with a tilt of his head.

Sarah introduced the man to Simon's brothers one by one, and when they were finished, Johnston turned his attention back to Sarah, his mouth quirked in something of a smile as his gaze took her in. Simon saw interest in that gaze.

He didn't like it.

He arranged the sheets of paper that were lying on the table in front of him and stacked them with loud taps on the polished wood surface. Johnston's attention snapped back to him.

"We've brought you here to ask you some questions. You are acquainted with the duchess, correct?"

"Yes, Your Grace. I drive her to the village often."

"When was the last time you saw her?"

Johnston tilted his head, considered. "Well, I'd say that'd be just over a week ago. Last time I drove for her."

"Did anything seem odd about her? Was she behaving differently in any way?"

"No, sir. She was kind and friendly as always. She gave me some pennies to go to the pub for a pint while she was at her ladies' gathering."

Mark snorted. "Of course she did," he said under his breath.

"And you drove her home after that?" Simon asked.

"Yes, sir."

"And there were no odd occurrences or incidents that you recall on that day?"

"No, sir. None."

Looking down at the papers he held, Simon blew a breath through clenched teeth. Not one blasted soul had seen or heard anything odd. His mother had seemingly vanished into thin air.

Johnston cleared his throat, and Simon glanced up to see him looking at Sarah again, who was giving him an encouraging nod. Johnston turned back to Simon. There was hesitation in his voice when he said, "There was one thing, though."

Simon set down the papers on the table. Very slightly, he leaned forward. "Tell me."

"I did see—and hear—something I'd count as odd. Not that last day I drove Her Grace, but days later. Two days, maybe." He scrunched his forehead as if trying to remember.

Everyone waited in suspended silence for him to continue.

He glanced at Sarah again as if asking permission, and she nodded again, urging him with her expression.

"It was early evening. It'd been pouring down rain all

day, but it had finally let up, and the moon was providing a bit of light, so I'd gone out to exercise one of the mares. I saw a cart in the driveway of the dower house as I passed it. I've seen carts there before, mind, when something's being delivered to Her Grace and such. But this cart didn't belong to anyone I knew, and it was drawn by asses, not horses. And the back was piled high"—he gestured above his head to demonstrate—"but I couldn't tell what with. 'Twas all covered by oiled woolen blankets, water from the earlier rain still dribbling off the pile down the sides.

"I rode on, not giving it much thought beyond that. I had ridden behind the dower house when I heard it."

"Heard what?" Theo breathed.

Johnston swallowed. "Well, sir...it was shouting. Coming somewhere from the upper story—I couldn't rightly tell which window it came from. It sounded like the duchess was yelling at someone."

"What was she saying?" Simon asked.

Johnston looked a little pink now. "I couldn't hear it all, Your Grace. But I thought I heard 'fool' and 'bloody idiot' and 'how dare he!'" Again, he swallowed, his Adam's apple bobbing. "I was...er... rather discomfited, sir, and I thought the duchess wouldn't like me eavesdropping. It wasn't my place to listen to a private conversation like that. So I turned the horse and rode away."

"Did she sound like she was afraid?" Sam asked.

"Why, no sir. She sounded very angry. Angrier than I'd have ever thought a lady like that was capable of. It sounded like she wanted someone's blood. Honestly..." Blushing full-on now, the tips of his ears scarlet, he said, "I thought she might be beating one of the servants."

Simon supposed that Johnston was new enough to Ironwood Park that he could forgive him for thinking that. Any of the older staff would never have considered such a thing.

"Did you hear anyone else?" Sam asked. "Was anyone else speaking?"

"No, 'twas just Her Grace. Or," he amended, "I thought it was." He frowned again. "It did sound like her, but her voice was raised so high and angry, I can't be completely sure of it."

"Oh, it was Mama, all right," Mark mumbled. "I'd bet my dinner on it."

Simon would, too. Their mother rarely lost her temper, but when she did she lost it monstrously.

"Have you anything else you can tell us, Johnston?" Simon asked him.

Johnston's forehead lined with thought. "Can't say as I have, Your Grace."

"All right. If you think of anything else, you must come to me straightaway."

"Yes, sir."

He dismissed the coachman, and Sarah walked him out. As soon as the door closed behind them, Mark asked, "What the devil could have made Mama so angry?"

Sam blew out a breath. "Who knows? Nothing that we found in the house gave us any clues."

His brothers continued talking, but Simon kept glancing at the door, wishing Sarah would return. He didn't like the way the coachman had looked at her. He didn't like her being alone with him.

"What do you think, Trent?" Mark was asking.

Simon dragged his attention from the door. "About what?"

"Do you think we should all leave Ironwood Park tomorrow?" Mark repeated.

Simon kept his gaze cool, and he leveled it on his brother. "Yes. Since we haven't unearthed any answers here, we'll all leave to our respective destinations tomorrow, as planned. Except you, Mark."

Mark nodded. Over luncheon, they'd discussed the need for someone to stay an extra week or two at Ironwood Park to ensure no stone had been left unturned here...and to oversee the unpleasant business of dragging the lake.

"Now that we know about the cart," Simon continued, "we can include it in our questioning. Odd as it sounds, it seems the Duchess of Trent disappeared from Ironwood Park in a cart drawn by asses."

"Good-bye, girl," Sarah's father said in a gruff voice. He gave her a quick, tight hug, then pushed her an arm's length away from him, still gripping her shoulders. "Be good."

She flashed him a grin. "I'm always good, Papa."

He smiled at that, though his blue eyes clouded with melancholy. "Too true, too true." He let her go, stepping back. "And you'll be good at watching over Lady Esme, too, I'm sure."

"I will," she promised. She leaned forward to kiss her father's cheek. Although he hadn't said so outright, he was proud of her rise in status. As far as he was concerned, she'd earned it first by proving her intelligence in the years

of lessons with Miss Farnshaw, then by her unceasing loyalty to the Hawkins family, which in turn had earned their
trust. Papa believed she deserved every bit of the new pres-
tige the title of "lady's companion" afforded her.

Sarah herself had doubts. She wasn't certain she'd be a
success at the position. Yes, she could make pleasant conversation with Lady Esme. She had an eye for fashion and
could advise the young lady on what to wear to any given
ball or dinner party. Miss Farnshaw had educated her on
etiquette in excruciating detail.

What Sarah wasn't as sure about was keeping up the
game with others. Those refined ladies of society who
would surely see through her pretense and know immediately that she had no right holding the position of
companion to a duke's sister.

She took a deep breath and pushed that thought into
the dark recesses of her mind where she stowed all her
insecurities. She *would* do this. She'd do it because her
father thought her worthy. She'd do it because Simon believed she could, and because Esme thought it "the most
excellent idea my brother's ever had!" She'd do it for the
Hawkins family, and she'd do it for her own selfish desire to wiggle her toes in the silky waters of the lives of
the privileged.

Most of all, she'd do it to be close to Simon.

She hugged her father again, as quick and short and
hard as he'd hugged her, then she hurried to the rear of
the two carriages, the one upon which Robert Johnston
had taken the position of driver. She opened the door, and
just as she had her foot on the step and was about to haul
herself inside, a sharp "Sarah!" had her leaning back and
looking toward the front carriage.

Simon stood beside the carriage, a slight crease between his brows. He glanced around at the other servants milling about, then, leaving the door open, he walked to her in a few long strides.

He leaned toward her and spoke so that no one else would hear. "You will be riding with us."

The flush burned, an instant reaction clear on her cheeks for him to see. "Oh," she mumbled. "Of course."

It had been natural to think she'd be riding with Amy, Esme's lady's maid. But she was a lady's *companion* now. Of course, she'd be expected to *accompany* the lady on the journey to London.

She grimaced at Simon, and he grinned in response, then shrugged and gestured toward the front carriage. "After you, Miss Osborne."

Miss Osborne. He'd never called her that before. But of course, it was the proper way to address one's sister's companion.

She followed him to the front carriage and then accepted his help as he handed her inside. Esme was already sitting on the forward-facing lavender velvet squabs, and Sarah settled in beside her. Simon climbed up behind her and sat on the opposite seat.

After greeting Esme, Sarah looked out the window. Sam and Theo had left early in the morning—Simon's departure had been delayed due to the time it had taken to pack all the luggage Esme had required. Now, Mark and the servants assembled on the lawn in front of the house to wish them safe travels. Slightly off to the side and behind the carriage, Sarah saw her father, clutching his wide-brimmed hat to his side. He raised his free hand, and with a curl of his fingers, gave her a little wave.

"Good-bye, Papa," she whispered.

Simon must have given the signal because the coach lurched into motion, and with that, Sarah felt the pull and then the snap, as if some connection had been severed. She was free. Cut off from the proverbial apron strings and letting them fly in the wind behind her as the horses trotted away from the place that had been her home for so long.

Sarah loved her father and hated to leave him alone. Yet she was literally leaving him in the dust to explore a new world, and she couldn't prevent the excitement that welled from a place deep within her.

When they turned down a bend in the road and she could no longer see Ironwood Park, she gave a soft sigh.

Simon gazed at her, an expression of understanding on his face. "We're not even to the village yet."

"I know. It's just...I know we're going to go straight through it. And," she said breathlessly, "I can no longer remember what's on the other side."

"Really?" Esme stared at her with rounded eyes.

"When we first came here, I was only eight years old," she explained, "and I was so sad to be leaving our old house in Manchester, where my mother died."

A deep crease appeared between Esme's brows. The young lady was one of those rare fortunate souls who had never lost anyone she loved, so she was sensitive to discussing death or those who'd died to begin with. Now, considering the fact that Esme's mother was missing, Sarah realized speaking of her own mother in the past tense wasn't the wisest idea.

"I pouted all the way from Manchester," she continued. "I was afraid of this new place, where I knew no one and had no idea how my days would be spent."

"I suppose you never predicted being attacked by a blackberry bush," Simon said.

Something in his smile made her breath catch so hard that she had to look away before responding.

"Not at all. The first few days here, my father was very busy, so I was left to wander about."

Esme frowned. "Until a blackberry bush attacked you?" Esme had never heard the story, and she had been too young to remember the incident.

"I fell deep into one of those bushes out by the stream. I was essentially stuck, and fortunate that His Grace came by before I caused myself permanent damage trying to climb out." Though the little scar remained on her knee, reminding her of that day every morning when she pulled on her stockings.

"And I took her back to the house for Mrs. Hope's salve, and she met our mother for the first time."

"...and Mama loved Sarah," Esme finished. She knew *that* part of the story.

"Precisely," Simon said.

Sarah smiled, her heart fuzzy with the memory, only to pang with the reality that the duchess was missing, and no one knew where she was.

She met Simon's eyes, and his expression grew serious. "I wonder what you will think of London."

Beside her, Esme gave a small shudder, but she didn't share her opinion of the noisy, smelly city with her brother.

Esme was still painfully shy in Simon's presence. She had the same problem with Luke and Sam, but one simply couldn't be shy around Mark—the second youngest brother could coax the most reticent turtle out of its shell. Of all her brothers, though, Esme was closest to Theo—fewer years separated them, and they were near identical in temperament. Both tended to keep to themselves and preferred academic pursuits over social ones.

Esme wasn't shy with Sarah, however, and Sarah knew all too well what Esme thought of London. But if Esme wanted to withhold that information from her brother, Sarah had no intention of breaking her trust and telling him about Esme's aversion to the city.

"I believe I will like London," she told Simon. She didn't know how she knew it; she just did. London would have to do something truly horrible to her to prove her instincts wrong.

And if Simon was there, how could she not like it?

Late that afternoon, Simon and Sarah had fallen into silence. Esme had tried to read but the motion of the carriage had made her queasy, so she'd fallen asleep, her cheek resting on a silk pillow wedged between the door and the back seat cushion.

Sarah possessed the boundless curiosity of a child discovering a part of her world for the first time, and Simon couldn't take his eyes off her. The scenery, each structure that they passed and each subtle change in landscape, entertained her endlessly.

She was so different from the bitter and cynical men who frequented Simon's club, those men who were weighted down by politics, their positions and their responsibilities. By the fact that America was close to declaring war on Britain, or by the fact that Wellington was taking the war on the Peninsula deeper into Spain.

Men who could no longer find joy from an early daffodil jutting up from the grass. Men like himself.

Sarah's fascination with the world around her reminded him of his humanity. Of the small things that were still worth looking at.

If he wasn't so consumed by looking at her, his gaze, too, might have been drawn out the window. But he was content to watch her stare out at the pastures and meadows and rolling hills of the Cotswolds.

"Endless green," she murmured without looking at him, quiet so as not to wake Esme. "And every shade encompassed, it seems, from yellow all the way to blue."

Simon glanced out his window. "Yes," he said simply. It was true—the expanse of land between Ironwood Park and London was quintessentially English and not unpleasant to look upon.

The carriage began to traverse the arched stone bridge that descended onto the high road of the town of Burford. "What river is this?" she asked, one of the many, many questions she'd asked today.

He didn't always have a ready answer for all her questions, but this time he did. "River Windrush."

She was silent as they passed through the village, studying the landmarks, the church and sandstone architecture. To Simon, Burford was just one of the many villages they passed through on the way to London—its only special quality being that it was near Oxford, where they'd spend the night before continuing on to London tomorrow. But Sarah saw something new and wonderful in it, her big, expressive blue eyes taking it all in. Her lips parted as she absently twirled a dark curl around her finger, her deep breaths showing in the rise and fall of her bodice.

Her lips were pink, plump, and her tongue peeked out and ran over them. God, he wanted a taste. He wanted to know if she was as sweet as he remembered.

She glanced at him, then quickly back to the window, a light pink flush rising on her cheeks.

So pretty.

Something clenched inside him at that thought. He'd thought of Sarah as pretty for years, but in a detached way. She'd been pretty to him like a painted landscape might be pretty, or even like he might describe his sister as pretty.

But this kind of pretty was altogether different. This kind made his body harden in places it should damn well be prohibited to harden in her presence. And, God forbid, in the presence of his sister, sleeping or not.

He tore his eyes away from Sarah to stare up at the ceiling of the carriage, willing his body to cool.

Chapter Four

❦

$\mathcal{S}$omething was wrong. Simon had turned inward. It had begun this afternoon and had continued this evening as they'd settled at the Angel Inn in Oxford.

Perhaps Sarah had been too exuberant in her expressions of delight as they passed through the English countryside.

Or...perhaps he worried for his mother.

Not wanting to upset Esme, Sarah tried to hide her fretting as they ate a sumptuous dinner that had been prepared especially for them and served in a private room. She pushed around the mashed turnips and pork roast on her plate until Esme eyed her suspiciously, and Simon asked in a low voice, "Is the food not to your liking, Miss Osborne?"

Sarah's head jerked up, and she glanced at the cook and Mrs. Stewan, the mistress of the inn, both of whom had been hovering since the Duke of Trent and his companions had sat down to eat. Both of them blanched in horror at the duke's question and stared at her fearfully in anticipation of her response.

"Oh, no. It is delicious!" To illustrate, she took a big bite of the pork, which was cold, its sauce rather congealed, and tried not to choke on it. After she managed to chew and swallow without even a hint of a grimace, she spoke in a low voice. "There are just so many worries."

"Ah. I see," Simon said shortly. He'd explained to them that he wanted to keep the duchess's disappearance quiet for as long as possible, so Sarah knew better than to mention it out loud.

Simon didn't believe they could keep such a secret for very long, as not only would he be hunting in London but his brothers would be hunting all over England. Soon enough, the rumors would begin. But Simon thought that whatever information they could glean before the gossip spread might be more valuable.

She looked him square in the eye. "I want to help."

The corners of his lips quirked up. He glanced to Esme and then back to Sarah. "You already are."

"Yes, but..." She sighed. "I believe you do know what I mean, Your Grace."

"I believe I do."

She glanced at Esme. The poor girl had hardly spoken all day, and despite having taken several naps in the carriage, she looked simply exhausted, with dark circles under her eyes. Alarm stirred in Sarah's belly. "Are you well, my lady?"

Esme gave a dismissive wave. "Oh, yes. Just a bit tired."

Sarah glanced at her plate. The food was cold, and she had no intention of eating any more. But then she glanced at the cook and Mrs. Stewan and chewed on her lip, not wanting to offend them by not partaking of the next course.

But Esme covered her mouth with a yawn, and when Sarah looked at Simon, he gave her a nod as if to say, "Go. I will placate them."

So Sarah rose. As soon as she did so, Simon rose, too. She stared at him across the table in shock for a second before she came to her senses.

Dukes didn't rise for servants.

She blinked, shaking it off, wondering if she'd ever grow accustomed to her new status.

She held out her hand to Esme. "Let's go upstairs, my lady. We have another long day ahead of us tomorrow."

Esme took her hand gratefully and let Sarah help her up. Upstairs, Sarah and Amy assisted her to undress and wash. When the younger woman was comfortable, yawning in her nightgown, Sarah dismissed Amy then led Esme to the bed and tucked the blankets around her.

"Thank you, Sarah. I'm sorry I am so..." Esme's voice trailed off.

Sarah trailed a hand over Esme's forehead. No fever. "Are you certain you're not feeling ill?"

Esme sighed. "It's not that. It's just...Mama. Trent. London. It's almost too much to take at once. Es-especially Mama."

"I understand," Sarah soothed. "But I know your brother will find her."

Esme's hazel eyes filled with tears. "Yes, you're right, but what good will that do if she's d-d—"

"Hush," Sarah admonished gently. "You cannot think

that way. We must continue to trust that your mother is alive and well unless someone proves it otherwise."

"But do you really believe that?"

"I do," she said firmly. "Now go to sleep, my lady. And I believe this will be good for you."

"Losing Mama?"

"No, spending some time with your brother. Maybe now you will finally learn to be more comfortable in his presence."

Sarah had always been comfortable in Simon's presence, so it was odd to think that his own sister found him so frightening. And yet she did.

"Maybe," Esme said doubtfully.

Sarah patted her shoulder and rose. "Good night, my lady."

"Will you be going to bed, too?"

Sarah glanced over at the door to the adjoining room, a small space with a tiny window—just a closet, really. She didn't feel like being cooped up in there just yet. "No. I think I'll go check on Amy, Robert, and Ned. Make sure they're settled."

"All right," Esme murmured.

"Sleep well," Sarah said before going out the door that led to the second-floor corridor. The Angel Inn was small, and Simon had let all the rooms on this floor for their party.

She went to the room Robert Johnston was sharing with Ned, a new coachman he was bringing to London to train to drive there, but neither answered the door. Amy didn't answer either, and Sarah realized they had probably all gone downstairs for dinner.

She had just descended the first step on her way to the

kitchen when she saw Simon climbing the narrow stairway.

She stepped back up onto the landing and waited for him. Deep in thought, he didn't realize she stood there until he reached the top.

"Sarah, what are you doing?" He looked past her to see if anyone else stood on the landing. Finding it empty, the parallel lines on his forehead deepened. She wanted to soothe them away. Press her thumbs to them and work them until his forehead was smooth again and a smile touched his lips.

"Lady Esme just went to bed, but I'm not tired. I was going to go downstairs to check on...everyone else." She knew that to Simon they were "the servants," but calling them that would set them apart from her, and she had always been one of them.

He stared at her, long and hard, then nodded. "I see."

She frowned at him. No one else was near, so she could be frank with him. "What is it, Your Grace?"

"I..." He shook his head. "It's nothing. I'm just not comfortable with you being out alone."

"I am not going out," she said, "just downstairs to see whether Amy, Robert, and Ned are settled and whether they need anything."

"Always taking care of everyone, aren't you?"

She couldn't tell whether he meant that in a positive way or a negative one, so she simply shrugged.

Suddenly, he raised his hand to the bridge of his nose and pressed hard, blowing out a breath.

On impulse, she reached out and touched his arm. His gaze dropped to the place where her body made contact with his.

"Sorry," she whispered, withdrawing her hand. "It's just…You have been out of sorts since this afternoon. I know how upset you are about the duchess. Tell me how I can help."

"It's not only my mother," Simon said on a sigh. "Flighty and peculiar as she is, she can take care of herself. While my brothers and sister may worry that something unspeakable has happened to her, I doubt that. I intend to go forward under the assumption that she is at some family member's house on a holiday and she simply forgot to tell us. You know how she is," he added, gaze dark.

"Yes, I do." Sometimes the duchess did seem to forget about her children. She loved them more than anything, but now that they were grown and on their own for the most part, she had become more absorbed in her own activities. She didn't always tell the family about everything she did and everywhere she went.

"So you understand why I am not worried."

"And yet you intend to find her."

"I do. To ease my siblings' concerns, and because she needs to know that it's unacceptable, not to mention irresponsible, to worry us like this." He blew out a breath between pursed lips. "Unfortunately, we probably won't be able to find her before the gossip mill starts to grind out the story, certainly with all kinds of embellishments."

"Ah," Sarah said. "So that's why you're frustrated."

He gave a cynical shrug. "What's another blemish on our family name? There have been so many. Between her and Luke, I'm surprised we're not the sole topic of every scandal sheet."

"Those blemishes heal with the work you do every day," she told him, certainty throbbing in her voice.

He gave a mirthless chuckle. "Thank you. There's much work left to be done, though." Then the laugh faded and he scanned her face. After a long, silent moment, he murmured, "I'll walk you back to your room."

But he didn't move, and neither did she.

She just stared at his handsome face, at the way his eyes narrowed as he studied her. At the heat in them. It prickled over her skin, building in her core. The look in his eyes was full of such…promise. Instinctively, she licked her lips, and his gaze flickered down to them.

And then he leaned forward and kissed her.

Simon remembered her taste—as fresh and sweet as the sunbaked grasses in a country meadow. Her mouth was warm and soft and dry, and he felt a little puff of air as her surprised "oh!" whispered over his lips in the gentlest caress.

Simon wrapped his arms around her slender form and drew her close.

His body screamed with need.

For Sarah. His friend. His sister's companion. The gardener's daughter.

He closed his eyes and stifled a groan as her arms came around him. Of course it had come to this. *Of course.* He'd been a fool to think he could keep his hands off her.

He pulled her closer until her pliant body was flush against his. He splayed his hand over the muslin covering the curve of her lower back and coaxed her lips open with

his. Wanting more of that sweet taste. Wanting to insinuate himself inside her in every way.

And then he heard voices. The softest whisper of
sound was like a slap, drawing him back to the world. He
tore himself away, immediately missing the feel of her
against him.

She blinked her wide blue eyes at him. Her cheeks
were flushed, her lips now damp from his kisses.

And guilt made a frigid wash through him. He averted
his gaze. Damn it. "I shouldn't have done that," he said
through clenched teeth.

She didn't answer him right away. The voices were
growing louder—there were people coming up the stairs.

Finally, she whispered, "I liked it." And then she
smiled.

A part of him—a very, very large part—wanted to accept that smile, to sink into it and bask in its warmth,
allowing it to burn away his guilt. A very large part of him
wanted to take more from her. Much more.

But he wasn't a man who took advantage of servants
and innocent young ladies. He left all that to his carousing
peers.

The voices came closer. He recognized one of them as
Johnston, the coachman. After an instant of confusion as
to why Johnston would be coming up here, Simon recalled
that he'd reserved the whole floor for his party—the suites
for him and his sister and Sarah, and the smaller rooms for
the servants. His family often frequented this inn on their
more leisurely trips to and from London, and the mistress
of the place tripped over her skirts to make certain all was
perfect for any member of the Hawkins family whenever
they chose to visit. Today had been no exception.

He didn't have much time.

"Listen to me, Sarah. That was a mistake."

She gazed at him, unapologetic. As lovely and sweet and innocent as she was, she was no wilting flower. She never had been.

"It can't happen again," he told her quietly, and took a step back from her. The servants were upon them now with bows and curtsies and "Your Graces." He greeted them all politely and wished them a good evening.

Then he disappeared into the silence of his room where he undressed to his shirtsleeves and crawled between the cold sheets to stare up at the dark ceiling.

Simon was twenty-nine years old—old enough to know better. A relationship between him and Sarah was impossible for a variety of reasons that would be too exhausting to explore. He was a member of the English aristocracy, which at times was prone to vice and debauchery, and he knew what happened when men like himself formed liaisons with women like Sarah. Nothing good could come of bringing her into his bed.

Yet, the more he was near her, the more he wanted to bring her there. That taste of her on the landing had not been enough to allay his thirst. It had only heightened his craving for her.

He was expected to marry; to produce an heir and a spare, hopefully a full bevy of children to fill his household. He'd always fully intended to meet those expectations, but he'd put it off for years—other issues had taken precedence over the task of hunting for a suitable duchess. For a year after he'd kissed Sarah the first time, he hadn't even been able to look at another woman.

But he *was* twenty-nine now, and his practical, responsible nature turned again and again to his duty to his title.

A few months ago, he'd decided that this was to be the year. This Season, he planned to attend the myriad balls, parties, soirees, musicales, and dinners to which he'd invariably be invited. And somewhere in the marriage mart that was the London Season, he'd find a woman suitable to be his bride.

The devil in him whispered to him, promised he could have it all: explore the lust with Sarah and continue the hunt for a proper duchess.

His stomach twisted from those thoughts, recognizing the wrongness inherent in them.

Still, that devil wouldn't stop its seductive crooning, and the only way Simon could shut it up was to fall into an uncomfortable, restless sleep.

Sarah's lips tingled, and it was a most pleasant sensation.

Vaguely, she wondered how long it would be possible to keep that feeling upon them. If she licked them, or if water passed over them, would it vanish? Or would it simply disappear over time?

She didn't want the sensation to go away. She wanted to hold onto it forever.

Half in a daze, she watched as Simon went into his room, closing the door firmly behind him. When she dragged her gaze from his door, she saw that Amy and Ned had disappeared into their respective rooms. Robert Johnston, however, was standing close by, watching her.

She drew her friendliest demeanor about her like a cloak. "Good evening, Robert. I trust your dinner was acceptable."

He inclined his head at her. "More than acceptable, thanks. May I walk you to your room?"

She glanced toward the door of her room, not ten feet away. "Of course."

He held out his arm, and after a slight hesitation, she took it. They walked the short distance in silence. He stopped before her door, and she disengaged her arm. "Thank you."

"Good night, Sarah."

"Robert?"

"Yes?" He turned back to her, his brows raised expectantly.

"I haven't checked in on you as often as I should." One of the tasks Mrs. Hope had given her was to keep track of the staff and to make sure everyone was content. "I do hope you have been happy at Ironwood Park."

"Quite happy," he said.

"You have visited London before, I gather."

He nodded. "I spent some time there with my previous employer."

"Do you like London?"

His smile was warm. He was quite a handsome man when he smiled—it made his brown eyes twinkle. He was dark and broad-shouldered—strong from working with horses. "I do like London," he said. "But it's a mite crowded. Think I prefer the open spaces of Ironwood Park."

"I can understand that," she said.

Her lips tingled, reminding her of Simon...the kiss he'd bestowed upon her not five minutes ago. She raised her fingers to her mouth as a light heat suffused her cheeks.

"Well, goodnight, then, Robert. Sweet dreams."

"You, too, Sarah."

She slipped inside the little room and closed the door gently, then leaned against it, letting a wistful sigh escape.

Simon had kissed her...*again*.

London was quite as dirty and busy and smelly as Sarah had been warned. But she didn't care. Her nose had been glued to the window as they'd traveled across Town and finally arrived at Simon's house in St. James.

Yesterday, they'd gone to church, and afterward, carrying their bibles, Esme and Sarah had gone for a long walk in Hyde Park, Esme awkwardly greeting a few acquaintances as they'd strolled along and taken in the spring air. Today was their second full day in the city, and when sunlight cracked through her curtains in golden rays, Sarah woke in the little bedroom that had been assigned to her.

She rose, made her bed—which was covered with the loveliest counterpane of yellow silk—washed, and quickly braided her hair before tucking it up into her cap. She secured herself in her stays and chose one of her serviceable muslins to wear, then drew the heavy curtains and peeked out the window that looked over the mews, grinning. Already the alley below was busy with servants and horses preparing for their daily duties.

Eager to see what her day held in store, she hurried downstairs for breakfast.

Simon was seated in the dining room, a newspaper spread open before him. He rose quickly, his chair scraping over the floor, as she entered.

She waved a hand at him, but she couldn't ignore the tremor of awareness that passed through her in his presence. "Please sit down, Your Grace. There's no need for such formality."

His frown bordered on a scowl. "Yes, there is."

He stubbornly continued to stand as she went to the sideboard and selected some toast and kippers and a fried egg.

He only sat after she'd lowered herself into the chair across the table from him. She took a bite of egg. Simon had obviously ensured the food would be hot and fresh. Not knowing when she and Esme would come down, he probably had tasked a footman with changing out the dishes every ten minutes.

He gazed at her with a small smile on his face. "What do you think of Trent House, Miss Osborne?"

Her lips quirked at the "Miss Osborne" designation. She'd probably never get used to him calling her that.

"It is lovely." From what she'd seen of it so far, Trent House seemed to be a smaller but no less opulent version of Ironwood Park. "It has the Hawkins mark upon it."

"True," Simon said. "Both houses were built by my grandfather, you know."

She did know but didn't answer because at that moment Esme came in, yawning as she crossed the threshold. "Oh," she murmured, her hand covering her mouth. "Please excuse me."

"I hadn't expected you up so early, my lady," Sarah said. Indeed, it wasn't uncommon for Esme to sleep until noon.

"I know." Esme glanced at Simon, who'd risen from his seat once again. She didn't take any food but sat at the table, taking the coffeepot and pouring herself a generous cup.

"That would be my fault." Simon pushed his newspaper aside. "I asked your maid to wake you because it's going to be a busy day. News has spread of our arrival in London. We have received an invitation to a ball on Wednesday."

Sarah and Esme stared at him. Wednesday was the day after tomorrow.

"I have already accepted the invitation," Simon continued. "I have attended every ball I've been invited to so far this year, and I don't want to raise suspicions by declining this one. For as long as possible, I wish to maintain a façade of normalcy in Town. When the truth about Mother's disappearance is revealed, that may change, but for now, I'd like to keep up appearances."

Sarah and Esme didn't say a word. So that was how it was to be—they were going to be thrown directly into the heat of London society with no time whatsoever to acclimate.

"Therefore," he continued, "you'll be visiting the dressmaker's, Sarah, because you're going to require a ball gown in two days. No doubt the dressmaker will have something on hand she can alter and have ready by Wednesday."

Sarah glanced down at her plain white muslin—its only decoration the big ruffles at the neckline and hem. A similar style to the other two dresses she'd brought—the only two other dresses she owned.

She should have considered the fact that she'd need proper clothing if she was expected to attend social gatherings with Esme. But so much had happened she hadn't given it a thought.

Simon leveled his gaze on his sister. "You will require

new dresses as well, Esme. Whatever you might have is from last year and out of fashion by now."

"Yes, Trent." Not meeting his eyes, Esme took a deep swallow of coffee as if to fortify herself.

Simon kept his gaze on his sister. "Neither of you are to spare any expense. After the immediate necessity of the ball gown, I want you to help Sarah acquire a proper wardrobe. And you must purchase anything new that you require as well. The Duke of Trent's sister and her companion will not be seen scampering about London in rags."

Sarah scowled—her clothes were old and somewhat worn, but they were clean and serviceable. Certainly to call them rags was a gross exaggeration. She would have told him so right then if a footman hadn't walked in to refresh the dishes on the sideboard.

Instead she shot Simon a glare that, if they had been seated on their bench at Ironwood Park, would have had him apologizing for his rudeness immediately. But he didn't apologize, just gave her a cool look in return and didn't say a word.

Something tightened in her chest. So, he saw her as some slattern wearing rags. Very well, then.

She dug into her kippers, stewing in her thoughts. Simon knew she didn't have the funds to purchase fancy dresses from haughty London dressmakers, which meant that he expected to pay for them himself.

A lady was not supposed to accept gifts from a gentleman. Miss Farnshaw had drilled that into her head as surely as she had drilled her in the steps of the quadrille.

Yet, Sarah wasn't a lady. And Simon wasn't giving her a choice. Furthermore, she wouldn't deliberately embarrass Esme or Simon by wearing inappropriate clothing in the presence of their peers.

Sarah recalled the specific reason why ladies were not supposed to accept gifts from gentlemen. It was because gentlemen usually offered them expecting something more—something *wicked*—in return.

She glanced at Simon, who had taken up his newspaper once more. He didn't offer to buy her ball gowns because he wanted something more from her. If he did want something more, he fought against that desire. He hadn't said anything to her about the kiss at the Angel Inn, but ever since then, she'd felt the skin-prickling heat of his gaze whenever they were in the same room together.

Sarah had never spent much time considering her reputation. Sheltered as she was in Ironwood Park, it had never been of primary concern, although Miss Farnshaw had told her that it should be. Without a reputation, one could not expect to find a worthy husband. Without a reputation, a woman was scorned and belittled.

Sarah never expected to find a worthy husband. In her mind, there was no man in the world who could measure up to the Duke of Trent, and she wouldn't marry some poor fellow and make him miserable by constantly comparing him to Simon.

Furthermore, at Ironwood Park, no one had ever scorned or belittled Sarah. The family wouldn't have tolerated it. Now in London, however, she knew they couldn't protect her so easily.

So Sarah would do what Simon told her. She'd shed her "rags" and shop for proper garments so that she could stand proudly beside Esme as her companion.

And as for the "gift" from the Duke of Trent—well, she would accept it. He'd never demand recompense for the dresses, especially not of a carnal sort. Honor, integrity, decency, propriety—those were all pieces of what made Simon who he was.

Melancholy welled in thick, dark bubbles inside her.

What an improper response. She should feel relieved. Happy. Safe. Pure. All emotions that a true lady would feel.

There was a certain quality of purity she'd never had that Miss Farnshaw had told them a true lady possessed innately. This feeling, this tingling, yearning desire that she felt for Simon—had felt for three long years—she knew very well what it was.

Lust.

More proof, then, that this was all a farce. She might speak like a lady. She might know how to pretend to be one. But deep inside, she was anything but.

Furthermore, she wasn't sure she wanted to be.

Chapter Five

On Wednesday evening, after a quiet early dinner in the Trent House dining room, it was time to prepare for Lady Bellingham's ball. Upstairs, two maids joined Esme, Sarah, and Amy in Esme's dressing room.

Everything Sarah would wear was new, from her stockings and shoes to the pins in her hair and her cosmetics.

Standing in her new chemise, she gazed at all of it—the results of the day they'd spent at the modiste's. The pile of hairpins and shiny ribbons. The lovely pearly silk cap that would be pinned onto her hair. The pink silk slippers, glittering in the lamplight. The crisp short stays and petticoat.

And the dress. It was a gauze robe dress of primrose over a pearl silk slip, with Chinese buttons down the front. It was so elegant. Finer by leaps and bounds than anything Sarah had ever worn before. She stroked a finger over the sleek, expensive, beautiful fabric.

"I am so pleased," Esme exclaimed. "Madame Buillard does lovely work. Do you know she designed my court dress last year?"

"I'm not surprised." Sarah looked over at Esme's dress, a white satin with a light pink slip overdress trimmed in black velvet and with black velvet sleeves. Satin slippers, white kid gloves, and a pink satin hat wreathed with fresh roses completed the ensemble. "Everything is so *beautiful*, my lady."

"Yes." When Sarah turned to the younger woman, Esme was watching her with shining eyes. She moved forward and wrapped her arms around Sarah.

Startled, Sarah almost stepped backward. But she came to her senses quickly and embraced Esme in return. "Sarah, you are like an older sister to me. You always have been. I'm so glad to have the opportunity to share all this with you."

Sarah's smile was watery. "Thank you," she whispered. "I will never forget it."

Releasing her, Esme stepped back. "This isn't temporary, you know. You shall remain my companion as long as you wish to."

"I would love that," Sarah admitted, but she knew better. "However, you shall marry soon, and I'll return to my old position under Mrs. Hope."

"No!" Esme exclaimed. At Sarah's expression of surprise, she clarified. "First off, I possess no high hopes of ever marrying."

"Why?" Sarah asked. "You have always said so, but I have never comprehended why."

Esme just shrugged. "After tonight you might possess a greater understanding. But even if I do marry someday,

Sarah, you must remain a lady's companion. You must never go back to being a housemaid. You are simply too good to hold such a position."

Something cold twisted in Sarah's gut at that. She knew Esme meant it as a kindness, but it was a brittle reminder of their essential difference. Sarah *wasn't* too good to be a housemaid. When she'd first ascended to head housemaid at Ironwood Park at the age of twenty, she'd been so proud. Someday she'd be qualified to be a housekeeper like Mrs. Hope. Truly, for someone with Sarah's pedigree, it was a great ambition to aspire to the position of a housekeeper at a great house like Ironwood Park.

She never thought she'd stray from that path. Certainly not to become a lady's companion, wearing a beautiful dress and attending a ball presented by one of the most esteemed patronesses in London.

It took a long while, even with the help of three maids, for them to dress. When Amy finished pushing the last pin into her hair, Sarah rose from her chair, smoothing her sleek skirts over her hips. She turned to look into Esme's large oval looking glass...and simply stared.

A primrose princess, dark-haired and pink-cheeked, stared back at her.

"You look lovely," Esme said.

Grinning, she turned to the younger woman and sighed with pleasure. Esme's black-trimmed pink dress was rich and warm and brought out the highlights in her dark hair and the shimmering hazel of her eyes. "So do you, my lady."

"Thank you." But then Esme's smile wobbled, and she whispered, "You'll help me to be brave tonight?"

"Of course. But only if you'll help me. It's my first time venturing into London society, you know."

"I do." Esme gave a wry chuckle. "We're quite the pair, aren't we?" She held out her arm. "Come. Let's go downstairs."

Arm in arm, they descended to the drawing room, where Simon awaited him. Sarah stifled a gasp when he turned to greet them. In his black knee breeches, velvet-trimmed black tailcoat over a striped and embroidered waistcoat, he was the most handsome and compelling example of masculinity she'd ever seen.

He stood frozen in a state of suspended silence, his gaze fixed on her.

The blush rose to her cheeks, fast and furious. Deeper, she was sure, than the rouge that one of the maids had brushed lightly over them.

"You look beautiful." He cleared his throat, and he seemed to forcibly move his gaze to Esme. "Ah...both of you. Are you ready to go?"

"Yes." There was a slight quaver in Esme's voice, and Sarah squeezed her arm in a gesture of strength and solidarity.

They left the drawing room and went out the front door and to the curb, where the carriage awaited.

Sarah had learned quickly that while London was vast, the area of the Duke of Trent's social sphere was somewhat smaller. The drive to Lady Bellingham's house only took a few minutes.

Nerves fluttered in Sarah's chest, but it was nothing to what Esme was experiencing. The younger woman had gone completely rigid in her seat, her hands clasped so tightly together that her knuckles were white.

Sarah didn't know how to help her.

Neither did Simon, apparently, or perhaps he didn't notice that his sister was sitting on the squabs as stiff as a mummified corpse.

Sarah couldn't quite fathom why this should be so terrifying to Esme, but she remembered the solemn looks on people's faces when they spoke of Esme's Season last year. Esme had never mentioned it to her, and Sarah hadn't dared ask.

Whatever it was, Esme still suffered from it—that much was apparent in her current pale-as-death countenance. Yet Esme had gone along with all the preparations for the ball with nary a complaint.

"Remember not to speak of the situation with Mother tonight," Simon reminded them as the carriage drew to a halt under a circle of golden-hued gaslight. "It is important for us to give the appearance that nothing is amiss. But keep your eyes and ears open for any information."

"Right," Sarah said.

Esme hadn't seemed to hear him. Instead, she was staring at the carriage door as a footman opened it.

"We'll do this," Sarah breathed into her ear. "I won't leave your side. I promise."

"Yes," Esme whispered, and she took the footman's proffered hand and stepped out of the carriage.

The house was a lovely Palladian structure, one of the few in London with a curving driveway and a front lawn—Trent House didn't have either, though it bordered on the Green Park which gave it a bit more of a feeling of openness than most.

Bright lamplight made the white façade of Lady Bell-

ingham's house gleam gold. People milled about everywhere, departing from carriages, gathering to converse in
the cool spring air.

It was chilly for Sarah, though, with her short sleeves
and no shawl to cover her arms, and she was glad Simon
led them directly to the open door. They passed through
the line, shaking the hands of a host of elegantly dressed
ladies and gentlemen, all of whom seemed to know Esme
and Simon and appeared pleased to meet Sarah.

She kept an eye on Esme throughout—despite her
rigid, silent demeanor in the carriage, she seemed to be
managing well enough now, smiling and nodding and
speaking quietly when spoken to.

They entered the vast—and already crowded—ballroom. Unlike outside, it was warm in here—and loud.
People milled about, drinking champagne, talking in
groups. With Simon's comforting presence just behind
them, Sarah's confidence rose. She stayed close to Esme,
almost pressed against her side, as she took in the visual
feast the ballroom provided.

An enormous crystal chandelier hung from the center
of the carved ceiling, flanked by two complementing
smaller ones, each holding what looked like hundreds of
wax candles. Gilded sconces dotting the walls provided
more light, creating the effect of a blazing sunlit day.

Sarah's gaze wandered toward the upstairs gallery and
the ornate bronze railing that lined the upper story of the
massive room. Scores of people stood there and chatted,
and a cluster of musicians took up the whole of one corner, warming their instruments.

"Your Grace!"

Sarah, Esme, and Simon turned to see a young man

bounding toward them. He pumped Simon's hand vigorously.

"Whitworth. Good to see you," Simon told him.

Whitworth laid eyes on Esme and smiled. But Sarah noted some tentativeness to it. "Lady Esme. I am so pleased to see you back in London," he murmured with a bow.

She curtsied, but her words were blunt. "I didn't expect to be here."

When she didn't add anything to soften her response, Sarah and Simon glanced at each other. Sarah knew she shouldn't speak since she hadn't been introduced to this gentleman yet, but Simon cut in, saving both her and Esme.

"I just brought my sister from Ironwood Park a few days ago. Thought it'd be good to have her and her companion visit for a while. Oh—have you met Miss Osborne? Miss Osborne, may I present Mr. Whitworth, Lady Bellingham's second son."

"Oh, yes, of course." Sarah curtsied. She could see the resemblance between this man and the regal lady she'd met as they'd entered. "I am so happy to make your acquaintance, Mr. Whitworth."

"And you as well, Miss Osborne," he said politely. He turned back to Esme. "Do you have a partner for the country dance, my lady?"

"No."

Whitworth hesitated, waiting, and when no further words were forthcoming he said, "Would you care to join me as my partner, then?"

Sarah watched Esme, whose gaze was on Whitworth. "Surely you've heard I'm a hopelessly wretched dancer, Mr. Whitworth?"

"What?" Sarah cried. "No, indeed you are not, my lady. You are a very fine dancer."

Esme gave her a bleak look. Simon cleared his throat. Whitworth's hand went to his cravat as if to loosen it, then dropped back down to his side, fingers curling. "I would like to dance the country dance with you, should you care to," he said quietly.

What a kindhearted man, Sarah thought, giving him a look of approval.

Where Esme had been pale as death ever since the carriage ride, she now flushed profusely, her round cheeks turning a mottled pink. "All right. Yes. Thank you."

He inclined his head at Esme, smiled at Sarah, and nodded at Simon. "Well, then. I'd best see if my mother has need of anything."

As he strode away, Sarah released a slow breath. She was beginning to see the nature of the problem with Esme. Odd, after so much instruction in etiquette with Miss Farnshaw, but then again, their lessons with Miss Farnshaw had occurred in the privacy of a quiet room at Ironwood Park, not in a crowded ballroom in London.

Sarah wished she knew how to reassure Esme, but she already felt the assessing gazes of the *ton* raking over them both. Anything she said to Esme here might be overheard. And she wouldn't add to Esme's embarrassment. Instead, she gave the younger woman an encouraging smile.

Esme didn't smile back. She looked stricken. "I was quite awful to him, wasn't I?" she whispered.

Sarah couldn't answer because more people were approaching them. Everyone wanted to greet the Duke of Trent, and by extension his younger sister and Sarah. By the time the dancing formally began, Sarah had been introduced to forty-three members of London society she hadn't previously known.

As the highest-ranking gentleman in attendance, Simon would open the ball partnered with Lady Bellingham. When he finally left them to escort the lady to the floor, Sarah and Esme found a pair of empty seats in the line of maroon-velvet-upholstered chairs that stretched along the length of the grand room.

For the first time in a good hour, no one accosted them. She supposed it was because Simon was no longer with them. Beside Sarah, a young debutante whispered to her companion as the dancing began, "That's the Duke of Trent. Oh, how I wish to be introduced."

"What would you say to him if you were?" her friend asked.

"I'd fall to my knees and kiss his toes and beg him to choose me for his duchess," the young woman said. Both girls tittered but kept rapturous eyes on Simon over their fan tops.

Sarah watched him, tall and handsome, as he switched partners, smiling down at the new lady. His lips moved. The lady, a plump woman a few years older than Sarah, gushed something Sarah couldn't begin to comprehend, then turned pink to the tips of her ears.

"Lady Esme!"

Sarah and Esme both turned. A beautiful young woman and her older counterpart were approaching. By the similarity of their features, Sarah assumed they were mother and daughter.

Esme rose, a bit of her dress catching between her seat and Sarah's, and she yanked it out as Sarah rose, too.

"Good evening, my lady." She gave an awkward curtsy over her chair. "Um..." She looked at Sarah. "This is my companion, Miss Osborne."

Sarah smiled, waiting for the ladies' names. But Esme was finished, so the older woman, after sliding her gaze one last time to Esme, said, "Miss Osborne, it is lovely to meet you. I am Lady Stanley, and this is my daughter, Miss Stanley."

"Good evening." Sarah curtsied, trying not to wince at the breach of protocol Esme had necessitated.

They stood there far too long in an uncomfortable silence. Sarah studied the young woman, who in turn studied Esme with an interested, coolly assessing gaze.

She was beautiful. A blond angel dressed in white with a shimmering silver trim. Blue-eyed, with a healthy glow in her cheeks. She was the quintessential maiden shopping in the marriage mart with her match-making mama. Sarah had heard of Baron and Lady Stanley—their country home wasn't far from Ironwood Park. But they'd never visited, and the duchess had never spoken of having them as guests. Sarah had no idea why, especially since the daughter appeared similar in age to Esme.

Finally, seemingly unable to bear the silence any longer, Lady Stanley said, "I hear you have only recently arrived in London."

"Yes, that's right," Esme said.

"We arrived just a few days ago," Sarah supplied.

"I see. I wouldn't have expected to see you in Town without your mother," Lady Stanley said. "Did she remain at Ironwood Park?"

"She is..."

Esme swallowed hard, and again, Sarah finished responding for her. "The duchess was unable to join us."

"Oh my. I do hope she is well."

Sarah looked closely at the older woman. Her face was a mask of polite concern, yet there seemed to be a slight insincerity to the way she'd said that. Had something unpleasant occurred between the women? Was that why the Stanleys never came to Ironwood Park?

"We will convey your good wishes," Sarah said simply, not wanting to lie and yet not wanting to give anything away, either.

Miss Stanley seemed uninterested in this topic. Her gaze had moved from Esme to the dance floor, where the musicians had just finished playing the last strains of the minuet. Moments later, Simon rejoined them. After greeting the lady and her daughter, he politely asked Miss Stanley to dance the quadrille. She accepted with a brilliant smile.

Simon had to leave to escort another lady into the next dance. Miss Stanley's partner came to claim her, and Lady Stanley spotted a friend and wandered off, leaving Sarah and Esme alone again.

As they resumed their seats, Sarah snapped open her new fan and fluttered it over her face as she watched the ladies continue to fawn over Simon.

Two more dances were punctuated by awkward conversations with acquaintances of Esme's from last Season. And then the quadrille came, and Sarah watched Miss Stanley dance with Simon. She didn't blush or simper as most of the other ladies had. She was open and gregarious and laughing with him, always brightening when she returned to him in the dance. She flirted with him in such a subtle yet entrancing way, Sarah couldn't tear her gaze away from them.

She wondered what Simon was thinking. He smiled down at Miss Stanley, but he'd smiled down at every other lady, too. Yet with Miss Stanley, it was different. Sarah couldn't quite put her finger on why, but it was, and it made her skin feel tight over her flesh.

She thought, not for the first time, of what it would be like when Simon married. When a new mistress came to Ironwood Park to take on the role of the Duchess of Trent. What would happen to their uncertain relationship then?

She wanted to ask Esme more about the Stanleys, but she couldn't, not in this environment. And she didn't want Esme to see how... well, how *jealous* she was.

So she sat there, loving Simon more than ever, envious of the ladies who so openly touched him and flirted with him, and pretended that none of it mattered.

Georgina Stanley gazed up at Simon, her light blue eyes encircled by a dark ring of blue and fringed with lashes that she swept downward as she turned away.

Her eyes were blue... like Sarah's. Yet so different. Sarah's eyes were a deep blue. When he looked into them, he saw so much more than their color. He saw understanding and interest and depth. Hers were eyes that could burrow under the shell of the Duke of Trent and understand the man that lay beneath. She *knew* him.

He clenched his jaw as he turned Miss Stanley. He shouldn't be thinking this way. Shouldn't be comparing other women to Sarah.

Miss Stanley didn't really know him. Despite the fact that they had danced countless times and conversed a significant portion of those, she didn't know anything about his family or his home. Or *him*.

Simon was acquainted with her father from Parliament and from his club. The man had been hinting at an association between their families for months. Simon had been noncommittal—he hadn't made public his intention to find his bride this Season. God forbid— if he had, the matchmaking mamas would wage a full-fledged assault.

He took the hand of the dark-haired lady to his right, and they walked to the center, meeting the other couples, stepping back, where they turned again, and he found himself face to face with a third lady, who murmured a shy, "Good evening, Your Grace."

He greeted her with a smile, then they separated.

Still, most everyone knew who he was. They knew his age, and they knew enough about him to know he intended to marry and father an heir one day. The Stanleys weren't the only family that had turned their focus on Simon as a potential husband for their daughter.

He reached for Miss Stanley again, resting his right hand firmly across her lower back.

Miss Stanley had been present at almost every event he'd attended in London since the beginning of the year. By now, he knew the feel of her hands as they clasped over his, how her waist curved beneath his fingers.

Yet she still didn't know him. For that matter, he didn't know her. He wasn't entirely sure he wanted to.

She was lovely—her beauty, frankly, was unsurpassed in society circles. She was the belle of the Season. She was also a daughter of an aristocratic family with money and connections. The Barony of Stanley was an old and

respected one. She would make a man a fine wife someday.

But she isn't Sarah...

He smiled down at her as he led her in another turn and
thrust that thought from his mind.

The truth was, no one could compare to Sarah. He
couldn't expect to find another Sarah from the pool of el-
igible ladies in London. Sarah was one in a million.

The thought depressed him. God knew he didn't want
a marriage like the one his mother and father had sub-
sisted in.

No, that would never happen. He'd never be like his
father. Or his mother, for that matter. Both of them had indulged in affairs—several affairs, in the case of his father.
He'd kept mistresses in Town while Mother had been left
on her own at Ironwood Park.

Many of his peers kept mistresses secreted away, to
be brought forward when a man was bored or in need
of sensual companionship a wife could not or would not
provide.

Simon had observed his mother's misery more than
once. Long ago, he'd resolved to never do that to his own
wife.

Holding both Miss Stanley's delicate gloved hands in
his own, he looked down into her bright blue eyes and
thought about a life with a woman like her. She was beautiful and virtuous and gregarious...all important compo-
nents of a respectable duchess.

The music ended, and he bowed to Miss Stanley and
then to the lady to his left. Turning back to Miss Stanley,
he led her back to her mama, responding to her chatter
but scarcely hearing it. When they reached Lady Stanley,

he asked Miss Stanley to accompany him to the supper, which she accepted with pleasure.

She did seem to enjoy his company, but he was no fool—he knew most of the time it was his title that held the allure. That was why he could count his true friends— those he was sure liked him for him—on one hand. Sarah, of course, was among those.

Leaving Miss Stanley with her mother, he sought out Esme and Sarah... and with an inward cringe, he remembered his sister's awkwardness. Why did she struggle with social gatherings? He didn't understand it. She'd been raised to shine in such settings, and yet she simply... didn't.

Whitworth had taken Esme for their dance, so he found Sarah sitting alone, watching the beginning strains of the country dance. He slid into the chair beside her, gazing out over the ballroom floor.

"Where are they?" he asked her softly.

"Near the potted palm."

Esme stood beside Whitworth, who gazed at her with a small, encouraging smile on his face. Good man, Whitworth.

Simon had been present at her final ball last summer. It had been a disaster. Not only had she fallen, sprawled over the wood floor, but two other people had tripped over her, causing the most unseemly pile of silk and wool and human limbs on the dance floor. He had protected Esme from seeing it, but there had been a very unflattering caricature of her in the scandal sheets the following day.

Glancing around, he saw they were still whispering about it. Several ladies scattered throughout the ballroom were pointing at Esme and giggling behind their fans.

In his mind, he catalogued the identities of those who laughed at his sister. He wouldn't make a scene, not here or anywhere, but he'd remember.

"She's so brave," Sarah whispered.

He glanced at her, wondering if she knew what had happened last year.

Sarah kept her gaze fastened on Esme, her eyes glassy, and Simon wished he could dance with her. He wanted her in his arms. He wanted her to be the one smiling up at him, looking at him with those honest blue eyes.

But a duke did not ask his sister's companion to dance.

He remembered the first time he'd seen Sarah dance, in the parlor at Ironwood Park. Miss Farnshaw had been pounding out a minuet on the pianoforte, and Sarah and Esme had been practicing in the center of the room. Hovering near the door, Simon had observed them, unnoticed.

Sarah had been seventeen years of age, and on that day, his gaze had been riveted to her. Watching the way she'd helped his twelve-year-old sister, her laughter, and her exuberance as she'd danced, Simon had felt the first stirrings of lust for Sarah Osborne.

It hadn't been three years ago, after all. It had started long before then, and over the years had grown into this powerful, pulsing need he felt for her now.

Esme began the country dance, not looking at Whitworth but at her feet, as if willing them to follow her commands. And her performance was, if not admirable, then adequate. No falls. Not even a trip. Through it all, Sarah studied her, and between speaking to people who came up to greet him, Simon covertly studied Sarah, taking in her profile, the lively expressions that crossed her face, her scent so fresh compared to the press of bodily sweat and heat that surrounded them.

She truly cared about Esme, that much was evident in the careful way she observed her, swaying gently to the music, then releasing little puffs of relief when Esme successfully executed a step.

At the end, Esme went so far as to smile at Whitworth for a moment before her shyness overcame her once again. Whitworth escorted her to Simon and Sarah and thanked her for the dance before disappearing into the crowd.

Sarah gave Esme a brilliant smile, and the two women shared something silent between them that Simon found impossible to interpret. He was glad that Sarah was proving to be such a fine companion for his sister.

It was time for the supper, for Simon to escort the Stanleys to the dining room. As he walked away, he felt the residual caress of Sarah's smooth voice washing over him.

Desire welled up within him. Desire to ignore Lady and Miss Stanley and escort Sarah to the supper instead, then spend the rest of the evening dancing with her. He wanted to push away the heavy societal burdens that had weighed on him for so long. The sudden longing to throw off the mantle of responsibility and, for once, do what he really wanted burned inside him.

Plastering a smile on his face, he doggedly approached the Stanley women instead.

Chapter Six

❧

They returned from the ball in the earliest hours of the morning. After seeing an exhausted Esme to bed, Sarah couldn't sleep. She wasn't tired. Her mind was too actively parsing out what had happened tonight, all the new things she'd learned, not only about London and society but about Simon and Esme.

Throwing her cotton robe over her chemise, Sarah left her room and tiptoed downstairs, making certain not to disturb any of the other members of the household. In the corridor outside the library, where she was intending to find a dull book to read to help her fall asleep, she stopped short. There was a line of light along the bottom of the door. Someone was inside.

It had to be Simon. Who else would still be awake at this hour?

Before she could think, before she could talk herself out of it, she'd knocked on the door.

"Come in."

Simon sat on a chair by the hearth at the far end of the long, narrow room, which was sparsely furnished except for the rows of bookshelves along the walls and two carved wooden chairs and a table near the hearth. He looked toward the door with a bemused expression that relaxed when he saw her hovering on the threshold. "Sarah. Come in," he repeated, setting his full glass on a side table and rising to greet her.

"It's not necessary to stand, Your Grace."

"Yes, it is, Miss Osborne."

She couldn't help the pull of a smile on her lips at the way he addressed her.

Simon wasn't wearing his coats. Only his shirt, open at the top and showing a vee of golden flesh, and the breeches he'd worn to the ball. Instantly, a tingling flush rose to Sarah's cheeks.

Tearing her gaze away from the sight of him so...*undressed*, she moved across the room toward the chair he was gesturing to, inhaling the pleasant essences of leather and cigar smoke. Simon had told her that his father had the habit of smoking cheroots in this room, and the smell had permeated into the walls and never faded away. He resumed his seat when she lowered herself into hers.

"I couldn't sleep," she admitted.

"Nor I."

"We both *should* sleep," she said. Their schedules were busy tomorrow.

He gave a soft laugh. "Probably."

She stared at the hearth, but feeling his gaze on her, she glanced at him. "Did you enjoy the evening?"

He'd danced with six different young ladies—twice with Miss Stanley. She'd counted.

His chest rose and fell with a deep breath. "It was . . . acceptable."

She cocked a brow at him, but only said, "Ah."

They sat in comfortable silence. Simon retrieved his glass from the table and took a few sips of the amber liquid. Sarah soaked up the heat of the fire and basked in the luxury of having Simon close to her without the presence of others.

"Lady Esme—" she finally began. Lord, how to finish that sentence? "She . . . struggled."

He nodded. "I know."

"Oh." She hadn't been sure he'd noticed his sister's extreme discomfort tonight, but she was glad he had. Sarah gave him a sidelong glance. "And . . . ?"

He fingered the rim of his glass. "I think her reticence is due to her being sheltered in the country. The more she is exposed to such gatherings, the more comfortable she'll become."

"Do you truly believe that?"

"I do."

"Perhaps your theory will prove true," she conceded after a minute. "In the meantime . . . she tried so very hard tonight."

"She performed . . ." he hesitated, then said, "adequately. Better than her last ball, by far."

Sarah didn't want to know what had transpired at Esme's last ball if this showing had been far better.

"She wants so desperately to please you."

He frowned. "Please me? Why?"

Sarah laughed. "How can you not know, Your Grace? You are her older brother, the head of the family. You are the Duke of Trent. Everyone wishes to please you, but probably no one more than Esme."

Except Sarah herself, of course.

Now it was Simon who stared into the flames. "I am just her brother. Just someone who wants the best for her. We'll keep trying. She'll continue to improve."

"I hope so."

"I have thought more than once tonight that her improvement was due to having you at her side."

"Oh, no. Your mother was at her side last year, and the duchess is a far more formidable ally than I."

"She is that, but she is also quite social and had a tendency to ignore my sister. Leaving her to the wolves, so to speak."

"Oh." Sarah's heart clenched. It made sense. The duchess knew everyone, spoke to everyone, was the most gregarious soul Sarah had ever known. She could see the older woman flitting from person to person, leaving poor Esme to fend for herself.

"But you remained by her side," Simon said.

"It is my duty to do so."

"Still—I wish you would have danced."

"What?"

His eyes met hers, held her steady in his gaze. "I would have liked to see you dance. I would have liked to dance with you."

"I do not stand at Lady Esme's side as her equal, Your Grace," she reminded him gently. As Lady Esme's companion, she could not encourage invitations to dance. Her duty was to be an observer, a protector of her lady's interests.

He was quiet for a moment, staring down into the liquid he swirled in his glass. "I know Miss Farnshaw taught you how. I watched you once, years ago."

"Did you?" she breathed.

"I did." He raised his gaze, met her eyes. "I watched you dance a minuet in the parlor."

"Oh." Something about the way he was looking at her sent a soft heat flushing through her from the inside out.

"I wanted to dance with you then. I wanted to dance with you tonight, too. Did you not wish you had danced this evening?"

She considered this. She would have liked to dance, yes, to take the place of Miss Stanley on Simon's arm. But how could she tell him that?

Suddenly, firmly, he set the glass on the side table and rose. He held out his hand to her.

She stood without thinking, reached out to take his hand. Like when he'd helped her into the carriage earlier, his grasp was warm and strong, but now was different. Now she touched his bare skin, felt the roughness of his fingertips under the sensitive flesh of her palm. His hand was warm and dry. Intoxicating. Touching him like this, skin to skin, was a heady feeling, indeed.

"A minuet," he murmured. "Dance with me, Sarah."

He stepped back and bowed formally to her. Entranced, she curtsied back. They both took a step, and he swept up her right hand once more in his firm grip. They turned to face the closed door at the other end of the room, and as he hummed the notes, they danced forward then began the figures and turns of the minuet. Throughout it all, Simon's lips pressed together, humming the notes in a low tenor, and his eyes never left hers.

In the minuet, the couple came in contact with each other infrequently, and when they were separated and dancing to the corners of the room or turning to complete their figures, Sarah ached for the moment when they would come together again, only their hands connecting, those strong fingers curving around her palm.

It was the slightest touch, the rarest contact between the two of them. But with his green eyes focused solely on her, his bare hand touching nothing but her, Sarah had never felt anything so erotic. Each time her skin connected with his, a deep shudder ran through her.

Finally he gathered both her hands in his, and as they turned, Sarah realized this was the end. The humming notes stopped, and he let her go, stepping back once more to bow.

She curtsied, and he straightened as she rose.

They stood there, in the center of the room, staring at each other. The depths of his dark green eyes held her in his thrall, so heavy with the weight of the world, and at that moment, she wanted to wipe it all away—the pressures of Parliament and government and his position. Worries about his sister...and his mother.

"I wished it had been me," she said softly. "When you were dancing with Miss Stanley and the others. I wished you were dancing with me."

He gazed at her unspeaking for a moment. Then he said, "I did, too."

He stepped forward, wrapped his arms around her, and pressed his lips to hers.

The feel of him, of their lips gliding against each other, sent fireworks exploding through her. She dragged him harder against her, heard his ragged whisper, "Sarah."

Their lips moved in a hot, sensual slide. His hand rubbed tight circles over her lower back...and lower, until he cupped her bottom, pulling her against him so the hard ridge of his arousal pressed against her abdomen. The feel of it, of that most primitive, masculine part of him, sent a carnal shudder racing through her.

His mouth moved down her chin, and she kissed his rough cheek, then tilted her neck as he moved her braid aside with his free hand to kiss her there.

His lips pressed against her jaw, then caressed the shell of her ear before kissing their way back to her mouth, seeking, exploring.

Sensation washed over her. Not only in the places his mouth touched, but all over and through her. Deep yearning. Longing. *Need.*

She gave a small whimper, clutched him tighter, kissed his bare, warm skin wherever her mouth could reach him. She wanted more. So much more.

His arousal grew, pressed against her lower belly, so hard and so hot she could feel the heat between the layers of their clothes.

His hand moved from her neck to the opening in her robe, cupping her breast over her nightgown, his thumb running over her nipple, hardening it into a sensitized nub that strained against the fabric of her chemise.

She pressed her body tighter against him, blindly seeking his lips with her own.

She caught them, moving against him in a brazen kiss that she hadn't known she was capable of. He tasted like man and desire. Cedar and spice. So delicious. She didn't know how she'd ever get enough.

Suddenly his hands moved from her buttocks and breast to her upper arms. With a low groan, he pushed her back.

"Stop."

She gazed at him, clawing through the haze of desire that had overcome her. "No, Simon."

He blinked at the use of the familiar name and, from a part of her deep inside, she froze.

Reality crashed in. Forcing her frozen neck to move, she swung her head away.

"Sarah, look at me." He cupped her hands in his palms, and warmth instantly flushed through her, combating the cold.

"I...Sarah, I *want* you. But I don't want to hurt you. I'm not the kind of man who...uses women."

"I know you're not." One of the reasons she adored him.

"So you see why we can't, why I can't...?"

"I'm not a fool, Your Grace," she said softly. Sarah knew that no matter what happened between them, no matter what power he had over her, Simon would never take advantage of her. "I know what I am doing. What I want."

Simon flinched. "I don't want to ruin you."

"I know," she whispered. "But sometimes I wish you did."

With that, and with a huge force of will, she turned and left the room.

On Tuesday afternoon, nearly a week after Lady Bellingham's ball, Esme and Sarah were sitting comfortably in the drawing room at Trent House when Lady Stanley and her daughter arrived for an unexpected visit.

Esme stared at the footman who'd announced them for a long moment. Then, she closed her notebook—she'd been working on one of the fanciful stories she loved to write—laid her pen on the mahogany side table, and said, "Please show them in."

Sarah tucked her own embroidery into its basket and exchanged a glance with Esme. Was the lady ready for this? These would be the first callers since their arrival in London—odd for a duke's sister to have so few visitors, Sarah thought, but probably not so odd for Esme, who had fewer friends in London than Sarah ever would have guessed.

"It'll be just fine," Esme said, reading her thoughts. Indeed, she seemed far more relaxed than she had during the ball. Still, there was a tightness around her mouth and a stiffness in her shoulders that belied her calm.

Moments later, the lady and her daughter were shown in.

Miss Stanley wore a fashionable white frock with a matching, fur-trimmed pelisse. Her beauty had not diminished after the ball. Indeed, she was just as lovely in daylight, if not more so.

Sarah watched her gaze skim over the room, taking in the light blue wallpaper, the marble hearth, the card table with a half-played game of chess, and the darker royal blue of the furniture upholstery, before her eyes came to rest on Esme. "Oh, Lady Esme, it is so good to see you apart from that crush at the ball," she told Esme warmly.

"Yes, it is good." Esme gave the lady a tight smile as Sarah turned to the footman to order some refreshments. With a bow, he left the room.

Lady Stanley, her face a mask of concern, gave Esme a full embrace, from which Esme stumbled backward, giving the woman an odd look. "Oh, my dear. We have heard. And we have come to offer our assistance in whatever form you may require."

"Heard?" Esme's expression was blank.

"The horrid news that your dear mama has disappeared, of course," Miss Stanley said.

Esme's eyes widened.

"And that no one has the faintest idea of where she's got off to," the baroness said.

"Oh. That." Esme swallowed hard. "Where did you hear that?"

The older woman waved her hand. "Oh, you know. Word travels so quickly in our circles."

Esme looked over the lady's shoulder at Sarah, who gave Esme a somber nod. They'd known this would happen eventually, and they had talked through with Simon how they would manage it.

Sarah glanced meaningfully at the cluster of silk-upholstered seats.

Esme gave a short nod and gestured to the sofa. "Please sit down."

"Why, thank you." Lady Stanley and Miss Stanley sat beside each other on the sofa, both of them still looking appropriately troubled. Sarah wondered if their concern was genuine. If it wasn't, they certainly did a very good job of pretending.

When Esme and Sarah had taken their seats in the armchairs across from the sofa, the baroness leaned forward. "Please tell me what happened. I've been able to think of nothing else since I heard the dreadful news."

Esme's chest rose and fell with a great breath as she prepared to speak. When she did, the words were careful and measured, and very close to what Simon had told her she should say. "Well, you see, my mother is prone to whimsy. As most everyone knows."

"Oh, yes," Lady Stanley said. "Even though we are neighbors, we have never been friends, which is a true shame. Though every time I have met your dear mama, I have seen how personable she is. But I have oft heard of her eccentricities as well."

"She supports many charity ventures across England, and even in Scotland," Esme continued. "And we have concluded that she must be off overseeing one of them." She shrugged. "We believe she merely forgot to tell us."

"Oh, how vexing!" Miss Stanley exclaimed.

"Indeed it is," Esme said gravely. "We are doing everything we can to locate her, just in case it is not what we think. But none of us is concerned." She raised her hands in a gesture of defeat. "That is Mama, after all."

Well done, Esme, thought Sarah. While Esme certainly wasn't as easy now as she was when alone in Sarah's company, at least she had been able to speak to the Stanleys politely. And in complete sentences. Furthermore, she'd handled relaying the situation regarding her mother with a calmness that would have made Simon proud.

"Well, it does seem extremely odd that she simply disappeared," Lady Stanley said. "Did she take servants with her?"

"She did. Two of them."

"Well, that is reassuring. May I ask what measures you are taking to find her?"

"Of course. It's quite simple, really. The duke has been searching here in London while my other brothers are searching in various places in England."

"Oh, I am quite certain His Grace will find her!" Miss Stanley exclaimed.

Sarah glanced at the young woman. She seemed in

earnest, her hands clasped tightly in her lap and her blue eyes shining.

A pair of maids entered with refreshments at that moment, and Sarah busied herself pouring tea for everyone. Esme and Lady Stanley took their cups with thanks, but Miss Stanley hardly looked at Sarah when she handed her the cup. Sarah was accustomed to being invisible to those outside the family as a housemaid, but since she had been elevated to lady's companion she had been treated with general politeness, and to be so blatantly ignored now gave her an odd, uncomfortable feeling.

"Well, if we can do anything, anything at all, you won't hesitate to let us know, will you?" the baroness asked.

"Of course," Esme said. "But truly, my brothers will find her. There's naught to worry over."

"I am so happy to hear that," the older woman said. "Indeed, I had heard otherwise."

Sarah felt the muscles in her shoulders stiffen. Esme frowned. "Oh? What have you heard?"

"It's probably nothing." When both Esme and Sarah simply stared at her, she added, "You know...gossip." She blew out a breath through her closed lips as if in exasperation.

"What kind of gossip?" Sarah finally asked. "Please do tell us."

Miss Stanley gazed uneasily at her mother.

"Well..." The older woman gave a dramatic pause. "Evidently, your brothers are concerned that she was *murdered*."

Silence. Then Sarah and Esme spoke at once.

"No evidence points to such a conclusion, my lady," Sarah said.

"Where have you heard that?" Esme asked.

Lady Stanley took a sip of her tea. Following her lead, her daughter raised her cup to her lips as well. Lowering her cup into its saucer, the baroness said, "My son is at Cambridge. He is acquainted with your brother, Lord Theodore. I received a letter from him this morning stating that Lord Theodore has taken him into his confidence and shared his and your other brothers' fears about the fate of your mother. My son, of course, is extremely concerned, as we all are."

"He exaggerated!" Esme exclaimed. "Theo has no such belief. He would have told me."

Miss Stanley's eyes narrowed on her. "My brother never exaggerates."

Esme shook her head mulishly. "And my brothers would have shared it with me if they harbored such concerns."

Would they? Sarah wasn't so sure. The brothers didn't want to worry Esme—she was already terribly fearful that something horrific had happened to the duchess. Still, she knew Theo. He was almost as reserved as Esme herself, and Sarah hadn't ever heard that he and Mr. Stanley were friends. It seemed unlikely he'd take Mr. Stanley into his confidence like that.

Lady Stanley gave a tight smile. "Now, girls. Georgina, you mustn't quarrel—we are guests here." She looked at Esme. "A misunderstanding, surely."

"Surely," Esme agreed, but her cheeks were flushed and her hands clenched over the sleek wooden arms of her chair.

Sarah racked her brain to think of something to smooth things over. "Would anyone like a lemon tart?" she asked brightly, reaching for the plate the maid had brought. Lady Stanley and her daughter swiveled to give her blank looks.

They were saved from answering by a knock on the door. Esme swung around. "Come in."

A footman entered. "My lady, there is a Mrs. French here from the Ogilvy School for the Blind to see you."

"Ah!" exclaimed the baroness. "Ogilvy is one of the duchess's charities, of course."

"A school for the blind?" Miss Stanley said incredulously, as if she'd never heard of such a thing. "But why would one bother to educate the blind?"

The baroness shrugged. "Well, my dear, as we discussed earlier, the Duchess of Trent did have her eccentricities." Setting her tea aside, she rose. "Come, Georgina. It is time for us to go. We are off to see Lady Morgan next."

Miss Stanley obediently rose, while Sarah stood more slowly, burning deep within at how the baroness had spoken of the duchess in the past tense.

She was glad for the interruption. A new visitor meant the current ones were given the cue to leave, and she was glad to be rid of the Stanleys. Not very many people caused her discomfort, but the baroness and her daughter certainly had succeeded in making her feel ill at ease.

"Good-bye, Lady Esme." Miss Stanley gathered Esme's hands in her own. "I am sure we shall see each other often over the next months...and even more often after that. We shall be great friends."

"Er...right," Esme said, and Sarah hid her smile. It seemed Esme felt the same about the Stanleys as she did.

Sarah curtsied and wished them a good afternoon, and the two ladies left.

Esme and Sarah hardly had a chance to exchange a relieved glance before Mrs. French entered. She was a tall, thin woman with gray-streaked black hair and thick spectacles. She held a flat leather satchel. Upon entering, she bowed low, clutching the satchel against her chest.

"Lady Esme. You might not remember me, but we were briefly introduced last year."

"Of course I remember you, Mrs. French. Mama and I visited your school and witnessed what an excellent job you have done with your pupils."

The woman flushed with pleasure. "Thank you, my lady."

Esme gestured to Sarah. "This is Miss Osborne. Miss Osborne, this is Mrs. French, the headmistress of the Ogilvy School for the Blind."

"A pleasure to meet you, ma'am." Sarah had heard about Mrs. French and her school from the duchess, who had been very pleased with the strides the headmistress had made in training and ultimately finding sustaining employment for her blind students.

"Would you like some tea?" Esme led the woman toward the sofa. "A lemon tart, perhaps?" Sarah noted that with this woman, Esme didn't need to be reminded of the common courtesies like she had with the Stanleys. Or maybe she just felt the slender woman could use the food.

"Oh, no thank you, my lady. I cannot stay long." Mrs. French perched on the edge of the royal blue sofa, laying her satchel beside her.

Sarah and Esme resumed their seats across from her. "I recall that you were commencing a program of teaching some of the more talented girls to sew. How is that faring?"

"Very well, my lady. Indeed, we have just had our first young lady hired as a seamstress here in Town."

Esme clasped her hands over her heart. "Well done, Mrs. French. I knew it would be a successful endeavor. My mother would be so proud to hear it."

"Why, thank you," Mrs. French said. There was a long pause, and then Mrs. French gulped and said, "I have come to see you today because I have heard that our benefactor the duchess is . . . er . . . *indisposed.*"

Esme's voice turned sharp. "Is that so? What have you heard of my mother being indisposed?"

Mrs. French clasped her hands hard in her lap. "The *Times* reported this morning that she is missing. Shocking news, indeed, and I am very sorry to hear it."

"The *Times*, you say?" Esme glanced at Sarah, who shook her head in bewilderment.

"His Grace left early this morning," she told Esme. When Sarah woke, two hours before Esme, Simon had already been gone. "Surely if he read it before he left the house, he would have warned us."

Esme turned her focus back to Mrs. French. "But why has this information compelled you to come to see me today?"

Mrs. French wrung her hands. "I'm so sorry." She rose abruptly. "I should not have come. It is not a good time for you—"

"Please sit, Mrs. French, and tell me why you came."

At that moment, Sarah saw a rare side of Esme that reminded her of Simon. That side that could command and lead.

Mrs. French abruptly sat down again. She opened the satchel on her lap and withdrew a sheet of parchment.

"It is all here, my lady," she said in a strangled voice. "The rents are due, and we haven't the funds to pay. The duchess wrote a promissory note for the amount of the rents. She assured me the funds would be sent in mid-April in time to pay the rents by the thirtieth, but..." She shook her head, not quite meeting Esme's eyes. "I am so sorry, but we haven't received them. We haven't enough in reserve to pay the amount due. We have acquired ten new students due to the outbreak of rheumatic fever in Holborn, and we've a new teacher to pay, and no means of paying the rents unless the duchess can help us."

She stopped speaking. Esme and Sarah stared at her, speechless. The thirtieth of April was the day after tomorrow.

Finally, Esme asked, "How much is it?"

"Seventy-four pounds, six shillings, my lady."

That amount was twice the sum Sarah made in a year at Ironwood Park as head housemaid.

Esme blew out a breath. "May I see the document?"

"Of course." Mrs. French rose to hand Esme the sheet.

Esme studied it for long, quiet moments, then she passed it to Sarah.

It was true—the Duchess of Trent had promised a hundred pounds to the Ogilvy School for the Blind by April fifteenth to cover the rents and other incidentals—presumably, in this case, the new teacher. Sarah recognized the flourish of the duchess's signature at the bottom of the sheet adjacent to another signature she didn't recognize.

Sarah slid Esme a glance. Esme was only nineteen years old, and Sarah knew that she had no access to those kinds of funds. Her fortune had been held in trust since her birth, and her brother managed her finances.

Esme surprised her again. "I shall have the amount promised delivered by tomorrow morning. The duke and I will ensure your school remains doing its good work, Mrs. French. Please do not spend another second worrying over it. I am so thankful you came to me."

When Simon arrived home that afternoon, Sarah and Esme explained the situation at the Ogilvy School for the Blind, and Simon arranged for the funds to be sent that very evening. To Simon, this served as disturbing proof that his mother hadn't planned her disappearance. If she had, she would have taken care of details like this before she'd left. His mother might be flighty, but she was rarely irresponsible in matters such as these.

Later, as they all sat down to dinner, he confirmed that the news of the Duchess of Trent's disappearance had traveled all over London.

"I am sorry the Stanleys surprised you like that," Simon told them. "I would have brought word to you sooner, but it was a busy day, and I'd no idea you'd be inundated with visitors." Inwardly, he chastised himself. He should have thought of that, knowing what he did of the vultures who inhabited London society.

"Esme handled it beautifully," Sarah said.

He smiled at his sister, then looked down at his plate to spear a piece of beef with his fork. "There is more news, or non-news, I suppose I should say."

The search for his mother had only resulted in non-news since he'd arrived in London. It was as though she'd disappeared without a trace, and his level of frustration increased with every day that passed with no gains made toward locating her.

"Oh?" Sarah asked. Esme just laid her fork down and waited.

"I received letters from both Mark and Theo."

The two young women watched him, waiting.

"Neither has found any information relating to our mother."

The breath left Esme in a whoosh. Sarah gave a low groan.

"Theo has begun the term at Cambridge," Simon continued. "Mark has completed his investigations at Ironwood Park"—he'd even supervised the dragging of the lake, which had resulted in nothing but waterweeds, thank God—"and he's traveling north to continue his search at Lake Windermere."

"What about Sam?" Esme asked.

"I haven't heard from him, but I know he's been occupied with his duties for the Crown, I doubt we'll hear anything unless he discovers something of note."

He glanced at Sarah. She was dressed simply, in one of her old white muslin dresses. For jewelry she wore only a strand of small paste pearls around her neck. Splashes of color on her cheeks spoke of her vivacity. Her dark hair, piled on her head haphazardly, with curling locks tumbling to frame her face, shone under the lamplight. Her blue eyes, fringed by dark lashes and full of compassion and concern, met his, and he caught his breath. She was a beacon of light. Of peace.

He wanted to kiss her again. No, he wanted more. He wanted all of her. To take that sweet light into him and hold it there.

When it came to Sarah, something inside him was wolfish. Predatory. Constantly assessing and calculating how to best conquer her. Reminding him that she seemed willing enough, so conquering her might be a mere matter of simple seduction.

Ever since they'd arrived in London, he'd waged a battle against these base needs of his darker nature every single time he saw her, but she seemed not to fear them. She *embraced* them.

Which only made him want her more.

Chapter Seven

In late May, Sarah and Esme went to the modiste's for their final round of fittings. By the time they left the dress shop, they'd loaded the carriage with several new dresses along with accessories: hats, gloves, stockings, slippers, and even hairpins. It was late afternoon, and Esme was in high spirits.

"Madame Buillard said a gold bracelet would go nicely with my new opera dress," Esme said. "Let's go to the jewelers."

They walked side by side, occasionally having to move aside to make way for other pedestrians—the streets in this part of London were very busy. The footman who'd accompanied them to the modiste's this morning walked a few paces behind.

"I've been to this shop with Mama," Esme explained, and Sarah was grateful that Esme was able to mention her mother without a sob welling. "Mr. Lamb is the master here, I believe."

And the man, nearly bald except for a tuft of white hair puffing out from the back of his scalp like a bird's tail, recognized Esme right away and hurried over to them from behind his counter. "Good day, Lady Esme," he said with a bow. "How may I be of service?"

"I'm looking for a bracelet," Esme said. "Something gold, but simple and delicate. Nothing too ostentatious."

"Of course. I have several pieces that might suit your needs. Follow me, if you please." Mr. Lamb turned to a table covered with golden jewelry. Esme perused the bracelets, but the adjacent table that contained necklaces of rubies and emeralds and other rare gems caught Sarah's eye.

She gave a wistful sigh. It was all so lovely.

And then her gaze snagged on one of the necklaces, and she turned her focus to it. The voices of Esme and Mr. Lamb faded as she stared at the lavender-colored gems for long seconds, the thudding of her heart the only discernible sound.

"My lady?" Sarah's words came out in a choked murmur.

Esme hurried over to her. Sarah didn't see her so much as feel her presence.

Slowly, she lifted her heavy arm to point at the one-of-a-kind piece of jewelry lying so innocently in its little bed of pink silk. "It's the duchess's amethyst necklace," she whispered.

Esme's gasp was audible. Finally, Sarah looked at the younger woman. Esme's eyes were wide and filled with tears, her hand flat on her chest as if to contain her own pounding heart.

She turned her wild-eyed gaze to Sarah. "What...? How...?"

"I don't know."

"What is it, miss?" Mr. Lamb was all proprietary concern, the wrinkles on his face deepening.

Sarah swallowed hard and answered for Esme, who was clearly incapable of speech. "That necklace...where did you get it?"

"I purchased it."

"When?"

"Why, just last night."

Sarah felt sick. "Who sold it to you?"

Mr. Lamb's lined face darkened. "What's this about?"

Sarah glanced desperately at Esme, not sure how much to reveal, but Esme was still staring at the necklace as if she hadn't heard a word of what they'd said.

Sarah straightened her spine. "We know that necklace, sir. It belongs to the Duchess of Trent."

The old man's eyes went wide. "What? But that's impossible."

"It would seem so," Sarah said, a dry edge to her tone, "and yet here it is. So if you'll tell us who sold it to you..."

A light sheen of sweat covered the man's face, and at her words, his face seemed to clam up.

"Please, sir. Where did this necklace come from?"

"I cannot say, miss."

"All we need to know is—"

"I'm sorry, but that is proprietary information."

"This is extremely important."

He just shook his head at her, his lips pressed together, his expression closed.

Sarah ground her teeth. "If you won't give us any information, perhaps you'll give it to the Duke of Trent."

She took Esme's arm. "Come, my lady, let's go find your brother."

An hour later, Esme and Sarah were back in the jeweler's shop, but this time Simon stood between them.

"Where is it?" he asked as he strode in.

Sarah led him to the display containing his mother's amethyst necklace. Simon stared at it for all of two seconds before turning hard green eyes upon Mr. Lamb, who was already hovering beside them, twisting his hands.

"You will inform me as to where you obtained this necklace, sir," Simon said by way of greeting.

Lamb dropped his hands. He looked furtively to the necklace, then back to Simon, not quite meeting his eyes.

"I purchased it from an independent supplier."

Simon raised a brow. Sarah could not help but notice how much larger Simon seemed than the other man. He towered over Lamb. And not only in stature. In *presence.* Lamb simply shrank before the duke.

"He is here in London," Lamb blurted.

"You will tell me his name and address."

"Of course, sir. The name's John Woodrow." He rattled off an address in London.

Sarah marveled at how easy it had been. Lamb hadn't been about to tell her and Esme anything about the necklace's origins earlier, yet Simon had hardly had to ask.

He is a duke, after all, she reminded herself. Sometimes she did forget. Most of England's population would bow and kiss his toes because he was the Duke of Trent. Sarah would do so as well, she acknowledged, though not because of the title, but because he was Simon. There was a marked difference between the two.

"You will remove that necklace from your display," Simon said. "After I speak with Woodrow, I will inform you as to how we shall proceed."

Lamb bowed. "Of course, Your Grace. I shall remove it immediately. It will go into my safe until this matter is resolved."

"Very good," Simon said.

As they turned to go, Lamb had already removed the necklace from the table and, clutching it in both his hands, scurried into the back room.

Outside, Esme turned to Simon. "Could Mama be in London?"

Simon shook his head. "I don't know. The address he gave is in the East End. I can't quite picture our mother in that part of town."

None of them voiced the greatest worry—that the necklace had been stolen. That whoever had taken the duchess from Ironwood Park was a violent criminal. But if that were the case, why hadn't she or the servants left signs of a struggle? Could it have been someone she knew and trusted but who had turned on her?

"There are so many things I don't understand," Sarah said softly, "but chief among them is that if the duchess is being ransomed, why have we received no word?"

Simon glanced at her, then opened the door to the carriage, handing Esme in first. "Exactly. It doesn't add up. It's why I find it difficult to believe she was taken against her will."

"Unless they took her, somehow preventing a struggle..." Sarah glanced into the carriage, where Esme was settling herself, turned away from them. "But she ultimately fought, and something horrible happened..."

A muscle twitched in Simon's cheek. "My mother isn't one to meekly submit when she feels as though she's been wronged, so it is a possibility."

They stared at each other for a second, then he held out his hand to help her into the carriage. She took it. Through their gloves, she could feel the strength of his grasp, in each finger, and a small shudder of awareness trembled through her. She could feel the heat of his eyes on her, too, but she kept her own averted. Her lips responded, though, an instinctual tingling in anticipation of another kiss.

She mused over this as the carriage jolted into motion.

Men were the aggressors. Miss Farnshaw had drilled that lesson into her and Esme. Miss Farnshaw had also given them a plethora of suggestions on how to divert masculine aggression in order to maintain one's reputation and purity.

Sarah watched Simon out of the corner of her eye. He would not be the aggressor, though she knew that it was in his nature. No, his notions of honor and protectiveness of her virtue were strangling his aggressive tendencies.

She wished Miss Farnshaw had taught her how to be an aggressor. She chewed on her lip, wondering if she could do it. Find a way to try...

Esme, who'd been gazing out the window, suddenly turned to Simon. "We're heading home?"

"Yes," Simon said. He didn't offer any further explanation.

Sarah shared a quick look with Esme before saying, "I thought we were going to the East End to inquire about the duchess's necklace."

"No," Simon corrected. "We're going home to Trent House, where you will be safe, and I'll be inquiring about the necklace on my own."

"Your Grace, I can hardly see how going to someone's lodgings in the middle of the city should be dangerous—"

"Have you ever visited a residence in the East End?"

"No," Sarah admitted.

"Well, then." Simon focused on a point on the carriage wall between Sarah and Esme. "I'll not put either of you in danger. Do not waste your breath arguing, Sarah. You will *not* be accompanying me to the East End this afternoon."

Sarah and Esme waited all afternoon in suspense for Simon to come home. A foggy dusk had wisped hazy fingers over London when he finally returned.

With no news.

The three of them sat in the drawing room drinking tea as Simon told them about his venture into the East End.

Esme let out a frustrated breath. "So you discovered absolutely nothing?"

"Nothing at all," Simon confirmed. "John Woodrow was nowhere to be found. The landlord said he was at home yesterday, but only briefly, before departing again. Evidently the man is seldom in residence and unpredictable in his habits."

"Where is he, then?" Esme asked.

"That is the question. No one seems to know where he goes."

"How will you ever find him if he's rarely at home?" Sarah asked.

"I've hired a youth to watch the neighborhood, specifically Woodrow's rooms. We'll know the moment Woodrow returns home."

That evening, Simon sat at the long dinner table in Lord Stanley's house. The table had been cleared for the dessert course. A servant had removed the many-footed, monstrous bronze epergne, and for the first time all night, Simon could see his old acquaintance, the Duke of Dunsberg, seated across from him. However, good manners kept his attention on the lady next to him, Georgina Stanley, precluding him from opening any topic of conversation with Dunsberg.

A servant refilled his champagne, and he took a sip. Champagne wasn't his beverage of choice, generally speaking, but it was close in the dining room, what with the body heat of the twenty-eight people seated around the table, the hearth behind his back, and the assorted servants milling about, and he was thirsty.

"Isn't this champagne wonderful?" Miss Stanley asked, watching him drink. "It is my papa's favorite."

He smiled at her. "Is that so?" He took another sip, and only now realized it had an exceptional flavor, as champagne went. "You're right; it is excellent."

"I don't know how he obtains it." She leaned toward him and dropped her voice to a whisper. "It's all very secretive, but somehow he has it shipped from France."

Simon carefully set down his glass. Everyone involved in politics knew of his long-standing outspokenness against the practice of smuggling. It disgusted him that even the lawmakers of the land turned a blind eye when it meant they could acquire the French spirits they couldn't seem to live without. Interesting that Stanley should choose to serve illegally obtained spirits tonight.

Miss Stanley took a small bite of her ice and gave a decadent sigh. "It is like I have died and gone to heaven. First the champagne, and pineapple is my favorite kind of ice in the whole world."

The way she looked through her eyelashes up at him and the way her pink tongue swiped over her lips to capture every drop of the ice...she was flirting with him, for certain. Georgina Stanley always flirted with him, and he'd always been unflinchingly polite in return.

Simon glanced at the head of the table, where his host presided over the festivities, watching everyone with a keen eye. Stanley reminded Simon of a hawk, intelligent and calculating, always aware of everything that occurred in his vicinity, and usually outside it.

He returned his attention to Georgina, who'd taken another bite of the ice and had closed her eyes in ecstasy. There was no doubt she was lovely.

Well-bred and innocent, too.

She isn't Sarah.

His gaze traveled past Miss Stanley, past Esme and her partner and down the long table until he saw Sarah, who'd been partnered with a curate. The lowest on the social strata of those present, they'd been the last to enter and had been seated far down at the other end of the table.

She wasn't paying any attention to the curate, who seemed to be enjoying his ice as much as Miss Stanley was.

No, she was watching Simon.

He tore his gaze away, choosing not to try to interpret the expression on her face.

"Do you like it?" Miss Stanley asked.

He looked down at his untouched ice. "Perhaps I should try it first."

She laughed prettily. "Perhaps so."

He took up a spoonful, and cold spiked with sugar and the unmistakable flavor of pineapple washed over his tongue. Damn good. An excellent choice to combat the stifling air he inhaled with every breath.

Not as good as tasting Sarah, though. He flicked another glance down the table. Sarah had turned away and was talking to the curate, gracing him with her wide, pretty smile.

His breath caught as jealousy swirled through him. He wanted to stalk over to the curate and forcibly remove him from Sarah's vicinity. Trying to calm the sudden possessive—and ridiculous—notion, Simon blinked hard, focusing on the dark strand of hair that curled around her ear. He wanted to rub that strand between his fingers, feel its sleek, silky texture.

God, how he wished things were different—that she was the one sitting beside him, not Georgina Stanley.

He forced his attention back to Miss Stanley and smiled at her as he took up another spoonful. "You're right. It's heaven."

But he lied. Heaven would be taking Sarah Osborne into his arms and keeping her there. Heaven was impossible. But as he sat here among these people he couldn't count as true friends, with the one person in the world he truly trusted sitting thirteen seats away from him, he began to question that.

He pretended to savor the dessert in silence for several moments. Then, Miss Stanley said quietly, "I am so glad you are as fond of pineapple as I am, Your Grace."

"Are you?"

"Yes." Her teeth ran over her lower lip. "It is important...I mean, for people to enjoy similar things." Blue
eyes blinked innocently up at him.

"I suppose it is," he said.

They finished dessert, and the ladies then retired to the
drawing room for coffee and tea while the gentlemen remained in the dining room and the port circulated clock-
wise around the table.

The men relaxed, a few of them drawing out their snuff
boxes, a few retiring behind a screen to make use of a
chamber pot. They talked about the recent earthquake
in Caracas, the loss of life, the implications to the British. They talked about the United States and how war—
again—had become inevitable. They talked about Bona-
parte and the French. Dunsberg, who had received a letter
from Wellington last week, updated all of them on the
push through Spain.

Simon was glad the political topics had outweighed
the subject of his mother's disappearance. He was tired
of repeating the story of what had happened and sick of
telling everyone his theory—growing less substantial as
the days passed—that his mother had simply gone off on
a holiday without informing anyone. He'd repeated the
story in Parliament, at two other dinner parties, in the
card room at a ball a few nights ago, and in his club on
more than one occasion. All the men here surely knew it
by now. And when they pressed for more information—
which also happened often—he could tell them in all honesty that he didn't have any.

Eventually, Stanley turned to Simon. "You are more

involved in the Season this year, Trent. Not avoiding the social events as you usually do."

Simon stiffened. "I'd hardly say I avoid them."

Lord Granger, a younger man who'd recently inherited his title, chuckled. "Can't say I'd blame you if you did, Trent. Damned tedious, the lot of them."

"The ladies seem to find them quite enjoyable," Dunsberg pointed out.

"Ah, but we are forgetting the point of the Season's events." Stanley gestured, rolling a finger to indicate the house around them. "This one included."

"Which is?"

Simon slanted a glance at Granger. The man could be more than passing dense sometimes.

"Why, to find matches for those of us who are as yet unmarried," Stanley said.

Simon felt more than one set of eyes on him, but he took another swallow of port and ignored them.

"The marriage market," Dunsberg said in a bemused voice.

"Exactly," Stanley said. "But you, Trent, I'd wager you do know the purpose of the Season. Ever since that year—What was it? Six, seven years ago?—you had that horde of matchmaking mamas prepared to battle to the death over which daughter would dance with you next, you've avoided it."

Simon made a noncommittal response. That year had been hell. He'd been green, hadn't yet understood the competitive natures of the ladies and their mothers. They'd ever so politely cornered him, called upon him, made subtle attempts to entrap him. They'd plagued him until he couldn't walk down the street without being accosted. Town gossip centered upon who would be the lucky lady he would select for his bride. He received piles of letters from secret admirers daily. Young ladies had burst into tears upon seeing him from across a street or a shop. One high-strung girl had even swooned when he'd greeted her one day.

He'd had to completely remove himself from the public eye. He'd temporarily moved into his half-brother Sam's lodgings, stayed indoors whenever possible, and went about his duties in unmarked carriages until the furor died down. It had taken many months, and in the years after that, he had dipped his toes into social life cautiously and with his eyes open, keeping strict control of who he spoke to and how, careful not to elicit unrealistic expectations.

If his plan for this Season came to fruition, all that angling would end soon. One thing about marriage he'd welcome with open arms.

"Oh, I remember that!" Sir Thomas Seton, another unmarried buck, announced. "Thought the ladies would never bother glancing at another one of us again."

Simon cocked an eyebrow at Sir Thomas. "Is that so? If I recall, you were still at Eton back then. I can't imagine how you could have heard about all that nonsense."

"Oh, everyone heard about it, Trent. *Everyone.*"

"I remember, too," the curate who'd been Sarah's dinner partner said. "I heard about it while I was at the seminary. All of London was watching on tenterhooks, Your Grace, waiting to see who you'd choose for your duchess."

"Every word you spoke in public that year was printed, pored over by matchmaking mamas searching for the one element that would give their daughters the edge," Dunsberg said with a chuckle. Dunsberg had experienced a similar situation years earlier and had commiserated with Simon on more than one occasion. Dunsberg had never married, though. It seemed the older man valued his bachelorhood more than most.

"The odd thing is"—Stanley's hawk-like gaze focused on Simon—"after all these years, you have finally returned to society in full force. Attended every event you've been invited to this Season, haven't you, Trent?"

"Thought he'd never come back after that." Granger shook his head as he poured himself more port. "I wouldn't've."

"You'd have been married thrice over if it'd happened to you," Sir Thomas told Granger, smirking.

"What are you driving at, Stanley?" Simon inquired politely of his host.

"I think you're on the hunt."

Simon fingered the rim of his glass with his thumb. "Before one hunts, one must assess the game and the potential for success."

"We all know hunting season is in its prime in the weeks after Easter, so you've had over a month to assess the game," Stanley pointed out.

"Indeed," Simon said.

Stanley smiled, showing the tobacco-stained whites of his teeth. "I think you've come to your conclusion. There is game in abundance but you shall bide your time until you decide upon a target."

"Surely the good duke will choose the plumpest, healthiest, most delectable bird to dress his table," Sir Thomas said, his smirk still firmly intact.

"Ah, you mean the *London* Season!" Granger proclaimed, the double entendre suddenly making sense to him. His eyes went wide as he turned to Simon. "Can it be true, old chap? You're finally looking to be leg-shackled?"

"Daresay it's about time," Sir Thomas said. "What are you now, Trent? Thirty? Go get yourself married, Your Grace, so the ladies of London will begin to pay attention to the rest of us."

"Twenty-nine," Simon corrected. "And perhaps I *will* endeavor to shackle myself to some willing lady before the end of the Season. But only for the sake of my peers and their *amour-propre*."

Everyone laughed, and conversation wandered to other topics. But Lord Stanley remained quiet, his fingers templed under his chin, gazing at Simon.

Assessing.

Chapter Eight

꧁꧂

"Your Grace! Your Grace!"

Simon sat up, instantly alert. Swinging his legs over the edge of the bed, he called out, "What is it?"

"It's your brother, sir. Come quick!"

"Which one?"

But Simon knew. He always knew. *Luke.*

As the man outside his door said, "It's Lord Lukas," Simon had already slung his robe over his shoulders and was striding toward the door. He opened it to find one of the footmen on his threshold.

"What time is it, Tremaine?"

"A little after four, Your Grace."

Simon sighed. They'd returned home from the Stanleys' just before two. "Where is he?"

Tremaine hurried down the corridor and led him toward the stairs. "Robert Johnston found him unconscious between the service door and the stable, and he informed me straightaway. I came directly to you."

Robert Johnston, the coachman. Simon frowned. He didn't like the way that man looked at Sarah.

A few moments later, Simon emerged outside and saw his brother curled on his side chin-to-knees against the iron handrail. Robert Johnston pushed himself off from the handrail when Simon approached. "Hasn't moved an inch since I first saw him, Your Grace."

Simon sighed. "Help me bring him inside, will you?"

The three men carried Luke inside. Not an entirely simple task, because Luke was as tall as Simon and deeply unconscious, a dead weight, awkward and flopping as they maneuvered him through the door and to the closest room with something comfortable for him to lie on—the drawing room. They laid him on the royal-blue silk sofa and stepped back, sweating, gazing down at him.

He hadn't budged, but his chest was rising and falling in a steady rhythm.

Simon passed a weary hand over his eyes. He had no idea if this was a drunken stupor or something worse, but he needed to find out.

"Have someone wake Miss Osborne," he told Tremaine. Out of all the people in his London household, Sarah had worked most closely with Mrs. Hope and therefore possessed the most medical knowledge.

"Yes, sir." The footman left, and Simon dismissed Robert Johnston, eliminating the possibility of the man seeing Sarah in any state of dishabille.

When both men were gone, Simon stared down at his brother.

"Damn it, Luke," he muttered. He lowered himself onto the foot of the sofa and rested his head in his hands, waiting for Sarah to arrive or for Luke to awaken.

Not surprisingly, Sarah came first. She hurried in, looking deliciously rumpled, her cheeks flushed as she fumbled with the tie on her robe. She took one look at Luke and her shoulders sagged.

"Oh." Her voice was flat as she came to a halt beside the sofa. She looked from Luke's peaceful face to Simon's no-doubt ragged one. "Are you all right?" she asked him softly.

"No. Yes. I just…" Hell, he already felt a thousand times better since she'd walked through the door five seconds ago. He made a helpless gesture toward his brother.

"How did he get here?"

"Robert Johnston found him by the back door."

She knelt beside Luke to check his heartbeat and his pupils, then laid the backs of her hands on his cheeks.

"Can you tell what's wrong with him? Is he drunk?"

"Yes, I think so."

"Fool," Simon growled.

"He's cold. There's no telling how long he was out there. We must warm him."

They set Tremaine and the pair of maids who had awakened Sarah to work warming Luke with hot bricks and warm towels. After his pulse settled and his skin returned to a more normal temperature, Sarah turned assessing eyes on Simon. "You must be exhausted, Your Grace. You should go to bed."

"So should you," he countered.

The edge of her lips quirked up as she rose. "Very well, but only if you promise to get some rest as well."

He nodded and told one of the maids to fetch him as soon as his brother woke. Side by side, he and Sarah trudged upstairs.

* * *

Sarah watched Simon closely. He looked—defeated. As if the appearance of his drunken brother had brought the weight of the world crashing down on his shoulders.

They came to Simon's bedchamber door first—her room was at the end of the corridor. She'd never walked with him upstairs before, and when Simon grasped the door handle, they both hesitated.

She looked up into Simon's face, into his haunted green eyes, and awareness flushed through her. Awareness...and a complex need that had everything inside her clenching tight.

"May I come inside?" she whispered. "There's something I wish to say."

His lips pressed together. His eyes scanned the dim corridor. It wasn't yet five o'clock, and most of the household was still abed. Finding no one, he gave a tight nod and opened the door.

She slipped inside the room. He followed, closing the door and locking it before turning to her.

She hadn't ever been inside this bedchamber. It was a far larger space than hers, with a marble hearth opposite the bed flanked by two doors, one perhaps leading to a dressing room and the other to a bedchamber meant for the duke's wife. A bedchamber, if the rumors were true, that would soon be occupied by the woman Simon chose to marry. The bed, still rumpled from him sleeping in it earlier, was simple, covered by a dark silk counterpane and matching covered pillows.

She tore her gaze away from the bed and turned to Simon.

Longing. Envy. Jealousy. Those were the emotions that

had run rampant through her during the Stanleys' dinner party last night. She'd watched Simon and Georgina Stanley conversing and laughing, and from her position way down at the end of the table with the lowliest of the guests, her heart had panged, heavy and sore in her chest. Every time Simon so much as smiled at the young lady, it was a painful reminder to Sarah of those deep, thick lines that society had drawn to keep them apart.

It hurt. She wanted so badly to be the object of his public smiles. She wanted to be the one partnered with him at formal dinners. She wanted to be the one he proudly led to the dance floor before hundreds of onlookers.

Society believed she was undeserving of all that, but she didn't agree. She *did* deserve it—as much as anyone fortunate enough to be born into the position.

This dangerous, brazen part of her had taken on a life of its own... It was running rampant, and she didn't know how to control it.

She squeezed her eyes shut and wrapped her arms around herself.

Last night, when the men had remained in the dining room to drink their port, the women had gone into the drawing room. The main topic of conversation had been the rumor that Simon was at last intending to give up his bachelorhood. That this Season, he was finally on the hunt for the lucky young lady who would become his duchess.

Afterward, while she was lying in bed in the earliest morning hours, Sarah had come to a realization. Once Simon chose his intended bride, there would be nothing left for her. He'd never, ever betray the woman he intended to marry. And she wouldn't want him to.

She knew she and Simon could never permanently breach the lines that divided them, but from the years of meeting him on the bench at Ironwood Park, from the three kisses they had shared, Sarah thought they might be able to *temporarily* breach them.

Their time was limited. If she didn't take control now, he'd marry, and she'd lose him before she even had a chance.

Now, she looked up into his face and spoke quietly. "Let me soothe you, Your Grace."

He was very still. Then, slowly, he shook his head. But his eyes flashed, sparking to life again after they'd been so dull and hopeless as he'd gazed at his unconscious brother. "You don't know what you're saying."

"I know exactly what I'm saying." She glanced down, then back up to meet his eyes, her resolve hardening. She untied her robe and let it slip from her shoulders. "I offer you care and comfort and love, to use in whatever way you see fit."

"No, Sarah," he said thickly, but his eyes raked up and down her nightgown-clad body, and the heat in them stroked over her. "That is too great a gift."

"It is one I wish to give you."

"You deserve better than what I can offer you."

She sighed. "What if you were to stop worrying and just listen to your heart? What if you were to just consider what you want at this very moment? What if I were to promise you that, no matter what happens, I won't have any regrets?"

"I don't want to hurt you," he murmured.

"I hear it always hurts, the first time," she told him in a near whisper.

"I don't want to hurt you that way." He stepped forward, reaching out to her. His hand moved to cover her heart, and he pressed down gently, his gaze moving to study her face. "But I don't want to hurt you here, either."

She covered his hand with her own. "I know."

He gave a helpless shake of his head. "How can I prevent it?"

"Whatever you choose to give, I will take it gladly and hold it close. I have no expectations, Your Grace. I promise. I just want to live for today. Enjoy today. Let's, for once, worry about tomorrow when it comes."

"I don't want you to have any regrets," he said. "We have been friends for so long. This will change everything."

She thought back to all those times they'd met on the bench at Ironwood Park, of their late-night discussions about Napoleon and France and the United States and Spain. About the challenges he faced in Parliament. About their fears for Sam, who'd spent so much time on the Continent, for England, and for the world.

He was right. This would change everything.

"Listen to your heart, Your Grace," she repeated. She reached up her free hand to cup his cheek. "I am willing to take that risk. Are you?"

He hesitated a moment. Then the word emerged, gruff and low but absolutely clear: "Yes."

She began to untie the strings of her nightgown. His gaze riveted to her chest, where the edges of the fabric gaped, revealing the curve of one of her breasts.

"No regrets, Your Grace. I offer you this with my eyes wide open. I know"—she took a deep breath—"our time together will be limited. But it can be for now. Just for now, we can offer each other comfort."

He was quiet.

"Please," she whispered. And then she did the bravest thing she'd ever done. She wrapped her arms around the Duke of Trent and pressed her lips to his.

Despite his "yes," his expression had still been infused with uncertainty. He was still waging that war within himself.

She half expected him to push her away. But he didn't.

Instead, as surely as if she'd thrown a bucket of water over it, her kiss seemed to douse the part of him that had been struggling against touching her.

With a small groan, he took her in his arms and pulled her tight against him. His mouth coaxed hers open, then his tongue flicked inside, licking at the inner flesh of her lips. One of his hands moved to her sleeve, yanking it downward and off her shoulder, and cool air whispered over her bare breast before it was engulfed by his hand.

She gasped, tightening her arms around him as his taut back muscles flexed beneath her palms. His lips moved to her ear. "Sarah, tell me you want this. Tell me this is what you want."

She arched her back, pressing closer, tighter against him, feeling the increased pressure on her breast and trembling at the flash of pleasure that rushed through her. "Yes. Yes, Simon. I want"—she punctuated her words with little kisses to the rough side of his cheek and his earlobe—"this. This is all I want."

His robe puddled on the floor, and suddenly, his lips traveled down the slope of her neck, over her collar bones, and then his tongue stroked over her breast in scorching swipes.

Oh, Lord. Her breasts felt heavy and needy, aching, wanting. His mouth brushed over her nipple, and sensation bolted through her, arching her body again. She grabbed onto his shoulders to steady herself. His arms locked around her lower back, her nightdress bunched in his hands.

"Is this what you want, Sarah?"

But then his lips closed around her nipple, and she couldn't answer. Sharp, sweet pleasure burst through her. Through hazy eyes, she looked down at his hair, filtered her fingers through it at his nape. Her breasts seemed to throb—how was it possible such powerful sensation could come from one spot on her body? Her nipples tightened into sharp, aching points. He sucked, nibbled, licked. Her knees wobbled as the pleasure permeated her muscles. She stumbled, but he held her firm, not letting her fall.

Keeping a tight hold on her, he straightened. His gaze met hers, his lips damp from his ministrations, his eyes the stormiest green she'd ever seen.

"Touch me," he rasped. "Feel what you do to me."

And, still holding her firmly, he guided her hand between his legs to cup the solid rod of his sex. Heat pulsed through the thin fabric of his drawers.

"It hurts when it's like this," he whispered. "There's only one way to soothe it. Is that what you want, Sarah?"

Her heart was beating so fast, she could hardly breathe. She certainly couldn't speak. But, holding his gaze—and tightening her fingers around him—she nodded.

"Are you sure?"

"Yes." She managed to make the one word sound firm and final. Because she *was* sure. She'd wanted him for so long, and she wasn't going to give up this opportunity to have him. Even if he were to find his duchess tomorrow, she would look back on this morning they'd shared with no regrets.

He blew out a breath and removed her hand from his shaft. "More of that later, then. Not too fast, or it'll be over before we even begin."

She had no idea what that meant, and she would have questioned him, but he took her hand and led her toward the bed. When they stood beside it, he said, "Take this off," then pushed the other sleeve of her nightdress over her arms. She tugged the sleeves over her arms, and her nightdress slid to her ankles.

"God," he murmured, and she heard the shakiness in his breaths. "You're so damn beautiful."

She stood still as his eyes devoured her, even though a whole life of training in the ways of demure behavior told her she must cover herself. But she wanted him to see her like this—raw, carnal, bared naked and wanting for him alone.

Gently, he put his arms around her, then lifted her and set her on the edge of the bed. He took a step back, remaining standing, gazing at her. Heat and need and desire seemed to radiate from his every pore.

"Have you ever shown your body to another man, Sarah?"

She shook her head.

"Another gift, then," he said softly. "One I'll be eternally grateful for."

Through her fluttering nerves, her lips quirked upward.

"Perhaps you'd like to bestow the same gift upon me, Your Grace?"

"Most definitely," he replied. Then he gave her a wicked smile. "But not yet."

"Tease," she whispered.

Dark promise entered his eyes. "You haven't seen anything yet."

And then he sat beside her. And he touched her. Everywhere. His lips and hands moved all over her, and she remembered what he'd told her on the bench by the stream at Ironwood Park: ...*all I can think about is putting my hands all over you. Tasting you all over again.*

He did just that. He left no part of her free of the soft press of his lips or the gentle caress of his hands. And then he slid his fingers between her legs. She was so sensitive there, she gave a little jump and squeak, and he met her gaze. "It's time for me to give you a gift of my own," he told her. "A gift of pleasure. Do you trust me?"

"Yes," she said breathlessly. She did trust him. She knew with all her heart that he would never purposefully hurt her, that fear of hurting her was what had kept him away from her for so long.

"Then open for me." He laid his hand on her knee, nudging it, and she understood. Slowly, she parted her knees, baring the most private part of herself to his view.

"Beautiful," he murmured. And then he gathered her against him in a one-armed embrace, and began to stroke her.

Sarah gasped, leaned against him, held on for dear life. She'd never experienced anything like this—such intense pleasure she felt like squirming out of her skin.

And then he pressed a finger inside her.

She had never considered such a thing. Had never dreamed that it was something anyone would ever conceive of doing.

And yet... it was heavenly. His fingers were hot on her and inside her, caressing and pressing in a place that was so sensitive, she felt as if a sweet-hot inferno were building within her, tightening, sending licks of sensation under her skin and through her limbs.

One finger stroked inside her, then two, his thumb pressing just above, circling the place that made her want to thrust against his hand and cry out at the blissful torture at the same time. His other hand remained around her, holding her firm around her hip, keeping her from squirming away, from jumping out of her skin. Keeping her anchored.

She thrust her hands into his light brown hair, its silky texture caressing her fingers. Her back arched, and she whimpered as his fingers stroked an oh-so-sensitive spot inside her. A finger circled that hot, needy place.

His breath whispered hot against her ear, his teeth bit gently down on her lobe, and he was saying all sorts of wicked things. The Duke of Trent was telling her she was beautiful. That she was so slick and hot. That he wanted to take her, to be inside her. To make her scream.

Her body began to shake as licks of heat shot down through her limbs, tightening her muscles. His hand around her firmed, keeping her still, keeping her somehow attached to the earth. Her eyes closed, because it required too much energy to keep them open. There was only the sensation, the absolute pleasure building within her.

And then... release. All of a sudden, the coalescing

ball of heat within her expanded, sending white-hot pleasure shooting through every inch of her body. She gasped,
then released a low moan, her body undulating unchecked
in the circle of his embrace.

Simon's lips pressed against hers. He kept moving his
fingers inside her and over her, but his movements gentled
as the powerful spasms that wracked her body receded.
And when she finally slumped, boneless and replete, he
caught her in his arms. Ever so gently, he laid her on the
bed, adjusting her limp limbs into a comfortable position,
then lying down beside her and drawing her close against
him.

She stroked his arm, feeling light and careless, as free
as a bird coasting on the wind. Smiling, she said in complete honesty, "Thank you. That wasn't what I expected."

His chest rumbled in a low chuckle, his arousal moving against her. "No? Did you expect me to lay you down,
hike up your skirt and simply take you?"

"I thought that was how it was done," she admitted.
"I'd no idea that a woman could be...could be pleasured
to...well, to such an extent."

"I'm glad to be the one to enlighten you," he murmured.

"I'm glad you were the one to enlighten me, too." She
gave a blissful sigh. Every muscle in her body felt full,
relaxed, satisfied.

"We're not finished yet." To punctuate that statement,
he pushed himself gently against her so she could feel his
erection pressing between her legs.

"I know," she whispered. "Now it's my turn to pleasure
you. Will you teach me how to do that?"

Smiling, he bent forward to kiss her lips.

"I will, love."

Pleasure flushed through her all over again. He'd called her "love."

"But touch me instead," he said. "Wrap your fingers around me."

"Like this?" She reached down to take his shaft in her hand again.

"Not exactly. Something's in the way." He turned away for a moment to shimmy off his drawers. "There. Try again."

This time when she held him, she could feel the heat of him, the softness of the skin covering the solid length of his erection.

He curled his fingers around hers. "Yes. And stroke it, like this."

He moved his hands up and down, and Sarah was fascinated by the texture of him, how the velvety softness covered such solid strength.

His eyelids grew heavy. "Yes, that's it, a little harder, love. Press your thumb over me when you reach the top."

She continued, feeling her own body growing impossibly needy and hot and wanting again as she stroked him. She tried to think about what it would be like for him to be inside her, but she couldn't even begin to imagine it. Still, her core grew warm and wet in anticipation as he began to thrust into her hand. She kept her eyes closed, kissed him as she learned about him, about every bump and contour. How was it possible that something this large could fit inside her? And yet she knew that it would. She was made for him, after all.

A sharp rap sounded at the door. Simon froze, and so did she, her hand still on him. Then he touched his lips to hers, gently disentangled himself from her, and turned his head toward the door.

"Yes?" he called.

"Your Grace," came the muffled voice from outside the door. "Lord Lukas is stirring."

With a hearty sigh, Simon moved to sit on the edge of the bed. "Go down and keep an eye on him, Tremaine. I'll be right there."

"Yes sir."

They sat still, listening to the sound of Tremaine's retreating footsteps.

Then, Simon turned to face her, his face filled with regret. "We'd best go down. I don't want him running off before I get a chance to tell him about our mother."

"Oh, Your Grace," she murmured, scooting closer to him to cup his face in her hand, "are you sure?"

He leaned in and kissed her again, this one long and slow and hot, his mouth claiming her lips, possessive and sure. When he pulled back, he murmured, "Soon, Sarah. Soon, I'll make you mine."

With her body still warm and sated from her release, her heart full, and her mind at peace, she knew, without a doubt, that she was already irrevocably his.

Chapter Nine

❦

Luke was stirring when Simon walked into the drawing room with Sarah on his heels. Simon held back as Sarah hurried toward him and checked his pulse and temperature. Luke's eyelids flickered, then he squinted at Sarah.

"Pretty," he croaked.

"Good morning, Lord Lukas," she said gravely. "How are you feeling?"

He gave a low groan. "Like hell."

"No doubt." She glanced at Simon, then back down to Luke.

"Sarah, is that you? Where am I?" Luke struggled up on his elbows and looked around the room. "Aw, damn. Trent House." He spat the words. "How the hell'd I end up in this bloody mausoleum?"

"Watch your language," Simon growled, stalking toward the sofa.

Luke sneered up at him. "Well, if it isn't my sainted brother."

"Hush, my lord," Sarah said, her voice warm but stern. "As to how you came to be here, I imagine you brought yourself. We found you unconscious at the back door."

"My mistake, then. I'll be going now." He struggled to rise.

"No," Simon announced. "You will stay."

Luke gained his feet, swaying a bit. "You've no right to order me about, Trent. Now get out of my way."

Sarah laid a hand on Simon's arm. "Stay awhile, my lord. You're not well."

It was true. Luke's eyes were bloodshot and his skin held a sickly tinge of yellow.

"I'm perfectly fine," he snapped. "Healthy as a damn ox."

Simon clenched his hands into fists. In his life, no one had ever been more capable of raising his ire than Luke.

"You're not fine," he bit out through clenched teeth. "And there are things we need to discuss. You will stay here if I have to lash you to the sofa."

Luke raised a brow. "Ooh. Sounds ominous, brother."

Simon cast a frustrated glance toward Sarah.

She took in a deep breath. "Why don't we have some breakfast." It was a command—to both of them—not a suggestion.

"Not hungry," Luke muttered. Raising his hand, he held his head as if in an attempt to keep it attached to his neck.

She patted his arm. "Food will do you good. Trust me."

He gave her a crooked grin. "I'd laugh at anyone else who told me that, Sarah. But you... very well. I'll trust you."

She gave him one of those smiles that made Simon's gut clench. Bright and sunny. A touch of heaven in the curve of her lips. He couldn't wait to take her back to bed. As soon as this business with Luke was over...

Luke frowned at her. "You're *here*. In London. Why the devil are you in this cesspool? London isn't worthy of you, Sarah. You belong at Ironwood Park."

She chuckled. "Well, that's a long story, my lord. If you wish, I can tell it to you while you're eating breakfast."

"Very well, then." Luke gallantly gestured for her to lead the way to the dining room, and he walked behind her, his steps decidedly unsteady. Simon followed his brother in case he needed to rescue any of the ancient Greek pottery in the corridor should Luke feel compelled to sway into it.

Sarah bustled them inside the dining room and had them both sit while she sent the servants off for hot food, poured coffee, and buttered toast. All the while, Simon and Luke sat, staring at each other in stony silence.

She set a plate of toast down in front of Luke. "Eat." Her tone brooked no argument, and with a negligent shrug, Luke began to eat.

Finally, she sat down, too, and told Luke about how she was now working as Esme's companion.

"A well-deserved rise in status for you," Luke said between bites of toast. "Congratulations."

Simon checked for any sarcasm or disingenuousness in his brother's expression or tone. He found none.

But then Luke scowled. "So I suppose that means Esme's here in London, too?"

"She is," Sarah confirmed.

Luke narrowed his eyes at Simon. "Why? Why would you bring her here? Why would you do that to her?"

Just like Luke, to question every damn decision he made.

"It was for the best," he said shortly, "considering the circumstances."

"What circumstances?"

Simon braced himself for what would come next. "Luke, have you been in residence in your townhouse at all?"

"Now and then. Why?"

"I sent you a message on the fourteenth of April, summoning you home."

Luke's blue eyes narrowed. "You did?"

"I did."

Luke snorted, then waved his hand dismissively. "For God's sake, Trent. You cannot expect me to come running at your every summons."

Simon ground his teeth and was about to open his mouth and inform Luke that he was not only a fool but also an ass...and then he felt it. The soothing hand on his thigh. Sarah's hand. But this was not an invitation—though his cock responded instantly to the proximity of her gentle touch—this was a plea for temperance.

So he sucked in a breath and took a second to loosen the tension that had knotted in his shoulders. "I summoned you, along with Sam, Mark, and Theo, to Ironwood Park for a reason. Did you even read the letter?"

Luke moved crumbs around on his plate, making it a point to look bored. "Can't recall."

After a few more seconds of tooth-grinding, Simon said, "Our mother is missing. She's been gone for almost six weeks."

Silence. No one moved. Then Luke looked up at him. "What?"

"Our mother. The Duchess of Trent. Has been missing. For over a month," Simon repeated. "No one knows where she is. We have been searching, but we have very few clues to work with. She simply disappeared, along with her servants. No one knows where they are."

"Well," Luke sputtered, "she probably just went to visit her sisters."

"No. We've checked."

"Her houses in London and the Lake District?"

"She hasn't been in residence at either one in over a year."

"So you're saying what? She was kidnapped?"

"It's possible."

Luke's blue eyes widened. "Murdered?"

Simon paused, then nodded. "Also possible."

Fury reddened Luke's face. "Who knows of this?"

The thin thread of control Simon had kept wound around his patience finally snapped. "For God's sake, Luke, the whole damn world knows it."

Luke smacked his hands down on the table. "And you didn't tell me."

"Lord Lukas, His Grace tried to tell you. He sent you a letter—" Sarah began.

"I didn't read the damn letter!" Luke roared.

Simon snapped to his feet. "You will not raise your voice to Sarah."

Luke jumped up, too, his narrowed gaze fixed on Simon. "Our mother is missing."

"Yes, she is."

"She could be *dead*."

Luke was the first person who'd said that aloud. The word hit Simon in the chest like a shard of glass. "Yes," he said coldly. "It is possible. But we—"

"And you didn't tell me. You sent me a damn summons you knew I wouldn't bother reading, but you didn't come by to tell me in person."

"We assumed that you weren't at home since you didn't respond to the letter. No one had any idea where you'd gone."

"Did you even look?"

"You mean, conduct a thorough search inside your whorehouses and gambling hells, Luke?" Simon's lips curled. "No, I didn't look. I have been too busy looking for our *mother*."

"It's as it always is, then. I am less of a brother, less of a son. I don't bloody matter, do I?"

What the hell? Luke always thought this way, and Simon never had the faintest idea why. He was the second son, the "spare," and he had been Simon's heir since their father had died. He had been treated as such by everyone, both in the family and outside it. He had always been given the honor and respect the position entitled him to, and yet he did everything he could to squander it. If anyone had the right to be bitter and resentful, it was their half brother, Sam. But Sam had never been this way.

"I sent everyone the same letter!" Simon shouted. "You, Sam, Mark, and Theo all received the exact same message. But Sam, Mark, and Theo *read* it. They cared enough to read it, and they cared enough to come."

"Please, both of you, stop!" Sarah exclaimed. Simon looked over at her to see that she was standing too, the color high in her cheeks. They all stood around the circular table, glaring at one another.

"My lord...please. The fact of the matter is that we didn't tell you, and perhaps"—she slid a look toward Simon—"we should have taken more pains to ensure you were informed. But now you know. And now you can help us find the duchess."

Luke crossed his arms over his chest, still glaring. He looked yellower than ever, and rather like he was about to keel over. The shouting hadn't done him any good.

Sarah saw it, too. "Please sit down." She walked around the table to urge him back into his seat. He didn't argue, just sat heavily and put his head in his hands.

Simon laid his palms flat on the table. "In your cups every night again, Luke? Is that what this is?"

"What's it to you?" Luke muttered.

Suddenly the energy left him, and Simon slid back into his chair, too. Sarah remained standing, watching them both. They stayed in their places for long moments, not speaking, not eating. And then there was a knock at the door.

It was Tremaine. "Your Grace, a George Turner is at the door insisting to see you."

Simon straightened in his chair. "Show him in. Right away."

"Yes, sir."

When Tremaine left, Sarah asked, "George Turner—is that the boy who's looking for Mr. Woodrow?"

"Yes."

Luke stared at him with a blank expression.

"We discovered this man—Woodrow—had sold our mother's amethyst necklace to a jeweler in Jermyn Street.

We've been waiting for him to appear at his residence in the East End in order to question him."

Luke gave a tightlipped nod.

Just then, George rushed in. He was a plump boy, with a round face and red apples for cheeks. The tall, thin Tremaine hovered over him.

"Yer Grace! He's home! Mr. Woodrow's come home!"

Simon and Luke went to the East End together, Simon filling Luke in on every facet of the situation regarding their mother's disappearance. Sarah had been right—food had seemed to strengthen Luke's constitution. That and sheer force of will, Simon thought, were what kept him standing.

Outside John Woodrow's house, Simon paid George Turner and sent him away. He didn't want the boy making enemies in his own neighborhood. Feeling the comforting weight of his pistol in his coat, and knowing his brother was similarly armed, Simon knocked on Woodrow's door.

The man who answered was huge. Tall and burly, the muscles in his arms straining against the dirt-stained linen of his shirt. Seeing the two gentlemen at his door, he raised bushy brown brows. "Wot's this?"

"I am the Duke of Trent. This is my brother, Lord Lukas Hawkins. May we come in?"

The man blinked stupidly at him, then stepped back to let them in. "Oh, aye, to be sure, yer lordships."

It had been a while since Simon had been called "your lordship." Clearly this man wasn't acquainted with many dukes and was unfamiliar with the correct form of address.

The apartment consisted of one room ripe with the scent of desiccated fish emanating from the plate of half-eaten food that the man must have been partaking of when they'd arrived.

"We're here to inquire—"

But before he could finish, Luke had the man by the throat and pressed up against the dirty wall. "Where the hell is my mother?"

The big man flicked Luke off him with a meaty hand. Luke went stumbling backward, tripping over a spindly wicker chair. As Simon helped him right himself, Woodrow said, "I ain't much o' one for violence, yer lordship, but I draw the line at bein' accosted in me own home."

"Please forgive my brother." Simon gave Luke a warning glare. "He is distraught. You see, our mother, the Duchess of Trent, is missing, and we are concerned for her welfare. We are given to believe you might have found yourself in possession of one of her belongings."

"Oh?" Woodrow rubbed his chin, suddenly looking thoughtful. "That right?"

"Yes."

"An amethyst necklace," Luke spat out, only being held back from lunging at the big man by Simon's grip on his arm. "Do you know what a bloody amethyst is?"

"Oh, aye, daresay I do." Now a sly look crept into the man's eye. "Mayhap even seen one or two of 'em in my time."

There was a pregnant pause as Woodrow eyed them.

Simon knew what he wanted. He drew a fat purse from his pocket, allowing the coins within it to clink loudly. Woodrow's beefy arm reached for it, but Simon held it back, meeting the man's gaze evenly. "Are you familiar with Ironwood Park, Woodrow?"

"The great house? Oh, aye."

"Ever been there?"

Woodrow's eyes went wide. "And you'd invite me in like a right proper guest, yer lordship?"

"Doubtful," Luke drawled.

Woodrow crossed his thick arms over his chest. "Nay, ne'er been out that far. I always keeps meself within a day's ride of London. Necessary for me work, you see."

"What work?" Luke asked.

Woodrow's gaze strayed back to the purse.

"I won't pay you for information if you caused her any harm," Simon said in a quiet voice.

Woodrow met his eyes evenly, but greed shone in his expression. "Told you I weren't one for violence, didn't I?"

"What do you think, Luke?" Simon didn't break his gaze from the big man.

"I think he's a bloody liar," Luke growled.

Woodrow shook his head. "I ain't one who'd harm a woman...One who ain't already been harmed, that is."

"What the hell does that mean?" Luke spat.

"So," Simon said, "you're a thief who chooses not to harm his victims."

"Not a thief, neither." He shrugged. "Well, not in the regular way, anyhow."

What the hell did he mean by that?

Woodrow eyed the purse meaningfully, then his gaze strayed back to Simon. "You're no' in league with the constables?"

"No."

"You won't go cryin' to the watch?"

"No. We just want information."

"What sort of information?"

"I will give you the contents of this purse—nigh on twenty pounds—if you tell me everything you know of the amethyst necklace that you sold to Lamb, the jeweler in Jermyn Street. And everything you know of the Duchess of Trent's whereabouts."

Woodrow blew out a breath through thick lips. "Mayhap you won't be liking what I've to say about it."

Something clenched inside Simon, but he said, "No matter. We need to know," in a tight voice.

Luke stared hard at the big man. "Tell us."

"Aye. I sold the necklace to Lamb. But I didn't injure the wearer. I...found her wearing it."

Simon narrowed his eyes. "You found her? Where?"

"Dug 'er up from a fresh grave in the Hillingdon churchyard." Seeing Simon's expression, Woodrow's fleshy face softened. "She was yer mam?"

"What did she look like?" Simon choked out. Maybe it hadn't been her...maybe it was someone else.

Woodrow shrugged. "Female. Dark hair. 'S'all I recall."

Luke stalked to the only window in the room. Upon reaching it, he yanked it open and leaned outside, taking deep gulps of air. Simon knew from experience that the air out on the streets of the East End wasn't much of an improvement over the close, fetid air in this room. He didn't move.

Woodrow's description didn't help at all. He could be describing half the people in England.

"You're a resurrection-man?" Simon pushed out.

"That'd be one way of puttin' it."

"You prefer grave-robber?" Luke said from the window.

"Rather prefer to call meself a man o' trade."

Luke turned, his blue eyes bright. "The trade of dead bodies, you mean."

Woodrow just shrugged again.

"How did she die?" Simon choked out.

Woodrow's lips twisted. "Sure you want to know, yer lordship?"

"Tell him," Luke spat.

"Slit throat."

The air was too close. Simon couldn't breathe. Suddenly, a meaty arm wrapped around him. "Best sit down, yer lordship. Over here." Woodrow led him to a wicker chair at the table and gently forced him to lower himself into it. Simon stared at the fish carnage on the plate in front of him.

"She's at peace now," Woodrow said, patting his shoulder awkwardly. "Remember that."

"Not if you exhumed her," Luke said coldly.

"Here now. She's furtherin' science. Bettering society."

"Where is she?" Luke's voice was low. Dangerous. "Who did you sell her to, you bastard?"

"I b'lieve that night's retrievals went to Thomas Caldwell, the anatomist."

"And at what price did Thomas Caldwell value my mother's body?" Luke spat out, dangerously, recklessly angry now.

"Nine guineas," Woodrow said simply. "If she were a bit fresher, she might have brought in ten—"

Withdrawing his pistol, Luke lunged for Woodrow.

"Luke!" Simon yelled, leaping out of the chair. "Stop!" He wrapped his arms around his brother.

Luke stopped struggling, looked up at him with streaming eyes. "For God's sake, Simon"—Simon sucked in a breath. Luke hadn't called him by his Christian name in years—"This man defiled her grave. Sold her to a god-damned anatomist—" He choked on his words. His body shook in Simon's arms.

"I know. I know. But he didn't put her in that grave to begin with, and we need to find out who did."

Because Simon would make whoever it was pay.

Still holding on to Luke, Simon looked over at Woodrow, who had tucked himself—as much as possible—into the corner, as far from Luke's weapon as he could get. "Where is Thomas Caldwell?" Simon asked him.

"London Hospital Medical College."

Goddamn it, their mother might have already been cut into pieces in the name of science. Simon loosened his hold on his brother. "Luke, we need to go there. Now. Before..."

His voice trailed off. They might already be too late.

The Duke of Trent wasn't stopped when he barreled in to the London Hospital Medical College—just one curt mention of his title opened every door in the place. Nor was it difficult to gain Thomas Caldwell's attention, de-spite the fact that he was engaged in a lecture in a small hall, his baritone voice ringing out over a crowd of fasci-nated young scholars.

Simon threw open the door just as Caldwell was say-ing, "Now let us observe the texture and the position of the stomach. I anticipate this to be a healthy organ, considering the age and the fact that the subject perished from unrelated causes."

The dark-robed students gathered closely around the body covered with a white sheet and lying on the cot in the center of the room. Caldwell raised one hand clutching a scalpel as his other hand poised to pull back the sheet.

"Stop!" Simon bellowed.

Caldwell straightened, turning toward him and Luke, bushy dun-colored brows rising in surprise. Fabric rustled as all the young men turned to stare at them.

Simon sprinted toward Caldwell, cutting a swath through the students with Luke on his heels, John Woodrow following with far less enthusiasm. When they reached the cot, Simon whipped off the sheet that covered the body.

He staggered backward.

Staring up at him from a gray face and with unseeing brown eyes was his mother's maid.

Beside him, Luke gasped. "Jesus Christ. Is that Binnie?"

Chapter Ten

Simon and Luke arrived at the churchyard at the Hillingdon Parish Church at dusk. It had taken them a while to question Caldwell and Woodrow to confirm that Binnie had indeed been murdered and that hers was the only body Woodrow had "acquired" on that particular night. It had taken more time for them to arrange for Binnie to be sent home for a proper burial.

When Simon and Luke rode into the town of Hillingdon, dusty and tired, worn in both body and spirit, a pedestrian directed them to the nearby vicarage, where the housekeeper answered to Simon's knock.

"Is the vicar at home?" Simon asked shortly. He was exhausted and dirty, tense from the day's events so far, and frustrated by the insufficient answers they'd received.

The housekeeper blinked. "Mr. Allen is otherwise engaged, sir."

Simon clenched his teeth, and Luke said, "We've come

from London, ma'am, and it's imperative we see him right away. Tell him the Duke of Trent is here."

Simon slanted Luke a glance. This was the most polite he'd been to anyone all day, Simon included. He'd barely spoken to Simon during the hours it had taken them to ride out here.

The housekeeper flicked a glance back to Simon, then nodded. "Yes, sir. I will see if he's at home."

She closed the door in their faces, leaving Luke with a growing scowl. Evidently his polite moment had passed.

"Patience," Simon muttered.

"It's almost dark," Luke grumbled.

"Yes." Simon gave a quick glance at the twilight sky. "I don't want to spend the night here." They'd return to London by lantern light if necessary.

Luke shrugged. "What does it matter?"

"Esme and Sarah have been left at home waiting in suspense. I'll not have them worry the night through."

Luke's lips twisted. "I understand you wanting to inform our sister. But Sarah Osborne? Why?"

Simon met his brother's gaze evenly. "Sarah is as much a part of the Hawkins family as any of us."

Indeed, while Luke was probably less connected to Sarah than the rest of them—like Simon, he'd been home for school holidays when she'd arrived at Ironwood Park and had only spent time at home infrequently since—he had always liked Sarah and was well aware of her deep ties to the family.

"For God's sake, Trent, she's a *housemaid*."

"She's no longer a housemaid," Simon reminded him, holding on to his patience by a tenuous thread. "And why should that matter?"

"I wouldn't give a damn," Luke said, "but you? The King of Hauteur and Contempt? I can't remember a time—ever—when you brought a servant into a private family matter."

"She is no longer a servant, technically speaking." Though it was a stupid argument—Simon had brought her into this matter before her status had changed.

"One day a housemaid, the next a lady's companion. One day in Ironwood Park, the next in London. Suddenly it's ever so important to keep her apprised of all the family news. Makes me wonder if there's something between you and the lovely Sarah—"

"She was the best choice for the position of Esme's companion," Simon bit out. "Our sister's ability to interact in society improves with every outing, thanks to her."

Simon's teeth were going to wear to the gums with the amount of grinding he was doing to them today.

"Do you mean Esme is not embarrassing you as keenly this year? Your beloved family name is not being incessantly besmirched by our sister's endless social faux pas?" Luke clapped his hands softly. "Bravo, Sarah."

Simon wanted to say that Luke had caused him more embarrassment than the rest of his family members combined, but he held his tongue on that matter, because he knew where that conversation always led—to Luke walking away and Simon not seeing him for months, only hearing about the waves of vice and corruption that he left in his wake. So instead, he said, "You know as well as I do that Esme finds public situations challenging. And no one understands her better than Sarah. Sarah has been at her side since she was weaned."

Luke huffed out a breath. "I'll grant you that. All those years spent together must have made them close."

Simon remembered his own childhood at Ironwood Park...and Luke's, although the years they'd spent together hadn't made them close. He didn't know why. When he was very young, Sam had been at home and when Simon was older, Mark and Theo had come along. But Luke had been his companion all along. His playmate. His companion in mischief. The only person who could lead the somber, serious Simon astray.

Just then, the door opened. The man standing there was short and wiry and wore spectacles. "Your Grace. I am William Allen," he said with a bow. "How may I be of assistance?"

"Thank you for seeing us, Mr. Allen. I am sorry to impose on you like this, but we come regarding a matter of great urgency," Simon said.

Allen invited them inside, and none of the men said much until the three of them were settled in Allen's cozy, if somewhat shabby, parlor and drinking a strong, hot tea that warmed Simon after riding for so long in the afternoon chill.

"Now, how may I help you?" Allen asked.

Despite the late hour and the knowledge that the ride home wasn't going to be pleasant, Simon took his time, telling the entire story of his missing mother, the chance discovery of the amethyst necklace that led to John Woodrow and Thomas Caldwell, and Binnie's lifeless body lying on a cot at London Hospital Medical College.

Allen listened attentively, his hands clasped at his chest almost as if in prayer, sometimes nodding, sometimes shaking his head. When Simon finished, Allen took a long, slow sip of tea before carefully setting his cup and saucer aside.

He took a deep breath. "These are disturbing circumstances, indeed, sir. And I fear that what I have to tell you won't be of much help."

"Anything you can tell us will help," Luke said.

"I will tell you everything I know, then. Your employee was discovered four days ago by one of our parishioners. The poor woman was found in the woods near the river, and it seemed clear to everyone who saw her that she'd been set upon by cutthroats. The parish did what it could to find someone—anyone—to identify her, but we failed. It was a mystery where she'd come from or what she'd been doing."

Simon nodded. A small parish such as this didn't have the means to conduct a full-scale search for the relatives of an apparently penniless woman whose body had been found in the woods. "No others were discovered with her?"

"No one. Nor any evidence that she'd been in anyone's company. The following day, I decided she must be buried. I presided over the burial."

Luke raised his hand. "Wait. Was she wearing any jewelry?"

At this, Allen flushed. "She might have been. If the necklace you mention was long, Your Grace, if it was tucked inside her bodice...well...I did not disturb her clothes. I am no coroner, sir, but a man of God, and such a thing would have been unseemly. And..." He went a little pale. "Well, there was so much blood, I—"

"Of course," Simon soothed.

Allen frowned. "But perhaps finding the jewels would

have prompted me to dig deeper into the truth of her identity." He passed a weary hand over his forehead. "Perhaps I should have searched her, or had someone...but my main concern was handing her into God's loving embrace."

"Do not question yourself," Simon reassured him. "You did what you should have done. You gave her a proper Christian burial."

The return to Trent House took far longer than the ride out to Hillingdon. Both Simon and Luke held lanterns. Though the moon was almost full, a shifting cloud cover dulled its light.

As the horses picked their way down the road, Simon and Luke mulled over what they'd learned.

"It's possible Mama wasn't with Binnie when she was killed," Luke said hopefully.

"True," Simon said. "I can't really see our mother just leaving her there." Unless she herself was in grave danger.

"But why would Binnie be in possession of her necklace?" Luke slanted him a glance. "Do you think she stole it, then ran off?"

Simon had known Binnie since she came to work at Ironwood Park when he was a child. By all appearances, she'd been a loyal servant who wouldn't think about robbing her employer. Then again, looks could be deceiving.

"I don't know," he admitted.

Luke was silent for a long moment, the only sounds the crunches of their horses' hooves on the gravelly road. "Perhaps she was carrying Mama's other jewels as well. Perhaps that was why she was murdered."

"Because she was flaunting the jewels she'd stolen from our mother?"

"Yes. And the highwaymen—or whoever—stole them and killed her. But they missed the necklace because they were in a hurry to get away."

Simon shook his head. "It seems farfetched."

"And yet it is the most plausible explanation given the information we do have."

"Such actions aren't consistent with Binnie's character."

"It could have been an elaborate ruse. Someone on the outside could have planned it and brought her in." Luke was quiet for a moment. His voice was firm when he spoke again. "We should return to Hillingdon. Question the inhabitants of the area. Search for any clues that might lead to her murderer. We should also delve more deeply into Binnie's background. Question her friends and her family. As well as the family of the male servant—what was his name?"

"James."

"James, too."

"James has no family, as far as we've been able to tell." Simon's head hurt. The deeper they dug into the mire that was his mother's disappearance, the murkier it became. He gave a great sigh. He wanted to go home.

He had the sudden fantasy of Sarah waiting in his bed for him. Naked. Warming his sheets with her silky skin. He'd climb into bed, draw her soft body into his arms. Then, as promised, he'd make her his.

Peace. Heaven.

They rode on in silence, concentrating on the road in front of them. Then Luke said in a low voice, "So, what is it with Sarah Osborne, Trent?"

Startled by the question, Simon glanced over at his brother. It was like the man had read his mind. "We discussed this. She was the best choice for Esme's companion."

Luke snorted. "If you weren't you, I'd be warning you about the repercussions of dallying with servants."

Simon stiffened. Looking straight ahead at the shadowy road, he said, "Well, I am me, so I expect warnings aren't necessary." Although if they were, Luke would be the proper person to issue them. Five years ago, Luke had engaged in a dalliance with one of the maids at Ironwood Park. Simon had managed to contain the scandal, but Luke had thoroughly compromised the young woman, who'd been sent back to her parents in Worcester in disgrace.

"Right. Of course, I would have no such qualms. To me, a beautiful woman is a beautiful woman, queen or housemaid. But you, Trent? You and I both know that your snobbishness has no bounds. You'd never sully yourself with a girl like Sarah."

Heat rose within Simon, boiling in his chest and rising to spread through his shoulders, neck, and face. His muscles tautened into iron bands across his shoulders and back.

Luke was doing this on purpose, Simon knew. Deliberately trying to raise his ire.

"Still," Luke continued, musing, "she's a pretty piece. She adores you—oh, I've seen the way she looks at you—so she'd be an easy conquest. And, knowing Sarah, she wouldn't make a peep of noise about it afterward. Not like—" He hesitated, then said, "Well, as dallying with servants goes, perhaps it wouldn't be such a bad idea, after all."

Simon was silent. He clenched his hands hard on the reins to keep them from wrapping around Luke's neck.

Luke laughed, the sound grating along Simon's nerves. "Come, now, Trent. I know you've thought about it. And I don't blame you. The woman has curves a man can't help but admire. Soft, luscious curves that would fit nicely into a man's hand. And a mouth meant to close over his—"

In one smooth motion, Simon had halted his horse and dismounted, lowering his lantern onto the ground beside him.

Luke stopped his horse a few paces ahead and looked back at Simon. "What?"

Simon wasn't sure he could speak. He'd never been so irate. He was shaking. Sweat broke out in hot pinpricks over his forehead.

He managed to growl out, "Get off the damn horse."

Luke stared at him, then slowly raised his eyebrows. The corners of his lips twitched upward.

"Get off the horse," Simon repeated.

Turning his horse around, Luke just shook his head. "What a sight. My brother and his oh-so-righteous fury. I'm so sick of it."

But Luke's earlier words keep hammering in Simon's skull. *"Easy conquest." "Pretty piece." "Dallying with servants."*

Worst of all: *"You'd never sully yourself with a girl like Sarah."*

He stared up at Luke, red crowding at the fringes of his vision.

"...a girl like Sarah..."

No more. He wouldn't have anyone speaking of Sarah—

his Sarah—that way. No one. Not even his brother, who he'd forgiven years of drinking and gambling and whores.

"Get down," Simon growled.

Luke shook his head. "You know, brother, I think this is where we must part ways. You see, you're heading home, back to the pretense of being a moral, respectable duke while you secretly lust after your housemaid. I have no desire to bear witness to that hypocrisy. I'm going to remain right here. First thing I intend to do is locate the closest pub, and after that, I intend to return to Hillingdon and get to the bottom of my mother's disappearance."

"Get out of my sight, then." Bitterness welled in Simon's voice. He couldn't count on Luke to find their mother. He couldn't count on Luke for anything except to get drunk, to offend everyone he cared about, and to find ways to besmirch their family name.

"Gladly." Luke turned in the direction from which they'd come, dug his heels into the horse's sides, and sent the animal into a gallop—recklessly dangerous this time of night, but wasn't that just like Luke to risk his horse?

Simon stood there for long minutes after the sound of hoofbeats faded into the night.

It was for the best that Luke was gone.

At least, he tried to convince himself of that.

Chapter Eleven

Simon paced the upstairs corridor of Trent House.

By the time he'd returned from Hillingdon, the household was dark, everyone abed, Sarah included. She must be asleep. He didn't want to rouse her. It would be selfish to do so, and none of the news he had to impart was good.

Simon went into his bedchamber and stared at his bed for long moments, but it looked so unappealing and uninviting, so cold, that he flung off the cravat he'd been untying and let it pile in a snowy heap on the floor, knowing Burton, his valet, would have fits about its wrinkles in the morning.

Simon turned on his heel and strode out of the prison-like confinement of his bedchamber. And then he paced. The corridor on the first floor was long and narrow. He didn't know why he didn't go downstairs, except for the fact that the ground floor provided a layout far less amenable to the task at hand, which involved striding down to one end, swiveling about, then repeating the process again and again.

Plus, up here, he was closer to Sarah. He could walk by her door and think about her lying in bed, her face peaceful in sleep. That thought brought him a bit of peace, too.

So he paced, avoiding the two floorboards he knew would creak if he stepped on them. He was silent and stealthy, a caged lion on the prowl. His mind would not settle. He couldn't stop thinking about the argument he'd had with Luke.

Was he being a hypocrite, as Luke had implied? When Luke had compromised that young maid, Simon had been furious. He'd railed at his brother, called him a stupid, selfish fool who couldn't keep his cock in his breeches.

And now he was engaging in the type of liaison he'd previously been so outspoken against.

Suddenly, her door opened behind him. He turned around, a part of him knowing that this was what he'd secretly wanted.

She stepped into the doorframe, wrapping a thin white cotton robe about her slender body. When she saw him, the tension in her face dissolved in relief. "Oh," she said in a small voice, "I'm so glad you're home safe."

"May I come in?"

She recognized his intent, for a blush instantly rose to suffuse her cheeks. "Yes," she said, but her voice now sounded scratchy and low.

She stepped aside and let him pass, and he entered her room, turning to her as the door snicked shut behind them.

"What happened with Mr. Woodrow?" she whispered.

They stared at each other for a long moment. He

couldn't get the words out. Turning away from her, he went to the window. Parting the curtains, he rested his hands on the sill and leaned his forehead against the cold glass.

After a moment, she came up behind him. She slid her arms around him and laid her cheek on his back. "Tell me it isn't the duchess. Tell me you didn't discover something horrible has happened to her."

"No, not my mother." He took a breath. "It was Binnie. She's dead, Sarah."

Sarah gave a little gasp, and he turned and took her into his arms. She held on to his shoulders, looking at him with wild eyes. "What happened?" she cried.

"She was found murdered outside London. She had the amethyst necklace in her possession, and it was taken from her. No one involved could give us any information about the whereabouts of my mother, or of James."

That was enough. He didn't need to tell her that Binnie's throat had been slit, nor of that nasty business with the grave-robber.

"Oh God," Sarah moaned. She buried her face in his shirt, and he felt her back move with silent sobs. Simon knew that Sarah and Binnie had never been close friends, but Sarah cared deeply about everyone who resided at Ironwood Park. Just as he did.

He'd had no idea how to comfort his sister when she'd sobbed in fear for their mother in the parlor at Ironwood Park, but now he knew exactly how to comfort Sarah. He held her tight, rubbing gentle circles into her back, throwing all the tenderness and compassion he could into his touch.

After a long moment, she looked up at him, her face

streaked with tears. "Why? What could Binnie have ever done to deserve such a fate?"

He shook his head hopelessly. "I don't know, love."

She sank back against his chest, and he stood there holding her, wishing desperately that there was something else he could do to ease her pain, until her tears subsided.

Finally she looked at him. Reaching up a finger, she gently traced the lines around his eyes. "I'm sorry," she whispered, her eyes shining, her eyelashes matted with tears.

He shook his head, confused. "Sorry for what?"

"That you had to make such a discovery today."

"I'm sorry, too." The image of Binnie's cold, naked body flashed in his mind, and he closed his eyes against it. "No one ever wishes to encounter death, but when it is the death of someone who has been a part of your existence for so long…"

"Yes," she said quietly. "Exactly." After a long pause, she asked, "Is Lord Lukas all right?"

How to answer that question? Honestly, he supposed. "No, not really."

"Where is he?"

"He returned to the town where Binnie was discovered. He wants to see if he can discover anything else."

"Oh," she murmured. "And you, Your Grace?"

He shook his head. "I just wanted to come home," he said simply. "To you."

Her arms tightened around him. She stared up at him with those big blue eyes, her lips parted. He had to kiss her. So he did just that, taking her face in his hands and tilting it up, then touching his lips to hers.

She was so pliant and willing in his arms. His body, which had been tense and prickly and generally out of sorts all day and all night, now roared to life. It commanded him to take her, to make her his in every sense of the word.

But no. Not yet. Not tonight, when she'd just heard about Binnie. When he finally took her, he wanted it to be special and memorable, not weighted down by tragedy and loss.

He pulled back, hooked a hand behind her knees, and lifted her. She wrapped her arms around his neck. Looking down into her face, her lips plump and pink from his kiss, her eyes still shining with tears, he whispered, "Sarah, let me love you."

She gazed up at him, utterly trusting, utterly accepting, and nodded.

She'd made her decision—she would accept whatever he wished to give. He knew Sarah well enough to know she wouldn't change her mind.

He walked to her bed—the sheets were still pulled back from when she'd left it to investigate who was making noise in the corridor—laid her gently upon it, and sat on the edge of the mattress.

"When we are alone from now on, will you call me Simon?" No one called him Simon anymore, but it was how he thought of himself—Trent was just the shell he inhabited—and he wanted her to think of him that way, too.

She smiled up at him, one of her wide, beautiful smiles that made his heart stutter, even though her eyes were still filled with tears. "In my mind, that has always been who you are."

"Then I would hear it from your lips, too," he said.

"Simon," she whispered, and the sound of his name in her voice sent a shudder through him and made his cock stir.

He bent over her and kissed her again, letting his hand move to explore the soft curve of her breast. He slipped beneath the opening of her robe, cupped the small mound, and thumbed her nipple, his shaft lengthening and pushing against the falls of his pantaloons as the tip of her breast puckered under his touch.

She squirmed a bit, releasing a sweet gasp into his mouth. He'd learned how very sensitive her breasts were; how responsive she was when he touched her here. He swallowed her gasp and kissed her harder, stroking her nipple to make her wiggle and gasp again and again before moving to the other side and giving it the same treatment.

He straightened to focus on untying the belt of her robe, then he separated the two edges and pulled them apart. She wore the same plain white nightgown she'd worn last night. It silhouetted her body in a way that nearly made him groan, outlining the slim shapes of her legs, the gentle rise of her mound, the curve of her waist, and the taut peaks of her nipples.

He kicked off his shoes and slipped into bed beside her, drawing her into his arms, pressing his own body against hers so she would have no doubt as to the level of his arousal.

More brazen than last night, her hands explored his back over his shirt, then his torso. He sucked in a breath when her fingertips passed over his nipples, and she pulled back in surprise.

"It feels good," he explained. "No doubt similar to how it feels when I touch you there."

Her lips curved. Seductive, even wicked. After one night, she'd already grown adventurous. Once she knew what she was about, she would be a spitfire in bed.

He ran his lips over her jaw, nuzzling her. "God, how I want you."

"And I," she said as her fingertips passed over his chest again, "want you."

If she kept doing that, he'd lose his mind in no time. So he took a handful of her nightgown in his fist and pulled upward until he could touch the silky skin of her thigh.

He trailed his fingers up her leg, reveling in the soft and smooth but muscled contours, getting near her most private place, testing and then retreating.

Ever so gently, he cupped his hand over her mound. She stilled. Her only movement was in the quick rise and fall of her chest with each short, jerky breath. When he slipped his finger between her lips, she gave a shuddering moan.

She was slick with desire, just like she'd been last night. She clutched the back of his shirt, bunching the fabric there, thrusting against his hand as he stroked her again then pushed a finger inside her.

He drew back a little to look at her face. Her eyes were closed, her mouth open in a rapturous O.

His cock was a solid pike, aching to take the place of his finger. But he didn't allow it to rule him. Sarah's pleasure was what mattered. He wanted to make her forget.

He stroked her, caressing her inner walls and pressing the heel of his hand over the nub above. He worked her, first with the one finger and then adding a second, until she was gasping, squirming, arching and begging him in sweet little pants. "Please. Please. Please."

God. He needed a taste. He crawled down her body, trailing kisses over her nightgown, taking time as he passed over her breasts, suckling each nipple over the thin cotton even as he kept working his fingers into her. Then he nudged her nightgown up her legs, pausing over the scar on her knee.

A lump formed in his throat as he realized that she'd received that scar the day he'd met her. He kissed the little raised half-moon-shaped scar tenderly, then moved upward to press his lips to the area just about the V-shaped triangle of hair that hid her womanhood.

Again, she stilled. "What are you...?" Her voice trailed off.

"Tonight," he murmured between kisses, "I'm going to enlighten you on another way a woman can be pleasured." He withdrew his hand from her center and nudged her thighs apart, settling into position between them.

Her thighs trembled, and she was so wet. She was already hovering on the precipice, so close to losing all control. He wanted her to come, to plummet over the edge, to lose herself to pleasure.

He kissed over her mound, then used his tongue to lick between her lips, drinking in the singular taste of her, fresh and sweet, with that hint of meadow grasses. Essential Sarah.

Her legs shook around him, and he sensed rather than saw her hands scrambling for purchase. He reached up and grasped her hand, settling her. Her fingers curled hard over his, and he licked over her nub, sending a jolt through her body that resonated through his own.

Holding the outside of her thigh with his other hand,

he pressed his lips over her, thrust his tongue into her. And then he focused on the nub, feeling the jolt of sensation spear through her whenever he caressed it with his lips or tongue.

Her fingers gripped his hand tighter; her legs clamped around his shoulders. As he kissed and licked, taking her sweetness into himself, she tightened, her muscles taut and straining, tighter and tighter. And then she found her release, her body undulating around him, her gasps harsh in the quiet of the night.

And, God help him, he nearly came against the bedclothes. But he held on to his control and coaxed her through it, keeping his firm, grounding grip on her hand.

When she emerged on the other side, he kissed his way back up her body, tugging down her nightgown over her legs as he nuzzled her neck and jaw and finally ended with a gentle kiss on her lips. Then he drew back to look at her.

He smiled. Her eyes were half-lidded, her lips soft and pliant, a dewy sheen on her cheeks.

"You look like a woman well-pleasured."

"Do I?"

He nodded.

She reached up, her arms wrapping around him. "Now I must pleasure you."

He pressed another kiss to her lips. "No, Sarah. Not tonight."

A frown furrowed her brows. "Why not?"

"Because tonight was for you."

"Are you saying you don't want me to pleasure you? Isn't that what women do?"

He chuckled softly. "What do you know of what men want and what women do?"

"Mistresses please their men. That is what they're compensated for."

"Do you wish to be compensated?" he asked, bemused.

Her eyes went wide. "No!"

"Because I'd be happy to." He pressed a light kiss to her nose. "Whatever your heart desires." Although he knew she wasn't much of one for material possessions.

"No," she repeated, more firmly this time. "It's not like that between us, is it?"

"You know it isn't."

He didn't like comparing her to a mistress. Although, he realized, with a sick feeling twisting in his gut, that was essentially what she'd become.

"Simon," she murmured. "Let me try. I probably will be inept and stupid, but I want to try..."

"Not tonight," he told her gently. "This is enough for tonight. I like to see a woman pleasured. I like to see *you* pleasured."

"But I want to..."

"What? What is it you wish to do?"

Her gaze wandered low, in the direction of his cock.

She bit her lip and looked back up into his face. "I want to please you," she whispered.

"You already have, love."

Whore.

Sarah lay in bed the next morning, thinking of that word. Of how, if all the people in London had known how she'd behaved last night and the night before, they'd label her with that awful word.

And yet, she did not feel like a whore. No bolt of lightning had struck her down where she slept. No pang of conscience had overtaken her. She was still Sarah Osborne. Her feelings about the world hadn't changed. Only her feelings about Simon had grown stronger.

No regrets. She'd told Simon she'd have none, and she didn't.

She'd lain in his arms in the darkest hours of morning. He'd held her through her grief about Binnie, made her feel comforted. Protected. Even cherished.

No one had ever cherished her before.

She'd fallen into a deep sleep with the weight of his arm over her. Just before dawn had begun to lighten the sky, he'd shifted away from her, then his lips had nuzzled into her hair.

"I must go," he'd murmured. "Sleep, love."

And she'd slept again. Deep and comfortable, warm, the languor from his lovemaking infusing her bones even hours later. Now, she could tell by the level of light in the bedchamber that she'd slept far past the hour at which she normally rose. But that didn't matter. She slipped out of bed, feeling warm and content.

Simon would be long gone, so she wouldn't be able to take her usual pleasure from breakfasting with him. She sat at her dressing table and gazed at herself. Her blue eyes were bright in the mirror, but there were dark smudges beneath that would tell the world that she'd been crying.

Poor Binnie.

She combed her hair with shaky hands, remembering the solidity of Simon's arms around her as she'd wept. Today would be a difficult day. She'd have to tell Esme and the household, and they'd have to write to Mrs. Hope and to Binnie's family.

But she'd get through it. The memory of Simon's embrace would sustain her.

Chapter Twelve

Simon sat alone in his drawing room, awaiting the arrival of Lord Stanley. The ladies were out shopping—they had no idea that Simon was here, because he rarely showed his face at home in the early afternoon hours. However, at Almack's last week after Simon had finished his second dance with Miss Stanley, her father had asked for a private meeting. Simon had accepted, though he'd no doubt as to what Stanley intended to ask him.

He wanted Simon to marry his daughter.

Simon had agreed to the meeting out of politeness, and because he wanted to clarify to Stanley that while Simon found his daughter lovely and an excellent dancer and dinner companion, he had no intention of taking things further than that.

Another time, another year, Simon might have given Miss Stanley serious consideration. She'd make a more than adequate wife for a duke; it was as if she'd been groomed to play the role. She probably had, come to think of it. But after a few days of visiting Sarah's bed, Simon's plans had changed. Simon had no intention of shackling himself to anyone—at least not this Season. He was enjoying this time he had with Sarah too much to put an end to it.

A knock sounded on the door and Tremaine informed him that Baron Stanley had arrived.

He rose to greet Stanley and offered him a drink. When they were both seated in the royal-blue upholstered chairs with brandy glasses in hand, he got straight to the point. "What is it you wished to see me about?"

Stanley took his time before answering, taking a slow sip of brandy, holding it in his mouth as if savoring its fine taste. When he swallowed, he gazed at the contents of his glass and said, "Thought you were against French spirits."

"Only those obtained illegally. This brandy is from the stores owned by my father before the war."

"Ah. I wasn't aware the old duke possessed such a keen sense of forethought."

Simon didn't answer. There was a full minute of silence. Then, Stanley carefully set down his glass on the round mahogany table beside his chair.

"I'm here regarding my daughter, Georgina."

Simon tilted his head in question and pasted a subtly concerned look on his face. "Oh?"

Stanley's gaze sharpened, his hawk's eyes keen as he studied Simon. "Despite your paltry attendance at the events every Season before this one, when you are present, you have always given my daughter a significant fraction of your attentions."

Simon sipped his drink. "Miss Stanley always seemed

to be in attendance at whatever function at which I chose to make an appearance. It is encouraging to see a familiar face in the crowd."

"Encouraging, eh?" Stanley gave a humorless laugh, and those narrow eyes glinted a steely blue. "No doubt. A familiar *beautiful* face, too. Do you fancy my daughter?"

Simon chose his words carefully. "She possesses a fair countenance, and she is a pleasant conversationalist. You have done a fine job with her, Stanley. She should make some gentleman an excellent match someday."

Stanley sat back in his chair. "So you make your intentions clear."

Simon raised a brow. "I assure you, I have no intentions regarding Miss Stanley. None at all, beyond neighborly friendship, of course."

"I see." Stanley studied him for a long moment, then spoke softly. "Georgina would benefit—indeed, our entire family would benefit—from an alliance with you, Trent."

Simon didn't say anything, because they both knew Stanley's words were very true. Stanley was a landed and moneyed baron, but the position Simon occupied was wedged into the very highest echelon of society, and Stanley's barony only permitted him partial admittance to that select bit of humanity that had the power to sway kings. Stanley had always wanted it, Simon knew this well. Hell, anyone would know it, just from looking at the man. His ambition was written all over his face. And if his daughter married Simon, that would give him—and his heir—greater access to all that power and privilege.

"But I think you would benefit from an alliance with us as well."

Simon didn't ask how. There was no point. Whatever "benefit" Stanley might see in it for him had no bearing, because Simon had no intention of marrying his daughter regardless. "That might be true," he said instead. "Believe me, I am honored that you'd consider me for your daughter. I know how fond you are of her." He didn't know that at all, but he assumed most fathers were fond of their daughters. "As I said before, she will make someone a fine wife. I am sure she will ultimately make a very good match that will benefit all parties involved."

Stanley heaved out a sigh. "That is unfortunate."

Simon gave the other man a tight smile. "I am sure the opposite is true. In the interests of her happiness, a match with me would not be ideal."

Stanley's brows arched into brown peaks. "Oh? Are you saying you'd make my daughter unhappy?"

"Not deliberately," Simon said, "but she doesn't care for me, Stanley. Surely you can see that."

"Not at all. When you are together, I see just the opposite. She is utterly taken with you."

Simon frowned. *No.* She was attentive and flirtatious—sometimes overly so. But Simon had always viewed that as an act, one that he'd seen duplicated by countless young ladies of her caliber. Surely Stanley couldn't believe that that behavior represented true affection.

Simon knew what it felt like to be really cared for—Sarah had shown him that.

Something in his gut clenched tight as thoughts and images of Sarah barreled through him in the midst of this talk of marrying Georgina Stanley.

Stanley leaned slightly forward, his hands clasped over

his flat stomach. "Tell me true, Trent. Can I harbor some hope that your feelings might change? Must I return home to my daughter and dash all her dreams?"

Dash her dreams? Good God, had it really come to that?

He shook his head. "I'm sorry, Stanley." He meant it.

"As am I." Stanley reached over to his glass and took a long drink of his brandy, his lids lowered. When he set down his glass and raised his eyes to Simon again, Simon didn't at all like the look on his face. "I am sorry for what I must do now."

"What do you mean?" Simon asked.

"I simply refuse to dash my daughter's dreams. Therefore, I fear I must take extreme measures."

Simon's hands tightened over the armrests of his chair. His cravat suddenly felt very tight. "Are you threatening me, Stanley? In my own home?" His voice was quiet. Dangerous.

"Not exactly threatening," Stanley said. "However, I fear I'm preparing to tell you something you'll not at all enjoy hearing."

For a second, Simon's thoughts seemed to scramble. Could Stanley know what had happened to Simon's mother? Was he about to confirm her death? But what did any of that have to do with Georgina Stanley and the reason Stanley had come to see him today?

Simon waited, his knuckles whitening over the chair arms.

"It has to do with your family. Your brothers, in particular." Stanley hesitated, then cocked his head, his eyes narrowing, both his hands clasped around his now-empty glass. "You see, I know the truth."

Simon waited for him to elaborate, but when several seconds had passed and he hadn't, he asked, "What truth?"

"About your brothers."

If it was possible to grow any tenser, Simon did at that moment. "What about them?"

Stanley's head tilted farther to the side. His lips parted, a light breath whooshed out, and then he said in a very low voice, "You don't know."

"What the hell are you talking about?"

Stanley drew back, his steely eyes slowly widening in true shock. "You don't know. My God. She kept it from you, all these years. Astonishing."

"Kept what from me?" Simon rose to his feet.

Stanley just stared up at him as Simon stepped closer.

"Tell me what the hell you're talking about, Stanley."

"I should have known. Ever so wily were the Duke and Duchess of Trent. Of course they wouldn't tell you. They knew better."

"Tell me *what*?"

Stanley still gazed at him, as if seeing him for the first time. "The prodigal son," he murmured. "So different from his parents."

Simon clenched his hands at his sides. If this man didn't get to the point soon, he wasn't going to be able to stop himself from throttling him.

Stanley raised his glass. "Another?"

His jaw working, Simon took the glass from him and stalked to the sideboard to replenish the brandy. He took the time with his back to Stanley to inhale several deep breaths and to calm himself. When he returned, handing the glass to the other man, he remained standing. "What

I'd like to know, Stanley, is if you intend to ever inform me what this is about."

Stanley took a deep drink, and when he lowered the glass from his lips, it was already half empty. "Since you clearly have no idea, I suppose I should start from the beginning. Sit down, Trent. You'll need to be seated for this."

Without a word, Simon resumed his seat.

"Your older brother, Samson, is a bastard," Stanley announced. "It is widely known that he is the illegitimate son of your mother and some unknown man."

Simon crossed his arms over his chest. He generally didn't tolerate people calling Sam a bastard—usually, no one dared use that word in his presence. Sam was his older brother by two years, and he was a man Simon admired and respected. Their mother had never stood for anyone speaking ill of Sam, either.

"It was surprising to most of England at the time, but your father still wanted your mother, even after her well-known indiscretion. Before you were born, they were touted as the wild duke and his whore."

Simon stared coldly at the older man. He knew all this, of course. He had spent most of his life attempting to clear the Hawkins family name of all that scandal his mother and father had thrived on.

"Shortly after you were born, the duke grew bored of your mother," Stanley continued. "He took a mistress in Town." He paused to take another sip of brandy.

Simon's lips tightened. His mother and father's relationship had been extremely complicated and difficult for his youthful self to understand. By the time Theo was born, however, they had seemed to come to some sort of arrangement that allowed them to live in peace—not as husband and wife, per se, but at least they could reside in the same country and even the same house at times—without the screaming and violent arguments he remembered from when he was younger.

"I know all this," he growled out. "Get to the point."

"Patience, boy." Stanley lowered his glass. "Your mother was distraught by your father's inattention. She turned elsewhere for comfort."

Simon didn't like the way Stanley placed emphasis on the word "comfort."

"She turned to *me*," Stanley announced. He gave time for Simon to absorb that, then continued, "I was young and unmarried at that time. A neighbor. A friend. We had a brief, torrid affair that consisted of many furtive, sweaty encounters in the pastures bordering Ironwood Park and my lands." He paused for a moment, then he added, "Alas, Trent, your brother, Lord Lukas Hawkins, isn't really a Hawkins at all. He is a Stanley."

Every word Stanley spoke seemed to compress Simon's lungs more. "You're lying," he choked out.

"Oh, I assure you, I am not."

"Then I don't believe you."

"You should." Now Stanley's voice was low and dangerous. The balance of power had switched to his side, and he knew it. "I've proof."

"Where?" Simon asked.

"Written documents," Stanley said. "An agreement witnessed by the Trent solicitor wherein I agreed that I would make no claim on the boy for as long as the old Duke of Trent was alive."

Simon's lip curled. "That makes no sense. Why would

my mother ever allow proof of her infidelity, not to mention an illegitimate child, to exist?"

Stanley gave a sly smile. "I plan ahead, Trent. I was prepared to reveal my link to the child then, but her position with the duke was precarious. He found out about our liaison and had threatened her with divorce. She convinced him otherwise, but she knew if I brought her dalliance to society's attention, he'd go through with it. So I demanded that we create this document, knowing that at some point in the future I might be able to use my paternity of Lukas to my advantage."

Simon's head was spinning. Luke couldn't know—if he did, he would have let the truth out during one of his many drunken rages in which he'd railed at Simon over the years.

If this was the truth, it would eviscerate him. Luke was already on the verge of complete failure. This news would push him over the edge.

"Don't you see me in him?" Stanley asked, and there was a dark shadow of humor in his voice. "I do. He takes after me, that is for certain." He gestured to his own face. "It's in the eyes."

Simon stared at Stanley's eyes. The resemblance, now that Stanley pointed it out, was absolutely undeniable. Luke's eyes were exact replicas of Stanley's, from their shape down to their shade. But it was more than that. The construction of their faces was nearly identical. Even their hair held the same blond shade.

"You look horrified, Trent." Stanley had relaxed again. The bastard had begun to enjoy himself, took pleasure from seeing Simon in distress. "But my story is only in its infancy. There's much more."

Simon's gut had twisted into a knot. "What do you mean? How can there be more?" Surely this was enough life-altering news for one day.

Stanley gave him a grim smile. "Regarding the agreement I made with your parents, know that I have no desire to claim Lukas as my own. I've no need of a bastard son, especially not one as depraved as that boy."

"Then why are you telling me this?"

Stanley didn't answer. He simply continued. "A few years passed, and your mother traveled to the Continent and was absent for quite a long time. Perhaps you remember—as I recall she left you and your two half brothers with your governess at Ironwood Park. Our affair had long since ended. When she returned, she was in possession of yet another 'legitimate' infant son."

"Mark," Simon said.

"Yes. Markus. And then, two years later, Theodore appeared."

Simon looked at him, waiting.

"Both of them are illegitimate as well."

"No," Simon said, his tone confident. "That is impossible."

"They're not of your mother's blood, mind. They are the product of your father and his mistress, Fiona Atwood. Your mother sent Fiona to France, then she paid dear for Fiona to hand over Markus the moment he was born. After Theodore, your mother had had enough. She gave Fiona a great deal of money to disappear and never show her face in London—or to the duke—again."

"You cannot know this."

"Oh, but I can." Stanley gave him a thin smile. "You see, lovely Fiona wasn't exclusively the Duke of Trent's mistress. When he wasn't busy with her, you see, he shared her with me."

"Oh, God," Simon muttered. Was there no limit to the lascivious, dangerous games his parents' generation had played?

Stanley still held on to that smile that was more of a grimace. "I comforted that woman as her belly increased from another man's seed, and I held her after her sons were taken from her. I know where to find her. If you really wanted proof, I can tell you where she is."

Theo and Mark's mother. No, it simply didn't connect properly in Simon's head. Their mother was his mother—the woman who'd been missing for over a month. The woman who'd raised them all.

Simon gave Stanley an unbelieving sneer. "Don't tell me Esme is illegitimate, too."

"Oh, I do believe she is. She has none of your father's features and looks nothing like you, after all. Not to mention the fact that your father was already deathly ill when she was conceived. It would have taken some grand heroics on your mother's part to encourage the duke to rise to the occasion, as it were." Stanley gave a dry chuckle. "That is only conjecture, however. I have no proof of your sister's illegitimacy. However, I do hold proof that all three of your 'legitimate' brothers are, in fact, bastards." He paused, that small smile curling his lips again. "How does that information sit with you, Trent?"

"Not well." Simon felt dizzy—as though the world had somehow tilted off its axis, and he was trying desperately to right it.

"I thought not."

Again, Simon gripped the carved wooden armrests of

his chair. "So. What compels you to tell me all these"—
lies, they must be lies—"things, Stanley?"

"It would be tragic to the Hawkins family if the truth
came out, wouldn't it?" Stanley said softly. "Devastating
to your three brothers, who have enjoyed the status of
lordship since their births. Especially my own offspring,
Lord Lukas. He would lose his position as your heir"—
he snapped his fingers—"in the blink of an eye. And
the scandal—" Stanley shook his head, giving out a low
whistle from between his teeth.

Simon stared at him.

"Therefore, Trent, I do believe it would be in your best
interests to propose to my daughter. It is the only way to
protect your family name. To keep Lukas as your heir.
To maintain Theodore's and Markus's positions in society and to assure their—very bright, I'm told—futures as
respected members of the aristocracy."

"Because if I do not marry Miss Stanley," Simon said,
his voice so low even he could barely hear it, "you will
inform the world that my brothers are by-blows."

Stanley's smile showed a row of tobacco-and-tea-
stained teeth. "Indeed. I'll include my suspicions about
your sister for good measure. Everyone will believe, for
everyone still remembers your parents'—how shall I put
it?—*vigorous* tastes. However, if they do not, I am in possession of my proof. There's no doubt your three brothers
will be ruined, and your sister will be eyed with suspicion
for the remainder of her days."

"I should like to see that proof you claim to possess."

"And so you shall," Stanley told him graciously. He
rose from his chair. "I do realize you are likely reeling
from all that I have said, Trent. Therefore, I shall give

you some time to absorb the truth. Think carefully on all I have told you. I shall come to this house next week at the same time, and then I shall expect my answer. I do heartily encourage you to choose marrying my beautiful, innocent, and worthy daughter over a lifetime of scandal and debasement for your brothers and sister." He strode to the door. "Good day."

And without another word, Stanley exited from the room, leaving a stunned Simon staring after him.

It was creeping onto midnight when he came to her that night. Rain pelted against the window, and the chill in the air had seeped through the spaces in the window frame. In her warm flannel nightgown, Sarah sat in her chair reading a novel, but she could hardly focus on the words laid out on the open page in front of her.

She was worried he wouldn't come—she hadn't seen him all afternoon—and so when she heard the door handle creak, she breathed out a long breath of relief even as her body tensed in anticipation of his touch.

"I missed you today." She set her book aside and rose to greet him as he entered and closed the door behind him, intending to wrap her arms around his solid body in greeting and to simply breathe him in.

But she stopped short when she looked at the thunderously dark expression on his face.

"What is it? Has there been some new information about the duchess?" Two days after they'd recovered Binnie's body, Simon had hired an investigator. Almost a week had gone by, and so far, the man had found nothing.

Simon stood in the center of her room, his arms limp

at his sides. He bent his head, closing his eyes. "No. Still no word."

"What, then?" she breathed.

He looked up at her then, his expression stark, his green eyes shining. "Come here," he said gruffly.

She did, and he drew her tight against him.

"I don't want to talk about it," he murmured into her hair. "I just want to be with you."

She reached up to trail her fingers through the silky strands of hair at his nape. "All right." She knew he'd tell her what was bothering him eventually.

His body shuddered against hers, and she gripped him more tightly. "It's all right. You don't need to tell me."

"Sarah," he whispered. He pressed his lips to hers, grinding against her mouth, a complete possession that would have ruined her for any other man, had she not already been ruined. She wanted all of it, accepted all of it until every nerve in her body sang with his possession.

With fumbling fingers, he worked the buttons of her nightgown, but she slipped out of his grip, stepped back, and pulled up the nightgown over her head and tossed it away.

She wore nothing underneath. Her breath caught as she raised her chin to look at him, his eyes devouring her with feral hunger. "Damn. You're so beautiful."

She blinked at the curse—Simon rarely ever cursed—and the strange juxtaposition of the word with the compliment. But otherwise, she didn't move or speak.

Holding her gaze, he removed his own clothes, starting with his shirt, baring his pale, muscled torso, and then working the buttons on the falls of his breeches before sitting on the edge of her bed to pull them completely off.

Sarah's breaths shortened, quickened. He was completely, utterly bare.

Her gaze slowly traveled down from his eyes, caressing his face, grazing his powerful shoulders, sliding over the tight, small, masculine nipples that made him shudder when she touched them. Past his rippling abdomen, over his trim, narrow hips.

Male beauty personified.

And there was his organ, jutting out from between his legs, its skin darker than the rest of him. Long and thick. He shifted under her perusal of it, and her gaze snapped back up to his face. A smile tilted one side of his lips, and she bit down on her lower lip as heat burned in her cheeks.

"I've never seen…Well, besides the Laocoön," she stammered out. "And yours…it's bigger. Longer. And darker."

"Laocoön is fighting for his life," Simon said softly. "I'd wager the sculptor decided he probably wouldn't be aroused at that moment."

"Right. Yes. Of course not."

His smile grew, deepening that dimple in his chin. "Come here."

She sat next to him on the edge of the bed. He wrapped a hand around her neck, drawing her in for another kiss, this one soft and seductive, caressing and stroking her with his lips and tongue until she sighed with pleasure into his mouth. His hand traveled from her neck down her shoulder and arm until he took hold of her hand and moved it over his member.

The heat of him made her draw in a quick intake of breath. He pressed his hand over her fingers so she curled them around him, then he moved up and down so that she was stroking him.

Steely hardness wrapped in velvet heat.

"Simon," she whispered.

He drew away from her lips and let her hand still over him. "What is it, love?"

Her breath caught, as it always did when he called her "love." She looked up at him. "I want to be yours," she whispered. "In every way. Tonight. Please."

She'd asked him before. He'd come to her whenever he could—three times in the past week. They'd kissed, they'd caressed. He'd worked her like an instrument, plucking the strings until her body hummed and pulsed, until her nerves sang and finally she reached pinnacles she'd never known were possible. They had been the happiest nights of her life, and that happiness had overflowed into her daytime activities so much that Esme had commented on her "glow."

But he hadn't taken this final step, and she didn't understand why. He hadn't allowed her to give him the same pleasure. She wanted to. She'd wanted to that first night, and her desire had increased every night since.

He leaned forward until his forehead touched hers. He cupped her face in his hands. "Sarah—" His voice broke as his breath whispered over her lips. "What if I told you that tonight was the last night I could come to you? The last night we could be together? Would you still offer me this gift?"

She hesitated, giving serious consideration to his words.

That day would come, she knew. The day this happiness—this perfection—would end. The day he could no longer be her lover. Even her friend. The day she'd be reduced to a simple servant in his eyes.

She couldn't harbor illusions of forever. She was soaking up this time with him into her skin, and she would make it sustain her when she was lonely later on. There was no other choice.

"I would still offer it," she said quietly.

"Why?"

"Because..." She reached up to stroke his cheek, rough from a day's growth of beard. "It is something I want you to have." Because if he took her virginity, he'd have it forever. "And it's not only that. It's for selfish reasons, too. Simply put, I want you."

She wanted to know what it was like to be loved completely. By Simon. There would be no one else.

He gave a low groan, but then he asked, "No regrets?"

"Never," she whispered. No matter what happened, that was the truth.

He laid her on the bed, and his green eyes sparkled in the sparse light from the one lamp flickering on the other side of the room.

"Then we won't think about what tomorrow might bring. Tonight belongs to us."

Chapter Thirteen

❧

Simon's touch was electric. It snapped over every inch of her body until she was a trembling mass of sensitive nerve endings.

"I want to please you," she protested.

"*This* pleases me." He worked his fingers inside her, feathering over that part of her that made her gasp with pleasure. His mouth seemed to be everywhere at once. On her lips. On her breasts. Caressing her neck, her stomach, her hips and thighs. Stroking her in tandem with his fingers between her legs.

"Watching you," he said. "Seeing your pleasure." *Stroke. Kiss. Caress.* "That pleases me."

And, not expecting that flush of ecstasy to overtake her so quickly, she came. He'd told her that was what it was, that pleasure undulating through her body, originating at her core and spreading outward to all her extremities. Her body shuddered, and his fingers slid through an increased slickness between her legs.

"I feel it when you come, Sarah. I feel your body's release. I feel your pleasure. *That* pleases me."

He stroked her until she squirmed, until her sated tissues were too sensitive for his touch, and then he finally drew away to lie beside her and pull her against him until their bodies were pressed against each other, skin to skin from her toes to her lips, and with every breath she nuzzled against him, inhaling his cedar-and-spice scent.

She might be sated, but he wasn't. He was tense and warm, his manhood hard and heavy against her thigh.

"What do you call it?"

"What do I call what?" he rumbled into her hair.

"This." She reached between their bodies, skimming it with her fingertips. "Do you call it your manhood? Your member? I don't believe I know of any other terms used to describe it."

He chuckled against her. "There are many. What would you prefer? The clinical penis, the erudite phallus?"

"Oh, right. I suppose I might have heard those two words, too, once or twice," she mused.

"Then there are the euphemisms. Rod. Blade. Sword. Horn. Knocker."

She gave a soft snort, and her body lurched with a laugh. "Knocker?"

"My schoolmates at Cambridge used that one often."

"I suppose I can see where that came from. It tends to...*knock*...on certain doors, after all."

"It does." He chuckled into the softness of her hair. "And to think—I hadn't even come to rolling-pin yet."

"No!" Her body shook with mirth.

"Yes."

"Are there more?" Her fingertips stroked over his silky flesh, and he shuddered against her.

"Ah, so many more. There are the more vulgar terms. Rump-splitter. Prick."

She made a small squeak, pressing her head into his shoulder.

"But perhaps we should start with the term I most frequently use. That organ which you are currently driving mad with your teasing is called a 'cock.'"

She looked up at him, confusion drawing her brows together. "Like...a chicken?"

His chuckle turned into a laugh. "There is a cock that is a male chicken, and there is the cock between my legs. But I assure you, there is little resemblance between the two."

"How very odd." A smile twitched her lips. "I shall never look at a cock the same way again. Although, I must agree, I cannot see any resemblance between the two. One has a bright red cowl and is feathery and noisy in the mornings, and one—"

His kiss cut off her words. He held her in a cocoon of warmth and strength, his arms around her, his leg hooked over hers, his *cock* nestled against her mound.

She held him tight, rubbing against him, watching the lines of tension on his face deepen. His self-control was powerful, but she could tell from those little lines that he'd put it to the test in the last few days.

No more. Not if she had her say.

"Take me," she whispered to him, and then she bit down gently on his earlobe.

He turned her to her back and moved so that he hovered above her. His body slid over hers, his heat stroking the dip of her pressed-together legs.

"This will hurt." His voice had changed, turned gruff and scratchy. He gazed down at her with eyes sparkling emerald green. "You know I don't want to hurt you."

And that was exactly what made it all right. "Yes," she whispered. "I know."

He nuzzled her hair, his lips skimming along her hairline above her ear. "My body is telling me that I must take you hard. Possess you completely. Make you mine in every way. Mark you."

She groaned aloud at that thought. She wanted that, too. She wanted to lose herself completely to his lovemaking. She wanted to feel possessed by him, consumed by him, and she wanted the marks to show it.

"But I can't. That will hurt you even more. I must take it slow. And you must tell me to stop if it becomes too much."

"Never," she promised him. She slid her legs out from under him and wrapped them over the backs of his thighs in a blatant invitation.

"Sarah," he said brokenly. Then, balancing himself on one arm, he reached down to guide himself into her. His fingers touched her first, and sensation shot through her, for her flesh was still sensitive from her earlier orgasm. She trembled, and he stopped. His lids, which had been lowered, rose so that he was looking into her eyes again.

He didn't speak, and neither did she. Instead, she arched into him, telling him it was all right, begging him to continue. And then she felt it. The broad tip of his cock pressing into her.

It didn't hurt in the beginning. But then, as he inched

into her, he seemed to grow bigger and longer, too big, and an instant of panic rushed through her, a sharp fear that he would tear her open from the inside out.

He sensed it. He pulled away, breathing hard now, and the terror receded. Again, she met his eyes. *No*, that feeling of panic had been wrong. Her body was meant for his. She *knew* that. Again, she arched into him.

He tried once more, pushing in slowly. It didn't hurt so much this time. He was solid and steely over her, but he was trembling. Sweat beaded over his brow. And she knew that it was torturing him to go slow.

He wasn't fully inside her, but he was retreating again, pulling away. She was sore, but she'd survive. The panic was gone. It had been groundless, in any case—no woman had ever died from losing her virginity to the man she loved.

"No," she whispered. At the same time, her hands slid down his muscled back to the top of his buttocks. She pressed him into her as she arched her pelvis up, wanting all of him.

And he surged into her. The wave of pain crested, and she let out a small cry. But then it broke and receded, leaving a dull ache in its wake.

She gasped. She'd never felt so full, like he touched all of her, inside her body and out, all at the same time.

Locked together. As one. A deep shudder of pleasure ran through her body. "Oh, Simon," she whispered. And suddenly she was on the verge of tears. She couldn't begin to comprehend why.

She forgot about the tears when he began to move. Stroking her inside walls with every surge forward and backward retreat, her own body tightening around him and drawing him in, wrapping around him in a fist of pleasure.

His fingers curled into her hair, but she doubted he noticed—she barely did. Her body was so alive with sensation. There was nothing beyond it. Nothing but the sweet, full feeling of him inside her. Finally, fully claiming her as his own.

Her body tautened around him. Her legs clamped over his thighs, her pelvis tilting up instinctively to allow deeper penetration.

"More," she whispered, because she could feel in the tension of his muscles that he still held back. "More, Simon. Give me everything. All of you."

It was like she'd unleashed the chains holding him back. He sank down lower over her until the tips of her breasts rubbed against his chest with every movement. His breath washed over her cheek in warm, harsh puffs. His hand tightened in her hair. And his movements became intense surges of power, deep and full.

It was what Sarah had wanted. What she needed. She wrapped her arms and legs around him and held on for the ride, her head nestled in the heated crook of his shoulder.

Simon had finally made her his. Pleasure erupted through her.

Her body stiffened around him, tighter and tighter, and then sweet sensation exploded in her blood, racing through her, making her body jerk and twist in the confines of his embrace. He responded to her orgasm, his motions growing stronger, then frenzied, and finally, with a low, guttural cry, he surged into her and held, his body contracting over her and within her.

The tension in his muscles bled away until he sank heavily over her, twisting to the side so he wouldn't crush her, but taking her with him. They lay facing each other, him still wedged tightly inside her. She knew he'd finished, but she was glad he stayed inside.

He gazed at her in wonder. "You came."

She nodded.

He blinked, his dark eyelashes sweeping down twice. "I've never heard of such a thing. A virgin orgasm."

"You haven't? You told me women sometimes come during the act."

"Not the first time," he said. "At least...not that I know of." He reached up to stroke her cheek with one finger, and his lips curved. "I suppose I can take that to mean it wasn't terribly painful?"

"At first it was. But it went away." Although now she could feel a not-too-unpleasant soreness setting in. "And then it felt so good, Simon. So right to have you inside me."

His smile was gentle. "For me, too."

She glanced away, feeling suddenly shy. Although that was surely silly, since they were lying naked together, and he was still inside her.

He moved slowly, making her gasp as sensation pricked through her. Oh, she'd thought she was sensitive before, but now the feel of him stroking inside her was so powerful she could hardly bear it.

"Too much?" he asked.

"Yes. No." She looked at him again. "I...don't know. It's just...the sensations are so strong..."

The finger that had been caressing her cheek smoothed back a lock of hair behind her ear. Then his hand drifted down behind her shoulder and back until his palm cupped her buttocks. "I could make love to you all night long."

She gave a small shudder. Her body was so alive, prickling with energy.

"But this is too new," he said, and she sensed the barest edge of regret in his voice. "You aren't ready." He began to pull away, but she stopped him by tilting her pelvis and pressing her hand on his lower back.

"Make love to me again, Simon."

And so, ever so gently, slowly and lovingly, he did.

Simon knocked on the door to his brother's townhouse. His manservant answered. Recognizing Simon immediately, the man ushered him inside, took his hat and cane, and asked him to wait while he saw if his master was at home.

Less than a minute later, he returned to usher Simon into Sam's study. Sam, who'd been sitting behind his parchment-strewn desk, stood when he entered. "Trent. Good to see you."

They shook hands warmly, then Simon took the seat opposite Sam's well-worn desk. He always felt at home here at Sam's. This was the place he'd hidden himself that Season he'd made all those mistakes and the female masses of London had been pursuing him with claws extended. Sam had graciously taken him in and had concealed him until the furor had died down.

Simon gazed at his brother, who looked hale and healthy as usual, his skin darkened from the sun to a shade far deeper than what was fashionable, his shoulders and chest broad and muscular from his exertions on his secret missions for the Crown.

"Sorry for disturbing you like this. I know you just arrived home and haven't had time to settle," Simon began. Sam had sent him a note yesterday afternoon, saying he was in Town for a few days before heading north again. He'd also mentioned that he'd encountered only blank stares and non-answers for his part in the search for their mother and had made no progress. "But there's something I need to talk to you about."

Sam gazed at him, very still in his chair. "Mother?"

"No." Simon blew out a frustrated breath. "We've found nothing since the recovery of Binnie."

They both sat in silence for a moment.

"Luke has gone off to search on his own," Simon finally said. "He might have discovered something, but he's angry with me at the moment, so I'm not entirely sure he'd let me know."

Sam shook his head. "I wouldn't count on Luke. He's likely to get distracted by the first thing in skirts that crosses his path."

"Perhaps. Though I'm not so certain in this case. He's taken our mother's disappearance hard."

Sam's brows rose. "Can it be that our younger brother has finally decided to become responsible?"

"Well, I wouldn't go that far." Maybe he was taking small steps, though. Then again, Simon remembered how the coachman had found Luke curled on the ground outside Trent House and doubted it. He sighed. "For my part, I feel as though I've run out of options. I've hired a man to continue to investigate, and he has turned up empty-handed as well."

"She couldn't have simply disappeared off the face of the earth."

"She's got to be somewhere," Simon agreed. "But this isn't why I'm here. I came to see you about another matter. I need your advice."

"Of course."

And here it was. He braced himself to tell his brother what had transpired between himself and Stanley and took a deep breath before saying, "I'm being bullied into marriage."

Sam raised a dark brow. "Not like you to allow yourself to be bullied, Trent. Who is it?"

"Our neighbor, Baron Stanley."

"Ah." Sam's lips tightened. "Never liked the man."

"Neither did I. Nor did our parents." Now he knew why. Geographically, the Stanleys had owned the closest house to Ironwood Park, yet they had never engaged in neighborly friendship with the Hawkinses.

"Right," Sam said. His gaze narrowed on Simon. "Who is he attempting to shackle you to?"

"His daughter."

"Don't believe I've ever met the girl."

"That wouldn't surprise me. They keep her sheltered." He gave his brother a bleak look. "They've been grooming her to be a duchess."

Sam leaned slightly forward, his eyes dark brown slits. "Why? What does Stanley have on you that he could possibly think would force your hand?"

Simon rubbed his temple against a sudden headache. "He is holding a family secret over my head. Says if I do not marry his daughter, he will expose it to the world."

"A family secret? I thought the well of our secrets had finally run dry. Our mother and your father's exploits have been bandied about publicly for years."

"Not this one." Simon met Sam's eyes. "This is one even you and I didn't know about."

Sam sensed the direness of the situation—maybe from Simon's tone or from his expression. He braced himself, his palms against the edge of the desk. "What is it?"

There was no choice but to lay it all out, plain and in the open for Sam to see. "He told me that our brothers are all illegitimate. That Luke is his son by our mother. And that Theo and Mark are the product of my father's relationship with a woman named Fiona Atwood. He claims to possess proof. And he claims Esme is illegitimate, too, although he admits to having no proof of that."

Sam stared at him, very still. A long moment of silence passed. Then he said, "That's ridiculous."

"Right. I thought so, too. But he told me exactly how it happened, in detail that wasn't easy to hear. He offered to show me the papers he signed promising to never acknowledge Luke as his. And he said he'd direct me to Fiona Atwood so I could question her myself."

"Papers can be forged," Sam said. "Women can be paid to lie."

"I know." Simon felt like he was choking out the words as he told Sam the one thing that had had his blood running cold since Stanley had left his drawing room. "But he looks like him, Sam. Luke looks like Stanley. His face. His eyes..." His voice faded.

Again, he felt sick, like something dark and poisonous was twisting around his innards.

Sam grimaced. "Do you believe him?"

"Yes," he said, his voice raw with the pain of admitting it aloud. "Yes, I do."

Sam blew out a long, slow breath between his teeth. "All right," he said quietly. "What are you going to do?"

"That's where I need your help."

"First of all, what are your feelings about marriage? About the lady?"

"I'd planned to find a suitable bride this year." Sam already knew that, because Simon had told him in one of their conversations just after the new year. "But even if I hadn't..." He hesitated, then began again. "Georgina Stanley isn't who I would have chosen."

Sam was too sharp to not pick up on Simon's small blunder. "So you'd already chosen another lady?"

"No," Simon said quickly. Then he hesitated, because that wasn't entirely true. He pushed a hand through his hair. Burton would blow out one of his long-suffering sighs when he saw Simon's hair later, but the valet would survive. "Perhaps. Not to marry, but..."

"I see," Sam said, but Simon was quite sure that he didn't. Simon didn't even completely understand how his feelings for Sarah had overlapped with his hunt for a duchess.

"We'll get back to that," Sam said. "So, you wouldn't have chosen Georgina Stanley. Why not?"

"She's a beautiful girl. Very proper. I'd thought before that she would make a perfect duchess—just not one for me. There's something about her that doesn't *fit* with me. I can dance with her. I can converse with her. Indeed, I can spend a pleasant evening with her. But marry her? No."

"That's understandable. Some people are compatible in every way but the ultimate finality of marriage."

Simon thought of Sarah. Of how he'd never been able

to strip off the shell of Trent so completely with anyone else.

"I wouldn't say I'm compatible with Miss Stanley. It's just...well, she's agreeable. But no more."

"And you have no wish to marry her."

"None at all."

Sam's gaze sharpened. "So then, what are you willing to sacrifice for our brothers and sister, Trent? How far will you go to save their names and their reputations?"

Simon met his brother's gaze evenly. "You know me," he said quietly. "You know how far I will go."

He'd spent his life protecting himself, protecting his siblings, and protecting his family name from those who would slander them. Where his parents had built themselves a house of cards and then proceeded to blow it down in hurricane fashion before burning the pieces with a flourish, from the moment he'd attained the title at the age of ten, he had built it back up slowly, fortifying the foundation and each wall with solemn maturity and propriety.

"Yes, I do know how far you'd go," Sam said. "But first, you must ensure his proof is solid. Check the legality of these papers he claims to have. Verify them with your solicitor."

Something suddenly struck Simon. "Did Prentiss work for our parents back then?"

"I think so."

"Well, there it is." Simon sank deeper into his chair. Prentiss had been a trusted member of Simon's staff ever since he'd become the Duke of Trent, and before that, the man had been employed by his father. "Prentiss supposedly signed that document. He wouldn't lie to me now, so

I can bring the alleged proof to him, and he can confirm once and for all whether it is a forgery."

"And the woman? Fiona Atwood?"

"I'll meet her," Simon said, though his throat seemed to tighten as he spoke.

"I'll go with you, if that would help."

"Yes." Simon lowered his head, trying to draw air. The dark, sick thing inside him tightened around his lungs, and his breath came in short puffs. "Is it so bad, Sam? Being labeled a bastard?"

There was a long silence before Sam spoke.

"Simon." Sam hadn't called him Simon in years, and that word coming from his brother's lips made the dark thing residing within him coil tighter. "I'm not sure Luke has the strength to bear the stigma of it. This news could be the thing that will ultimately destroy him."

"I know."

"He is our brother."

"Yes."

"And Mark and Theo... That label will snatch their futures from before their very eyes."

Simon nodded, but he still didn't meet his older brother's gaze. He was going to confirm Stanley's statements—and the sick feeling entwined in his gut gave him a dark assurance that everything Stanley had said was true—and then he was going to propose marriage to Georgina Stanley.

And he was going to break Sarah Osborne's heart in the process.

And his own.

"You've done it," he choked out, a drowning man reaching, searching for that floating debris that would keep him alive. "You've surpassed all expectation. You're a success."

Sam shook his head slowly. "At too much cost," he said. "Too much. And what do I have to show for it?" He gestured at his shabby office. "Really, it's not much."

And Simon realized it wasn't. Sam had been gifted with moments of happiness and of fulfillment, he knew, but they had all been stolen away for one reason or another. And what did he have now? A small apartment in Town and one dangerous secret assignment after another for the Crown. No one to come home to. Few friends outside his family.

"And then there's Esme," Sam said quietly. "We both know her, her difficulties, her reputation, which is only kept sterling due to your influence. But even your influence couldn't protect her from this. Our sister will be ostracized if even the lightest whisper of 'Esme Hawkins is a by-blow' was unleashed into the air. You can't let it happen."

Simon raised his bleak gaze to his brother. "I know."

"You do. I know you do. If you can think of a way out of the marriage without Stanley spewing his venom…"

"I can't." Simon had thought about it, wracked his brain, in fact. But Stanley wouldn't be convinced. His plan had been in the making for years—probably since his daughter's birth. A plan that had taken that long in its execution could not be so easily dismissed.

Sam gave him a faint smile. "At least she's not disagreeable."

It was a feeble attempt to make him feel better. And it didn't work.

"Ah. I see how it is. Who is the other lady, Trent?"

Simon looked away.

"Do I know her?"

He wouldn't betray Sarah. That simply wasn't going to happen.

Sam sighed. "And you're not a man who will continue an affair while you're married to another."

"That would be our parents," Simon said bitterly. "Not me."

"I know."

They sat in silence for a long minute. Finally, Sam murmured, "Luke I might believe, but Theo and Mark? Mama raised them like they were her own."

"I know. What kind of a mother raises her husband's mistress's children as her own flesh and blood?"

Sam hesitated, then shrugged. "Ours."

"Right."

No one was quite like their mother. And no one, not Simon, not his father or any of his siblings, had ever been able to understand some of the choices she made. She was one of those people who actively avoided conformity. Some of the kinder gossip about the Duchess of Trent proclaimed that she was an utterly one-of-a-kind woman, and no one in her family had ever disagreed with that.

Ultimately, it was within her character for her to whisk away the sons of her husband's mistress to raise as her own. Hadn't she done a similar thing with Sarah? If something had ever happened to Sarah's father, Simon had no doubt that his mother would have officially made her part of the family.

Simon looked up. "Once I've verified the truth, should I tell them? Theo and Mark? Luke? Esme?"

"If it were you, would you want to know?"

"Yes." Simon's answer was instantaneous.

"But you're not Luke. You're not Esme. Theo and Mark…"

Simon's lips twisted. "Luke wouldn't believe it if he heard it from my lips."

"And if he did?"

He met his brother's eyes. "He wouldn't take it well. But he deserves the truth."

"I don't think you should tell him," Sam said quietly.

Simon disagreed—all he knew was that he would want to know, and everyone deserved to know where they'd come from, even if the truth was difficult to bear. But he was willing to let it go, for now. Theo and Mark were busy with other things, and Luke—well, God only knew when he'd be seeing Luke again. He wanted proof first, to know for certain, and then he would have time to think about how best to approach that particular facet of the problem.

"We'll talk about it later, then," he said tiredly, rising to leave.

For now, he had other concerns. Verifying Stanley's proof. Proposing to Georgina Stanley.

Telling Sarah.

Chapter Fourteen

Sarah lay naked beside Simon in bed, her arms wrapped around him, sated and drowsy from their love-making but still awake.

Something was wrong, she knew. Something had been wrong for almost a week now. She had tried to ignore it after that first time he'd told her he didn't want to discuss it, but each time he'd come to her since that night—the night they'd made love for the first time—it had been present. A near palpable darkness that had seemed to hover behind him, press down on his shoulders. The heaviness of whatever it was pressed into her as well, a crushing heaviness on her heart.

"Simon." She drew back to look into his face. "Tell me what happened last week that weighs on you so."

He gazed at her, then sighed. "I have tried not to bring it here with me. I see that I have failed."

"Not exactly." He'd never seemed distracted or anything but completely focused on her when they were together. "But I do sense a black cloud hanging over you. And it builds and grows more thunderous every day."

"I'd planned on telling you tonight." He turned and swung his legs over the edge of the bed, then looked back over his shoulder at her, his expression grim. "I'd still like to pretend it doesn't exist, but you have to know."

She looked at him in rising terror, but he turned away, not meeting her eyes. "Dress. This will require clothing."

The pressure on her heart deepened as she obeyed him, slipping her nightgown over her head, then, even though it was warm enough without it, she pulled her robe on, wrapping the edges tightly around her body before cinching it closed with the belt.

When she'd finished, he'd drawn on his trousers, and his long, white shirt was draped over his torso, making him look like a half-naked pirate, dangerously handsome with his tousled light brown hair and piercing green eyes.

He dragged a chair next to the bed, then sat on the edge of the bed and gestured to the chair. "Sit."

She sat, looking at him warily, every nerve in her body brimming with trepidation.

He stared at her for a long moment, his hands clenched in the mussed blankets. Then, he said, "We both knew this would happen. I'd just hoped it wouldn't have to be so soon."

She stared at him, uncomprehending. Surely he couldn't be talking about them. Their discovery of each other had only just begun.

"After tonight...I can't come to you anymore. What is happening between us must end. It is over."

"No." It came out as a harsh whisper before she could

stop it. A tidal wave of pain crashed through her, and she closed her eyes and clenched her fists to combat it.

It struck her...she'd thought she loved Simon before. Now, since he'd started coming into her bed, she realized how much she truly did love him. How quickly he had become her universe.

"I'm sorry," he said quietly.

She opened her eyes and looked at him. His gaze was stark, his hands still clenched. He didn't want this, either.

"Why?" she asked, her voice hoarse.

"Circumstances beyond my control are forcing me to offer marriage to...someone."

She blinked at him, the different scenarios running through her mind, all of them so uncharacteristic of Simon. She shook her head. "How...? Did you compromise her?"

"No!" he choked out. "Sarah..." He slid off the bed and came to her, kneeling before her chair and looking up into her face, only open honesty showing in his. "There has been no one but you this spring, no one but you for a long time. It's nothing like that. There are other compelling reasons—none that have anything to do with her or me or any prior relationship between us, but with my family's reputation and my brothers' and sister's futures."

She shook her head, unable to make sense of his words. The dukedom wasn't in financial peril—or was it? No, it couldn't be. And why marry to protect a sibling's future? Had Luke ruined some lady, and was Simon offering himself in lieu of another type of payment?

It would be like Luke to make such a dire mistake. It would be like Simon to do whatever he could to save his brother...and the family name.

Her eyes filled with tears, and she blinked furiously to not allow them to spill. She was an expert at deceiving the world when it came to her feelings about Simon. She must continue to be so, now more than ever.

He slid his hands up the outsides of her thighs and pressed his forehead to her knees. "Don't...look at me like that," he said brokenly.

"Like what?"

"Like the world is coming to an end."

My world *is* coming to an end, she thought.

"We knew. I tried to warn you. Warn myself—"

"Who is it?" she whispered, cutting off his words.

He seemed to deflate a bit against her. "Georgina Stanley." With seeming great effort, he pulled back and stared at her from his position on his knees.

"Oh."

Beautiful, proper Miss Georgina Stanley. She was exactly the sort of lady Sarah had always thought Simon would marry. Until recently. Until he'd started coming into Sarah's room at night and had somehow put ideas into her head that his wife would be more like...her.

His lips were so tight their usual pale pink tinge had faded. "I don't want this. I don't want her. I want..." His voice faded, then he shook his head. "It doesn't matter what I want," he said softly. "It is what it is."

"When will you arrange for the betrothal?" It was astonishing how smooth and clear her voice sounded. How she could pretend that the sharp dagger of pain hadn't stabbed a hole into her heart. How it was possible her lungs were still capable of drawing breath.

She knew he wasn't betrothed yet. Simon was the sort

of man who wouldn't go near a woman once he was bound to marry someone else.

"Tomorrow."

She let out a little cry of pain before she could stop it.

And he was drawing her off the chair, onto his lap, and cradling her close.

Don't cry. Do not cry. You will not cry in front of him, because you knew this was going to happen. You knew *it, Sarah.*

This was the last time he'd ever hold her like this. It hurt. More than she could have ever comprehended it would.

He held her face against his chest, pressed his own face into her hair.

"I have to do this. For my family." His words came to her, fractured and broken. "Please understand."

She did understand, or at least a part of her did.

Mostly, she understood that her life loomed before her, a bleak and desolate wasteland without him.

And then he was kissing her. Everywhere. His lips were frantic, his movements erratic, like he wanted to touch every part of her at once. One last time.

That, she understood completely. Because she was kissing him, too, her movements equally jerky, equally fumbling. Everywhere. Her hands moved over his jaw, his night beard rasping against her palms. Down the front of his chest, then dipping beneath his shirt and moving up again until they reached his heart, hesitating there for seconds while she felt the frantic pounding beneath her fingertips. His fingers worked toward the hem of her nightgown, or her robe, or both, and her hands pressed around his sides.

Unchecked tears ran freely down her cheeks now, and as he laid her on the carpet, he bent down and kissed them away. And then he pressed inside her, and she gasped at the rush of sensation.

The trembling started in her core and spread in long fingers outward. She couldn't control it. She was a mass of nerves, her skin more raw and sensitive than it had ever been, her heart speared open and laid bare.

Simon's mouth moved over her, furiously frantic. He collected her into his arms so that she was somehow cradled beneath him. His body pressed firmly over hers, but he supported the majority of his weight on his forearms and knees. He was heavy and warm, but he trembled with her, his chest heaving with the harsh breaths he made with each deep plunge his body made into hers.

She was lost, swirling in a chasm of pain and desire and ecstasy. Her shudders deepened, and then her womb contracted hard, and she cried out and arched beneath him, completely at the mercy of her body's demands.

He groaned, and somewhere from deep within the chasm, she heard his words as his seed spilled into her body.

"Sarah. Sarah. It's you I love. *You*."

Simon entered Baron Stanley's London drawing room. Lord and Lady Stanley rose from their pink-upholstered chairs to greet him, along with Georgina. He greeted them all politely.

The room was papered in pink, and a pink carpet blanketed the floor. Even the fire glowed pink, a garish reflection of the surrounding color.

"And good afternoon to you, Your Grace," Lady Stanley gushed. "A very good afternoon, indeed."

For her, perhaps.

Ever since he'd told Sarah he'd need to end things last night, he'd felt rather as if he'd been skinned alive and was bleeding all over the place. This felt unreal, like some kind of nightmare he wished he could wake from. And he wished he'd wake in Sarah's bed. Then, he'd turn to her, pull her tight against him, take comfort from her sweet smell, her sweet body...

"Your Grace." Miss Stanley gave him a very proper curtsy.

He took her hand and squeezed it. "Miss Stanley. I'm so glad you are here."

He'd known she would be. He and Stanley had planned all this yesterday, when Stanley had called on him to hear his answer. Simon had neglected many of his duties in the past week to seek out Stanley's proof. First, he and Sam had ridden to Croydon to seek out Fiona Atwood. They'd found her in a small hovel. The place reeked of cheap gin. And although Stanley had named the high price it had taken the duchess to buy Theo and Mark and assure no one in London would ever set eyes on Fiona Atwood again, it seemed the woman had squandered it in spirits and gambling.

And still...beyond the smell of alcohol emanating from the overweight, wheezing woman as she told them her story, of how she didn't want to give up her "dear boys" but the duchess had left her with no choice, Simon saw undeniable hints of his brothers in her. The brown eyes and the hair—which on this woman now hung gray and limp, but Simon could see the hints of the light brown curls it had once held.

Sam had seen it too. In the end, both of them believed the woman was Theo's and Mark's mother.

The next day, Simon had retrieved a copy of the agreement Stanley had signed regarding Luke, and he'd taken it to Prentiss, his solicitor. After giving Simon his heartfelt wishes that none of it had ever happened, Prentiss had verified the veracity of the agreement.

Lukas Hawkins was the illegitimate son of Baron Stanley and the Duchess of Trent. The truth of it still sat like a sour pit in Simon's stomach.

Lady Stanley gestured to the table. "There is hot tea. And a peach marmalade, which is quite delightful. Georgina, dear, will you serve His Grace?"

"Of course, Mama," the young lady said demurely. She stood behind the tea service—a replica of the tea service at Ironwood Park, the one Sarah had served him from.

Simon's feet were rooted to the floor as images of Sarah, her smooth white body, her long limbs, her head thrown back in ecstasy, her hands roaming over his skin, whipped through him. Her bright smile, and those lovely blue eyes that had burrowed so deeply under his skin... The fresh, sunlit taste of her. The sweet smell of her...

"Do sit down, Your Grace."

Stanley offered him a raised brow. "I'd perhaps offer you something a bit stronger, Trent. A nip of sherry, perhaps? I'd choose brandy, myself, but I know how much you despise spirits obtained in the manner in which I have obtained mine."

Simon didn't answer.

"Nonsense." Lady Stanley gave Stanley a dark look. "Why, look, Georgina is already pouring the tea."

Miss Stanley remained focused on her task. Stanley cast his wife a look that was less than affectionate. This was all a touch surprising, but then again, while Simon had attended functions of theirs before, such as the dinner last month, he realized he'd never seen them actually communicate prior to this moment.

And should he be surprised? Stanley had admitted to Simon that he'd shared a mistress with Simon's father. And Fiona Atwood probably wasn't the only one. Simon's stomach soured even more, and he wondered if he'd be able to manage even the tea.

"Tea will be fine, thank you," he said brusquely, meeting Stanley's blue hawk's eyes. *Luke's eyes.*

Stanley gave a short nod. "Well, then, Charlotte. I've some correspondence to attend to, and I believe you have a scheduled meeting with the housekeeper. Shall we leave the two young people alone?"

Simon fought not to cringe. The situation was so fabricated, it was almost laughable. He cut a glance at Miss Stanley. She was looking at her parents wide-eyed, the expression on her face bordering on panic. Not for the first time, Simon wondered how much she knew about her father's plan.

Lord and Lady Stanley bustled out, leaving him and Miss Stanley in utter silence. Finally, she handed him his tea, looking up at him with eyes that reminded Simon of her father... and of Luke. But at least they were not so jaded—they held a far greater degree of purity of expression.

"Thank you," he said, and took a sip of tea.

"Honestly, I don't know what's got into them." She gestured toward the door. "They certainly aren't prone to disappearing like that when a guest arrives."

Simon wondered whether he should trust her act of

innocence. Then he decided he should. Distrusting his future wife from the beginning did not bode well for a happy marriage.

Happy marriage. What a joke, he thought bitterly.

"They know why I have come to your home today," he told her in a low voice. "I believe that's why they made such a hasty departure."

"Oh? But why have you come here today, Your Grace?"

Hell. He didn't want to do this.

He took another sip of tea to hide his hesitation, and then he looked up at her, setting the teacup and saucer aside. He was no coward. He wouldn't be one today.

"Miss Stanley, you have honored me with the pleasure of your company at many events this Season."

She clasped her hands in her lap. "I do enjoy your company immensely, Your Grace. Every moment of it."

"I am glad."

He gazed at her. She wore a light blue silk that brought out the color of her eyes. A white sash was tied high on her waist, and a white vine was embroidered in a twisting fashion around the skirt. Surprisingly, she wore no gloves or jewelry, but the lack of both made her look younger—perhaps that had been a deliberate choice to make her appearance more appealing to him.

Her hair was swept up to show multiple hues of blond, and tendrils curled around her face. Her lips were quite pink and bowed, and she seemed to have a permanent flush on her cheeks as well as a dark rim around her eyes that brought out their size and shape. Her lashes and brows were several shades darker than her hair. Her skin was porcelain-pale except for the blush that spread over her cheekbones.

She looked like a blushing bride. Exactly how a young duchess should look. No one would deny she was lovely.

She did absolutely nothing for him.

"You would make a fine Duchess of Trent," he said in a low voice, not breaking his gaze from hers. It was the truth. Her reputation was spotless. She was a much sought-after young lady, talented in drawing and music, trained to run a household, and came from a family with money and connections.

A fine Duchess of Trent.

She stiffened. Her pink lips parted, but she didn't speak.

It was completely up to him, then.

"Your father has given his permission," he said quietly. "And now I ask for yours. Miss Georgina Stanley, will you be my wife?"

For a long moment, she didn't move. Then the slender column of her throat moved as she swallowed. She pressed her lips together, then nodded. "Yes, Your Grace." Her voice was modulated low and wasn't quite even. In that moment, Simon truly believed she hadn't been part of the plan that had set this proposal in motion.

He forced himself to smile, because any woman who'd just accepted a proposal of marriage deserved at least a smile. He stood, went to her, then reached out for her hand, helping her up. She wasn't as tall as Sarah, nor as hardy. He looked down at her, this delicate porcelain doll, and tightened his fingers over hers.

She gazed up at him, blinking her blue eyes. Brighter eyes than Sarah's, but they seemed glassy and transparent in comparison.

He had spent several nights this week staring into

Sarah's eyes, falling into the complex facets of her soul.

God help him. He'd just proposed to another woman. He shouldn't be thinking of Sarah now. But still, her image swam in his mind, transposing itself over Georgina Stanley's face.

Trying to shake it off, he raised her hand, turned it over, and pressed a kiss to her bare palm.

"Miss Stanley. You have made me the happiest of men," he lied.

"Georgina," she whispered. "You must call me Georgina, now that we are engaged to be married, Your Grace."

She gazed up at him, pink-cheeked and shiny-eyed, and he knew what was expected of him.

"Georgina," he confirmed. "And you must call me...Trent."

Not Simon. No one but Sarah called him Simon. She was the only one with that right.

He shook himself. No, not even Sarah would call him Simon anymore. He'd taken that from her last night.

"Very well...Trent."

She looked up at him, tilting her head. Oh, God. She was angling for a kiss.

He stepped back, still keeping hold of her hand. He couldn't kiss her. Not now. Not yet.

He twisted his lips into a smile. "Well, then. Shall we find your parents and tell them the happy news?"

Dismay flickered over her features before they smoothed out again. He tried to give her hand a reassuring squeeze.

"Oh, yes," she said brightly, "let's!"

They left the overwhelming pink of the drawing room

to search for Lord and Lady Stanley. Simon straightened his spine and faced his fate head-on, but a part of him felt like this was a death sentence.

Another part of him had already died.

Sarah had pulled herself together. She had taken some time—more than she'd anticipated she'd need—to allow herself to fall apart. She'd claimed a headache that morning and risen very late, and as they'd sat in the dining room and shared a meal that would more accurately be called a luncheon, she'd begged Esme to cancel their planned social calls for that afternoon. Esme had agreed to do so, but concern was etched into her brow.

"What is it?" she'd asked Sarah. And then her frown had deepened. "Is it that coachman? Robert Johnston? Has he taken liberties—?"

"Oh, goodness, Esme, no," she'd murmured, stabbing at a kipper with her fork. "Robert Johnston? Why in heaven's name would you think that?"

"He fancies you." Esme's hazel eyes glinted over her chocolate.

Sarah shook her head. Since she'd arrived in London, she'd scarcely spoken to him except out of politeness whenever he drove her and Esme somewhere. "I don't think so."

"Oh, he does." Esme seemed more confident in this than she had in anything all summer. "Did you see how he looked at you when he helped you into the carriage after we visited Mrs. Templeton yesterday?"

Sarah rubbed her temple. She really did have a headache, as well as a heartache. "No, I didn't," she said quietly. "How was he looking at me?"

"Goodness, Sarah! You are completely blind. He is utterly besotted."

"Not at all." Sarah glanced up at the two impassive footmen flanking the door. Neither man met her eye, but she knew both were friends of Robert's. The servants of the Duke of Trent always behaved at the height of discretion, but this was gossip directly pertaining to one of them. He'd hear some rendition of this conversation.

"*Humph.*" Esme leaned forward conspiratorially, a devilish grin on her face. "You know, Sarah, your behavior has been quite odd lately. I'm starting to think there must be something between you and Mr. Johnston." She took a meaningful bite of toast, chewed, swallowed, took a sip of chocolate, and grinned again. "Say what you will, Sarah, but I do believe you're in love."

"My lady!" Sarah widened her eyes in the direction of the footmen, a clear warning, but Esme just laughed, unapologetic.

"You are both charming. And if it takes a little nudge from me for something to finally happen, then so be it."

Sarah had simply stared at the younger woman. Esme would never, ever know how right she was...and how wrong. She assumed Robert—a man to whom Sarah had hardly spoken—was responsible. It would never cross her mind that the man who'd caused the change in Sarah was actually her brother.

Esme would never believe that Simon cared for her, because dukes simply didn't care for their gardener's daughters. But coachmen did. A gardener's daughter and a coachman—that was something Esme could understand.

She gave Esme a weak smile. *Thank you, Esme, for reminding me of my place.*

After breakfast, they went into the drawing room, where Esme began to scribble in her notebook. Sarah tried to read, but every word seemed to be surrounded by a halo, and she closed her eyes and put the book away. She picked up the basket of stockings she'd been knitting for the residents of the school for the blind and got to work on those. Her eyes blurred, and she made mistakes, something she rarely did when knitting, but she stared at the stockings and diligently pressed on.

"Sarah?"

"Hm?"

"I'm...doing better, am I not?"

Sarah frowned up at Esme, who held her notebook clasped against her chest. "Better?"

"I mean, better than last year. I'm improving. With people."

Sarah's expression softened. "Yes, my lady. You improve with every day that has passed since we arrived in London."

Esme's sigh was replete with relief. After a pause, she said, "I'm trying so hard."

"I know."

"It's just...Without Mama, I feel that it is my duty to take her place. And you knew Mama. She was so effusive. With everyone. No one in the world intimidated her."

Sarah wondered when they'd all started speaking of the duchess in the past tense.

"Very true. And truly, my lady, you've done so very well. Not only socially, but in taking over all your mother's charitable endeavors as well. She would be so proud of you."

"Do you think so?"

"I know so. And I know your brother is proud as well."

Esme's expression brightened. "Is he?"

"Yes," Sarah said firmly. She and Simon had discussed Esme's progress at length and had agreed that she was making great strides.

Esme waved her hand. "Oh, you wouldn't know that. When do you ever talk to Trent? He's never even home, and when we do see him at social events, he hardly speaks to us."

Sarah looked down at the sock she was knitting and shrugged. "I can see his pride in you every time he looks at you," she murmured.

There was a knock on the door and Tremaine entered. "My lady, Lady Stanley and Miss Stanley are asking if you are at home for visitors today."

Sarah froze. Everything in her went still as death, except her heart, which surged in her chest, beating so hard it was a wonder Tremaine didn't hear it from across the room.

"Of course." Esme was evidently feeling confident from the conversation she and Sarah had just had. "Please show them in."

Tremaine bowed, and when the door closed, Esme gasped and turned to Sarah, wide-eyed. "Oh, Sarah. I'm so sorry. I forgot about your headache."

Sarah stared at her knitting needles. "Don't worry." She tried to make her voice light. She failed.

Georgina Stanley was going to be the Duchess of Trent, the lady of Ironwood Park. Sarah needed to become accustomed to her. Still, she hadn't expected she'd have to face her so soon.

Sarah's weak words hadn't convinced Esme in the

least. She frowned. "Perhaps you should go upstairs and rest. I can manage the Stanleys on my own. I think."

That was an excellent idea.

"Yes, that might be best," Sarah managed weakly. She pushed the stocking, yarn, and knitting needles from her lap, not caring that she didn't put it all away properly in her basket, and rose unsteadily. But at that moment, the door opened, and Miss Stanley, apparently having sprinted all the way from the front door, burst inside.

She bounded toward Esme. When she reached her, she reeled to a halt, clasping her hands in front of her.

"Lady Esme," Miss Stanley said, breathless, "we're going to be sisters!"

Esme frowned up at her. "Sisters? Wha—"

Lady Stanley appeared at the door, huffing a little but beaming. "Georgina has just accepted a proposal from your brother!"

"The Duke of Trent!" Miss Stanley said, in the event that Esme had forgotten her brother's identity.

"Ah...oh!" Esme cast a look of wide-eyed surprise toward Sarah.

Sarah didn't respond in kind. She was too busy gathering the frayed edges of her composure and wrapping them tightly around her.

Slowly, Esme rose. Miss Stanley threw her arms around her. "Sisters!" she repeated. "I am so happy! We have been such good friends, and now, sisters!"

Esme cast Sarah another look, this one rather bewildered. Sarah didn't blame her. Esme had never thought of Miss Stanley as a friend, much less a good one.

"Er...well. Congratulations," Esme said awkwardly.

Lady Stanley came forward and took over embracing

Esme after Miss Stanley finally released her. "You may call me 'Mama,' dear," she told Esme.

Esme went stiff in the lady's arms. Even from several feet away, Sarah could see it.

But Georgina didn't. "And you must call me Georgina!"

Esme pulled away from the older woman. "Oh. Well. All right." She did not offer for either woman to call her Esme.

"How wonderful," Sarah told the ladies. She tried so hard to keep the stiffness out of her voice. "What lovely news." She gestured to the sofa. "Please do sit down. Shall I call for tea?"

"Thank you, Miss Osborne. Yes, tea would be splendid, just splendid," Lady Stanley said.

Woodenly, Sarah went about arranging for tea. When she returned to her seat, Lady Stanley was saying, "...agreed to an autumn wedding. The sooner the better, I say, and an autumn wedding in the Cotswolds is always a lovely thing."

"And the best part of it is that we will be residing at Ironwood Park until the wedding takes place," Miss Stanley said.

"Oh?" Esme asked.

Miss Stanley shrugged. "Yes. There is no reason to stay in London now that I am engaged to be married. Plus, the air here is so *rancid*, and Mama thinks that country air will help me to perfect my complexion prior to the wedding."

Sarah rather thought the young woman's complexion was already perfect. How could it possibly be improved?

"Why not go to your father's home?" Esme asked.

Miss Stanley wrinkled her nose. "We'd planned to stay in London until August, at least, because the walls at Hartledge are being stripped from top to bottom, repapered, and repainted."

"Ah," Esme said.

Lady Stanley waved her hand in front of her face. "Paint and wallpaper do ruin good country air. I have determined the house will not be fit for habitation until December, at least."

"So, Trent asked you to come to Ironwood Park instead?"

"Indeed he did. We will both be in residence through the summer," Lady Stanley said. "His Grace has agreed to be present as much as possible until Parliament adjourns, and then he'll join us there. Permanently!" Clasping her hands together, she leaned forward. "He told me that he shall send you home next week, to be with us and to help Georgina learn all the ins and outs of her new home. Isn't that wonderful?"

"Oh, Esme," Georgina said, dropping the "lady" without Esme's permission. "It'll be absolutely delightful— my own personal introduction to the environs before I take over the household."

Sarah did not like the sound of that.

Then again, ever since she'd moved to Ironwood Park, she'd known that this was inevitable. That one day, Simon would marry and the duchess, who'd treated her almost as one would treat her own child, would be displaced.

"Well. Of course," Esme said, clearly attempting to be polite but thrown too far out of kilter for it to sound completely real.

"Don't tell me you wish to remain in London?" Lady

Stanley said. "It is well known that you are quite...un-comfortable here." She leaned forward to pat Esme's knee. "We are so sorry about all the talk regarding your public awkwardness. I'm sure it'll be such a relief for you to get away from it all."

Esme blanched, and fury rose in Sarah like a flash flood. Clenching her fists in her lap, she schooled her expression to neutrality, but inwardly, dislike of Lady Stanley boiled within her.

Miss Stanley gave a vigorous nod. "You will certainly be more in your element at Ironwood Park."

"I daresay I will be," Esme said faintly. And Sarah knew that all the tenuous confidence Esme had built in the past few weeks had just been shattered.

The tea arrived, and the ladies drank and chatted effu-sively for another fifteen minutes before bustling out of the drawing room, saying that they had many more peo-ple to call upon to share their wonderful news, and many, many letters to write. They promised they'd come to see Esme again before their departure for the Cotswolds.

When they left, Esme and Sarah sat in silence for a few minutes. Esme seemed to be composing herself as Sarah wondered how Simon could possibly need to marry Miss Georgina Stanley to save his family. Her original thought that Luke had compromised her didn't seem at all feasi-ble.

Finally, Esme looked over at Sarah, and they locked gazes. Esme's lips twisted. "Well," she mused, "Miss Stanley wouldn't have been my choice for my brother. But I suppose it's not my choice to make."

Nor mine, Sarah thought.

"And she's very beautiful and accomplished. She's just

the kind of lady Mama expected him to marry." Esme shrugged. "Ah, well. Those ladies were right, I suppose, about me and London. I am happy we're leaving early, before I make a true faux pas like I did last year and embarrass my brother again." A sad smile tilted her lips, and her shoulders seemed to deflate, whether in relief or defeat, Sarah could not tell.

"We're going home, Sarah. And to be honest, I won't complain if I never have the opportunity to set foot in London again."

Chapter Fifteen

Parliament hadn't finished its business until somewhat later than usual that year, so it wasn't until the first week of August that Simon returned to Ironwood Park without any immediate plans to return to London.

He would remain in the country until November, which would be a month after his marriage, when the next session of Parliament would commence. He did not know if his wife would be returning to London with him; many ladies preferred to remain in the country for most of the year, and he wouldn't complain if that was her choice.

By all appearances, Georgina had been ecstatic to see him when he'd arrived at Ironwood Park. But Sarah, who'd always been one of the first to greet him whenever he arrived home, was nowhere to be found.

No doubt that was for the better. Still, her absence bothered him. Ironwood Park simply didn't feel like home without Sarah.

Sam had accompanied him to the country—he had been given a month's holiday after his latest assignment. After his trip to the Lake District, Mark had continued the search for their mother from Ironwood Park, so he was already home. Theo had been home for a few weeks, too, since the term at Cambridge had ended the first week of July.

The night Simon came home, he sat in the parlor after dinner, surrounded by his family and the Stanleys. It should have been pleasant but for the three marked absences. First of all, Luke was still gone. No one had heard from him since his disappearance the night they'd discovered Binnie, but Simon had tasked the investigator he'd engaged to search for his mother to keep an eye on Luke as well. The man had reported that Luke was in London, asking questions about their mother's whereabouts on the rare occasions he was sober, but spending more time than ever carousing.

Secondly, Simon's mother wasn't there. She'd been missing for nearly four months now, with no trace, and Simon was beginning to accept somewhere deep inside him that she was gone forever. He knew his siblings felt the same way, that acceptance coming over them slowly and with no small amount of grief but seemingly at the same pace as his own.

And, finally, there was Sarah. She'd never dined with them at Ironwood Park, but as Esme's companion, she'd taken all her meals with them in London, and he'd quickly grown accustomed to having her present during meals. Now, he felt her absence keenly.

Finally, when the port he was drinking began to loosen the muscles of his shoulders that had been strained by the hours on horseback, he turned to his sister, who was laughing at something Mark had said, and asked casually, "Where is Miss Osborne?"

Esme's laugh stopped abruptly. She slid a glance at Georgina, who was sitting on the plum-colored sofa beside him, and then returned her gaze to Simon. "She is with her father in their cottage, I expect."

"A quite *exceptional* girl." Lady Stanley sipped her tea. "Why, when Georgina and I discovered that Esme's companion was just a housemaid, we were quite impressed. A maid? Can you imagine? Such stature the girl possesses for one born so low."

Simon stared at her, not trying to hide the faint frown on his face.

"We thought it very wise of you, Trent, to raise her to the position of lady's companion, as Esme tells us in no uncertain terms that there was no other reasonable choice at the time. However, now that we are home, it is neither proper nor necessary. I told the young woman as much, and she understood the temporary nature of her rise in status and the necessity to reassume her prior position in this house."

So many reactions ran through Simon in response to this—surprise, annoyance, full-on anger—that he couldn't speak for a moment. He took some time to compose himself, forcing a swallow of the port that didn't want to go down.

"I see," he said tightly, aware of his siblings watching him, gauging his reaction. None of them knew the extent of his feelings for Sarah, but they all knew he had always been fond of her. As were they.

Lady Stanley had no authority in this house. How dare she meddle with his staff?

Soon enough, the staff would be entirely Georgina's responsibility. But not now. Not yet.

Bitterness rose within him, sharp and potent, but he would not contradict his future mother-in-law publicly. He wasn't one to make a spectacle, and he wasn't going to start tonight.

"Georgina and I are Esme's companions now, and she has need of no other," Lady Stanley finished with no small measure of smugness.

"Of course you don't," Georgina told Esme, her voice warm, yet there was a condescending edge to it. Simon turned to look at her, but there was nothing but affection in her expression as she beamed at Esme. Perhaps he had been mistaken, was inventing behaviors that didn't exist because his intuition told him to like or trust neither Lady Stanley, nor—unfortunately—his future wife, though Georgina hadn't done anything improper. Unlike her mother.

"I suppose I do not," Esme said quietly, not quite meeting Georgina's eyes. Instead she looked at him and gave him a small smile. Was he inventing things again? Because, to him, that smile was a sad one. A regretful one. One that told him she'd rather have Sarah as her companion than the Stanley women.

"Did you know we all grew up with Miss Osborne?" Mark asked Georgina and her mother.

"Oh, yes. Esme told us," Georgina said.

"Just another example of your mother's eccentricity." Lady Stanley laughed, a high-pitched noise that Simon had never noticed before but now grated on his nerves. "The gardener's daughter raised and educated in the nursery of one of the greatest houses in England alongside the offspring of a duke. Imagine that!"

Mark shook his head. "Oh, but you are quite mistaken, my lady."

"Oh?"

"Indeed, none of us ever went into the nursery. It's a dark and dusty place. Our mother chose to keep us with her most of the time."

"Really?"

"It is quite true," Theo added. "Wherever the Duchess of Trent was on any given day, that was where we would be. And our mother despised the nursery."

Mark grinned at Simon. "Remember the time we all popped out of her skirts, scaring Mr. Beardsley and his wife half to death?"

Standing at the corner of the room—Simon wondered if his brother ever sat down except when forced—Sam nodded. "I do. They'd come in here thinking they were calling on the duchess and that she was alone—"

"And then...pop, pop, pop, pop, pop! The five of us all jumped out of her skirts like jack-in-the-boxes," Theo said.

Sam frowned at his youngest brother. "How can you remember that? You couldn't have been more than three."

Theo's grin didn't fade. "One tends to remember such moments in one's life. We were all laughing so hard while Mr. and Mrs. Beardsley looked so aghast..."

"Mama laughed so hard tears ran down her face," Mark said.

Simon glanced up to see Sam looking at him, a small smile curling his lips. As the two oldest siblings, they probably remembered that day the best, and the many other similar days they'd spent with their mother, flustering, surprising, or simply shocking others. But even though Sam's memories shone in his face, Simon found it difficult to remain engaged in this conversation.

Sarah was a housemaid again. There would be no more fashionable silks and London ballrooms for her.

That discomfited him. No, it more than discomfited him. It *infuriated* him.

He was glad Mark had changed the direction of the conversation. If he hadn't, Simon might've reinstated Sarah to her position at Esme's side.

He should do that in any case, because it was deuced presumptuous for Lady Stanley to think she could control his household. And it was unacceptable for her to think she could control Sarah.

Lady Stanley was smiling and laughing with the brothers. "Oh, how I wish your dear mama were here now to laugh with all of us. That business of her disappearance, it's a shame, I say. An utter shame."

They all sobered at that. Eventually, Mark raised his glass. "That it is, my lady," he said solemnly.

Everyone was silent for a long moment. Then, Georgina turned to Simon and said in a very bright tone, "Well, I loved my nursery. I shall endeavor to make the nursery at Ironwood Park a welcome place for my children. My happiest days as a little girl were spent in my nursery, and I believe that children are safest, happiest, and most at home in the one place they may call their own."

Her words stabbed a reality that he'd been avoiding straight into his chest. She would be the mother of his children. Someday, his and Georgina Stanley's children would be scampering around Ironwood Park.

Or perhaps they wouldn't be scampering about. Perhaps they'd be imprisoned in that attic room that his mother had told him was a haunted, nasty place. Mother used to say that if they slept in the nursery they would hear the children who'd once died there crying for their mothers. It was why she'd allowed them to sleep in her room with her until they were all old enough to keep their own bedrooms.

It didn't matter. Their mother *had* been eccentric, and she'd liked to tell them outlandish stories as they'd crowded around her at night. The nursery wasn't haunted. It was a very suitable room, and if Georgina remodeled it, it would be a perfectly acceptable place to keep children. *Their* children.

He finished his port, managed to say something proper, and then allowed the conversation to flow around him, all the while feeling heavier and heavier, like he was swimming like mad to stay afloat but had giant boulders tied to his ankles.

He'd never shirked his responsibility before. He'd stay afloat, no matter the cost.

"I want to reinstate you to the position of Esme's companion."

Sarah stood in the door of her father's cottage. She turned back to glance into the dusky interior. "I'll be just a moment, Papa."

Her father, who'd been eating his breakfast, gave a gruff, "all right, then," and Sarah stepped out, closing the planked door behind her to stand on the small stoop.

Simon looked resplendent in his riding clothes, tall Wellingtons that had been polished to a high shine, buff breeches, and a dark wool coat that hugged his body, showing off his broad shoulders and trim waist. Behind him, the early morning sun sparkled on the water drops from last night's showers, making the hedges and trees glimmer in various bright shades of green. She straightened her spine and looked him in the eye. "Good morning, Your Grace. Welcome home."

"You were not there to welcome me like you usually are." There was a hint of accusation in his voice.

"I am sorry. I was engaged in a task for Lady Stanley." The lady had decided the Stone Room was her favorite place at Ironwood Park. She had taken to spending an hour there every afternoon to bask in its cold grandeur. When sitting on one of the marble benches yesterday, she'd found some smudges on the statue of the Laocoön and had tasked Sarah with scrubbing it until the marble was a perfect uniform hue.

Marble was never perfect, nor was it uniform, but Sarah had done the best she could, cleaning the crevices of the carved bodies of Laocoön, his sons, and the serpent until every muscle in her body ached.

Simon blew out a breath. Beside him, his horse tossed its head and whickered, and he pulled gently on the reins he gripped in his dark-gloved hand, bringing the animal to heel.

"Sarah..."

She looked down at herself, clasping her hands in front of her. She was wearing one of the old muslins she'd brought to London but had never worn there after the modiste had delivered her new dresses. Today would probably be another day of heavy cleaning, and even if it wasn't, she wasn't sure she could ever wear those London clothes again. Nor would she ever have reason to.

Simon removed his hat and brought it to his side. "I want you to be Esme's companion."

"Is that what Lady Esme wishes?" she asked quietly.

"I am sure it is."

It was what Sarah wanted, too. But it was too late. She was no fool. Being Esme's companion would put her in the constant company of Lady Stanley and Miss Stanley. Lady Stanley would hate that Sarah had returned to a station so clearly above her and resent Sarah for going above her to reclaim the position. And Sarah could hardly be in the same room with Miss Stanley without feeling nauseous.

Furthermore, as Esme's companion she would be more frequently in the company of Simon. She wasn't sure if she could bear being with Simon any more than absolutely necessary, but being with him and Miss Stanley, seeing them together—

Well, she had always prided herself on her personal strength and resilience. But perhaps she was not that strong, after all.

So she looked at Simon, remembering the look in his eyes when he'd gazed at her after they'd made love. Remembering his lips, so soft as they'd caressed her body. And she shook her head.

"No." The word was soft but firm. Final.

He blinked at her, his long lashes fluttering in surprise. She was surprised, too. It was the first time she'd refused him anything.

She shook her head. "I cannot. It wouldn't be proper."

A muscle worked in his jaw, but he kept his voice at a low pitch. "What isn't proper," he ground out, "is you standing here. Wearing those clothes. Behaving like a *maid*."

"I *am* a maid. Your Grace."

He looked away from her, down at his hand clutching the reins, his shoulders taut underneath the fine fabric of his coat.

She had no idea what he was thinking. She wished he'd tell her. Even before they'd come together, he'd always been easy in sharing his thoughts with her.

But she had no right to know his true thoughts. She never had, really. She'd always known that his friendship was a gift that could be snatched away from her someday. Men in his position weren't meant to befriend women in hers.

He raised his head. "Perhaps," he said in a near-whisper, his gaze meeting hers, "that is for the best."

Oh, it was. That was certain. But she only gave a tiny nod in response.

"Sarah?" Her father was calling her from inside, and she glanced back.

"I must go, Your Grace."

"Yes, of course. I'll see you later."

"Ah...yes." Maybe. Hopefully not. Even now, it felt like blood was tumbling around in her body, a windswept sea in a violent storm, with no veins or heart to contain it.

"Good day, then, Sarah."

She managed a curtsy. "Good day, Your Grace."

And then she turned her back on him and went inside. But as she started another pot of tea for her father, she nudged the curtain aside and watched him turn down a winding path that led into the forest. Inside, she wept, her broken heart raw and pulsating, a reopened wound, but outside she pasted on a cheerful smile and chatted with her father about his proposal to plant a hedge of hawthorns near the stream.

* * *

Two days later, Simon asked Georgina to walk with him at dusk.

He'd seen Sarah a few times by then. Even though she'd refused his offer to reinstate her position as Esme's companion, she'd been performing her duties with her trademark cheerfulness, clearly managing their separation far better than he was. Seeing her calmed him, though. Gave him the determination to proceed with his duty.

It was a fine twilight, with enough fluffy clouds for the sun to cast dramatic streaks of pink and purple across the sky as it descended for the night. He led Georgina toward the bank of the stream, pointing out features in the gardens and outside grounds that had been designed by the famous gardener Capability Brown in his grandfather's day and improved upon by Mr. Osborne.

"Mr. Brown wished to eliminate the garden completely," Simon told her as they walked along a row of buttercup yellow roses, "but my grandmother would have none of that. She loved her roses and spring blooms far too much. So they came to a compromise."

"A very lovely compromise, indeed," Georgina replied. He opened the garden gate for her, and they stepped out onto the path that led to the far reaches of Ironwood Park. This was where the land abandoned the geometric structure of his grandmother's English garden and the landscape began to take on more of the sweeping grass-and-tree characteristics in the style of Capability Brown.

They walked down the curving path that led in the direction of the forest in the far distance. "Brown loved to use water, and in Ironwood Park, he had a natural source," Simon said as the path turned at the bank of the stream and the blackberry hedge opened to allow them a good view. For a moment, they stood there, looking down into the clear water bubbling over smooth stones below.

"I imagine Mr. Brown found everything about Ironwood Park to be idyllic."

He turned to her. "Do you find it idyllic here?" he asked her seriously. Ironwood Park, after all, was to be her home for the remainder of her days.

"I do. It is. It is a grand home befitting the Duke of Trent."

"Some find it…cold, at times." His mother had incessantly complained of its sterile coldness, though she'd done her best to put her mark on it in the few places she felt she could. Many rooms she'd never touched, and Simon knew it was out of respect for what Ironwood Park was—a testament to the greatness and power of England and its aristocracy. The Stone Room, with its disconcerting statue of the Laocoön, was one example of a room she'd left alone.

"Oh, I do not find it cold at all," Georgina reassured him. "Most of the spaces are so very elegant, and must remain so. A duke's seat must clearly display his wealth and position. Some of the rooms need to be modernized and formalized, but there is plenty of time for that, and it is a task I shall happily take on, because I know how busy you are."

Simon turned away from the stream to look back at the house looming on the low-sloping hill in the distance. It was lofty, even forbidding with its gothic cornices and domes. But he had been born here. It was his home, and it would be his family home for generations to come. If nothing else, those truths alone made him love Ironwood Park.

He turned back to his wife-to-be, and she gave him a demure smile. He held out his arm, and she slipped her little hand over his coat as they began to walk again, taking the path as it curved to follow the natural bank of the stream.

They walked for several minutes, until they'd gone downhill a ways. He steered well clear of the bench where he'd spent so many hours talking to Sarah. He had no desire to relive his memories of his conversations with Sarah with another woman on his arm. That would be unfair to them both.

Just past his and Sarah's bench, the stream turned sharply, and the house was no longer visible behind them. There, he paused once again on the bank of the stream.

He turned to Georgina, and she tilted her face up to blink at him, her cornflower blue eyes innocent and lovely.

Slowly, he stroked his hands down the outsides of her arms and grasped her gloved hands in his own. "You are very beautiful, Georgina," he said, knowing that his attention toward her had been scattered and even somewhat deceptive, and while he'd done his best not to be unkind, he feared she had sensed his ambivalence toward her.

"Thank you," she breathed, a slight smile forming on her lips in response to the compliment.

And he bent down and kissed her.

His body tried to recoil, but he held himself stiff, focusing on the movements of his lips against hers.

She surprised him, though. He'd thought her an innocent in all ways. He'd expected her to freeze, like gentle young ladies were supposed to.

Instead, with a little gasp, she wrapped her arms around him, and within a fraction of a moment, her lips thawed, became pliant and warm and supple beneath his.

Oh, God.

He didn't want this. Didn't want *her*.

A violent tremor began somewhere deep inside him, a rebellious, sour thing that told him in no uncertain terms he was betraying everything he'd ever cared for.

But that was wrong. He wasn't betraying anything; no, he was *protecting* what he cared for.

Except Sarah. He wasn't protecting her. And he *did* care for her, damn it.

A twig cracked loudly behind Georgina, causing both of them to jump back. Simon's stomach roiled, and a cold sweat broke out on his forehead.

Over her shoulder, he saw swift movement near the direction of his and Sarah's bench.

She ran away, darting deeper into the forest. But not before he identified her. It was the color of her hair, shining like dark polished ebony in the twilight. It was her carriage, upright and nimble as she hurried over the obstacles in the path.

Sarah had just heard him tell Georgina she was beautiful. She'd just seen him kiss her. Everything in him cried out for him to go after her, to hold her in his arms and tell her everything he did and said to Georgina was false.

"What was that?" Georgina asked, breathless. He realized she still had her arms wrapped around him.

He looked down at her. She was flushed, her lips shining from his kiss, and he shrugged even as guilt and regret boiled in his gut.

"A deer. Must have been grazing nearby, then saw us and ran away. I don't see it now." He reached down, gently disengaging her hands from his sides, and tucked her hand into the crook of his arm. "Come. Let's return to the house."

Chapter Sixteen

Sarah waited in Miss Stanley's dressing room for the lady to appear. Evidently, Miss Stanley's lady's maid often suffered from headaches and had taken to her bed with a particularly violent one tonight, so Sarah had been ordered here to help her dress for dinner.

She wasn't looking forward to the task. She'd done her best to keep her distance from the Stanleys since Lady Stanley had removed her from her position as Esme's companion.

Last evening, she'd had some free time and had gone to her and Simon's bench to think. She wished she hadn't. The encounter between Simon and Miss Stanley had proved a few things to Sarah—the foremost of which was that watching Simon marry Georgina Stanley was going to be the most difficult thing she'd ever have to endure.

Minutes ticked by, and the lady didn't arrive. So Sarah busied herself with tidying—straightening the various undergarments and accessories that had been strewn about the dressing room when she'd entered. It seemed Miss Stanley had had a difficult time determining exactly what to wear this morning. She'd torn the room apart in a stormlike fashion before deciding on the lovely green striped muslin Sarah had seen her wearing this afternoon as Robert Johnston had helped Miss Stanley, Lady Stanley, and Esme into the carriage, presumably for a visit to the village.

She was tucked behind the door to the clothes press smoothing out one of the lady's dinner dresses when she heard the voices of the lady and her mother as they entered the adjacent bedchamber. The ladies were talking to each other in hushed, low tones, and Sarah paused, resting her hand on the yellow silk, her head tilted in curiosity. She'd never heard either of them speak in such serious voices.

As the door snicked shut and they stepped closer to the dressing room, Sarah began to be able to discern their words.

"Mama, it is far, *far* too dangerous."

"Your papa believes otherwise."

"Oh, he is utterly blind," Georgina said dismissively. "Do you realize how close Bordesley Green is? It's less than ten miles away! For heaven's sake, I could walk there."

Bordesley Green? What was that? Sarah racked her brain, knowing she'd heard the name somewhere before.

"It is quite a private place. Extremely discreet. And Bertram goes by a different surname. There is nothing to connect him to us. Nothing whatsoever."

Miss Stanley gave an unladylike snort. "Smith. Right. I remember."

"Now, Georgina," Lady Stanley said soothingly. "Nothing will be exposed. You know how important this is to your father, and to me as well. We have kept him hidden from the public eye for this long. After all this time, surely we are all safe."

"I'd just rather he was farther away." Miss Stanley's tone grew surly—a vocal feature Sarah had never heard from her. "In Abyssinia, perhaps."

"Alas," Lady Stanley replied, taking her daughter's suggestion seriously, "I doubt your father would send him so far, and I'm not sure they have such places for people like Bertram in Abyssinia. But I shall ask."

"Oh, *why* does Papa insist upon allowing him to remain so close to us? I shall be so *very* embarrassed if anyone ever finds him." Now she was whining. "I should simply *die*."

"We would all be gravely embarrassed if anyone connected him to us, I am sure," Lady Stanley said. "I will discuss this with your father, but I am certain he will dismiss our worries. Anyhow, you know your father. He likes Bertram close so he can keep a close eye on him. Now," she added brightly, "we must dress for dinner. Where is that wretched maid? I told her to come up to help you."

Sarah stood very still. She was well hidden behind the door of the clothes press, but if someone entered the dressing room...Quickly, she weighed her options and decided to stay put and pray they went away.

Sarah tilted her face to the ceiling, squeezing her eyes shut, and spoke in her head. *"Dear Lord..."*

Miss Stanley sighed. "I've no idea where she is. And I don't even know what to wear."

"Wear the yellow silk," Lady Stanley said distractedly. Then, she added, "Perhaps she is with Esme."

"Please encourage them to leave," Sarah beseeched.

Miss Stanley groaned. "She is always with Esme."

"They needn't go far," Sarah continued, and a little devil popped up from somewhere deep inside her and added, *"Although they might fare quite splendidly in Abyssinia."*

"Even now. I'd hoped to never see her again," Miss Stanley added, "as she has so obviously forgotten her place, but Esme is always keeping her close, asking her to do things."

Yes, that was true. Esme had taken to asking her to perform simple tasks, like ordering and pouring tea, or stoking the fire, to keep her close. It was a simple truth— Sarah had spent more time with Esme than anyone else, and it followed that Esme was easier when Sarah was nearby.

"She certainly does have poor Esme under her spell," Lady Stanley said, a clear note of censure in her voice.

"I can't understand it. I have tried so hard with Esme, even though she is perhaps the dullest lady I've ever met in my entire life. Have you seen her scribbling her stupid little stories?"

Sarah closed her eyes, picturing Miss Stanley's lovely little shudder. She pressed her lips together to hold back her defense of Esme's writing.

"These things take time," Lady Stanley said. "But I must give you one word of advice: You must never drop your guard with that lady, Georgina. I've the feeling she'll turn on you in an instant."

"What?" Miss Stanley seemed surprised.

"This Hawkins family—they aren't quite right. Well, allow me to amend that. The duke has done his best to restore some respectability to the family name. He is quite a proper and decent gentleman. But the rest of them—" She made a little noise of disapproval before continuing. "They all possess a hint of their parents' insanity, I think."

"Their papa was insane?" Miss Stanley asked. "I knew their mother was—what kind of mother would encourage a servant girl into the family, for heaven's sake? But their papa, too?"

"Yes," Lady Stanley said, her voice very serious. "When I was your age, I was ordered to stay well clear of that man. His horrid reputation and behavior was put forth as an example of debauchery and as a warning to all young ladies of character."

"But he was a duke!" Miss Stanley exclaimed, as if being a duke forgave all impropriety.

"That he was." Lady Stanley sighed. "I admit it is rare, Georgina, but there are times when even a man's title cannot restore his good name."

Miss Stanley seemed to mull this over. "And do you think Esme is mad, too?"

"It is quite possible."

Sarah sent a quick thought up to heaven. *"Abyssinia truly might be the best place for them, Lord."*

Lady Stanley continued, "She is young and inexperienced now, and perhaps it is true that the madness has not yet taken hold. We must use that to our advantage. We must do everything possible to insinuate ourselves into her good graces."

"Honestly, I do not see why," Georgina argued. "She

is only Trent's sister, and they don't appear particularly close. He doesn't listen to her."

"That is because she doesn't speak to him," Lady Stanley said. "She hardly speaks to anyone. But what if she did?"

Miss Stanley hesitated. "Well, in that case he might listen to her," she conceded.

"I think he might. So do endeavor to become her bosom bow, Georgina. At least until you are married. Then, you will be a duchess, and you may do whatever you wish."

"Yes, Mama. Oh, I cannot wait until October," she said wistfully.

"It'll come soon, I promise. Until then, we shall both be on our best behavior with these peculiar people."

"It is true that Trent does stand out as the most proper of all of them," Miss Stanley said.

"You're very lucky he is the one you will marry, Georgina. Very lucky, indeed."

"Yes." Miss Stanley gave a breathy sigh. "I am the luckiest girl in the world."

"So you see why we mustn't give Trent any reason whatsoever to change his mind."

"Oh, he won't change his mind. He would never jilt me! He is far too honorable."

Lady Stanley laughed softly as Sarah's stomach twisted. "Probably true. Still, there is no reason to antagonize him."

"I know. And in any case, I've no wish whatsoever to antagonize him. He's kind and generous."

There was a short silence. Then Lady Stanley spoke in a wistful voice. "Ah, my dear. I do envy you the match you have made. I am so very proud that you were able to catch the eye of a duke—although, indeed, I knew all along that you would succeed in doing so. When I was a girl, I always dreamed of making such a match for myself."

"And you made the match with Papa."

Miss Stanley said that like it was a positive thing, but Lady Stanley made a low, derisive noise. "Your Papa is not a duke."

"Too true." Miss Stanley laughed, and it was a sound that made Sarah's stomach twist. For it wasn't a happy laugh, it was a laugh of victory, as if Simon were a conquest she had been fighting with the whole of England for, and she had emerged the victor.

Sadly, there was much truth to that. Sarah had spent years sheltered in Ironwood Park, but she had observed the way ladies behaved toward Simon during the time she'd been in London. Those months had showed her in no uncertain terms that he was considered the premier catch of all the aristocratic bachelors in England.

"Now, let us go find Esme. If that girl is with her, I shall give her a proper set-down for disobeying me."

They left the room, closing the door behind them.

Sarah sagged against the clothes press for a minute, her eyes squeezed shut to thank the Lord for finally nudging them out.

And then she opened her eyes and studied the now-clean dressing room. After hearing that conversation, any residual hope that she'd ever like Miss Stanley or her mother had evaporated. They'd called Esme's stories stupid. They'd claimed that madness ran in the Hawkins family.

They were both simply awful.

She deliberately turned her thoughts to the beginning of their conversation. Bordesley Green...where had she heard of that place before? What was it? She'd have to ask Mrs. Hope.

And Bertram Smith, whose last name was counterfeit. Who was he, and why did Georgina wish he were in Abyssinia?

Perhaps it was someone who had compromised Georgina somehow, and the Stanleys had paid him off to disappear...and he'd gone to this Bordesley Green place, and Georgina thought it was too close, that Simon might discover she wasn't the innocent miss she pretended to be...

Goodness, her mind was running away from her. She had to speak to Mrs. Hope quickly before she invented an entire story, one that would end happily for all—with Georgina Stanley and Bertram Smith eloping to Abyssinia together.

She continued tidying up the dressing room, and when the door to Miss Stanley's room opened again, she hurried out of the small room, her hands full of clothing, and made her voice innocent and bright. "Oh, Miss Stanley. Good afternoon! I've been sent up to help you dress for dinner."

Miss Stanley frowned at her. "Where have you been?"

"Why, waiting for you. Your lady mother told me to come up to wait for you, and I did right away...well, as soon as I'd run a quick errand for Mrs. Hope. I was just tidying your dressing room as I waited." She held out the armful of pantalettes as evidence.

Miss Stanley puffed out a breath and strode past her

into the dressing room, yanking open the clothes press. "Mama said I should wear the yellow silk."

"Excellent choice, miss," Sarah said quietly. The yellow silk was the dress she'd set aside before the ladies had first entered the bedchamber.

Another puff of a sigh.

Standing in the center of the little room, Miss Stanley held her arms out straight from her sides. Taking this as a cue to begin undressing her, Sarah approached.

She removed Miss Stanley's clothes wordlessly, touching the younger woman as little as possible. First, her green striped muslin came off, followed by two petticoats, her stays, and last of all, her chemise. Sarah went to one of the drawers and pulled out a clean silk chemise, holding it up for the lady's approval.

"No, not that one."

"Which one would you prefer, miss?"

"There is only one other silk, of course. The one with the lace trim around the bottom."

Sarah searched the drawer while Miss Stanley watched her, but she could find no such chemise. Finally, she looked up, empty-handed. "Do you know when you last wore it, miss?"

"No, of course not. I never remember such things."

"Perhaps it is downstairs being laundered. Shall I check for you?"

"For heaven's sake, no! We are already late, you know, due to your silly task for the housekeeper." Miss Stanley heaved a disgusted sigh. "Very well. The other silk will have to do. Although Missy could have found it for me."

Missy was the lady's maid who'd taken to her bed this

afternoon. It was suddenly very clear to Sarah why Missy suffered from headaches.

She finished dressing Miss Stanley with two additional bursts of temper—the first when she tied the lady's short stays "too tightly," although Sarah had been tying stays her entire life and was sure she knew exactly to what level of tension to adjust the ties. But she said nothing and loosened them until Miss Stanley voiced her grudging acceptance. And then, the dress. There was a tiny smudge of something—dust, perhaps, on the sleeve.

"Oh, no," Miss Stanley cried. "My dress is ruined!"

Sarah tried brushing out the light smudge, and she'd thought she'd done a good job of it, but Miss Stanley outlined the shape of it with her fingers, her eyes welling with tears.

"What will Trent think if I come to dinner looking like a common ragamuffin?" she wailed, and Sarah was forced to call in a very busy Mrs. Hope for assistance.

But, finally, it was done. The "horrid defect" had been taken care of, and now it was time to do Miss Stanley's hair.

Sarah didn't want to touch those shining golden locks. She really, really didn't want to.

So, when Miss Stanley sat at the dressing table and looked expectantly up at Sarah in the mirror, Sarah hesitated. Then she said in a low voice, "Miss, I must admit, arranging coiffures is not my forte."

Miss Stanley's blue eyes narrowed as she shook her head.

"Of *course*. I am not surprised. What *is* your forte, may I ask? What did you learn in the nursery—sorry, not in the nursery, but wherever it was the family governess taught you as you scampered about inside the duchess's skirts? French? Drawing? Playing on the pianoforte? Of what use are those skills to a housemaid?"

Sarah wasn't sure how to answer. True, she had been taught French—which she was good at, and drawing—which she could do with passable skill if she never used a person as a subject. Miss Farnshaw had given up on teaching her music as soon as Sarah had opened her mouth to belt out a note and the governess had deemed her tone deaf. But Mrs. Hope had taught her many skills as well, and Sarah prided herself on her housekeeping abilities.

So she didn't answer Miss Stanley, just bowed her head.

And then, although Sarah thought her heart couldn't be shattered any further, Georgina Stanley pushed the dagger deeper and then drove it home.

"A maid incapable of arranging hair," she spat. "Really, it is beyond bearing. When I am the duchess, I shall not tolerate such ridiculousness from my staff." Miss Stanley turned around fully in her chair, and a sticky sweetness overtook the venom in her voice. "That is in two months' time, Sarah Osborne. I do hope you are already looking for another position, because in two months, you shall be leaving Ironwood Park forever."

Sarah lay in bed, staring up at the ceiling. Sleep was elusive—had been elusive since that last night she'd spent with Simon in London.

Her future was so uncertain. So...bleak.

She was a cheerful, happy person—had been her entire

life. She always saw the positives in a given situation or a person.

Now she stood on the verge of losing everything that was dear to her. Simon and the Hawkins family as a whole. Ironwood Park and everyone who lived here...including her father.

For the past sixteen years, those things had composed her entire sphere of existence. And now Georgina Stanley threatened to take them all away.

The ceiling was dark, its details obscured by the black velvet of night, but she continued to stare up at it, unmoving.

There was no way to escape this mire, she realized now. No way to prevent the loss. The only thing that she could do was face it with her head held high.

She would do that, if nothing else.

She *would*.

She should have known this was coming. She had been stupid to think that she'd remain at Ironwood Park forever. Impossible, given her feelings for Simon. In fact, it was best she left. She could find a good position elsewhere. Any member of the Hawkins family would provide her with a good reference, as would Mrs. Hope.

Unlike some girls who found themselves in similar situations, she had the luxury of options. She could probably find a position anywhere in the United Kingdom. Perhaps even for a British family in the West Indies or India.

She closed her eyes to the daydream of sailing away from England on some elegant ship.

Something at her window rattled, and Sarah froze.

It rattled again, and she took a deep breath. There was

nothing to be afraid of. For goodness' sake, she had freely traipsed about Ironwood Park at night for most of her life.

She slipped out of bed and went to the window. She reached out to part the curtains, and jumped back, gasping, as she saw the dark form hovering outside. She blinked hard, and the figure came into clearer focus.

Simon, his face pale in the moonlight.

She stared at him in shock for a moment. It was unlike Simon to skulk about late at night. Before, whenever he'd wanted to speak to her, he'd simply knock on her door or approach her during the day. Or meet her at their bench.

She hastened to open the window. "Your Grace, what is it?" she asked in concern, and then she remembered the night they'd found his brother at the back door in London. "Is something wrong? Is it Lord Lukas? Your mother?"

The expression on his face, which had been taut with tension, softened. "Nothing's the matter," he said, then he flinched. "Well, nothing of that nature, anyhow. I just need to speak with you."

She took a small step backward, feeling the frown deepen between her brows.

"Please," he said quietly. "It is nothing untoward."

"Of course. Will you give me a moment to dress? I'll meet you at the front door."

"Yes. Thank you." He stepped back from the window.

She pulled on her cloak hurriedly, trying not to confuse her mind with what he could possibly want from her. He waited by the door as she exited. She closed the door behind her as she stepped out into the cool evening air. "What is it, Your Grace?"

He held out his arm. "Let's walk."

She looked pointedly at his arm, then up at his face. She didn't want to torture herself by touching him.

He dropped his arm, regret flashing over his features. "Right."

He began to walk. She stayed at his side as he led her toward the stream, not stopping or speaking until they reached their bench. He stopped there, at the edge of the bank, but didn't sit. "I looked for you here earlier," he said. "But you weren't here. I realized how odd it was that every time I used to feel the need to speak with you, I'd find you here."

"Sometimes I knew when you'd come," she murmured. She'd seen it in his expression as they'd passed each other in the corridor or when she'd served him tea.

"But you didn't know I'd come tonight," he said.

She shook her head. "I decided that perhaps it would be best if I never came here again."

He crossed his arms over his chest. Turning away from her, he looked out over the water. "We're always thinking of what would be best," he said quietly. "But what if we're wrong? What if I'm not making the right choices? What if I'm seeing this through a lens that is giving me a warped perspective?"

"What do you mean?"

"I don't know." He dropped his hands to his sides and turned to her. "I brought you out here tonight to apologize."

She stared at him, waiting.

"Last evening. You shouldn't have seen that."

She tore her gaze from him. "It is a sight I should force myself to become accustomed to."

Even now, the memory of him calling Georgina Stanley beautiful, of their passionate kiss, threatened to tear her apart. She'd spent the day trying to scrub the sight from her memory. She'd failed, of course. Now, nausea swirled in her gut, and she stared straight ahead, trying to swallow the sensation down.

"I'm sorry, Sarah."

She didn't answer.

"I have to do this," he said. "I must marry her." But he sounded wretchedly unhappy about it.

"Why?" she whispered. "You never told me why."

"I'm not sure you knowing will help things."

"Maybe it would help me to understand. I think you owe me that much, at least." She looked up at him, her eyes stinging. "You don't love her, do you?"

Her heart throbbed, raw and painful in her chest as she awaited his answer.

"No." The word was solid, a rock, something for her to grasp onto.

"Then why?"

"Come. Let's sit down."

They sat, side by side, as they had so many nights before this one.

And he told her about how Lord Stanley had come to him. About how the baron had claimed paternity of Luke. About how Theo and Mark were the sons of a London courtesan who'd been mistress to both the duke and Lord Stanley. About how Simon had sought out verification of these accusations, and it had all proven true. About Stanley's theory that Esme, too, was illegitimate.

Every word Simon said was like a spoonful of her soul being dug from her, until he finished speaking and all that remained of her was an empty shell.

"If I do not marry Miss Stanley," he told her finally, "my family will be ruined. My brothers' and sister's futures will be ripped away from them."

He'd trusted her with this devastating information. That fact did not escape Sarah. The fact that the Stanleys were a devious, cruel, and manipulative lot didn't escape her, either.

They sat in silence for seconds that formed into long minutes, the only sound the whisper of the nearby stream.

Finally, she looked up at him. "Can you be happy with Miss Stanley, Your Grace?"

"Not as happy as I am with you." His answer was automatic. But then he seemed to shake himself. "Perhaps one day, I'll learn to...love her." He grimaced as he said "love," as if the word tasted bitter to him.

"Learn to be happy with her?"

"Perhaps." But he sounded doubtful. He heaved out a sigh. "She seems a decent enough young lady. I've no evidence that she knows anything of her father's despicable plot."

From what she knew of Miss Stanley, Sarah wasn't so sure. But how could she tell Simon that? She had no proof. Indeed, she had nothing but petulance and peevishness.

She should tell Simon she hoped he'd find happiness and love with Miss Stanley. After all, his happiness was more important to her than anything else in the world. But she was selfish, too. She couldn't bring herself to wish them happiness together. She just couldn't.

"Do you understand now, Sarah?"

"I do." She did understand. Simon was too good a man to allow his family to fall into ruin around him. She tried to smile up at him. "I'd invented a story or two as to why you'd chosen this path. I was wrong." She shook her head. "The truth of it is more fantastical than my imaginings. Poor Lady Esme. Your poor brothers, Lord Luke most of all."

He sighed deeply. "I still can hardly believe it. If I hadn't seen the proof firsthand..." He gazed at her, some of the softness she'd seen in bed with him returning into his green eyes. "What had you guessed?"

"That perhaps you'd made a terrible investment and had suddenly found yourself insolvent and you faced ruin if you didn't marry a lady with a sizeable dowry immediately."

"Me? A terrible investment?"

"I was desperate for answers, as you can see very well." A smile twitched at her lips. "I thought also that Lord Luke had perhaps debauched Miss Stanley, and her father caught them *in flagrante delicto* and was demanding his blood, but you offered your bachelorhood up as payment instead."

"Well, that one is closer to the truth of it, at least," Simon said.

"Still a rather great distance from it, though."

They sat in quiet, companionable silence for another few moments before Simon said in a voice so quiet she could hardly hear him, "I want to make love to you again, Sarah."

She stiffened. With great effort, she turned to him and looked him in the eye. "But you won't."

"I can't."

She knew he couldn't. His loyalty was one of the reasons why she loved him. Why she'd always love him.

She rose from the bench. "Take me home, Your Grace."

"Of course."

Side by side, they walked back to her father's cottage in silence.

Chapter Seventeen

Sarah sat straight up in bed. She hadn't had the time to speak with Mrs. Hope about Bordesley Green yesterday. But now, on some edge of her fractured sleep, a dormant part of her mind had awakened and remembered what Bordesley Green was.

Her blanket had dipped around her hips, and she was wearing her lightest nightgown, but the morning wasn't cold. Vestiges of dawn seeped in through her curtains, bathing her room in a shadowy gray light. All was silent; even the birds had not yet begun their morning song.

Bordesley Green was a private asylum. James, the duchess's manservant who'd disappeared when she had, had supported his mother who lived there.

Sarah had never spoken to him about it. She'd over-heard him talking to Binnie one day, had heard only the fringes of their conversation. She'd gathered from the bits and pieces of information that he sent funds monthly to Bordesley Green for the care of his mother, who'd forgotten who she was...and who her son was. It had been his day off that day, and he was leaving to visit her.

"So that's where you go every month," Binnie had exclaimed, as if that solved some great mystery.

"Aye, it is. Even if she doesn't remember me...she's still blood," he'd said gravely.

Sarah dressed herself hurriedly, ate a quick breakfast despite the rumbling in her belly, left a note for her father, and headed to the stables.

As she'd expected, Robert Johnston was already awake. She found him in a stall where he was saddling one of the mares for a morning ride.

"Robert?"

She'd startled him. His head jerked up to her, but then his lips spread into a grin, and the tension seeped out of his shoulders. "Sarah! Good morning. What are you doing up so early?"

She glanced around to make sure no one was listening—surely the stable boy wasn't—he was humming as he shoveled muck out of a stall at the far end of the stables.

"I need to ask you a favor," she told him, slipping into the stall. "A rather enormous favor, I'm afraid."

"Anything for you," Robert said, his voice warm.

"It's Thursday. It's my day off today. I believe it's yours, too?"

"Aye, it is."

"Did you have important plans for the day?"

"None but a bit of riding." He gestured to the horse he'd been saddling.

"Would you mind..." She took a deep breath, then plowed on. "Would you mind taking me somewhere?"

"Be happy to."

"It's a place called Bordesley Green. I don't know where it is, exactly—Mrs. Hope would probably know. But..." She gave him a cringing look. "...I have heard it's about ten miles away."

"Of course. I'll ready the old duke's phaeton."

She released a relieved breath. He'd agreed readily, and with no questions asked. He turned back to the horse standing beside him to unsaddle it, and then he went to ready the phaeton while Sarah hurried to the house to ask the way to Bordesley Green. Though Mrs. Hope looked at her askance, she told Sarah where the asylum was located, and by the time Sarah had returned from the kitchen where she'd packed a luncheon they could eat, Robert was ready to go.

"Thank you," she told him with feeling as soon as they were underway. "This was so important to me. I cannot thank you enough for taking your day off to help me."

"It is my pleasure," he told her.

The journey took two hours. During that time, she kept talking, as if engaging him in conversation about mundane things like the weather and the breeding of horses at Ironwood Park would prevent him from asking her too many questions.

When they finally arrived at the high gates that marked the entrance to Bordesley Green, the sun had peeked out from behind gray-toned clouds that had threatened rain all morning.

She'd given Robert a highly abridged explanation of why they were coming here, focusing on the fact that it might help in the investigation regarding the duchess, and now he gave her a sidelong glance. She said nothing, just watched the scene unfolding before them.

He stopped the phaeton outside the tall iron fence. While Sarah held the horses, Robert stepped out to inspect the closed gate, and he glanced back at her. "It's not locked, but I imagine we are expected to leave the horses and phaeton here."

"All right."

He came back to take the reins from her, and he secured the horses while she descended from the phaeton to take a good look at Bordesley Green. The brick building stood about a quarter-mile from the gate, three stories rising in dark, gothic lines from the center of a vast green lawn. There was no one out and about on that lawn. The place just stood there, still and haunting and quiet under the looming clouds.

Determinedly, Sarah began to walk down the long, straight path that led to the front door. And then she saw that Robert had hurried to her side.

She slowed. "Robert, I'm sorry. Will you wait for me out here?"

He glanced at the quiet, imposing structure ahead of them and then back at her. "Sarah—"

"I'll be all right. I just need to ask after the man I was telling you about. It'll only be a few minutes."

He hesitated, then nodded. "Very well. I'm remaining right here, though. And if you are gone longer than an hour, I'm coming after you."

"Thank you." On impulse, she squeezed his forearm in thanks.

The air was growing warm and thick around her, and she glanced up at the sky. It really was possible that it would rain. She hoped Robert didn't get soaked waiting for her.

She reached the tall, heavy wooden front door. It loomed up dark and silent in the gloom, and with seemingly no other option, she knocked.

After a long moment, a swarthy woman dressed all in black with her hair pinned back severely at her nape opened the door. "How might I help thee?"

"Good morning," Sarah said with the brightest smile she could muster. "I am here to visit one of your residents."

"Which patient wouldst thou like to see?" The woman's manner of speaking and her sternness of dress marked her as a Quaker.

"Bertram Smith," Sarah asked automatically. And then she did something rare for her—she outright lied. "He is my cousin."

The woman raised her brows. "Friend Bertram doesn't receive many visitors."

Sarah nodded. "I haven't seen him in years. I've come from London, you see, and I've never had the opportunity to travel to Worcester before now." When the woman was silent, she added yet another lie. "We often played together when I was a child. It has been a very long time."

She hoped the woman would not try to verify all this information with Bertram Smith. She'd no idea even if he was able to understand the concept of a cousin. Or if he'd ever played.

"Your name?"

"Sarah. Sarah Stanley."

Recognition flared in the woman's eyes. Interesting. So the lady did possess knowledge of the link between Bertram and the Stanleys.

"I am Hannah Mills, the matron here. It is a pleasure

to meet thee. However, I am afraid today is not a visiting day. The second Friday of the month—tomorrow—is the day we accept visits from family members. On the day before such encounters, we provide a calm and serene atmosphere for the idiots so that they might be in a proper state of mind to see their loved ones."

"But I am only passing through—"

The woman raised her hand, and with a small smile on her face, added, "However, since Friend Bertram sees visitors so infrequently, it'll do him good to see someone from his childhood. I shall do my best. Please, follow me."

Sarah trailed after the woman into a dim, quiet corridor and up a flight of stairs. They passed only one other person, a young woman dressed in the same crisp black that Mrs. Mills wore, carrying a tray of dirty dishes.

"Good day, Hannah," she said to Mrs. Mills.

"Good day, Prudence," Mrs. Mills responded, crisp and polite.

Prudence nodded at Sarah as they passed in the corridor. Mrs. Mills led her into a stark, white-painted reception room scattered with wooden chairs, a large brick fireplace on one wall and a row of tall gothic windows on the other. The woman stopped by the door and gestured inside. "Pray, be seated. I shall go inquire whether Friend Bertram is prepared for a visit with a family member this morning."

"Thank you very much."

As Mrs. Mills exited from the room, Sarah selected a chair with a good view of the doorway so she could see Mrs. Mills and Bertram when they returned.

If they returned. That was a big "if."

But Sarah couldn't know. She sat there, chewing her lip in nervousness. She didn't have any experience with idiots, and she didn't know what to expect. Her plan had ended at gaining entrance to Bordesley Green and convincing them to allow her to see Bertram. Since she still didn't have anything but guesses about who he was or why Georgina Stanley wished for him to remain a secret, her plan had reached its limit.

The door opened, and Mrs. Mills entered, followed by a man-sized boy.

Sarah looked up at him, slowly rising from her seat, her heart pattering against her ribs. For the man-boy looked unnervingly similar to Georgina Stanley.

A flattened-out, plumper, doughy version of Georgina Stanley.

As soon as he saw her, he grinned. Two of his teeth were missing. "It's my birthday! For me!" he announced with a lisp so marked, it sounded like he'd said, "Itsch my birfday."

"Come inside, Friend Bertram," Mrs. Mills said patiently, and he obediently strode into the room, looking around with interest, his cornflower blue eyes shining.

Although his white gown looked freshly starched and had probably been snow white this morning, there were dribbles of something—gravy, perhaps—spattered across its front.

He didn't look quite right. It was like looking at a male version of Georgina through drunken eyes. His face was too round, his ears and teeth too small, his eyes too perfectly almond-shaped and too close together.

Mrs. Mills looked up at Sarah and shrugged. "Whenever something he considers to be a happy event occurs,

he believes it's his birthday. Of course, we do not cel-
ebrate such things as birthdays here, but that day must
have been a special one for him when he was a boy, and
he hasn't forgotten."

Sarah nodded. She swallowed her fear. Surely if the
man were dangerous, Mrs. Mills would have taken pre-
cautions. And in any case, fear wouldn't help her in this
situation.

She stepped forward. "Bertram," she said, "it is so
good to see you."

He stopped and stood still, his gown fluttering over the
floor, and looked at her with bright-eyed interest. His eyes
were the exact same color as Miss Stanley's but contained
none of the malice Sarah had seen the last time she'd encountered the lady.

"You?"

"I'm Sarah," she said quietly.

"I like cousins," Bertram said. Mrs. Mills must have
told him his cousin had come to visit. And then he released his words in a rattle so fast Sarah couldn't keep up.
Not only did he have a lisp, but he also slurred his words.
He said something about papas with a scowl, and brothers and sisters. And people named Gertrude and Mary and
William, and their mamas and papas and cousins. Then,
suddenly, he stopped cold, frowning as if he'd lost his
train of thought.

Mrs. Mills patted his arm. "Friend Bertram has become something of a pet to many of our patients' families."

"Oh?" Sarah didn't know what else to say.

"Indeed. Thou might recall his humble, happy nature.
He seldom requires restraints, he doesn't complain or cry,

and his only ambition in life appears to be one of the simplest, yet one of the most important for all of humankind: to be happy."

"Oh," Sarah said in some surprise. Bertram grinned at her, showing his little gapped teeth.

"It's my birthday! Cousin Sarah! Happy, happy!" he exclaimed, clapping and bouncing on his toes.

"And how old are you today?" Sarah asked him.

The question appeared to confuse him. He looked to Mrs. Mills for help.

"Why, Friend Bertram, thou art four and twenty. Dost thou not remember?"

"Four and twenty," he told Sarah brightly. "Four and twenty, four and twenty, four and twenty," he sang.

And, with that, it all became clear.

In the parlor at Ironwood Park one day, Sarah had overheard Miss Stanley telling Esme that she'd had an older brother who'd died at the age of nine when she had been five years old.

This was the brother who'd "died." The Stanleys had hidden him away here, somewhat close to their properties so Lord Stanley could keep an eye on him, but far too close as far as Miss Stanley was concerned. She'd prefer it if her embarrassment of a brother was sent to Abyssinia.

Even more potentially scandalizing for the Stanleys, Georgina's younger brother—Lord Stanley's current legal heir—was only nineteen years old and at Cambridge.

Bertram was Lord Stanley's true heir. The Stanleys were deceiving the world, pretending Bertram had perished when he was, in fact, right here in England, giving her a gap-toothed grin and singing about how he was four and twenty.

Sarah took a deep breath and forced a smile. "I am so glad to see you again, Bertram."

"Four and twenty!"

"Your family...misses you."

The smile turned into an instant frown. "Don't like papas and mamas."

Sarah looked at Mrs. Mills. "Have they visited?" she asked softly.

Mrs. Mills shook her head, her expression grave. "Not for many years."

Sarah blew out a slow breath. "Do you remember your mama and papa?" she asked Bertram.

She held her breath as he looked up as if the answer dangled from the ceiling and he might pluck it down. Then he looked at her, his lips twisting, and leaned forward, close enough that she could smell him. His scent was an odd combination of harsh soap and sweat.

"I'm fat," he told her, making circular motions around his girth. "Papa is skinny. Papa has blue eyes like me."

"Do you remember your sister, Georgina?"

"Little tiny babe in mama's tummy," he said. "Big, big tummy like Bertram's, but full of baby, and she went away forever and ever, and pop! Georgy!" He shook his head vigorously. "Bertram can't hold Georgy. Bertram might break Georgy. Bertram can't play. Bad, bad Bertram."

His movements and words were growing more slurred and more frantic, and Sarah cast Mrs. Mills a hopeless look.

"Wouldst thou like to return to the common room, Friend Bertram?" Mrs. Mills asked.

"Cousin Sarah!" he exclaimed.

"I'll come back and visit you again," she told him gravely. It was a promise she vowed to keep, too. No matter where her new position took her after she left Ironwood Park.

"Common room, then." Mrs. Mills turned him around and, with a hand on his back, firmly pressed him toward the door. He looked back over his shoulder at Sarah.

"Cousin Sarah, cousin Sarah black hair!"

Only then did she notice that two attendants had been waiting just outside the door. Mrs. Mills handed Bertram off to them, and he ambled away down the corridor, talking about cousins and papas and Sarahs until he was out of her hearing range.

Sarah just stood there, willing her heart to calm. Mrs. Mills reentered the room. She gave Sarah a small smile. "I should have warned thee that speaking of his family tends to agitate him. He sees so many other families here on visiting days. I believe a part of him pines for his own."

"I am sorry," Sarah said. "I didn't know..."

"Yet his father has asked us to remove them from his memory," Mrs. Mills continued. She looked at Sarah with a shadowed, wary expression.

"What do you mean?"

"They wish us to invent a new family for him so there will never be a chance of him being connected to the baron." She gave Sarah a wistful look. "That was why I was rather surprised to see a cousin here today. I've been led to believe they meant to sever all family ties."

Sarah blinked, then nodded slowly. "My...uncle and his family are prideful people."

"Too proud to bring an idiot into their midst, certainly."

"Right. But he seems happy. They have chosen well in his home."

Mrs. Mills's smile was genuine. "Thank you, Friend Sarah. My husband and I toil under the belief that all of us, even—and perhaps especially—the idiots, are God's children and deserve to be treated with love and humanity."

"A truly noble belief," Sarah said, meaning it.

"Come. I will see thee out."

"Thank you."

As Mrs. Mills walked her down the long, silent corridor, Sarah gathered the courage to speak. As they began to descend the staircase, she asked, "I believe I know another of your residents as well, Mrs. Mills."

Mrs. Mills glanced back over her shoulder. "Oh?"

"Mrs. James. She is the mother of a . . . well, someone I once knew."

"Ah, yes. Liza James."

"Is she still here?"

"Yes," Mrs. Mills said in a clipped tone.

"Would it . . . be possible to see her as well?"

"No." They'd reached the bottom of the stairs, and Mrs. Mills drew to a halt. "Thou must not be truly acquainted with Liza James, Friend Sarah, for she is one of our most difficult residents and requires restraint nearly all the time."

"Oh." Sarah swallowed hard. "I am sorry to hear that. You're right—I've never made her acquaintance. I only know her son . . ."

"Of course." Mrs. Mills gave a short nod. "We have

believed for some time now that she is not suited for an idiots' home and should be transferred to a home better equipped for lunatics, but despite the hopelessness of her condition, Mr. James refuses to move her and continues to visit her monthly. He is a very loyal and devoted son."

Sarah's heart began to race yet again. "You say he visits every month—when was the last you saw him?"

"Why, on visiting day last month. He arrives when the doors open at ten, like clockwork."

Heavens. James had been here last month! Sarah spoke through her suddenly dry throat. "And you expect him tomorrow?"

"Oh, yes. He hasn't missed a visiting day in the five years his mother has resided here."

"Thank you," Sarah breathed. She began to walk quickly down the corridor toward the exit. At the door, she thanked Mrs. Mills profusely and promised to come again to visit her "cousin."

She hurried down the path toward the phaeton, trying to refrain from lifting her skirts and running, hardly noticing the first drops of rain splashing against her cheeks.

The duchess had been missing for almost four months now. James had been seen last month, which meant he surely had some information on the duchess's whereabouts.

She needed to hurry home. Tell Simon all that she had learned.

Robert pushed off from where he was leaning against the side of the phaeton as she rushed up, breathless, and moments later, they were once again under way. He'd put up the hood, but soon the infrequent drops evolved into a shower. The hood only provided partial shelter from the rain—they'd both be soaked by the time they arrived home.

Not home. She had to stop thinking of Ironwood Park as home. Something fluttered in her stomach at that thought. A feeling she'd been having often in the past week or two—a rumbling stomach, like she hadn't eaten in a week. She glanced down at the sack she'd brought containing their lunch. No, that wasn't it. The odd feeling had come and gone seemingly with no connection to how full or empty her stomach was.

What, then?

She thought hard.

And then it hit her. Her courses. She must be about to begin them. How awkward it would be to start them on the way home with nothing—

Wait.

When were they due? Her breaths began to quicken as she calculated, and she felt the blood rushing from her head as she came up with the answer.

She was late. For goodness' sakes, she'd completely skipped her courses last month. So much had been happening, between her heartbreak over Simon's engagement and the move back to Ironwood Park, she hadn't even noticed.

She swayed toward Robert, then jerked herself upright. *Oh, God. Oh, God.* It was the eighth of August. The last time she had lain with Simon was the eleventh of June—a date she'd never forget.

Two months.

Robert glanced over at her. "Are you all right?"

"Yes." She'd meant the word to sound like a firm, confident statement, but it emerged instead as a breathy wisp of air.

Robert reined the horses to a stop and turned to her, a frown wrinkling his brow. "Sarah, what is it?"

She passed the back of her wrist over her forehead, soaking up beads of water she knew were not raindrops.

"It's just... what I learned today."

"Can you tell me?"

No, she couldn't. She couldn't speak, couldn't think beyond the rushing tide of blood as it swirled in her head in a descending whirlpool, leaving her dizzy and faint.

You are two months gone with child, Sarah.

Simon's child.

Chapter Eighteen

❦

The family was sitting in the parlor before dinner, along with Lord Stanley, who'd arrived from London late last night. Earlier today, Simon, Georgina, and Lord and Lady Stanley had had a picnic on the northern banks of the stream and had then gone for a ride through the property, Simon pointing out the features and borders of his lands. When it had begun to rain, they'd raced home, but not before all of them had received a good dousing. They'd bathed and dressed for dinner, and now they relaxed on the royal-blue silk upholstery of the parlor, comfortable and warm, with Simon's brothers and Esme.

Talking about the wedding.

Simon secretly wished he were still out riding in the rain. But no, Georgina and Lady Stanley were going on and on about whom to invite to the wedding breakfast.

"Yes, Lord Granger, for certain," he said in response to Lady Stanley's question. He wandered over to one of the windows to glance out at the rain, which was now coming down in sheets. Mark and Theo gave him twin sympathetic looks as he walked past them.

Mark and Theo were so alike. More alike, really, than any of his other siblings. Now he knew why—they were probably the only two with the same two parents.

And they didn't know. It plagued him that he hadn't told them the truth. But how to go about it eluded him.

He sighed, parted the curtains, and looked out into the gray.

It had been a long day. Tedious, really. The air between him and Stanley had been stretched taut since breakfast. On the verge of snapping.

Simon's hatred for his situation grew daily. He was determined to grit his teeth and face it with stoic acceptance, but every time he saw the smug expression of victory on Stanley's face, he wanted to tackle the man to the ground and beat the snide look off his face.

He missed Sarah, damn it. Missed her smile and her scent. Her soft skin, dewy after they'd just made love. He'd only had her for two weeks. But those weeks were imprinted upon every inch of his skin and had seeped deep into him. He'd never forget. He wondered if he'd ever stop longing for more.

"What do you think, Trent?"

Stanley's voice jolted him out of his reverie. He turned to the older man. "What's that?"

"Georgina would like to do something different at the wedding. Instead of one bridesmaid, she'd like to have a dozen," Lady Stanley said.

A dozen bridesmaids. This was going to be the spectacle of the decade.

He inclined his head at Georgina. "Whatever you wish, of course."

She clapped her hands. "I'm having them all wear plain white, so the beauty of my dress, which will be silver, will be a shining star among them."

Simon wondered if his smile appeared as pained as it felt. "Excellent."

The door burst open and banged against the inside wall. Simon jerked his head in the direction of the noise as someone—Esme, perhaps—gasped in surprise.

Sarah stood at the threshold wearing a dripping wet gray pelisse, her black hair in whipped wet clumps, and her blue eyes wild. Her gaze searched, secking, then latched on to him. "Your...Grace."

Her voice was choked. Full of some indefinable emotion.

"For heaven's sake!" Lady Stanley exclaimed. "What is the meaning of this?"

From the corner of his eye, Simon saw that she'd risen from her chair. But he couldn't tear his gaze away from Sarah. His chest clenched tight. When she wore her public face, Sarah was always restrained, never dramatic. Something was very, very wrong.

"Sarah...what is it?"

"Your Grace," she pushed out. "I need to...we need to..." Her gaze darted around the room. She was trembling. Cold and wet and terribly upset about something.

He strode forward. "What is the matter?"

"I...I..." She wrapped her arms around her body as if to contain its shuddering. "I need to speak with you."

"Is it so urgent you cannot take a moment to dry yourself off?" Lord Stanley asked dryly.

"You are dripping all over the Persian carpet, girl," Lady Stanley snapped.

As if from far away, he heard Georgina say, "What insolence, to thrust herself upon us in such a fashion. Can you imagine?"

Simon turned on his wife-to-be. "Miss Osborne is a valued member of my household. If she has something to say to me, she will be given leave to say it."

"Trent," Lady Stanley said, "this is highly improper. She is a mere housemaid and should not be bursting in on the family with the impudence of some dirty wild thing. If something important has happened, she should go to her superior, who will then address you if she deems it of enough consequence. But I cannot abide a servant behaving so freely—and this one, in particular, has forgotten her place more than once in my presence."

"Mine, too," Georgina added primly.

Sarah stood at the door, looking so alone, so vulnerable. She needed him right now.

First, he turned to Lady Stanley. "This is my house and I shall treat everyone who resides here as I see fit, my lady. Do not ever presume to know more about my household than I do."

"Of course I—"

"And you," he said, interrupting her and turning on Georgina, "will treat everyone at Ironwood Park with respect."

He didn't wait for a response from her. He turned to Stanley and his brothers. "Please excuse me. I've no idea if I'll return in time for dinner."

Finally, he looked at Esme. "Have Mrs. Hope fetch warm towels and tea and have them sent to the library."

She nodded. "Of course."

Was it his imagination or were the corners of her lips twitching? He didn't have time to analyze his sister's expression. He turned back to Sarah. "I'm sorry about all that."

"It's...all right." Her teeth began to chatter, and she clenched them together to stop.

"Hurry, Esme. She's ice cold."

As they left the parlor, Esme was on their heels. She turned toward the kitchen and Mrs. Hope's office while Simon steered Sarah in the opposite direction toward the library. As they walked, he unbuttoned his tailcoat and laid it on her shaking shoulders, hoping it would help keep her warm until the towels and tea arrived. Burton would have a fit about the ruination of this particular coat, but Simon didn't give a damn.

Keeping his hands on her shoulders, he led her into the library and to one of the warm rose-colored velvet chairs by the hearth, then he bent to stoke the fire. After a few moments, he turned, brushing his hands. Crouching in front of her, he took her cold hands in his own and began to chafe them as he looked up into her face. Her expression could only be called haggard.

"What is it, Sarah?" he asked quietly. "What has happened? Why were you out in the rain?"

"I..." She bowed her head, breaking their eye contact. "I found out something...about the Stanleys and about the duchess...and I think there's more." She looked back up, but her gaze shifted, not quite meeting his. "We might be able to find your mother."

He rose and pulled a chair beside hers. "Tell me what happened."

"I overheard Miss Stanley and Lady Stanley talking about a place called Bordesley Green."

"Yes, I've heard of the place. It's a home near Worcester."

"They were talking about someone they knew who lived there whose identity they didn't want to expose."

Simon kept trying to work some warmth into her hands, moving up to rub her wrists and forearms.

"I had no idea what they were talking about, but I'd heard of Bordesley Green before, I knew it. It wasn't until this morning that I remembered where. You see...your mother's manservant, James, keeps his own mother there. I went this morning to investigate. And I discovered that James was there to visit his mother last month, and he's due again tomorrow. It seems he's very much alive, Your Grace. I don't know where he lives, but he'll be at Bordesley Green tomorrow. He might have all the answers. If you intercept him there, he might be able to tell you once and for all what happened to your mother."

Simon sat quietly for a moment, taking all this in. Then he looked at her and asked softly, "You went all the way out there on your own?"

"Yes." She flinched. "Well, Robert Johnston drove me. It took some time to return home. The rain and the mud—"

"Why didn't you tell me, Sarah? You needn't have taken this on yourself."

"You were busy with Miss Stanley," she whispered.

Her pain was raw in her eyes, and he had to close his own in sheer self-preservation.

"And...I found the man the Stanleys are trying to hide."

His eyes opened, and he stared at her.

"Bertram Stanley. The eldest brother. He's alive."

"What?"

"They tell everyone he's dead, but he's not. He's alive and living at Bordesley Green."

"What the hell?"

"Because they don't want an idiot to inherit, Your Grace. If Bertram is 'dead,' Miss Stanley's younger brother is the legal heir."

"Good God," Simon murmured. "Their selfishness and deviousness knows no bounds."

He glanced at Sarah, but she was gazing into the fire, her eyes welling with unshed tears.

There was a knock on the door, and he pulled his hands away from her. It was a maid and a footman bearing tea and towels. While the maid laid out the tea service, Simon took the towels from the footman and wrapped them around Sarah. She was sitting stiffly, her back straight, blinking hard and staring at the hearth, obviously trying to hide her emotions from the two who'd just entered.

"You may go," he told them.

They hurried out, and Simon finished pouring the tea. He added a bit of sugar, the way he knew she liked it, stirred it, and handed it to her.

"Will you be all right?" he asked her.

"Yes," she said shakily. That was a lie. He frowned.

"I'll go to Bordesley Green tomorrow," he said.

She nodded.

"I'll speak with James and I'll see Bertram Stanley."

"Yes."

He took her hand again. It was warmer now. "I'll

take care of everything, Sarah. I'll find out whatever it is James knows about my mother."

Her teeth closed over her lower lip.

"Everything will be all right."

She looked away from him. She didn't believe him.

"What is it? Is there something else?"

She took a long moment to answer. Finally, she turned to him slowly, as if moving through pudding.

"No, Your Grace. There is nothing else."

"It's Sarah Osborne, isn't it?"

Simon snapped his head up from his drink and squinted at his brother. He sat slouched in one of the velvet armchairs in the dark library. The fire had long since stopped giving off heat, and there was a chill in the air he hadn't noticed before.

"What are you talking about?" he asked Sam.

With a sigh, Sam did something most rare: he sat, lowering himself into the chair Sarah had occupied earlier. It was likely still damp, but Sam didn't complain. One thing about Sam—he never complained. He had come home once from the Continent with a gunshot wound to his shoulder that had festered and taken months to heal, and he had never spoken one word of complaint.

"Sarah Osborne," Sam said. "The other woman whose identity you wouldn't reveal to me the day you came to tell me about Stanley's threats."

Good God, had he been that obvious this afternoon? If so, what were the rest of them thinking?

And then, a realization jolted through him. He didn't care. He didn't give a damn if the whole world saw how he felt about Sarah.

A great weight lifted from his shoulders, and he gazed at his brother, stone-faced. "Yes."

Sam tilted his head. Simon couldn't really see his expression in the gloom, but his brother's dark eyes shone.

"Trent," he said, his voice ever so quiet, "it is unlike you to dally with the servants."

Fury built in Simon so quickly he snapped out of his chair, still gripping his brandy in one fist. Cool liquid splashed over his hand. "Don't push me, Sam."

Sam remained seated, gazing up at him. "Why? Isn't that what you're doing?"

"No!" he roared. The bloody drink was in the way, so he stalked over to his desk and slammed it down. Then he rounded on his brother. "I am not dallying with anyone. And hell, if another person refers to her as a servant, he's going to be receiving a mouthful of my fist."

"Then what is it, exactly, that you are doing with her?"

"What are *you* doing?" Simon growled. "You come in here and accuse me of dallying with servants when you know damn well that's not what this is."

"If not a dalliance, what is it?" Sam pressed. "Don't tell me you had intended to propose marriage before all this Stanley nonsense."

"Marriage...?" Shaking his head to clear the sudden fog in it, Simon stared at his brother.

"I see," Sam said mildly. "The thought never even occurred to you. Of course it didn't. She's too far below you to consider such a preposterous idea."

"I..." Simon shut his mouth. Sam was right. The thought hadn't occurred to him. Not once.

"She'd make an unacceptable wife, of course," Sam continued. "Her breeding isn't of the proper sort, after all.

She's not remotely close to possessing an aristocratic lineage. And only a true lady could be a wife to you, right, Trent? Only someone who's been groomed for the task, who has the correct aristocratic bloodlines. You could never marry a woman like Sarah Osborne. You must consider yourself lucky to have had Georgina Stanley fall into your lap instead."

A vague part of his brain registered that Sam had grossly insulted him, but the greater majority was overwhelmed by the concept that swirled about. *Marry her.* Marry Sarah.

Make her his wife. Spend his life with her. Fall asleep beside her every night and wake beside her every morning. Have children with her. Grow old with her. Possess the freedom to love her openly. Make her his duchess.

The thoughts grounded him; calmed him. It wasn't like considering his marriage to Georgina, which always left him vaguely angry and slightly ill. No, the idea of marrying Sarah was a balm to his soul.

All his life he had assigned such importance to aristocratic bloodlines and lineage, just like Sam said. But not anymore. He didn't give a damn anymore. He'd learned there were things far more important than having the blood of the aristocracy running through one's veins. In any case, from the evidence he'd gathered this summer, that blood was mostly tainted.

Marry Sarah.

But it couldn't happen. He was betrothed to another.

He pushed a frustrated hand through his hair and turned away from his brother. "This conversation is moot," he said harshly. "It is too late for such talk."

"Right. Of course. Then tell me, Trent, what *are* you doing with Sarah, if it does not qualify as a dalliance?"

"I am..." His voice trailed off. He rubbed his temples. "I am trying to do what is right. What you advised me to do. Marry Georgina Stanley to save my brothers and sister from disgrace."

"But what about Sarah?"

Simon swallowed hard, emotions he dared not name churning within him. After a long moment, he murmured, "I'm hurting her."

He was hurting himself. Hurting them both.

"I am fond of Sarah," Sam said quietly. "All of us are."

"Not the Stanleys."

"You know I don't mean the Stanleys. I mean all of *us*. None of us wishes to see her hurt."

"Nor do I, damn it."

Sam's eyes glinted in the dim. "Are you saying that you care about her? That your aristocratic pride is willing to stoop down so low?"

Simon straightened. "Society might think her lower than me, but she isn't. She is...my *equal*. In all things."

Sam sat back in his chair as if Simon's words had slapped him across the face. A long moment of stunned silence filled the room.

Finally, Sam said, "If you're hurting her, Trent, you're going to need to put a stop to it."

Simon leaned on his desk, both hands flat on the sleek mahogany surface. "And what do you propose I do? Please, gift me with your wisdom, because I'm bloody well in dire need of it at this moment."

Slowly, Sam shook his head from side to side. "There is no solution that will result in everyone's happiness.

Worse for you, perhaps, is that there is no solution that won't result in a scandal worthy of our mother."

Simon stared down at his hands.

"But you must fix this, Trent."

Slowly, he raised his gaze until he met his brother's eyes. "You're right."

The next day, while Sarah was eating her midday meal, Robert Johnston entered the kitchen. She tried to smile a greeting at him.

Forcing her lips into upward tilts had been a difficult exercise for the past day. Ever since she'd realized she was with child, she'd brought a dark cloud into every room she entered. People had noticed her dour mood, but she didn't have any idea how to clear away the gloom.

A pregnancy should be a time of joy and anticipation, but all she could feel was fear and dread. The simple fact was, Georgina Stanley was going to force her to leave Ironwood Park. Yesterday morning, Sarah had believed she had options, would find another situation in another house, and while she'd miss Simon, she'd survive. But now that she'd be bringing an illegitimate child with her, her options fluttered away, as fleeting as dandelion seeds whisked away on a strong breeze.

She hadn't the faintest idea what she'd do. Where she'd go. Who'd accept her now.

How she and the babe would survive.

She'd thought about telling Simon yesterday afternoon when she'd revealed her discoveries at Bordesley Green, but she hadn't been able to do it. Who knew what his powerful sense of duty and propriety would compel him to do? If he jilted Georgina Stanley and married Sarah because he considered it the "right" thing to do, the scandal would destroy him and his family. She couldn't do that to him—to any of them.

Or, he might never even consider marrying her. He'd go forward with marrying Miss Stanley, but his sense of duty might compel him to "keep" Sarah, perhaps set her up discreetly in a small house far away with an allowance for her and the babe.

That thought, when she'd had it just after breakfast, had given her such a sour feeling in her gut that she'd run to the privy to release the contents of her stomach.

She had remained slumped against the door of the privy for a long while as she'd come to terms with this additional verification of her pregnancy, and while she'd stood there, she realized that she couldn't accept the option of being Simon's "kept woman." She was too proud to be hidden away somewhere. To be Simon's embarrassing secret.

Although once her practical nature regained control, she admitted to herself that it might be her last resort. If it came to accepting his charity or the poorhouse, her pride would just have to endure the blow.

Now, she pasted a smile on her face and directed it to Robert Johnston. "Good afternoon, Robert."

"I was hoping I'd find you here," he said.

She wiped her hands on her napkin and pushed her plate away. "Here I am. How may I help you?"

He glanced around the kitchen. One of the housemaids was eating with Sarah at the table. Two kitchen maids were kneading dough, and the cook had poked her head out of the larder and was watching them with interest.

He looked back down at her. "Do you have time to walk with me?"

She didn't want to walk with Robert Johnston, but her mind was too muddled to invent an acceptable excuse not to. "I might be able to spare half an hour."

His smile was brilliant. "Wonderful."

The summer day was fine, and she didn't need a coat. They walked the garden path, then out onto the lawn, headed toward the stream and the line of trees marking the forest. They reached the line of blackberry bushes along the bank of the stream, then Robert cut behind them. Toward her and Simon's bench.

"Let's sit for a while," Robert said when the bench came into view.

At his expectant look, she lowered herself woodenly. She hadn't wanted to come here ever again, but to come here with Robert and not Simon—a part of her felt like she was being unfaithful.

"I enjoyed our day together yesterday," he said as he sat down beside her.

She looked at him in some surprise. She'd hardly noticed him all day, so selfishly focused as she'd been on her own revelations. "It was very kind of you to drive me all that way."

"I was happy to do it for you." He paused, then added in a low voice, "I'd do anything for you, Sarah."

Sarah's heart began to pound, and her stomach roiled, reminding her of the tiny life growing there. She pressed her hand flat against her bodice. Her baby. Simon's baby.

Her luncheon tumbled around in her stomach. If she vomited here, she would be mortified.

"Robert, I don't—"

He held up his hand. "Please. Let me speak."

She shut her mouth, stanching the impulse to beg him to stop talking, to take her back to the house.

He turned to face her. "I can't stop thinking about you, Sarah."

She tried to remember to breathe, forcing air in and out, in and out. She shook her head in silent denial, pleading him with her eyes to stop, stop now, before he said something they'd both regret.

But he didn't seem to understand her silent pleas, because he continued. "You are lovely. You are kind and honest and pure."

"No—" she gasped, but he raised his hand, stopping her again.

"In short, you'd make the most perfect of companions for me. I have asked your father for your hand in marriage, and he has given his consent." He took a deep breath. "Sarah Osborne, will you make me the happiest of men? Will you marry me?"

She opened her mouth, but now that she'd been given leave to speak, words failed her. She scrambled through the cackles of laughter from the devil in her soul—"Pure? You? What a wonderful farce!"—and tried to find the words she could string together into a coherent sentence.

Finally, she spoke, her voice low and scratchy. "You...hardly know me."

"I've spent a full day in your company," he answered readily, "and we've seen each other on countless other occasions. I observed you in London. You behaved admirably, given the challenging situation the duke and his sister put you in. You remained composed in every circumstance, and through it all, your grace, your gentle and compassionate nature shone through."

She blinked at him, feeling like she was in some kind of warped dream. His words sounded so formal. Had he rehearsed them? Again, she shook her head. "No, you don't understand."

He looked up at her, his brown eyes dark and serious. "But I do. I know you, Sarah. I know you will make me a fine wife. Your father agrees."

She rubbed her forehead, trying to eliminate the awkward image of Robert asking her father for permission to marry her.

"Oh, Robert." She squeezed her eyes shut. As much as she hated to hurt him, it had to be said. "I cannot marry you."

"Of course you can."

"No. I can't. I truly can't."

The first lines of concern deepened between his brows. "I'll give you whatever time you need. I will court you properly. I will do whatever it takes—"

"No. It will never...It can never be. I am so sorry."

"If you take some time to think it over—"

"No, Robert."

"Give me a chance to prove myself to you, then."

"No," she repeated as her heart wept. Wouldn't it have been wonderful if Robert were the man she'd fallen in love with? But, no, she'd lost herself, lost everything to an impossibility.

He shook his head. "I can't accept no. There is no logic to that answer."

"But there is. I don't love you."

"I will earn your love. It'll come in time."

She simply shook her head. "I am sorry."

A frown marred his lips. When he spoke, all softness had melted from his tone. "Why, then?" His dark eyes bored into her. "Tell me why."

"I...can't. I'm sorry."

Sorry, Robert. I am so sorry. But she knew all the sorrys in the world wouldn't save her from Robert's probing gaze.

She looked away from him and felt the hardness of his stare for long moments. She gazed down at her hands twisting in her lap.

Finally, he said in a low voice, "It's the duke, isn't it?"

Every nerve ending in her body jolted as though each one had been struck with a tiny bolt of lightning.

"What?" she gasped, swiveling her head to look at him.

"It's the duke. You fancy yourself in love with him."

Oh, Lord. Oh, Lord.

"I..." She shook her head vehemently, gathered her wits, and then stilled and growled out, "I daresay that is none of your business."

"And that's enough of a confirmation for me," he said in a gravelly voice. Then, he added, "Sarah, even if you have engaged in some sort of liaison with the Duke of Trent, you must know nothing can come of it."

She couldn't do this. She couldn't sit here and discuss her love for Simon with Robert Johnston.

"He would never marry you," Robert continued. "He'll never give you his home. I want to share my life with you, Sarah. My home. My children."

She met his eyes, her own stinging with tears. "You don't understand, Robert. It's too late." It had always been too late for the two of them. "Too late for any of that."

Robert understood. She watched as understanding dawned in his eyes.

"Hell," he whispered. "You gave him everything, didn't you?"

She didn't answer.

"Your love. Your body."

She closed her eyes as his gaze lowered to where her hands were pressed against her stomach.

"You're with child, aren't you? His child?"

Bending her head, her shoulders slumping as her body closed in upon itself, Sarah burst into tears.

Chapter Nineteen

To everyone's surprise, Luke had arrived at Ironwood Park sometime between midnight and dawn. When Simon and Sam had gone down to breakfast, Luke was slouched in the breakfast room drinking coffee and talking to Theo and Mark. The Stanleys were not yet up, nor was Esme.

Luke seemed sober, but black bags puffed beneath his eyes, and he was in a dour mood as he reported that his search for their mother had not resulted in any revelations. Simon had known that from the investigator he'd hired, so it came as no surprise.

Luke didn't offer any apology, an excuse, or even an acknowledgment of the last time he had seen Simon, and for that, Simon was grateful. He had enough on his shoulders at the moment without being dragged down by an old encounter with his brother. He was content to start fresh.

Over poached eggs and coffee, Simon told his brothers how Sarah had learned that James would be at

Bordesley Green today. Again, Simon wasn't surprised when all of his brothers insisted upon going there with him. Half an hour later, they were packed tightly in the family carriage.

Last night, Simon had decided that he would take this opportunity away from the presence of the Stanleys to tell his brothers the secret that had been weighing on him. He was glad they would all be together in the privacy of the carriage, and he was especially glad for Luke's arrival. Having Luke remain the only brother in ignorance seemed wrong.

So as the rattling carriage progressed in a northerly direction, Simon told his brothers everything. About how Stanley had come to him and suggested marriage. About how he'd refused, and about how Stanley had pretended to be regretful about "being forced" to give him this information.

He told Mark and Theo that they were the result of an affair between their father and Fiona Atwood, who now dwelt outside London. Mark and Theo stared at Simon in stunned amazement as he told them how he and Sam had gone to see the woman and she'd corroborated Stanley's story.

Theo swallowed hard. "Does . . . does she look like us?"

Simon looked away, sighing. "She is an old woman now, clearly one who has led a difficult life."

"There was a near-empty decanter of gin on her table, and she reeked of the stuff," Sam added flatly. Their oldest brother was never one to mince words. "She was jaundiced and generally unhealthy in appearance."

Theo cast an alarmed look at Mark, who still hadn't moved.

Simon winced. "She doesn't look like you, per se, but she does share features with you both."

Theo stared at him.

"You are still my brothers," Simon said. "That will never change."

"But we..." Theo breathed. "We aren't... We aren't legitimate." He looked terrified, like the thought of losing the "lord" in front of his name would be akin to ripping off a limb.

Mark finally spoke. "Mama never treated us as anything less than her own, Trent. How do you explain that? If we weren't hers, she should have shunned us, not spent so many years with us practically tied to her skirts."

"Our mother is still our mother. She took you in and made you her sons. And we must take something away from that."

Luke snorted. "What's that?"

"That we are all members of this family. That we all carry the Hawkins name. That we are brothers, and shall remain so until the day we die."

Luke leveled a cold blue gaze on Simon. "That's not all of it, is it, Trent?"

Simon slid a glance to Sam, who sat beside Luke. But this was Simon's responsibility. He was the head of this family, which meant it was his duty to tell his family members news that they didn't want to hear. News that could devastate them.

"You are illegitimate as well, Luke," he said quietly. "I am sorry."

"Let me guess—I am the son of some other whore our father yanked out of a London gutter."

"No," Sam said.

"You're not our father's son at all," Simon said. "You're the offspring of our mother and Lord Stanley."

The silence was instant and thick, the only sounds the rattle and groan of the carriage and the clomp of the horses' hooves as they traveled down the road, the air the brothers shared in the carriage redolent of shock and dismay. Simon watched Luke take in the information. His face was stony, impossible to read, but his eyes— so much like Stanley's—glimmered ice blue in the dim light.

Finally, Luke licked his lips. When he spoke, his voice was raw and jagged, like his throat was coated with shards of glass. "You'd best bloody tell me that you are joking."

"He's not joking," Sam said quietly.

Luke bent his head forward and laughed. It was the bitterest sound Simon had ever heard. "So first I have one bastard for a father, and now I have another. And not only that, but I am now officially a bastard as well." He looked up. "How validating. I'll bet you weren't surprised, were you?"

"I was deeply surprised," Simon said truthfully. "I still am."

Luke gave another one of those bitter laughs. Simon glanced up at Sam. "Will you tell them about Esme?"

Sam did, his voice even and low. Their brothers listened. And then Simon explained Stanley's plan to extort marriage from him. Finally, he told them how Sarah had learned about Bertram Stanley.

An hour later, as they walked along the path that led to the front door of the looming gothic structure, Theo and Mark still looked pale and shocked—stumbling and weaving in their steps as if Simon were to tap them on the shoulder, they might tumble over. It would take time for them to absorb what they'd learned this morning.

As for Luke, he looked angry. But he also looked bemused. He definitely seemed the least surprised of the three of them. And as they'd climbed down from the carriage, he'd made a sneering remark about gaining another idiotic brother today and that he was looking forward to meeting Bertram Stanley.

A half an hour later, they sat in a Spartan private receiving room drinking tea. There were no decorations on the walls and no furniture save the chairs they were seated on and two plain, square wooden tables. Once the master of the place, a Quaker named Mr. Mills, had learned Simon's identity, he'd been more than accommodating. He told him that James was already here visiting his mother, and he'd send him in immediately.

A few minutes later, James himself opened the door and entered the room. When he saw the five brothers gazing at him from all angles, he stopped short, his mouth falling open.

"Close the door, James," Simon said quietly.

James turned, fumbled with shaking hands to close the door, then he turned back to face them. "Y-your Grace. I...er...I didn't expect to...see you here."

"I imagine not," Luke said dryly.

"We have some questions for you," Simon said.

James glanced furtively from one brother to the next. His Adam's apple bobbed as he swallowed.

"Just bloody tell us where our mother is, if you please."

Simon cast a surprised look at Mark. He was always

the most lighthearted of the brothers, and Simon couldn't remember ever hearing him swear. But right now, he stood tall and squared his shoulders, and his expression was black.

She wasn't even his mother. Not really.

But she was his mother in spirit. Always had been. And while Mark must be angry with her for a lifetime of lies, Simon knew he still loved her.

"Er." James swallowed again. "I...uh...don't know."

"You disappeared the same night she did," Simon said. "You never came to us to give us any information regarding her whereabouts. Indeed, you remained hidden despite the fact that we've been searching for you for almost four months."

"Perhaps you murdered her," Luke said, his voice as sly and wicked as a snake's. "Perhaps it was you who stole her jewels, and then you killed Binnie as well. That's a rather fine coat you're wearing today, James."

"No!" James gulped in a breath. "She paid me..."

Sam had been standing in the corner, but now he stepped forward.

"Stop this nonsense," he told them all. His gaze narrowed in on James. "Tell us everything. From the night the three of you disappeared. Spare no detail. We need to know why you left Ironwood Park, what happened, and where the duchess is now."

James shook his head. "I might not be able to—"

Sam raised his hand, cutting the man off. He gestured to a chair that faced the brothers. "Sit there. Start at the beginning, if you please. The night you left Ironwood Park."

"Very well." James wrung his hands as he lowered

himself into the chair. "Er, well…" He looked at each of them, then down again. He cleared his throat. "Well, her Grace was preparing for bed that night, and a stranger arrived at the dower house. I wasn't sure if he was a gentleman, or someone pretending to be one. He was quite intent upon speaking to Her Grace. She agreed to see him in the upstairs drawing room."

"What was his name?"

"He introduced himself as Mr. Morton," James said. "Roger Morton." He took a breath. "After a while, they began to argue. The duchess grew very angry. Binnie and I went to see what was the matter, but she commanded us to go. We didn't know what to do. When she finally returned downstairs, she told us we were leaving; we were all going on a long journey. Binnie and I packed quickly, and we left at around two o'clock in the morning.

"We traveled through the night and the next day, heading west, into Wales. Her Grace and Mr. Morton hardly spoke. Neither Binnie nor I understood what was happening; why we were leaving Ironwood Park. Truly…" He gave Simon a frightened look. "Her Grace seemed resigned and worried, but she also seemed to be in control. She would order Mr. Morton about, and he would obey. I didn't understand it.

"We came to Cardiff, where the duchess secured lodgings in a house. We remained there for almost a month— the duchess never venturing outdoors—and then, one night, Her Grace brought us into her room. She handed a bag of jewels as payment to Binnie and another to me, and she said we must leave that very evening. That we must go to London and sell the jewels, but we must never return to Ironwood Park or show our faces to any of her family. She made us promise to never reveal ourselves to anyone associated with the Hawkinses."

"Good Lord," Simon muttered.

"We obeyed her, Your Grace. She was our mistress, our employer, and she'd compensated us well. We traveled to London, but..." He looked down at his lap. "In the stagecoach, Binnie was showing off the jewels Her Grace had given her. Said she was going to sell them in London and she was going to be a fine, rich lady. Just outside London, we stopped at a coaching inn for the night. The next morning, she was gone."

He stopped talking, rubbing his hands up and down over his thighs, sweat gleaming on his brow.

"What did you do?" Sam asked.

"I looked for Binnie that morning, but I couldn't find her. I figured after all that showing off, something bad had happened, and I feared that whoever'd got Binnie was after me, too. I was too afraid to continue on to London, so I turned around and went to Birmingham. I sold the jewels there." He glanced over his shoulder at the door. "I knew I could not return to Ironwood Park, but I wanted to remain close to my mother," he said awkwardly.

Simon leaned back in his chair and steepled his hands in front of his chin. "Where is the duchess now?"

"Cardiff? I'm not sure. Binnie and I left her there. She and Morton—well, I had the feeling they were waiting for someone, or perhaps something to happen. But I didn't know who or what—Binnie and I just performed our duties, and they never shared that kind of information with us."

"So you left her with this man, Morton," Luke said dangerously. "With no help or protection?"

James cast a nervous glance in Luke's direction. "She ordered us to go," he said in a voice not much louder than a whisper.

"Do you believe Morton had evil intentions toward her?" Sam asked.

"I..." James shook his head. "I couldn't be sure, but no, sir. He deferred to her."

"Could it have been a master plot to kidnap her?" Theo mused. "This Morton fellow was working for someone else?"

"I could not say," James said. "Her Grace's behavior was...odd. Angry one minute and smiling the next. Binnie and I didn't know at all what to think."

The brothers continued to question James, but they weren't able to get much more out of him. Finally, they had him give them his address in Birmingham in case they needed to find him again, then they dismissed him.

When Mills's wife came in to offer them more tea, Luke rose. "I should like to see Bertram Stanley now, madam."

Simon said, "He means Bertram Smith, of course. Please forgive the error."

"Of course." Mrs. Mills gave a shaky smile. "Friend Bertram isn't expecting visitors."

"We'll just be a moment," Simon told her.

She looked from one brother to the other, all of them poised to follow her to Bertram Stanley, and then she gave a firm shake of her head. She didn't question why they wanted to see him; instead she said, "I fear facing such a great number of men will agitate him. One of thee may visit with him, but no more. And I shall be present as an observer."

Luke crossed his arms over his chest. "I'll go." He cast Simon a daring look, but Simon didn't challenge him. If Luke wanted to be the one to see Bertram Stanley, Simon wasn't going to stop him.

Luke was the man's brother, after all.

During the return drive to Ironwood Park, the brothers discussed what they'd learned from James. Thanks to Sarah, they'd received the most important clue they'd been given since their mother's disappearance. She was alive, or had been until late May, and she'd last been seen in Wales.

"I'll be traveling to Cardiff," Luke announced.

Luke had been quiet and contemplative since he'd returned from seeing Bertram Stanley. He told the brothers nothing of their meeting save the fact that the man was indeed a Stanley. Most definitely Georgina's older brother and Lord Stanley's son.

Now, hearing Luke's declaration that he was heading to Wales to find their mother—the first time he'd said much of anything in the past hour—Simon just nodded.

The rest of the ride home was quiet. It seemed like everything that needed to be said had been said, and now there was nothing left for Simon to do but give each of his brothers time to absorb all that they'd learned.

And it gave Simon time, too.

Fantasies about a future with Sarah ran through his mind, a continuous play, scenes repeating themselves. Sarah in his bed. Sarah in his arms, smiling up at him. Sarah comforting him after a long day spent debating in Parliament.

Sarah gazing with adoration into the tiny face of their newborn son.

Now that Sam had opened the floodgates of Simon's mind to the possibilities, he indulged in them. And as he indulged, certain truths sharpened and became crystal clear in his mind. Sarah Osborne was the only woman who moved him. Who he admired. Who could engage him, body, mind, and spirit.

He loved her.

And he wanted it all.

He daydreamed about going home and calling off the engagement with Georgina. He was somehow going to convince Stanley not to reveal the Hawkins family secrets. When that unpleasant business was done, he'd see the Stanleys out of Ironwood Park and into their carriage back to London, or wherever they wished to go.

Then, free of the Stanleys forever, he'd go to Sarah.

He leaned back against the carriage squabs, closing his eyes, rehearsing his words in his mind.

"I want you in my life forever. I want to make you mine. You're my life, Sarah. Marry me. Be my duchess."

All throughout, bleak warnings nudged at the back of his mind: *Stanley is stubborn. Stanley won't allow you to sever the engagement. Stanley will ruin you.*

He closed his eyes for a long moment, then he looked at his brothers.

"I can't marry Georgina Stanley. I'm going to find a way to end our engagement."

They all stared at him as if this news, after a day full of revelations, was simply too much to take in.

"I can't do it," he told them.

"How will you get out of it?" Sam asked, seemingly the only one of Simon's brothers still capable of speech. "Will you use the existence of Bertram Stanley against them?"

Simon didn't want to lower himself to Stanley's level—to use extortion to fight extortion. And yet he was the head of this family...How far would he go to save his brothers and sister? Far enough to compromise his principles?

Probably.

Yes.

"I don't know," he told Sam softly. "Should I?"

"No!" Theo roared.

Everyone swiveled to face Theo.

"Don't do it, Trent. That kind of coercion is not in your nature. You are the most honest, honorable person I know. I'd rather see the truth about me exposed than to see you renounce your morals."

"So would I," Mark said, his expression hard.

Luke stared out the window to avoid meeting Simon's gaze. "And I. Wouldn't want to be the cause of you tarnishing your spotless morality, Trent."

"I've no desire to see Stanley spread rumors about our family," Simon told them. "But I don't love Miss Stanley. I never will. I can't marry her."

"Then don't," Luke said, as if it were that easy.

"There's someone else," Simon said in a low voice. "Another woman I care deeply for. After I break it off with Miss Stanley, I intend to propose to her."

"Really? Who is it?"

Simon glanced at Theo to see him frowning in confusion.

He took a deep, steadying breath. Other than Sam, their reactions would be filled with shock, surprise, disbelief. Even Luke's reaction would be so, given how shallow he believed Simon's feelings for Sarah were.

This would be the first set of reactions of many that would come, from everyone he knew and from people he didn't know as well. He'd deal with them all, starting with his brothers right now. Because he'd changed. He would no longer hesitate to shout his love for her from the rooftops. He wanted everyone to know.

"Sarah," he said, his voice steady and firm. "Sarah Osborne."

Simon's confrontation with the Stanleys had to wait due to the ball at their neighbor's house that night. Canceling their attendance at the ball would have set tongues wagging, and when word got out about the breaking of his betrothal, Simon wanted it to be on his terms.

Simon could only stomach one dance with Georgina, but that didn't stop every other gentleman in attendance from dancing with her. Mr. and Mrs. Beardsley were holding a house party this summer, and several men Simon hadn't seen since he'd left London approached him.

The Duke of Dunsberg was one of them. Simon had retired to the card room for a brief respite from it all when the older duke approached with a grin on his heavily weathered face.

"Well, Trent. I've just finished dancing with your lovely betrothed. I must congratulate you—she is a rare find indeed, a true diamond of the first water." Snatching a glass of brandy from the tray of one of the passing servants, Dunsberg settled in the seat beside him and gave him a rueful glance. "Now that you're joining the ranks of our fellow peers wallowing in connubial bliss, I suppose that'll leave me as one of the few unattached dukes in the country."

Simon wasn't going to correct Dunsberg about the status of his engagement. But he felt itchy and unsettled, like thousands of tiny ants crawled under his skin. God knew, he wanted to tell the man. He wanted the whole damn thing over with. Now.

"Why did you never marry?" Simon asked him instead, deliberately turning the direction of the conversation.

Dunsberg regarded the liquid, swirling it in his glass. "Ah, well." He slid Simon a wry look. "I was like you once, though I didn't lose my own father until I was forty. But all the ladies were well aware that I would be a duke one day, and for ten years, at least, the matchmaking mamas emerged in full force every Season to plot my downfall."

He took a sip of brandy. "But I wasn't interested in marriage then. Those were wild times. No doubt you've heard much about them from stories of your parents."

Simon made a small noise of agreement.

"And…" Dunsberg frowned into his glass. "Well, I suppose I found all of it a trifle distasteful. As if I weren't a human being but my title was some kind of prize they were all vying for."

"Yes." Simon understood that completely.

"So I avoided being shackled at all costs. Eventually they gave up, for the most part." Dunsberg chuckled softly. "Now, at the age of forty-nine, I finally feel ready to find a wife…but…" He shrugged. "I suppose I just haven't found the right lady as yet."

Simon raised his glass. "I wish you the best of luck in your search."

Dunsberg chuckled. "I should concede defeat. I am too

old. Ladies are attracted to the young and virile. Look at me"—he gestured to his wrinkled and pitted face—"the years have not been kind."

"You're still a duke."

"Right. Yet to find a creature as lovely as the one you have snagged for yourself... well, I doubt such a blessing is in store for me."

"You never know," Simon said.

They talked for a while longer, then Simon excused himself to return to the ballroom.

The evening felt interminable, but he managed to endure it without anyone—besides his brothers—knowing something was amiss. Still, it was closing in on dawn when they returned home. Exhausted, everyone went straight to bed, except Simon, who paced his bedchamber, wanting to go outside, find Sarah, take her in his arms, and tell her everything.

But he needed to break with Georgina first. When he went to Sarah, he wanted to be a free man, a man who could lower himself on one knee and proclaim his neverending adoration to the woman he loved.

Tomorrow. Tomorrow would be the day he'd reveal all.

Chapter Twenty

$\mathcal{S}$imon awoke from a short, restless sleep and asked one of the footmen to have Lord Stanley meet him in the library after the older man breakfasted. Simon was still in the library just before noon, mulling over accounts at his desk, when a knock on the door finally heralded a haggard-looking Stanley.

After he bade the man to be seated and offered him a drink, he got right to the point.

"I'm not going to marry your daughter."

Stanley's eyes went ice cold. He stared at Simon. Simon gazed back at him, keeping his expression blank. He didn't know how long they sat there, staring at each other.

Finally, Stanley's lips twisted. When he spoke, his words were soft. Calm. "Are you sure that's what you want, Trent? Are you prepared for the repercussions of this decision?"

"The only repercussions should be the increased happiness of the parties involved, Stanley. Mine and your daughter's."

"Her happiness revolves around her upcoming marriage. To you."

"That's nonsense. She feels nothing for me."

Stanley raised a brow. "Do not tell me you have fallen victim to romantic tripe regarding your future wife, Trent. You know, perhaps better than I do, that in our class there are more important factors than romance when choosing a bride. You have a dukedom to consider."

Simon almost smiled. He did indeed have a dukedom to consider. One that Sarah would manage with grace and aplomb. One that he wished to continue to manage only with her by his side.

"I have come to the conclusion that for the overall happiness and well-being of all the people who depend upon me, Miss Stanley is not the right choice."

Stanley's expression soured even more. "You're deranged. Of course Georgina is the right choice. I have groomed her for this very position."

Simon leaned forward, resting his forearms over the papers on his desk. "That's just it. You've groomed her to be a peer's wife, Stanley. But not *my* wife. With my title comes my family and its reputation, and all the eccentricities weaved into that."

Stanley shrugged. "Georgina's entry into your family will only help its reputation."

Simon's smile was wry. "I don't care about that. You see...I have spent most of my life trying to clear my family's name. And do you know what? I am finished with that. My family is odd, certainly. We have struggled with more than our share of difficulties. But my family is mine, and if anyone dislikes them or wishes to judge them, I would thank them to stay well clear of the Hawkinses."

"Are you implying—?"

"I'm not implying anything. I am telling you that I am sick and tired of people trying and convicting my family members of crimes against polite society. I am finished. From now on, I will no longer try to correct my family members' alleged wrongs. From now on, I have only one thing to say to those of you who will condemn my siblings or my parents: to hell with you."

"Is that what you're going to say when the truth about your brothers' and sister's parentage is revealed?"

"I am hoping that, as a man of honor, you will see the wisdom in my decision not to marry your daughter, and that you will choose not to reveal that information. There is no point. Unless the idea of ruining the lives of innocents appeals to you."

"We had a deal, Trent."

"Not exactly. You attempted to extort a marriage out of me, and I allowed it for a while. But no more."

Stanley tilted his head, gulped the last of his drink, and smacked his glass down on the desk as he rose. "You will regret this decision. Mark my words, you will regret it."

He swiveled and stormed out, slamming the door so hard the window rattled. Simon sat there for some moments, composing himself, then he went to look for Georgina. He found her on the far reaches of the lawn with her mother, Esme, and his four brothers, who'd clearly taken pity on him and brought the ladies out into the lovely summer day. Servants had set up a variety of archery targets, and they were taking turns at shooting.

As he approached, Georgina let an arrow fly, then squinted at the distant target and squealed. "Ooh! I do believe I hit it that time!"

Mark grinned at her. "I do believe you did."

Seeing Simon, Georgina hurried toward him. She was dressed in white muslin trimmed with cornflower blue ribbons that matched her eyes. Her blond curls shone beneath her crisp white wide-brimmed hat, and a healthy color glowed on her cheeks.

She was a flawless English rose. On the outside, at least. Even now, he wasn't sure about the inside. She hadn't shown him anything of herself but what she wanted him to see.

"Oh, Trent! Where have you been? We are having such fun!"

"It certainly looks like it," he told her, taking in the scene. Theo was helping Lady Stanley nock her arrow. Esme carried a bow slung over her shoulder and was selecting an arrow from the long table. Even Luke was there, but he hung back from the action, standing under the shade of a sycamore tree, a faint smirk on his face as he studied the proceedings and sipped at a glass of what appeared to be lemonade.

Luke met his gaze and gave him a slight nod, but the cynical expression on his face didn't change.

Simon turned back to Georgina. "Will you walk with me?"

"Oh...of course." She cast a longing glance back toward the table, where Esme was talking to Theo about the arrows. "Mama," she called, "Trent and I are going for a walk. We'll be back..." She gave Simon an enquiring glance.

"Soon," he supplied.

"Soon!" she said.

"Oh, do take all the time you need," Lady Stanley crooned, waving them off.

Giving Georgina his arm, Simon turned his back on his family and began to walk, taking care not to enter the area where Esme and Theo were shooting.

They were well out of sight of the party when they stepped onto the bridge over the stream, heading back toward the house. At the top of the arched bridge, Simon stopped, then rested his hands on the rail and gazed down at the flow of the stream. Georgina duplicated his every move.

Ahead, the willow trees that grew on the banks sloped toward the water, their long branches reaching across the stream toward each other, like lovers seeking a caress.

He felt no need to use small talk to delay the inevitable. Instead, he spoke quietly and got right to the point. "Georgina, I think it would be best if we called off our engagement."

Her pink lips parted, and she blinked at him several times.

"What?" she finally breathed.

"I cannot marry you."

"Yes you can!"

"I'm sorry. I cannot."

"Why?"

He tried to make his voice gentle. "I don't love you. I am sorry."

"Oh." Her chest seemed to deflate, and she matched his gentle tone with hers when she spoke again, patting his hand. "That's all right, Trent. I don't love you, either.

That little thing shouldn't get in the way of our marriage, though."

Her words stunned him for a moment, but he gathered himself quickly. "You don't understand. I don't wish to enter into a marriage without genuine affection."

"Why not?"

"I just don't, Georgina."

"If that is the case, then why did you propose to me?"

Well, then. She really didn't know the reason. He considered his answer for a long moment, then told her a half-truth. "Your father thought it would be the perfect match. He made me an offer I couldn't refuse at the time. But now... things have changed."

He thought of Stanley's rage. How the baron wouldn't hesitate to spew his venom about all of Simon's siblings.

He closed his eyes, remembering how his brothers had demanded that he not compromise his morals to save them.

Georgina had been pondering his words, and now she asked, "Why did you change your mind?"

Her reaction was far less emotional than he'd expected. Obviously he did not know or understand this lady at all.

"I've learned in the past few weeks how important it is for me to have someone I love at my side."

Her eyes narrowed. "Is there someone else? A mistress, perhaps? Mama taught me that I should never begrudge my husband his mistress. She has got along quite well for years with my father and his mistresses. She told me it is better if he has someone to turn to for physical release, because it removes the burden of his unwelcome advances."

Simon tried not to grimace, not wanting to think about the carnal lives of Lord and Lady Stanley. He remembered his parents screaming at each other about their paramours. Whenever one of his parents learned about one of the other's lovers, it lodged another shard of glass into that parent's soul. By the time his father had died, they'd both been so broken, Simon could hardly look at either of them without feeling their pain inside himself.

His mother had healed somewhat after his father died. She'd let her children—even her husband's mistress's children—help with that. He knew now that that was part of why she'd become so "eccentric" in her decision to always keep them close.

"So," Georgina continued, "if you should decide to keep your mistress once we are married, I shall not be put out."

Put out? Really? He raised a brow, remembering his mother sobbing, flailing out with fists at his father, his father's retaliatory hit, and his mother's blackened eye the next day.

"Georgina, you're not understanding me. We're not marrying. I've made the decision and it's final." When she didn't have a ready answer for that statement, he added, "I am sorry."

She turned back to the rail and gazed out over the stream. The afternoon sun shone on the water, making its ripples sparkle and glitter.

"I thought you should be the one to formally break our engagement to the public. It will be the best way to keep the scandal contained."

She gave a short, scoffing laugh. "You have informed my father of this, I assume?"

"I have."

"And?"

Simon sighed. "And nothing. He's no choice but to accept it. As do you."

"No," she said quietly. Then she pushed off from the railing and turned to look up at him. "No. I won't accept it."

"You must."

"But I want to be a duchess!"

"I am sorry I cannot assist in your endeavor to become one."

"I was promised a duke, and I will accept nothing less."

"So it is true, then." Simon wasn't surprised, but to hear confirmation of it voiced out loud felt like sandpaper scrubbing his skin. "I *am* just a title to you."

Her eyes seemed to shoot icy blue sparks at him. "You are a duke."

"I am a *man*."

Her lips were tight, but her voice was deadly quiet. "You will *not* do this to me, Trent. You cannot offer everything and then just turn around and throw it all away based on some ridiculous notion that you don't love me. I won't accept it, I tell you!"

"You haven't any choice," he said again.

She stamped her foot. "Change your mind. I insist!"

"No. I'm sorry."

"Ugh!" she cried in frustration. "I'm going to my father. *He'll* make you change your mind."

"You may go to your father," he said calmly, "but I won't change my mind."

"Then he'll make you suffer. We'll all make you suffer!"

He gave her a bland stare. He could manage the wrath of all the Stanleys combined with Sarah by his side.

She stamped her foot again. "This is your last chance," she growled, rage deepening the color on her cheeks.

"Threats against me won't work for you. Nothing will. I will not marry you."

She made another frustrated *humph*, stamped her foot again, and spat, "Rot in hell, Trent," before spinning away and storming off toward the house.

The sun had settled high overhead, beating down on the cart Robert Johnston drove with Sarah seated beside him. She dipped her head so her bonnet brim would shade her face from the penetrating rays.

When Mrs. Hope had asked her to make this journey to Birmingham to fetch a collection of new linens she'd ordered last month, Sarah had agreed, thinking that a brief time away from Ironwood Park would be good for her. She hadn't expected Robert would be her driver. She'd also expected one of the housemaids to accompany her, but Mrs. Hope said that everyone was busy with the houseguests, and two maids had the day off, so she'd be shorthanded as it was.

So the day after rejecting his proposal and accidentally pouring out all her wretched misery to him, Sarah found herself side by side with Robert Johnston on the bench of a cart on an errand that would last well into the evening hours.

They'd traveled mostly in silence all morning, Robert working the horses, Sarah turned away from him and staring out over the landscapes they passed. Green, fertile farms. Tiny villages with timbered houses. Willow-herbs blooming with splashes of pink. Fields of clover and forget-me-nots, and clumps of blue fescue. Copses of elms...sycamores...oaks. She could name almost every plant and tree that they passed, thanks to her father, and she passed the time by listing them in her mind and categorizing them and saving the details of those she couldn't name to ask her father about later.

That way, she didn't have to think about how mortified she was to be sitting beside Robert Johnston, the person she'd least wanted to come in contact with today.

It was now past noon, and they were still driving. She'd never been to Birmingham, but she'd heard from the other servants that the drive took about half a day. They'd left at dawn, which meant they were closing on seven hours now. Seven interminable, miserable hours.

She glanced at Robert. "Are we almost there?"

"Ah...not yet." He didn't look at her but doggedly remained focused on the horses.

Suddenly, every alarm bell in her body seemed to go off at once. She stiffened in her seat.

"Robert?"

"Mmm?"

"Is something wrong?" She looked in the direction he was staring—the team of four horses—but they all looked hardy enough. Though she wasn't an expert on horses like he was. "Is something wrong with one of the horses?"

"No, Sarah. Nothing is wrong with the horses." Gradually, he slowed the animals to a walk. When they were plodding along at a far more sedate pace, the sounds of their clomping hooves subdued, he stared straight ahead and said, "I need to speak with you about something."

She stifled an inward groan. In a way, she wished

he'd hated her after what she'd revealed to him yesterday. She wished his image of her perfection had been shattered. Instead, he'd gently comforted her. Whatever anger he had possessed seemed to be directed toward Simon, not her.

Gripping her hands in her lap, she nodded.

"I went to your father yesterday."

She flinched. Oh, good Lord. "Again?"

"Aye. I told him everything."

"What?" she gasped. No. Oh, no. Her father... She knew he'd learn about her pregnancy at some point, but she wasn't sure how he'd respond to it. She'd wanted to have a firm plan in place before she told him to limit his worry... and his disappointment in her.

Robert's expression didn't change. "I told him you were with child by the duke."

Heaviness settled thickly in her chest, like someone was pouring cooling iron into her lungs. Her father knew. He hadn't arisen this morning to see her off. She hadn't even seen him last night—she'd worked late at the house, and when she'd returned, he'd already been abed. Did he hate her now? Think of his own daughter as a whore?

Who knew how Robert had portrayed her relationship with Simon?

She turned slowly, looking at Robert with new eyes. He'd revealed her secret. He'd told her father something it was her right alone to reveal.

"How could you?" she whispered. She shook her head and looked away from him, her hands clenched tight in her lap, her eyes stinging, unable to communicate to him how betrayed she felt.

"It was for your own good, Sarah. Did you think you

could hide it from him forever? Better sooner than later, I say. So we can protect you. Save your reputation."

Foolish men. She had no reputation to save.

"We spoke at length and finally determined our best option," Robert continued. "*Your* best option."

She swung her head around to stare at him with narrowed eyes.

He took a deep breath. "We came to the conclusion that you and I must marry. Immediately. It is the only way."

"The only ... *way*?" she repeated faintly.

"Yes. To save your position and status at Ironwood Park."

Her mouth dropped open.

"It is also the only way to legitimize the child—everyone will believe that he is mine," Robert continued, "and I will not deny it. I'd do that for you, Sarah."

"Oh, God," she whispered.

"Your father was thankful that I would sacrifice so much for you."

He said it as if he believed she should be thankful, too. But her mind was swirling—full of betrayal and fear and hopelessness. "So you ... you're kidnapping me?"

His eyes widened. "Of course not. I'm simply taking you to Scotland so we can be married without delay. Without wasting the weeks it would require for the reading of the banns were we to marry in England. Before you swell with child and the speculation begins."

She didn't say anything. She couldn't think, couldn't process what was happening.

"Your father said you would come to your senses on the journey. That you would ultimately agree."

She stared at him in wide-eyed disbelief. Was that what this swirling madness in her head was? The process of coming to her senses?

"Mr. Osborne and I spoke for hours. Believe me when I say this is the best solution for you. The only solution that will assure your future. The child's future. You don't wish to raise a bastard, do you?"

"I..." She closed her mouth, still unable to speak through the jumble of words cluttering up her throat. She stared ahead. So...they weren't going to Birmingham, after all. They'd passed Birmingham and were headed north. To Scotland.

"Mrs. Hope?" she managed.

At that, Robert grinned. "Your father and I went to her with our idea. Don't worry—we didn't tell her about the child, though."

Oh, thanks for that, Sarah thought bitterly.

"As soon as she heard the plan to whisk you away to Scotland so we could be married, she thought it was all very romantic. She told us she'd help us in any way we required."

"So...she lied to me."

"I wouldn't put it like that."

"She tricked me." Even Mrs. Hope had betrayed her.

"She *helped* us," Robert said quietly. "You know all the servants were well-aware of our courtship."

Sarah closed her eyes, remembering the snide comments from the other maids, the smirks from the footmen, the comments from Esme...She'd simply brushed them off.

A courtship? Was that what this had been?

She gazed at the winding ribbon of road stretched out

before them. The road to Scotland. Had she been on this road all along?

If only she could find a way off of it. But towering walls stood on both sides, hemming her in. There were no forks in the road, no intersections. No options.

Perhaps Robert was right. There was no other way.

Chapter Twenty-One

❦

Simon hadn't seen any sign of Sarah all day, and after Georgina stomped off in her temper, he itched to hurry off in search of her. Her father would know where she was. Or perhaps Mrs. Hope.

But he lingered at the stream for a few minutes, shaking off his surprise at Georgina's behavior, bracing himself for the inevitable unpleasantness that the Stanleys would lay on the Hawkinses now.

Except for his mother, his whole family was still here. Tonight he'd bring them together—with Sarah, of course—and devise a plan about what to do.

But first...Sarah. He needed to reveal his heart to her. It couldn't wait any longer.

He began walking in the direction of her father's cottage, but he hadn't gone far before he saw Mr. Osborne's telltale straw hat peeking over a box hedge. Simon had always liked Osborne—the man took a special pride in the appearance of Ironwood Park and was passionate about his work. He worked hard and made good decisions, and Simon respected him for those qualities. He also respected the close relationship that Sarah seemed to have with him. Never once had Sarah made a disparaging remark about her father. By all appearances, he seemed to be a doting parent. Sarah had told him that was because she was the only family he had left, and that she doted on him as well, for the same reason.

Hurrying toward the older man, Simon found him heatedly discussing the use of stable manure as fertilizer with one of the under gardeners.

"Mr. Osborne," he hailed.

Osborne went silent at the sound of his voice. Slowly, he turned his head and looked at Simon. Then, he turned back to the gardener, speaking in lowered tones. The other man immediately strode off after a quick bow in Simon's direction.

Osborne turned fully to him and gave him a perfunctory nod. "Your Grace. How may I help you?" His words were polite but his tone was not, and though Simon had believed that the man knew nothing about his relationship with Sarah, he now wondered if that were true.

"I'm looking for Sarah," he told Osborne. "Do you know where I might find her?"

"Yes."

Simon waited for the man to continue, but he just stood there, looking at him, his eyes squinting at him under the shade of his hat brim.

"Where is she?" he asked.

"Scotland."

"Scotland?" He shook his head in confusion. "What do you mean?"

Osborne's leathery skin twitched in the vicinity of his jaw. When he spoke, it sounded as if he was forcing each word out through a tiny tube.

"She is going to Scotland to be married."

"Married? To whom?" Simon asked in bewilderment.

"Robert Johnston," the man gritted out.

No. That was...*No.* Impossible.

Osborne's eyes narrowed further, and he pointed a dirt-smudged finger at Simon. "I would thank you not to look at me like that, Your Grace. As if you are surprised. Your actions led to this. *Your* actions forced my daughter into this."

"What are you saying?" Simon pushed the words through his closing throat.

Osborne shook his head in disgust. "You compromised her. My sweet, innocent, lovely Sarah. You..." He turned his face away, then turned back, his blue eyes—eyes like his daughter's—shining with unshed tears. "Never mind." His voice was lower now but rough with emotion. "I promise you, once she is married, she will keep her distance from you. I hope you will show her enough courtesy to do the same."

Simon's mind worked rapidly. Why would Sarah do this? She'd told him she possessed no aspirations of marriage, and he was certain she didn't have feelings for Johnston. How had Simon's actions forced her into marriage? Unless...

Oh, God. *Unless Sarah was with child.*

Sarah's child. *His* child.

But if that were the case, why go to her father? Why go to Robert Johnston? Why hadn't she come to him?

Those questions would wait. For now...he had to find her. Had to stop the damn wedding.

Unless it was too late.

"When did they leave?" he snapped at Osborne.

"This morning."

Simon gave him a short nod, then he took a step forward. "Listen to me, Osborne, and listen closely. I am leaving this instant. I am going to Scotland. I am going to stop this marriage."

Osborne opened his mouth to speak, but Simon cut him off.

"She cannot marry Robert Johnston," he said, spitting out the other man's name. "Because she is going to marry me."

Osborne spluttered in surprise. "But you're —you— engaged—someone else—can't—"

"There is no one," Simon informed him. "There never has been anyone else for me. I love her...and I... love..." The child. *Their* child. Emotion welled up in him so fast he could hardly speak. When he did, it emerged as a shaking whisper. "Sarah is everything to me."

With that, he swiveled around and headed toward the stable, his chest vibrating with the truth of his words.

Simon rode like the hounds of hell nipped at his heels. He rode for long hours, stopping only to change horses and only late at night when he was so tired he worried he might fall off the horse.

On a foggy late morning two days later, he rode into the village of Gretna Green, not knowing what he'd find. Maybe Sarah and Johnston were here now. Maybe they weren't here yet. Maybe they'd already married and were heading back to Ironwood Park. He hadn't encountered them, but there were those bits of time he hadn't been on the road and there were certainly other times they hadn't been on the road. It was possible they'd passed one another unknowingly.

But he hoped not.

The hard riding had stripped him of all emotion, all feeling. Except hope. Hope was all he had left.

He rode to the famed inn where the blacksmith of Gretna Green had married runaway brides and grooms for the past sixty years. The man had died last year, and the position of the Gretna Green Parson had been handed over to his grandson-in-law, a Mr. Elliot, who performed ceremonies in the inn, the largest establishment in the village, set among a tidy row of mostly old clay cottages and a few modern stone houses.

As Simon dismounted, a sallow-faced young man appeared at the door of the place. Securing his horse, Simon removed his hat and greeted him. "Are you Mr. Elliot?"

"Aye, sir."

"Have you performed any marriages here in the past twenty-four hours?"

Elliot regarded him for a moment, then said, "Nay, I havena. Much to that lad's disappointment." He angled his pointed chin toward the lawn. Simon followed the movement, squinting at the dark figure slouched beneath a tree in the distance.

He strode toward the man, and as he drew closer he recognized Robert Johnston's bearing and his dark hair.

The coachman straightened as Simon approached, and his features drew tight as he recognized Simon.

"Your Grace," he said quietly. Then he shook his head, blinking as though Simon were some apparition he was trying to make disappear. "What are you doing here?"

Simon hadn't ridden all this way to have a pleasant chat with Robert Johnston. He ignored the man's question. "Where is she?"

"Sarah?" Johnston squinted his eyes at him as if he was confused. "You're looking for Sarah?"

Simon's hands fisted at his sides as he struggled for calm. "Where is she, Johnston?"

"Why would you come here...to Gretna Green... looking for Sarah? You're the one who..." Johnston's features went taut again, and his eyes narrowed.

Simon took a step closer, tapping the brim of his hat against his thigh. He addressed the man with slow speech, as if he were speaking to a child. "I need to speak with Sarah Osborne."

Johnston's lip curled. "Why? So you can ruin her all over again? So you can leave her broken and scattered to the winds, with no one to turn to?" He shook his head and added bitterly, "I'm not going to be there to pick her up the next time."

Simon stared at the other man, shaken. Had he done that? Broken her and thrown the pieces to the wind?

"I am trying to make this right."

"Right? How do you intend to make this right, Your Grace?" Now patent dislike shone in Johnston's gaze. "What will you do? Set her up in some fine townhouse in London as your secret mistress while you show off your high-and-mighty lady wife to the world? She's too good for that." He poked a finger into the air in emphasis. "Too. Good."

Only now did Simon see the half-empty bottle of whiskey nestled among the roots at the base of the tree. He looked back at Johnston. "You're drunk."

Johnston gave a negligent shrug.

Simon stepped forward, his gaze narrowed on the coachman. "She didn't go through with marrying you, I presume."

Johnston scowled and looked away.

Simon pushed his hand through his hair, which was already sticking up straight from the lack of both a comb and Burton's fastidious care. "Why did she refuse you?"

Johnston pressed his fingers to his temples. "Accused me of kidnapping her. Of not knowing her mind. Her heart. She left this morning on the mail coach."

"Where was it headed?"

"To England. Manchester."

"When did it leave?"

"Nine o'clock."

Hell. He'd passed the mail coach on the road less than an hour ago. Sarah had been inside.

That put him more than an hour behind it now.

He secured his hat and turned toward his horse.

As he walked away, Johnston called out to him. "For what it's worth, I quit. I shall never darken your doorstep—or your driver's seat—again."

Simon didn't answer him. Moments later, he turned back onto the road to England, spurring the horse into a gallop.

Sarah clutched her hands in her lap and stared at them. There were three other passengers in the mail coach—a married older couple and a young man heading to London. They'd tried to make conversation with her, and while she'd usually be eager to get to know other travelers, she didn't have it in her today to converse with strangers.

So she'd let their talk flow around her while she sat gazing at her clenched hands, feeling the enquiring gazes they sent her way, knowing they understood the significance of the mail coach fetching a single young woman from the inn at Gretna Green.

Robert had been kind to her during their journey north. He hadn't tried to touch her, had given her the time he thought she needed to come to terms with marrying him.

She'd remained quiet, for the most part. Trying to find some acceptance in her heart of what she couldn't deny was the best solution for her and for her baby. But she hadn't been able to.

Finally, as Robert had discussed their situation with the parson at Gretna Green, she realized she couldn't do it. Not to herself, and not to him. He deserved a woman who cared for him as much as he cared for her. Marriage might be what he wanted, but she knew she would never grow to love him in the way he thought she would. As much as she might like him—and she couldn't even say she liked him after how he'd betrayed her to her father— she could never love him.

He'd been hurt and confused. It was only providence that had the mail coach arriving at just the right time for her to slip onto it, paying the driver with part of the funds that Mrs. Hope, playing her part to the letter, had given her for the "draper" in Birmingham. As she'd reached into the purse to find the coins she needed, her hand had brushed over a tiny, folded paper.

When the coach was underway, she'd withdrawn the paper and unfolded it to find a note from Mrs. Hope.

Dearest Sarah,

I am so happy for you, my dear. Mr. Johnston is a lovely man and I wish you both many felicitations and happy years together. Please accept this little purse as a wedding gift from the staff at Ironwood Park, and I insist you take the next week off as a honeymoon for you and your new husband to enjoy together.

With all my love,
Mildred Hope

Swallowing hard, Sarah had refolded the note and tucked it back into the purse. She'd need to return all the money once she returned home.

And that was the plan. She'd return to Ironwood Park to tie up everything there. As soon as Simon was married, she wouldn't be welcome there anymore, but she intended to be far from the place by then.

But before she left, she was going to tell Simon how she felt. She was going to tell him that he was going to be a father—not because she wished to manipulate him or threaten him, but because he deserved to know.

The carriage jerked to a halt, and Sarah looked up in surprise. "What is it?" she asked no one in particular.

Mrs. Jones, the only other female occupant of the carriage, exclaimed, "Well, I never. Now we'll certainly be late!"

The single man—Sarah could not recall his name—pushed aside the curtain and peered outside. He bent closer, then turned to the rest of them, eyes wide. "There's a man on horseback outside. He looks rather wild. I think we're being robbed!"

Mrs. Jones pressed her knuckles to her mouth. "Highwaymen?" she squeaked.

And then a shout came from outside, in the vicinity of the driver. "Sarah? Sarah Osborne?"

The three other passengers stared at her. She raised her gaze to theirs.

Good God, what was Robert doing? She'd thought him above making a scene on a dusty country road.

The door of the carriage flew open, and the passengers all found themselves looking at a set of bright, wild green eyes staring out of a dirty face.

Not Robert Johnston, but a very dirty, very rumpled Duke of Trent.

He stared into the carriage. They all stared back at him. And then his eyes moved to Sarah.

"Sar-ah," he said in a broken voice, reaching his hand out to her.

"Y-your Grace. What are you doing?"

"I've come for you," he said simply.

She shook her head, blinking hard to make sure it was Simon, not Robert. She couldn't quite wrap her mind around the idea that she was gazing at him, that he was here.

Why was he here?

"But why?"

The corner of his lips cocked up ruefully. He glanced at the other occupants of the carriage and then back to her. "Come stand outside with me for a moment."

She let him lift her from the carriage and set her on the dusty ground. Then he grasped her hand and led her a short distance away. Off to the right, she saw his horse, standing with head hanging and dusted with foam from nose to tail. Wherever he'd come from, he'd been in a great hurry.

She looked up at him in concern. "I don't understand." She couldn't conceive of an emergency occurring at Ironwood Park that would send him chasing after her in the far reaches of the country.

He gazed down at her, his eyes softening. He cupped her cheeks in his hands, tilting her head up so she faced him.

"I've missed you so much," he whispered.

He'd never been demonstrative with people watching. And she knew people were watching—she could feel the fascinated gazes coming from the direction of the mail coach.

"Wha—what are you—?" she stuttered.

And then he bent down and kissed her.

She forgot the eyes watching them. She forgot she was standing in the middle of a road. She forgot that Simon was marrying someone else.

There was only him. His soft lips caressing hers, tentatively seeking, tasting. Moving against her with exquisite gentleness.

She wrapped her arms around him and returned the kiss, pouring all her love into it. Pouring all the secret hopes and desires she'd ever had into it.

He pulled away, touching his forehead to hers, and for long moments, they just stood there, sharing a space in the world they hadn't dared share for too many weeks, trading whispers of breath between them.

It felt so right.

And then reality returned. There were people watching. People who'd heard her call him "Your Grace." They were on a road somewhere in the far northern reaches of England.

And she wasn't sure what on earth Simon was doing. It wasn't like him to behave so openly. He was ever conscious of listening ears, of seeing eyes, of the potential for scandal.

Reluctantly, she pulled away from him. He dropped his hands from her cheeks.

"I don't understand," she whispered.

"Why..." He glanced down in the vicinity of her stomach. "Why didn't you tell me, Sarah?"

She stiffened.

"No," he said, sliding his hands up and down her arms. "Don't."

"Who...?" she choked.

"No one told me. Your father..." He shook his head. "He didn't tell me, exactly, but I was able to derive the truth from what he did say."

She closed her eyes.

"Why didn't you tell me?" he repeated.

"I didn't want to put you in an untenable position," she said dully. "I didn't want to force you to make choices that would hurt you... or your reputation."

He blew out a harsh breath and his fingers tightened over her arms. "My reputation has no importance when compared to you, do you understand that?"

Gazing at him bleakly, she shook her head.

His chest rose and fell. "Sarah, I love you. So much."

She looked hard at him, trying to see, to understand his words. The expression on his face, open and raw and honest, made her breath catch.

"I love you," he repeated. Then, in a louder, stronger voice, "I love you."

She struggled to breathe—because he'd said the words so loudly everyone from the mail coach must have heard. There was no air in the atmosphere. It had all been sucked away. Her breaths came in little gasping spurts.

Silence, and then she pushed out the only word she could manage through the thick well of emotion in her throat. "Why?"

Simon blinked at her, then shook his head, a slight smile on his face. The dimple in his chin winked at her. "Why do I love you?"

"Yes...why?"

"There are too many reasons—reasons I intend to spend the rest of my life making you understand. For now...Because you are kind and honest and loyal. Because you see beneath Trent straight through to the man I am. Because you understand me. Because you love me for who I am, not because of the title I hold. Because I can reveal my heart to you. Because you are the person I want to lie beside every night, and you are the only person whose face I want to see when I wake every morning."

She blinked back tears. "It cannot be, Simon," she whispered. "You are betrothed to another."

"No. I ended the engagement."

"What?" she gasped. "But...your family. Your brothers...The secret..."

"My brothers understand. I could never love Georgina Stanley, could never be happy with her. They have supported my decision. There is only one woman I want. You."

A tight sensation pulled at her chest. "Is this because of the child?"

"I broke it off with Georgina before I knew about the child."

She inhaled a full, deep breath—somehow the air had returned to the atmosphere. Relief flooded her as she realized he hadn't come all this way with the intention of hiding her away somewhere to cover up her pregnancy.

"I finally learned to listen to my heart, Sarah. To really listen, like you told me to that night in London. The child didn't affect my decision in the least. But I am not unhappy. I want you to be the mother of my children." Suddenly, he sucked in a harsh breath. "I just realized something. My God."

"What is it?"

He looked down and spoke in a low voice so that the people in the carriage, yards away, couldn't hear. "I never...came inside a woman before you. I was meticulously careful to prevent conception—with every woman, it was always at the forefront of my mind." He blinked hard. "I always thought of Sam and what he endured as a boy and how I wouldn't do that to a child. But with you...I wanted you so badly, to be as close to you as a man could be to a woman. That concern never crossed my mind. Now I know why."

She gave him a quizzical frown. "Why?"

"Because I knew even then...at least a part of me did. My body knew that you were mine. My heart knew. It just took a while longer for my head to catch up, for me to listen. But now that I have, I know the truth. I want you as my one companion for life. My wife."

"Your..." Her voice drifted away.

"Yes." His green eyes latched onto hers, and he sank to one knee before her, his hands trailing down her arms until his fingers wrapped around hers. He looked up at her, his green gaze overflowing with warmth and hope and love. "Sarah Osborne, will you marry me?"

She stared down at him for long moments that turned into minutes, her mind grasping onto the truth in bits and snatches.

Simon loved her.

Simon wasn't marrying Miss Stanley.

Simon wanted her. To be his wife.

"I love you, Simon," she finally breathed. "So much." She always had, ever since that day he'd rescued her from the blackberry bush.

He was still gazing up at her, but he closed his eyes in a long blink. When he opened them again, they were the shimmering green of emeralds. "Marry me, Sarah."

She nodded. Then she said, in a low, scratchy voice, "Yes."

Rising to his feet, he enfolded her in his arms. And as their lips met, cheers and shouts of "bravo!" erupted from the direction of the mail coach.

Chapter Twenty-Two

❖

$\mathscr{S}$imon and Sarah turned around once again and headed back up to Scotland, where there was no sign of Robert Johnston and where a seemingly unsurprised Mr. Elliot married them in a most efficient manner.

Simon spoke his vows solemnly and listened to Sarah as she said hers, her sweet, calm voice always such a balm to his soul. All the agony of the past few weeks slipped away as Elliot solemnized their bond before God.

Still dusty and dirty, they retired to the finest bridal chamber in the inn, where they bathed and ate their dinner, a simple meal of mutton stew, pigeon pies, and fresh bread.

Afterward, Simon removed Sarah's clothes and kissed her belly, marveling at the life that was being created within her. Then, he spent the night making love to his wife until they both fell asleep in sated exhaustion.

The next morning, Simon procured a carriage for them

to make the return trip to Ironwood Park. They moved diligently south, aware of the looming difficulty with Baron Stanley, but Simon refused to rush. They rose late and breakfasted, then paused on occasion to view the scenery and for picnic luncheons. In the evenings, they stopped at pleasant inns, where Simon gloried in bathing his wife, in feeding her morsels of dinner by hand, and then in worshiping her sweet body again and again.

Finally, on the fourth afternoon after their marriage, they entered through the tall iron gates that opened onto the vast property of Ironwood Park.

He glanced at Sarah, who stared straight ahead. Tiny lines of tension had formed around her mouth.

He took her hand in his. "Don't worry," he murmured.

She gave a shaky laugh. "I am trying not to."

He knew she had many fears regarding her return to Ironwood Park—from her father's reaction to how the staff would respond to her sudden elevation in status. In truth, he thought this might be even more difficult for her than the ultimate necessity of facing the *ton*. These were the people who mattered to her. The people she loved.

They rolled onto the graveled drive and the carriage drew to a halt. He turned to her and kissed her gently on the lips before slipping out of the carriage and holding out his hand to her.

She smoothed the skirt of her dress—one of the plain dresses she'd often worn before he'd taken her and Esme to London. Much to Sarah's chagrin, Johnston and her father had taken it upon themselves to pack her luggage in preparation for her abduction. They'd included her hairbrush and hairpins, her underthings, and her two extra muslin dresses. They'd avoided the clothes Simon had bought her in London, probably thinking them too rich for a Gretna Green marriage to a coachman.

She looked at Simon with desperate eyes.

"They'll hate me. They'll think I trapped you."

"If they believe that, then they're undeserving of your respect."

"I know...I'm just..." She looked past him to the stately façade of the house. "Mrs. Hope is waiting at the door," she gulped.

"Of everyone, you can face Mrs. Hope."

"Esme is there, too."

He glanced over his shoulder as his brothers came out of the front door to stand on the portico beside Esme and Mrs. Hope. Even Luke appeared—Simon had expected him to have gone to Wales in search of their mother by now.

Sarah's father emerged from the house—a place he seldom visited—wearing his broad-brimmed straw hat and looking decidedly uncomfortable.

And then the servants began to line up on one side of Mrs. Hope while Simon's family and Mr. Osborne clustered on the other, everyone's gaze directed toward the carriage. And the two of them.

"Oh, my Lord," Sarah squeaked.

But Simon grinned. His brothers had done this for him. They'd prepared Mr. Osborne and the staff so Sarah wouldn't have to face their shock and questions.

He grasped her hand. "Our people have come out to greet us. Our family."

She gave a small nod and allowed him to hand her down from the carriage. They walked between two of the massive columns and up the steps, Simon holding his wife's hand in a reassuring grip and feeling his grin grow-ing wide. This was the perfect way to present his duchess to his household. With everyone waiting for them, stand-ing with looks ranging from a stable boy's awe to Mrs. Hope's glowing happiness.

They reached her, and she gave a low curtsy. "Wel-come home, Your Grace," she said gravely.

Simon acknowledged her with a nod. Then he said, in a loud enough voice for them all to hear, "Good after-noon, Mrs. Hope. I would like to present my wife, Sarah Hawkins, the Duchess of Trent."

"Oh!" Mrs. Hope cried under her breath. She turned to Sarah, and her smile split her wrinkled face as she curtsied again. "And welcome home to you, too, Your Grace."

They walked down the line, and Simon watched ev-eryone, from Fredericks the steward to Burton, Simon's valet, all the way down to the most junior of the scullery maids, bow and greet their new mistress. None of them seemed surprised or upset to find Sarah in this position.

His talk to his brothers on the way home from Bordes-ley Green—about how he intended to erase the lines of separation society had drawn between him and Sarah—had sunk in. His brothers had prepared the household well.

Simon and Sarah circled back around to greet their family. His brothers slapped him on the back and gave Sarah brotherly kisses. Simon watched Mr. Osborne blink back tears as he gave his daughter a gruff hug. And then Sarah turned to Esme.

Sarah had told him that this was the relationship she worried for the most. Out of everyone, she feared Esme might never understand why Simon would marry some-one like her.

Esme looked at Sarah for a long moment. Then, a small smile curved her lips. "When Luke told me Trent had gone after you, I didn't believe it at first," she told Sarah softly. "I thought you and Mr. Johnston...well, I needed to mull it over for a while. You and Trent—the both of you hid it so well, Sarah, but the more I thought about it, the more I recalled those subtle clues. The way you looked at each other. The way you spoke to each other..." She gave a rueful shake of her head, but then she smiled a real smile that went all the way through to her hazel eyes, and whispered, "I once said you were the clos-est thing to a sister I have ever had. And now you really are my sister. I am so happy."

"I've always longed to have a sister like you," Sarah said. And they embraced.

Esme looked over Sarah's shoulder at Simon. "And thank the *Lord* you didn't marry that awful Georgina Stanley! She was the most horrid little brat I have ever had the displeasure of knowing!"

Not only was the statement utterly true, but such a hearty declaration coming from Esme's lips was so un-characteristic, Simon burst into laughter, as did his broth-ers.

They meandered inside, Mrs. Hope shooing everyone away and commanding Simon and Sarah to go upstairs to bathe away the grime of travel and to dress for an infor-mal luncheon that would be served in the parlor.

Inside his bedchamber, Sarah stopped to gaze around, her blue eyes round with wonder. Simon chuckled. "You look as though you've never been in here before."

"I *have* been in here before," she told him. "Many, many times. To change the linens or iron the draperies or dust the mantel."

"But this isn't the same," he said.

"Not at all."

"You'll come to know it in a different capacity now. But if you wish to do any ironing, I certainly won't begrudge you that."

She turned to him, grinning, but their conversation was interrupted by the servants carrying the bathtub and water to bathe and Sarah's London clothes fetched from her father's cottage. Burton entered wielding a pair of freshly shined shoes which he arranged in exact precision beneath the clothes that had been laid out for Simon to wear.

Then the valet turned to Simon. His brown eyes widening, he let out a heartfelt sob. "I am a failure, Your Grace. Look at you, just look! Your outward appearance as a duke of the realm is my duty, my responsibility, and you look like a...like you've been rolling about in a meadow." With an expression of supreme disgust, he plucked a piece of grass out of Simon's hair, then held it between his thumb and forefinger and gazed at it as though it were a particularly revolting species of insect.

Simon grinned at Sarah, and she glanced away, smiling and blushing. He had, in fact, tumbled her in a meadow earlier today when they'd stopped for a picnic luncheon. He'd laid her on a blanket and tasted every inch of her sun-kissed skin. He'd made her come with his mouth and his tongue. Then he'd taken his pleasure with her on her back, then on her knees, then riding him, her hair tumbling around her shoulders and shining blue-black in the sunlight.

With effort, Simon turned his attention back to his poor, fastidious valet. "Burton," he said reasonably, "I have been traveling." He gestured to the steaming bathtub. "And please note that I am attempting to remedy my unseemly appearance. If you would kindly go away, then I could proceed."

Burton sniffed. "Very well, sir. I shall return in half an hour to shave you and assist you in dressing."

"Oh, no. You shall come when I summon you." Simon slid Sarah a look filled with heat and promise. "And you can be sure it'll be far longer than in half an hour."

"Yes, sir." Burton bowed stiffly to Simon and then to Sarah before slipping out the door, closing it with a tidy snap behind him. The other servants soon followed him out, and moments later, Simon found himself finally, blessedly, alone with his wife, who pushed a dark lock of hair out of her face and cast a longing glance at his enormous linen-lined copper bathing tub.

He gave her a wicked grin. "My bathing tub is large."

She gave it a considering look. "I've always thought it to be excessively so. Its size makes it all the more difficult for servants to fill."

"Be that as it may, a large tub does have some advantages." Reaching her, he began to undo the simple buttons of her dress.

"Such as?" she asked innocently.

He'd been right about her proclivities when it came to the bedchamber. She learned fast. And she was a vixen.

"Such as giving a certain duke the ability to share a bath with his wife."

The dress slipped off her shoulders, and he stroked the palms of his hands down her arms, pushing her sleeves all the way off as he did so. Her dress pooled on the floor, quickly followed by her petticoat and her stays and chemise, and finally, she stood before him, naked save her stockings and shoes.

He stepped back, taking in her long limbs, the curve of her waist, the high breasts, each one just large enough for his hand. "Do you know what an erotic vision you are?" he asked softly. "So beautiful."

Color rose in her cheeks as he came forward again and bent to his knees to remove the ribbons that held up her stockings and slowly rolled each stocking down her slender legs, his fingertips stroking her warm skin, his palms cupping the backs of her calves.

When the second stocking rolled past her knee, he saw it. The little scar from the scratch the blackberry bush had given her all those years ago. He pressed his lips to it, closing his eyes, remembering that day, how brave and sweet she'd been, even with deep scratches all over her. Her big blue eyes had roused his protective senses more than anything, made him want to take her home and make sure she was taken care of.

Slowly, he drew away and looked up at her, seeing the memory of that day in her eyes, too.

"Hold my shoulders," he commanded as he lifted her foot, removed her shoe, and finished rolling her stocking off. He felt the gentle pressure of her hands on him as he took off the other shoe and stocking in the same manner.

Now she was naked. Still in a crouch, he looked up at her again. She was gazing down at him, and now her blue eyes were full of heat.

She narrowed her eyes and shook her head slowly from side to side. "This is hardly fair."

"Oh?"

"I am completely naked."

"Oh yes, you are," he said, his voice saturated with pure male satisfaction.

"And you are fully clothed."

He looked down at himself. "So I am."

"I insist you join me in nakedness. At once."

He grinned up at her. "Demanding now, are you, little wife?"

"Not demanding," she said, "just willing to make a stand for justice."

"Then we shall have to remedy this atrocious wrong," he said.

He rose from his crouch, but he took his time, kissing the insides of her thighs, her mound, her hips, and her stomach where their child grew. He lingered there, thinking of her with his baby in her arms. He knew she'd be no Georgina Stanley—he'd had the distinct sensation that Georgina had intended to stow away their children in the nursery like most aristocratic mothers tended to do. Sarah would be as loving and attentive as his own mother had been. More so, because Simon would make damn sure she wouldn't have to bear any of the pain his mother had suffered from her and his father's infidelities.

"There is no one in the world more suited to be the mother of my child," he murmured.

He rose to his full height and discarded his clothes in short order. She watched him, her eyes dark with desire... and with love.

He went into the hot water first and pulled her in after him, settling her on his lap facing away from him, where he used one of the soft cloths covered with lavender-scented soap to bathe her, knowing that even lavender couldn't cover her innate fresh, sweet scent. Or taste.

He paid special attention to bathing the area between her legs, touching the tiny peak above her entrance with soft but sure strokes, knowing how wild it made her when he touched her there. She writhed, making ripples in the water as she gasped, "Simon!"

With his arms wrapped around her hips, he worked her with two hands. With one, he continued to stroke her with the cloth. Using the other, he parted her folds and slid two fingers inside her, feeling the slickness of her arousal despite the water that washed around her.

He was still learning her body—would be learning it forever, he knew. His own arousal, nestled between the cheeks of her bottom, was tight and throbbing, aching to fill her, to take her again.

He stroked the outer nub as he slid his fingers into her, through her folds, back inside again, moving his fingertips against her inner walls. He played her like a violin, until she was thrumming with pleasure, gasping with it, flushed with it. And then she came, her back arching, her body convulsing around him. He kept her still in the water with his arms tight around her body and felt every shudder, every contraction, as she moaned her release.

She came down from it, slumping back against him, her hands stroking the outsides of his thighs as the remnants of her orgasm shuddered through her. When she was finished, relaxing completely against his chest, he murmured into her hair, "We're not finished yet."

"Mmm," she said.

With a low laugh, he turned her around, lifting her and

adjusting her until she straddled his body over his thighs. She looked down at him, at his arousal, and gave him the wickedest erotic smile he'd ever seen. Somewhere in the water she found the cloth he'd used to pleasure her, and she took her time to cover every inch of it with copious suds.

He looked askance at her. "What are you planning to do with that, love?"

She didn't answer but laid the cloth out so it covered her hand and then plunged both her hands into the water to take his cock into her grip.

He was already so hard, so hot. She felt it, too, her eyes widening at the hardness, at the seeming impossible length of it.

And then, she began to stroke him.

With a low groan, he leaned his head back against the edge of the tub. Heat rushed through him, starting from her hands and licking up through his torso and out through his limbs. He thrust into her grip, a purely instinctual move his body couldn't control. And then his ballocks tightened, and he felt the bloom of pressure at the base of his spine that told him he was close to exploding.

With a swift movement, he thrust her hands away from him. Her eyes widened, but before she had a chance to say anything, he hauled her forward with one arm, lifting her so he could position his cock beneath her entrance. He found the notch of her sex and wedged his cockhead into it, grunting a little at the exquisite pleasure of that most sensitive part of him stroking her hot folds.

He grasped her hips and pressed her down over him.

Both their breaths released in a harsh rush. She froze. He froze. They stared at each other.

Then, she began to ride him. Leaning forward, she placed her hands on his shoulders for leverage, and with long, slow drags, she raised and lowered herself over him again and again. He kept his hands on her hips, guiding her, his fingertips kneading the tops of her buttock cheeks.

Now the water did splash over the edge of the tub, but Simon couldn't bring himself to care as Sarah bent forward to take his mouth. Her lips met his in a kiss that took his breath, and his awareness of his surroundings. There was only Sarah now. The sweetness of her enveloping him, covering him, bringing every part of him to levels of pleasure he hadn't known existed before she'd come into his life.

The pressure at the base of his back returned, this time a thousand percent more powerful than the last. It grew and tightened, a ball of roiling lust and love that centered around the woman in his arms, who loved Simon just as intensely as he loved her.

When he came, it poured from every physical part of him, and also from his heart and soul, his body wrenching in pleasure and release.

She collapsed over him, wrapping her arms tight around him, her cheek pressed to the side of his head. He gathered her tight against him, both of them trembling.

"I love you, Simon," she said, her breath a tickle against his earlobe. "I love you so much."

He buried his face in her hair and held her close, never wanting to let go.

It was two hours later when they came downstairs, Simon shaved and dressed in perfect, unwrinkled fashion by

Burton, and Sarah dressed in one of her London dinner gowns, her hair done elegantly by one of the maids, who'd gushed to her the whole time about how wonderful and romantic it was that she'd captured His Grace's heart.

She glanced over at him and felt the warm wash of his love. It was unavoidable—just from looking at him one could tell that he loved her. He made it clear to everyone that she had been charged with the care and keeping of his heart. He either couldn't hide it or didn't care to. Either way, it strengthened her, made her feel confident and...complete. She'd always wanted Simon, but she'd pushed that love for him into a corner of her heart, never even allowing herself to dream of one day being his wife.

"Come with me into the library for a moment," he told her, and she followed him into the dim room.

He went to the desk and unlocked it, pulling something from the drawer before straightening. "Give me your left hand."

She reached her hand out to him and watched as he slid the ring they found in the dower house onto her finger.

"But it's your mother's—" His fingers pressed over her lips, stopping her protest.

"This ring belongs to the Duchess of Trent. First my grandmother, then my mother. It was meant to be my bride's next. I know that wherever she is, she would want you to have this."

He brought her hand up to his lips and pressed a soft kiss to the ring on her finger. Then he let her go, and she felt the weight of the diamond-encrusted gold.

"I'll wear it until we find her," she said, "and if she wants it back—"

"She won't." Smiling, Simon enfolded her hand in his. "Let's go to dinner."

They walked into the parlor, and Sarah's heart brimmed as she looked at her family. She'd always secretly considered the Hawkins family hers, but now it was no secret. They were *legally* hers. And she adored each and every one of them.

Simon fetched them plates and went to the sideboard, where she pointed at various dishes and he filled their plates. And then they joined the family, sitting on the silk sofa—the same sofa the duchess had asked Sarah to sit upon so many years ago, when she was dirty and bleeding from the blackberry bush. This was the very room where she'd met all of them that day so long ago. This was the room where she'd discovered the identity of the boy who'd saved her.

She smiled at Simon as he handed her a plate, and they ate in silence for a few minutes.

It was Sam who spoke first. "The Stanleys are gone."

Simon nodded. "I expected they'd go."

"Ah, but I'd wager you didn't expect the manner in which they departed," Luke said with a chuckle. He raised his glass of wine and took a healthy swallow.

"What do you mean?" Simon asked.

The brothers exchanged looks, and Sarah's heart began to pound. Slowly, she lowered her fork to her plate.

"Well, who wants to be the one to break the news to him?" Luke asked, glancing around. When no one answered him, he said, "Me? Oh, very well." Shrugging, he turned back to Simon. "The day after you ran off to Scotland," he said, "so did Miss Georgina Stanley. With the Duke of Dunsberg."

"What?" Sarah gasped.

"That's right. Seems she was so intent on becoming a duchess, it didn't matter which duke she attached herself to. So she grabbed the first one that came along. Dunsberg called the afternoon you left, Trent, when all in the house was still in quite the uproar, and I expect she poured her poor broken heart out to him."

"What did her parents do when they found out?" Simon asked.

"Absolutely nothing," Mark said cheerfully.

"They wanted their daughter to be a duchess, and when she succeeded, they had no complaints," Luke said.

"But she didn't succeed in the way they'd planned!" Sarah exclaimed.

"And they're not going to like the scandal, surely," Simon said.

"If anything," Esme said, and they all turned to her, because it wasn't like her to speak up when they were in a group, "Georgina will be thrilled by this particular scandal. Imagine...jilted by the Duke of Trent only to fall into the arms of the Duke of Dunsberg. She'll simply thrive off all the attention she's bound to receive."

"I hope Dunsberg knows what he's got himself into," Simon said, shaking his head.

Luke waved his hand in dismissal. "Oh, I know Dunsberg. He can manage women. Even one as obnoxiously spoiled as Miss Stanley."

"I saw them together the night they disappeared," Mark said. "He seemed, well, quite *taken* with her."

Simon gave his brother a contemplative look. "He seemed taken with her even when she was engaged to me. But I don't think they know each other well."

Luke shrugged. "Does it matter? He is a duke. She wanted to be a duchess."

"And for Dunsberg's part," Sam said, "how could a forty-nine-year-old man resist the wiles of a twenty-year-old beauty proclaiming her undying love?"

Mark gave Sarah a blinding grin. "Well, let Dunsberg have her, I say. I'm much more pleased to have Sarah as my sister-in-law."

"Always thought of you as my sister when I was a boy," Theo said. "And I have to say, I always found it a little odd to think of you as a housemaid. Even Esme's companion. Now..." He shrugged and said simply, "it feels right."

She gave him a warm smile. "Thank you, my lord."

"Theo. Call me Theo."

Her smile widened. "Theo. I admit to being apprehensive about your reactions, but I am..." She took a deep breath and tried to control her roiling feelings. "I am so glad you have accepted me."

"As far as I'm concerned," Luke said, "this is the first time my brother has shown sense in a long while."

"Do you think so?" Simon asked.

"Of course."

Simon's thumbs moved in small circles over the edge of his wine glass. "It's just that Stanley still intends to reveal your parentage, Luke." He looked at Esme, realizing that she might not know about any of this. "Did they tell you?"

She gave him a solemn nod. "Yes. The night you left."

"Good. The fact is, we all need to come to a decision about how we're going to manage the repercussions of Stanley spreading his bile to the world."

Sam, who'd been leaning against the mantel, pushed off and stepped forward, holding out what looked like two sheets of parchment in his hand. "You have received a few letters, Trent."

"I'm sure I have many—"

"You'll wish to read these," Sam interrupted, "immediately."

With a bemused look, Simon took the two folded pieces of stationery. He read the first one in silence and then handed it to Sarah.

Trent,

   I am leaving this wretched place and finally marrying the duke who deserves me.

   If you, or anyone in your family, ever mentions the existence of the idiot Bertram Smith, and his link to my family, I shall bring down the wrath of the entire Dukedom of Dunsberg against you. Mark my words, Trent. You do not wish to trifle with me.

   Good-bye, and may we never see each other again for the remainder of our days on Earth,

                              Georgina Stanley,
                              Future Duchess of Dunsberg

"Goodness," Sarah whispered. "But how did Miss Stanley know you knew about Bertram?"

Simon glanced up at his brothers, who all looked away, except for Luke, who gave him a grin worthy of a Cheshire cat. "Bit of a slip of the tongue, perhaps?"

"Luke," Simon said warningly.

"What? The lovely Georgina is my half sister, after all."

I simply asked her what she thought of our eldest brother. When she looked confused, I clarified I meant our dear brother, Bertram Stanley, the idiot who resides at Bordesley Green."

"Good God. So not only did you tell her we knew about Bertram, but you also revealed that you were her half brother?" Simon asked.

Luke gave a soft chuckle. "It was fun, really, to see how many shades of green she could turn before she went off crying to her papa."

"We believe the second letter is a result of that conversation," Sam said, passing it to Simon.

Simon bent his head to read the second letter, and then, as he had before, he passed it to Sarah.

Trent,

No thanks to you, my wishes for my only daughter have come to fruition, and I am a happy and proud man. Her chosen duke, though neither as young nor as sound in body as you are, possesses a maturity and sense that I feel certain you never shall.

Regarding the unpleasantness we have discussed in multiple circumstances—I have changed my mind. I think it's best if society is left in the dark regarding certain people's *parentage.*

Therefore, the secret shall remain in my safekeeping. But understand this: it shall only remain safe for as long as you keep the secret regarding the identity of a certain B.S., who resides near Worcester. If, at any time, you reveal that man's identity, I shall not hesitate to publish the proof I carry with me regarding certain people.

I trust we are in understanding on this issue, but should you have any questions regarding our agreement, I shall remain in London for precisely one month, after which time I will be heading to Hampshire to Dunsberg's seat for a house party celebrating my daughter's nuptials. You may contact me in London, but I suggest you do not show your face in Hampshire, for yours will be an unwelcome visage indeed.

Stanley

Sarah looked up from the letter as Simon said, "They think we've turned the tables on them. Threatening them with openly revealing Bertram's identity."

"But we're not!" Theo exclaimed.

"No." Luke shrugged. "But why deny it? To give Stanley leave to blab all over England that he's my father." A sour look crossed his face. "No, thank you."

"Luke is right," Sam said. "We do as we planned—which is to remain quiet regarding Bertram Stanley, and Stanley will keep quiet, too."

"It is a reasonable solution." Simon pinned his three younger brothers with stares, one by one. "But that doesn't mean the secret is safe. Too many people know it."

Theo sighed. "In other words, our 'legitimacy' is safe for now, but it could be revealed at any time that we're baseborn."

Luke gave his youngest brother a scowl. "I take offense to that, Theo. I'm not baseborn." Giving a negligent shrug, he added lightly, "Just a bastard."

Theo rolled his eyes heavenward.

"But what am I?" Esme said softly.

They all turned to her.

"The only one who knows that is our mother," Simon told Esme.

"And we still don't know where she is," Sarah said with a heavy sigh.

"But," Luke said, "we have a lead. I have a name and location. I'm going to bring her home so she can damn well explain everything to us." Luke glanced at Sarah, and she saw the touch of gentleness behind the steel of his blue eyes. "I wanted to ensure you were safe and sound before I left."

"Oh, Lord Lukas. I *am* safe and sound."

Luke flinched. "Don't call me Lord Lukas anymore, Sarah. You're my sister now, so just Luke will do."

"Very well, Just Luke."

He gave her a wry look then turned back to Simon. "I'm pleased you did the right thing, but now I need to leave. I'm heading to Cardiff. I'll be gone by the time you wake tomorrow morning."

"Do you require anything?" Simon asked.

Luke raised a sardonic brow. "From you, Your Grace? From your unending wealth of resources? Why, thank you, but no. I'd prefer to do this one damn thing on my own."

Simon regarded his brother in silence for a moment. They all did. Finally, Simon gave a slow nod. "Very well. I suppose all I can do for you then is hope for you to return quickly, and with our mother at your side."

"Hear, hear." Sam held up his glass. And they all drank to Luke and their mother's swift return.

* * *

Sarah woke to see Simon standing by the tall window that looked out over the winding drive that led from the main road to the house. The heavy velvet curtains were parted, and the soft light of dawn seeped into the room.

She watched him for a long moment. He stood there, his form tall and powerful. He was a powerful man, inside and out.

One who could have had almost any woman in England. And he'd chosen her. She wondered when she'd stop feeling so awed by that. Probably never.

Rising, she slipped a robe over her shoulders and went to stand beside him. He moved her in front of him, tucking her against him so the hard length of his body pressed against her.

Safe and sound. Now, enclosed in Simon's arms, she realized she'd never felt safe in her life, until now. It was a heady sensation.

It wasn't difficult to see what he was gazing out at. She looked down just as Luke finished tightening the straps of his saddlebag and then mounted his horse.

They watched in silence, Sarah secure in Simon's embrace, as Luke walked the horse down the road that led away from Ironwood Park.

Then she whispered, "He'll find her."

"Do you think so?" Simon's voice was musing.

"Yes."

But her own voice wasn't as confident as she would have liked it to be, and she felt the heaviness of Simon's sigh behind her.

"I engaged Grindlow's services again. I asked him to follow Luke. To conduct his own investigation regarding this Morton fellow Mother left Ironwood Park with."

"How do you think Luke will feel about that?" she asked him.

"He'll probably be infuriated. But it's not my duty to pander to Luke's self-absorption. I want to find my mother, and I'll use whatever means I have to do so."

Sarah could understand that. "I still hope that Luke is the one who finally finds her."

"So do I."

"He seems better. Than he was in London, at least."

"Yes." Simon sighed. "Sometimes it's hard to say, though. Is he still drinking too much? Gambling? There's really no way to know."

"I don't think he is doing any of those things. At least not to the extent at which we found him in London."

"I wish he'd just stay here. Fewer things about to lead him astray than in a place like London."

"And yet he always has complained of boredom here at Ironwood Park." That was one thing she'd never really understood about Luke.

"True."

They watched Luke ride until he turned a bend lined on both sides of the road with thickly wooded elm trees and disappeared through the iron gates. After they could no longer see him, they stood there a few moments longer in silence.

"Let's go back to bed," Simon finally said.

She went gladly. In the warm cocoon of blankets, Simon made slow, sweet love to her, worshiping her body with his hands and lips. She would never tire of this, of the way he touched her and kissed her like she was the most precious thing in the world.

He brought her to her peak and then reached his own.

They drifted off to sleep again until the sun blazed in a slanted, golden ray through the open curtains of the window and across the room.

She turned over to look at Simon, who lay on his side gazing at her. Reaching up, he pushed a lock of hair out of her face and tucked it behind her ear.

"Our life together truly begins today, my love," he told her in a low voice. His hand wandered to her stomach, where their child grew. No one at Ironwood Park knew besides Sarah's father. Sarah and Simon had decided together to keep the child their special secret for now. They'd tell the rest of the household in a few weeks.

The truth of it all swept through her, invigorating and simply wonderful. She and Simon were making a family together. A life. She smiled at him. "The first day of a new life. One I never imagined I'd be blessed with."

"Nor I," Simon told her. "But I shall thank God for it— and for you—every day."

They rose and performed their morning ablutions before going downstairs together. The first day of their life together was a perfect one, the first of many that followed.

The scandal, as expected, rocked England, its details whispered in the far reaches of the empire, but no one seemed to be able to shun Sarah for long. Soon enough, she was accepted into society as if she'd been born into it, and her marriage to Simon was touted by many as the love match of the decade.

And for as long as he lived, nothing made Simon Hawkins, the Duke of Trent, happier than to fall asleep beside Sarah at night and for her face to be the first thing he saw when he awoke in the morning. To Simon, nothing could be sweeter.

Please read on for a preview of
The Rogue's Proposal ...

Chapter One

❧

*L*ord Lukas Hawkins wasn't drunk enough. Not yet. He gazed at the glass of ale sitting on the table before him and dragged the pad of his thumb through the drops of condensation on its lip.

He would have preferred something stronger, but the ale was beginning its work. All his sharp edges, those phantom blades that sliced so ruthlessly at him when he was sober, were beginning to dull. The noises of the tavern had faded into an agreeable drone rather than the piercing, headache-inducing racket of when he'd first arrived.

Luke took another generous swallow of the cool amber liquid and leaned back, letting his eyelids descend to a pleasant half-mast.

He'd asked enough questions for tonight. He'd made no progress in his hunt for Roger Morton, but that didn't surprise him. The villain who'd taken Luke's mother from her home at Ironwood Park was a wily man, slipping through Luke's fingers all the way from Cardiff to Bristol.

Luke wouldn't find Morton here. It was hopeless. What he needed now was to gulp down another three or four tall glasses of ale, unearth some pleasant companionship for the evening, and plummet into a dreamless sleep.

Only to wake up tomorrow and begin the whole fruitless endeavor over again.

Taking his ale in two hands, he brought it to his lips, closed his eyes, and tossed back the whole bloody thing.

His eyes reopened as he lowered the empty glass.

Well, well, well.

Straightening his spine, he brought his glass down until it landed with a decided *clunk* on the worn wooden tabletop. His lips curled into a wicked grin. It seemed like his pleasant companionship had unearthed itself.

A vision in black and white had seated herself on the other side of the narrow wood-planked table. She was the loveliest thing he'd seen in a very long time. Brown eyes shot through with polished gold gazed at him, their expression inscrutable. Thick, burnished waves of bronze hair escaped the little annoyance of a prim, white cap and framed a heart-shaped and pink-cheeked face. Her lips...hell, just edible. Gazing at those lips aroused Luke's senses—the deep red of cherries in the summertime, their sweet scent, the decadent, juicy burst when he bit into one.

Just one glance at those lips was enough to bring Luke's sluggish body to sudden, alert life.

"Well," he said, infusing his voice with a lazy edge of suggestive slyness. He'd perfected the tone over the years, and it had a dual purpose: It told a lady of loose morals exactly what he wanted, while simultaneously warning an innocent maiden to escape while she still had a chance. "It's about time. I've been waiting for you."

To her credit, her only reaction was a slight widening of her eyes. He wouldn't have seen it if he hadn't been looking carefully. Otherwise, she didn't move.

"Have you now?" she asked.

Lust jolted through him. God, that voice. Potent and smooth, like the finest brandy. It evoked images of the bedroom, mussed sheets, a rough tumble, erotic pleasure.

His body hardened all over. His cock pressed against the falls of his breeches. Between her lovely face, her calm, unperturbed demeanor, and the husky sensuality of her voice, he was done for. He wanted to take her upstairs. Immediately.

But Luke wasn't one to rush things overmuch, especially when he was so intrigued. He possessed some restraint, some patience. Not much, but some.

He cocked his head at her. "What took you so long?"

"Well—" She took a deep breath. The action drew his eyes to her bosom—her full breasts strained at the top edge of her bodice as if they yearned to be set free. He'd be happy to perform that task for her.

"—I was detained," she finished.

"Oh? By what? Or whom?"

The corner of her lip quirked upward. She was playing with him. He was the one who usually toyed with females. But in this case, they were toying with each other. He liked that.

"By ignorance," she said.

Ignorance. Loose women usually didn't use such words, especially not with such inflection. Her throaty voice had spoken the word as only an educated woman would.

Luke settled back in his seat, pushing past his arousal and drunkenness to study her. He'd only noticed her cap before—when he'd wanted to toss it to the floor and push his hand through that bounty of burnished hair. He hadn't noticed the pearl earrings, the fine silk of her dress, white with black velvet trim.

She was no whore. She was a lady.

He stiffened, quickly scanning the area surrounding them. The tavern was crowded with men and women drinking, eating, conversing. The atmosphere was boisterous, and the smells of charred meat and hops and yeast permeated every inch of the place. No one was watching them—at least not overtly. But, hell, ladies like this didn't just waltz into pubs and plunk down across from the first drunkard they encountered. This woman knew something.

None of these revelations made her less appealing. In fact, they fascinated him. She was brazen, lady or not. Luke liked his women brazen. That kind of woman was fearless, more likely to take risks, in bed and out.

He leaned forward, placing his elbows on the sleek, well-worn surface of the table. The table was so narrow his face ended up only a few inches from hers. "And now you're no longer ignorant?" he asked her. "Someone has enlightened you?"

She nodded sagely. "Indeed."

She'd probably heard he'd been asking questions about Roger Morton. "So then. You have information for me?"

"Hm," she said. Her fingers drummed on the table, drawing his gaze downward. Her brown kid gloves hugged each long, elegant finger as they tapped the wooden surface. "I thought *you* might have information for *me*."

He raised his brows. "Is that so?"

Her brows mirrored his in a haughty reaction. "It is."

He laughed, the rare feeling bubbling up in him and spilling over. His smile widened. This was not how women generally behaved in his presence. They either ran crying to their mamas like abused little kittens or dragged him straight to bed like lionesses on the prowl. This woman was a different kind of creature altogether.

"Therefore, I have a proposal for you, my lord."

Ah, so she knew who he was, as well. Or, he amended, she knew who he spent his life pretending to be.

"And I have a proposal for you. Miss...?"

"Mrs."

"Mrs.," he repeated. But he didn't believe for a second that she was married. No, he possessed the skill of sniffing out married women. And this woman—she smelled of lavender soap, but there was more. Something raw and sensual, something in her gaze that spoke of warm, womanly flesh and dark, languid nights.

No, definitely not married.

So that meant that she was lying about her marital status...or she was a widow. She was very young to be a widow, though. He narrowed his eyes at her, trying to see beneath that calm surface, to delve underneath and find some clue that would tell him what this woman was about.

"Mrs. Curtis," she told him.

"Mrs. Curtis," he said, "*I* have a proposal for *you*."

That corner of her lip quirked again. Her eyes sparkled the most fascinating shade of amber at him.

"Do you?"

He reached up to drag a finger across her lower lip. Softer than the velvet of her dress ribbons. Plump and red as a ripe, sweet cherry. He wanted a taste.

"Come upstairs with me," he whispered.

She didn't react to his touch, or his words. She was very still. Too still. Then, she drew back from his touch and gave the slightest of nods. "Very well, my lord."

Terse and businesslike, she rose. He rose instantly, too, out of long-ingrained habit more than anything else. "Always rise when a lady is standing," his governess had told him, "or you shall be considered the rudest of gentlemen."

These days, he *was* considered the rudest of gentlemen, but it still didn't prevent him from rising.

"Please"—Mrs. Curtis gestured in the general direction of the exit—"lead the way."

"Of course." He turned away from the table, seeing his empty ale glass from the corner of his eye. How odd— he'd forgotten to hail the serving girl to ask her to refill his glass. But that seemed utterly unimportant now.

They threaded their way in silence through the crowded pub. No one paid them any mind. They left the large room and walked down a long corridor, taking the narrow stairs at its end.

Nighttime had descended, and with it, a bitter autumn chill. It was cold in the dimly lit stairwell, and Luke had the urge to draw Mrs. Curtis close to warm her. But he was sober enough to realize that that kind of advance in plain, public view might be unwelcome to such a lady.

On the other hand, he was foxed enough to imagine

how exuberantly she'd accept his advances behind a closed door.

He strode up the stairs, pausing on the landing to gain his bearings. It was a large inn, and the corridor branched in three directions from here.

She paused beside him, quirking a bronze-tinted brow at him. "I believe it's this way, my lord."

He followed when she turned to the rightmost corridor and began to walk again. So, he mused, she already knew where his room was located. She grew more intriguing by the second.

She stopped at the very last room. "Here?"

"Yes, Mrs. Curtis. Here."

He withdrew the key from a pocket in his coat and unlocked the door, then stepped inside.

The room was Spartan and cold. Unlike his exalted brother, the Duke of Trent, Luke didn't have the means to set aside entire floors of inns for himself and his party and employ maids and other servants to stoke fires and light braziers to keep them pleasantly warm. Besides, he had no party. There was just him. Always had been, always would be. Especially now that he knew he wasn't a true Hawkins.

He opened the door wider, and she stepped inside behind him. She made to move around him, but he shut the door with a firm *click*, then held up an arm to stop her. She retreated until her back pressed against the door.

He boxed her in, placing a firm arm on either side of her and flattening his palms against the door. "There," he said softly, "now you're my prisoner."

Something flared in her eyes. Heat or fear? Heat, probably. From what he'd seen of her so far, she wasn't a woman who was easily frightened.

He leaned down to whisper in her ear, "You like that idea, don't you? Do you like to be bound, Mrs. Curtis?"

Her reaction was slight—an infinitesimal tremor that ran through her body. It was enough.

He moved his mouth to a hair's breadth from hers. The warm wash of her breath fluttered across his cheek. Other than that soft release of air, she didn't move.

His body was an inch from hers. Not touching, but so close he could feel their heat combine and simmer in the narrow gap between them.

Slowly, painstakingly, he touched his mouth to hers in the lightest of kisses. His eyelids sank shut. Her lips were plump and soft, forgiving against his.

He dragged his lips against hers in a back-and-forth motion, a slow, sensual slide. She didn't move, but her flesh yielded beneath his, and he released a low groan. She tasted so good. Sweet. Ripe. He sipped at her unresponsive lips, then touched the tip of his tongue to the corner of her mouth, urging a reaction, but still she didn't move.

God, he wanted this woman. His body screamed at him to haul her against him and take all the wicked pleasure her supple flesh could offer him. But he didn't only want her compliance, he wanted her to be an active participant.

He kissed his way from the edge of her lips, across the upper portion of her jaw—such supple, smooth skin—until he nuzzled the tender lobe of her ear.

"Now," he whispered, "are you ready to hear my proposal?"

He feathered his lips over her earlobe, bit down over it

gently, then drew back to study her. Her expression didn't change, but her eyelids were lowered. She didn't speak for a long moment.

As she formulated her response, he formulated his own words in his mind. *I believe you have information for me, Mrs. Curtis. I believe you might want something from me in return. But those are things that can be saved for later. Right here, right now, I want you. I want your lovely body beneath mine. I want to strip that dress from you and lick every inch of that delectable skin. I want to make you scream my name in pleasure again and again until we're both in such a delirium that there's nothing either of us can do but to sleep. And then, when we wake—*

"No," she said, finally looking up at him.

"No?"

"I *don't* wish to hear your proposal, my lord."

God, her voice. It scraped his every nerve into a raw, needy thing that only her touch could soothe.

"I think you do."

"I know I don't," she countered. "Because I know the essence of it."

"And it's not a proposal you believe you'll accept?"

"Absolutely not," she said.

"Why not?"

She looked deliberately down at the arms that caged her, first his right arm, then his left. Then she looked back at his face, her eyes coming to sparkling golden life, brimming with determination. "Because I've more important things to do."

He laughed, long and loud. "Trust me, Mrs. Curtis. At this hour, there is nothing more important than what I intend to suggest."

"There is," she said simply, and the soft curve of her lips firmed.

He'd humor her, then. "What could it possibly be?"

"The proposition *I* have for *you*."

He sighed. "Very well. Tell me what it is."

"You've come to Bristol looking for a man named Roger Morton, is that correct?"

He gazed steadily at her. This didn't surprise him. She knew who he was. She knew the location of his room. Obviously, she'd been watching him since he'd ridden into town yesterday and knew exactly why he was here. He hadn't made a secret of it. He was looking for any information that would lead him to Roger Morton.

"Yes, that's true. I am searching for Roger Morton."

"I can help you find him."

His lips curved. "Could you?"

"And that is my proposition. I will give you the information you shall require to find him if you allow me to come with you."

"Allow you to come with me." He said the words slowly, tasting them in his mouth as images washed through him. Taking this lovely specimen of womanhood with him in his hunt across England for Roger Morton. Sampling the beds of different country inns. Long nights of feasting on her pale, curvaceous flesh, of vigorous lovemaking...

He studied her face. The color was high on her cheeks now, and her implacable features had hardened, giving her an expression of iron resolve. He stood close enough to her to feel the thrum of purpose under her skin. Whatever this was about, it meant a great deal to her.

"Why would you wish to travel with me? *Alone* with

me?" He put emphasis on the word "alone" to remind her of the potential permanent repercussions to her reputation. She was a lady, after all, and ladies simply did not travel alone with gentlemen unless they were married to them.

"Because," she said, her voice throbbing with certainty, "I want to find Roger Morton, too."

He narrowed his eyes at her.

"And then I want to kill him."

Dear Reader,

When Sarah Osborne, the heroine of THE DUCHESS HUNT, entered my office for the first time, I thought she was a member of the janitorial staff and that she was there to clean.

"I'm sorry," I told her. "I'm going to be working for a few more hours. Can you come back later?"

Her flush was instant, a dark red suffusing her pretty cheeks. "Oh," she said quietly. "I'm not here to clean...I'm here as a potential client."

Now it was my turn to blush. But you couldn't really blame me—she wore a dark dress with an apron and a tidy maid's cap. It was an honest mistake.

I rose from my seat, apologizing profusely, and offered her a seat and refreshments. When she was settled, and neither of us was blushing anymore, I returned to my own chair and asked her to tell me her story.

"I'm the head housemaid at Ironwood Park," she told me. Leaning forward, she added significantly, "I work for the Duke of Trent."

I'd heard of him, and of the great estate of Ironwood Park. "Go on."

"I want him," she murmured.

I blinked, sure I'd missed something. "Who?"

"The Duke of Trent."

"You are the *housemaid*."

She nodded.

"He is a *duke*."

She nodded again.

I shook my head with a sigh. The housemaid and the duke? Nope. This wouldn't work at all. The chasm between their classes was far too deep to cross.

"I'm so sorry, Miss Osborne," I began, "but—"

Her dark eyes blinked up at me and she held up her hand to stop my next words. "Wait! I know what you're going to say. But it's not as impossible as you might think. You see...I am His Grace's best friend."

I gaped at her, for that was almost more difficult to believe than the thought of her being his lover. Dukes simply didn't "make friends" with their maids.

"We have been friends since childhood. You see, the duke's family is quite unconventional. The dowager raised me almost as one of her own."

Now this was getting interesting. I cocked my head. "Do you think he would agree with your assessment?"

"That the House of Trent is unconventional?"

I chuckled. "No. I know the House of Trent has been widely acclaimed as the most scandalous and shocking house in England over the past several decades. I meant, would he agree with your assessment that you are his best friend?"

She folded her hands in her lap, and her dark brows furrowed. "If he was being honest?" she said softly, and I could see the earnest honesty in her gaze. "Yes, he would agree."

I leaned back in my chair, drumming my fingers on my desk, thinking. How intriguing. Friends to lovers, to…*love*. What a delightful Cinderella story this could make.

My lips curved into a smile, and I flicked open the lid of my laptop and opened a new document. "All right, Miss Osborne. Tell me your story. Start with the story of the first time you laid eyes upon the Duke of Trent…"

And that was how my relationship with the wickedly wonderful family of the House of Trent began. I've loved every minute I've spent with them, and I hope you enjoy Sarah and the duke's story as much as I enjoyed writing it.

Please come visit me at my website, www.jenniferhaymore .com, where you can share your thoughts about my books, sign up for some fun freebies and contests, and read more about the characters from THE DUCHESS HUNT and the House of Trent Series.

Sincerely,

Jennifer Haymore